Iguana

Also By Vincent Traughber Meis

The Long Journey to You

Colton's Terrible Wonderful Year

First Born Sons

Far From Home

The Mayor of Oak Street

Iguana

VINCENT TRAUGHBER MEIS

Cover design: Vincent Traughber Meis
Printed in The United States of America

FIRST EDITION
Fallen Bros. Books
1920 Bradhoff Ave.
San Leandro, CA 94577
ISBN-13: 978-0-9976728-9-3

Contents

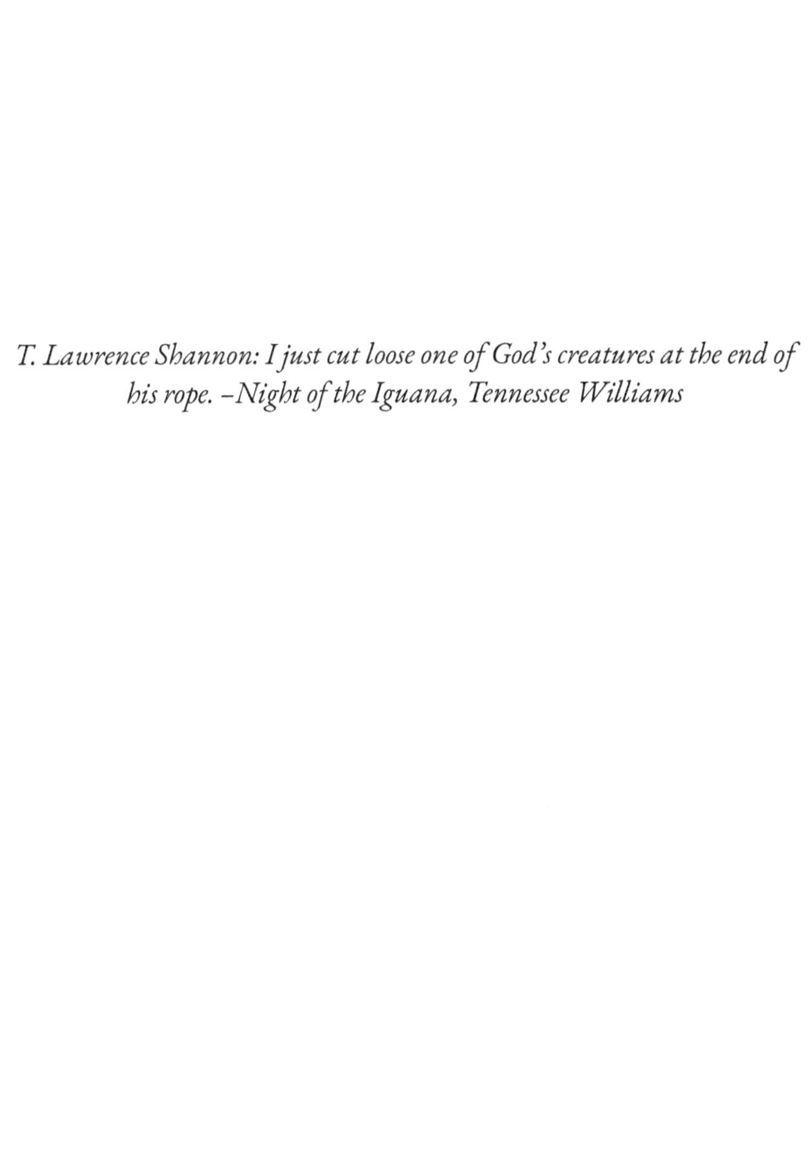

T. Lawrence Shannon: I just cut loose one of God's creatures at the end of his rope. –Night of the Iguana, Tennessee Williams

One

A rustling in the dry undergrowth and the crackling of twigs indicated a large-ish animal. It spotted me before I spotted it, but even with its camouflage, it couldn't hide in the sparse surroundings. The iguana slithered up the embankment to higher ground with its long black and tan striped tail fanning back and forth to aid its escape. It climbed a tree and moved out on a branch that hung over the sidewalk in front of me.

I stopped. It stopped. I took a step forward. It crawled out a little further on the branch as if it was a gatekeeper. I had never been that close to an iguana, just ten feet above me, looking fierce with a torso about three feet long and a dewlap of variegated skin fluttering under its throat. A row of spikes ran down the spine, getting shorter as they reached the long tail. I'd been told they were harmless as long as they weren't threatened. Some people even took them on as unlikely pets, putting them on leashes and charging tourists to take a picture with them.

But there was something about the way it stared at me that kept me frozen there on the pavement, wondering if it was safe to walk under its perch on the branch. I stared back. For what seemed a long time, we stared at each other. And then, its scaly eyebrow closed over the black marble pupil in a bed of yellow iris. If we had been playing a game of who blinks first, I had won. I didn't feel like a winner, though, and the iguana didn't seem to care as it continued to observe me, blinking as if bored with the relative newcomer on the planet. I nodded, acknowledging I was an invader in its land. Not just as a foreigner but as a human carving into the jungle habitat of the animal.

I was in Mexico for a new beginning, walking down the hill to do my shopping, if this beast would let me. Sweat began pooling in the middle of my chest, and I needed to move on. As I passed under the branch, I swear the iguana shrugged and looked away as if it was done with me. I felt dismissed. And then I began to laugh, a laughter of relief and surprise, thrilled with this new experience, one more in a long list that seemed a daily occurrence since I had moved here.

The day had begun with clear skies broadcasting hope, the balcony slightly cooler than inside the house as I lingered over my breakfast, feeling the view of the Bay of Banderas from Punta de Mita to Los Arcos like a physical thing that coddled me. We were in the dog days of summer, with the dog-star, Sirius, rising and setting about the same time as the sun. It was the hottest time of the year, and relief only came, I was told by my neighbors, when afternoon showers again pelted the corrugated roofs of the neighborhood down below. Everyone talked of the rains coming late this year.

Before the heat and humidity became too oppressive, I planned to walk down the hill to the market and buy food for the next few days when the forecasters insisted the heavy rains would come, ushered in by thunder and lightning. I would get back up the hill before the church bells struck ten in the plaza below.

I stepped out of the apartment into the stuffy hall, which smelled of fried onions and spices I couldn't identify from the apartment across the hall. I summoned the elevator and watched the short countdown from the rooftop to my floor. When the doors opened, Ivan in his company logo polo shirt and jeans stood chewing on one of his fingernails. He dropped his hands and folded them in front of his crotch as he stepped aside and made room. "Buenos días, señor Dawson."

"Hola, Ivan." I leaned against the back wall and watched his blurry reflection in the shiny metal of the doors.

On the next floor, he got off, and as the doors closed, I let out the breath I didn't know I had been holding. The tension I felt when near him made no sense. Ivan had been hired a few months before as the day manager who oversaw daily operations in the twelve-unit building curiously named Paradiso, which sounded both presumptuous and unsettling. He handled everything from delivering packages to residents' doors to coordinating cleanups to keeping the place secure. Everyone found him friendly and efficient. Everyone loved him. Why did I often see him joking and bantering in English and Spanish with other residents when he was all business and cold with me? Why did my packages sometimes go undelivered when everyone else got theirs the same day?

Ivan continued to occupy my thoughts as I started down the hill with my sneakers crunching the leaves blown across the sidewalk by a balmy breeze. His dark, brooding good looks reminded me of a character in a book I edited recently, Darius, whose brown eyes could be soft or turn hard at a moment's notice. When Darius showed up at the home of the female protagonist, she decided she was going to marry him. But it was not to be. He took her brother and his friends out on a fishing expedition and a sudden squall swept Darius overboard, according to her brother's report. The story didn't sit right with her, and in the rest of the novel, she embarked on an investigation that took her to dark and haunting places.

I laughed at myself, knowing I spent too much time immersed in the characters of books that I read for pleasure and books I edited for work. Not enough time living. That was why I was in Mexico. To live. To be the character in my own story. There was nothing about Ivan that indicated he should be a fellow character in my life, and yet, there he was, dancing around in my brain as I walked down the hill to the shops.

My experience with the iguana pulled me out of my musings, the eye-to-eye with this mysterious creature replacing my encounter with Ivan. It would stay with me all day.

Further down the hill, I came upon the corner boys outside a small store, some of them sitting on a wall, smoking and drinking soda while others straddled small motorbikes, ready to take off at a moment's notice. In cooler times they kicked a soccer ball around the intersection until a car came, waiting until the last minute to get out of the way. Sometimes one of them would cradle a wad of bills in his hand and shout to a companion across the street or make mysterious hand gestures. I tried not to jump to conclusions. They didn't bother me and sometimes afforded me a nod or a mumbled "Hola."

On the main avenue running parallel to the beach, I entered a place selling locally sourced coffee, a rustic, wood-paneled café and store, a throwback to another era with the musky smell of patchouli in the air. Rough shelves held jars of herbs, the walls decorated with dream catchers and mandalas and the atmosphere untainted by artificial air conditioning. It was the kind of store my parents would frequent, and my mother would probably tell me again the story of using patchouli oil to cover the scent of marijuana back in the day. Other stories she told me of protesting the government and sexual experimentation made me cringe, and I went through a rebellious period in college where I registered as a Republican and declared that the only drug I needed was beer. Once in the real world, I saw that my parents were right about a lot of things, and in my late twenties, I found with them a common ground where we could be friends. Now, I would give anything to hear my parents' stories again, but COVID-19 took care of that.

The shopkeeper's friendly greeting in English took me out of my moment of sorrow. With his long, pulled-back hair and a scraggy beard, he looked as if he had just arrived from one of the intentional communities I grew up in, and for a second, the familiarity made me think I might have known him as a child. It was highly unlikely. I smiled and pointed at the vacuum-sealed bags of coffee on the wall and asked where the coffee was from.

"It's organic and mountain grown not far away in the state of Nayarit by indigenous people. Flavorful and robust with earthy tones and hints of berry," he said. My parents surely would have been pleased that I was buying organic coffee grown by indigenous people.

"Are you looking for ground or whole beans?" His teeth were crooked and yellowed, but his smile was warm, and he had a gentle, natural demeanor.

"Ground, please."

As I paid, we chatted about the neighborhood, and he mentioned how things were changing, new places opening and others closing, old buildings being torn down and new ones being built. I was part of that change, a change that had ramped up during the COVID pandemic with digital nomads and remote workers making their way south to Mexico in droves.

I continued to the market down the street, where a plump, cross-eyed woman greeted me as if we had a shopkeeper-shopper relationship that went back years. She asked if I was there for the eggs. When I nodded, she assured me they had just arrived fresh. I bought a dozen eggs, two mangoes that she promised would be perfect for eating in the next day or two, and half a large papaya wrapped in plastic. I also picked up zucchini, carrots, tomatoes, and a bunch of cilantro. At the fish stall next door, I selected prawns as thick as my big toe. With the satisfaction that comes with doing business with local people as opposed to the large supermarkets, I strolled down the street, staying in the shade as the heat surged.

Next stop was the bakery with whole grain bread and French-style pastries, owned by a woman from Quebec but still a small business that hired locally. I got two croissants and a pan au chocolat that left a buttery stain on the snug paper bag she slipped them into. I came prepared with a plastic-lined shopping bag, dropping the pastries in before laying them on top of my other purchases in my backpack.

I left the store and peered across the street at groups of beachgoers with towels thrown over their shoulders, the invaders sporting a variety of hats and outfits in blaring shiny colors. They headed for the sand past shop after shop that advertised "ropa tipica y artesanal," though there was nothing typical or locally made about them. The bright colors and synthetic fabrics only seemed to add to the heat of the already baking sidewalk on the sunny side of the street.

In cooler weather, I liked exploring the neighborhood and discovering new shops and cafes, but the hour was approaching when sane people ducked into darkened homes and switched on the air conditioning if they had it. I turned around and began the trudge up the hill, taking a series of streets where I could stay in the shade and break up the monotony of always taking the same route.

A third of the way up the hill, I entered a corner store, partly because I needed a few more things and partly because the kind, hairy man behind the counter always greeted me in a playful way. "Hola, güero," the man said. The counter fan was on the highest setting and swept across his features without moving a single strand of his thick black hair.

"Hola."

"En qué le puedo servir?" he said with a wink and a charming grin, belying the formality of the language. A smile crossed my lips as I thought of ways but only mentioned the few things I needed. I tacked onto the list a bottle of cold water. After I paid for the items, the clerk wished me "Good luck with the hill" in English. "Hasta mañana," the man continued as if sure he would see me the following day.

The first half of the climb was a steady grade and not taxing, but the last half got the sweat glands working and the legs aching. I glanced at the tree where I'd seen the iguana, but the beast was gone. In the gutter along the sidewalk, a clucking mother hen and her chicks pecked at leaves and garbage.

I reached the building, punched in the key code, and entered the lobby. In the elevator, I scanned the walls for mosquitoes that tended to roam the corners waiting to attack. To avoid bites, I had developed a little dance, moving arms and legs for the short ride to the fifth floor. The door opened on my floor as I was mid-dance step, where I must have looked like I was practicing John Travolta's *Saturday Night Fever* dance. And there was Ivan again.

"You're here." My face flushed as I pointed out the obvious.

"Till seven," he said in a monotone but with a glint in his eyes, perhaps amused at my embarrassment.

"Long day."

"I don't mind. I like being here."

I jumped to the assumption that he had nothing to go home to.

The elevator door started to close with me still in and Ivan out. I stuck out my arm, causing the door to ding and retreat into the slot. We sidestepped around each other, resulting in another impromptu elevator dance, until he switched places. As we brushed by each other, I was hit with the essence of his soap, or maybe the last bit of cologne he put on that morning, mixed with the sweat of a day's work. The scent lingered, and I breathed it in, a tiny shiver of excitement running through me.

"Hasta luego," I said, wanting to remind him that, yes, I was a foreigner, but one who tried to speak Spanish. The door closed before he could respond. I walked to my apartment door, rubbing a knot of tension that had flared up suddenly in my shoulder.

I spent the rest of the day working on a manuscript until I felt the pull of the Malecón, craving my sunset walks along the boardwalk with its carnival atmosphere, the waves splashing against the seawall, and the sun putting on a show. The last few days, the damp woolen skies of the afternoon led to brilliant sunsets as the fiery ball slid down through layers of clouds, scattering light into orange, magenta, yellow, and purple splotches. If I timed it right, I could watch the sun dip below the horizon from the balcony and still make it down the hill to see the aftershow of deepening colors painted on the broad sky.

The cicadas began their sunset ritual, a rising drone-like vibration that announced the end of daylight. And like previous nights, the sun did slip through bands of clouds, but the last minutes before its disappearance, it was hidden by a dark bank along the horizon.

As I headed out the door, I received a text from Stef and Ray, a couple who had become my best friends in the town. We often met for evening walks, and the text announced they had arrived at our usual meeting place in the plaza in front of the church. I answered that I would be there soon.

I met Ray and Stef a month after moving to Puerto Vallarta. Determined to know more about my neighborhood, I signed up for a Wednesday evening art walk, combining exercise with art appreciation and possible social interactions. What could be a better way to fall into this new life? In one gallery, I stood in front of a large painting that, because of the colors and the angle, didn't immediately invoke a reclining male nude. *Oh yes, the curves of tangerine skin emerged as buttocks, and the triangle was a bent leg, and the beach he lay on was chartreuse, and the sea beyond purple.*

As I deciphered the image, an imposing figure came up beside me. "There seems to be a preponderance of male nudes in these galleries," he said.

To what felt like a come-on line, I debated whether to engage and flirt back or to agree with a noncommittal "yeah" and move on. Curiosity, as usual, made the decision. I turned to acknowledge the baritone voice of a handsome Black man, perhaps in his fifties, some gray at the temples of his close-cropped dense coils, warm eyes, and a killer smile.

"I've noticed that," I said.

A second later a short woman with frizzy blond hair and blue eyes arrived on my other side. "Don't mind my husband. He likes to accost strangers with his art opinions."

"I'm Ray Burnside," the man said, offering his hand. "And this is my wife, Stef Gould. Sorry if we interrupted your concentration."

"No problem. I was beginning to wonder if talking was allowed on these walks," I said with a snicker.

"Only after you've bumped into the same people at four galleries," Stef deadpanned. "Ray broke the rules. He always breaks the rules."

"I'm Dawson, by the way. Dawson Wozniak." Then their names caught up with me. "Wait. Did you say Ray Burnside?"

Stef smiled. "Here we go."

"The writer?"

"I've been called worse," replied Ray. "My mama always taught me to introduce myself with my full name. In most cases, it doesn't spark any reactions."

"You have to be careful who you talk to at these things," I said with a laugh.

"Next you're going to tell me you read my book."

"Book? I read all three."

"I had forgotten there were two more after the one," he said, gripping his chin between his thumb and forefinger. "Tried to forget."

"Don't be so hard on yourself. You're not the first writer who hit a homerun with the debut and then had to suffer the cruelty of critics when the following books didn't reach the same level." In my nervousness, it had come out all wrong. Had I just said Ray's second and third books didn't measure up just like the critics had? "I didn't mean..."

Ray put a hand on my shoulder. "I'm flattered beyond words that you read all my books."

"Who is this guy?" said Stef. "Not only is he a reader, but he's clearly intelligent, not to mention good-looking."

Oh, my God. They're both coming on to me.

"Yes, you seem to know more than the average Joe reader," said Ray.

"I work for a publisher. I'm an editor."

"Which one?"

"Caliber House. Small press. You probably haven't heard of it. It's in Los Angeles."

"Are you just visiting PV then?" asked Ray.

"No. I live here. I came down during the pandemic. A perfect job to do remotely, which also means I got absolutely no time off. I liked it so much I bought a place."

"What do you publish?" asked Stef.

"Anything that will sell," I said with a smirk. "We're supposed to focus on literary fiction and historical nonfiction, but I recently worked on a YA fantasy written by the daughter of a famous actor whose name shall go unmentioned. I love to do literary. The other stuff not so much."

"Then I'm particularly flattered you found *Night Dancer* worthwhile," said Ray.

"Worthwhile? Are you kidding me? You deserved every bit of the praise."

Stef and Ray nodded at each other with big smiles, sharing a silent conversation.

"We would like to invite you to dinner," said Ray. "We're starving and were thinking of going to a place we like in Versalles."

I was thrilled at the invitation to go out to dinner with a writer I admired, but it had all happened so suddenly. "I...uh...was going to fix something at home."

"Look, I know," said Ray. "A bit of a hard come-on. We don't normally do this, I mean, invite strangers we've just met out to dinner. We're excited about meeting someone with a brain. It's nothing fancy. Just a gourmet-ish taco place with a rad patio."

"Does sound better than the boring thing I was going to fix." And exactly like the kind of new experiences I was hoping to have when I moved here.

We closed the restaurant and solidified our friendship with a couple of bottles of wine.

Two

With memories of that first meeting with Ray and Stef putting a smile on my face, I headed down the hill, past the tree without its iguana, past the corner boys who sat on a wall and stared at me. But the last couple of blocks before reaching the Malecón, it became clear there would be no aftershow. The sun's light was swallowed by a monster of dark clouds as if heavy theater drapes had fallen mid act, cutting the audience off from the performance. And yet, as I got a half block from the seaside walk, I saw that the crowds had not been dissuaded from their nightly stroll and vendors still displayed their wares.

The moment I reached the wide pedestrian walkway, the ocean in the sky, after building for days, finally found a rift and poured down in sheets. People scurried in all directions as if a bomb had gone off, rushing to escape the sudden downpour. Sellers hurried to pack their artisan goods into plastic bags and food in plastic bins.

On a side street, I found cover under a plexiglass awning jutting out above the entrance of an art gallery where the lights were on, but a closed sign was on the door. Rain pelted the awning with a deafening racket, and in a matter of minutes, water cascaded down the hill, filling the streets to the curb. I imagined the accumulating river reaching a flood stage that could carry me along with everything else in its path out to sea. Lightning tore across the sky, and thunder shook the buildings around me. It was everything I had been told to expect by long term residents. Since moving into my place in January, the weather had been mild and predictable. Now I feared for my life. A lot of my neighbors in Paradiso had already fled the town to their home countries, avoiding the heat and humidity of summer, as well as the heavy rains, apparently feeling it wasn't "paradiso" in the summer. "Wimps," Ray called them. He and Stef had lived in Puerto Vallarta year-round for the last five years.

I sent Ray a text. **I will try to make it to you.**

Ray responded. **This isn't going to let up. We're looking for a taxi home.**

You're not being wimps, are you?

Trust me on this. You should go home, too. Check for leaks. First big rain and all.

I knew I should listen to him since my building was new construction and hadn't gone through a rainy season yet, but I wasn't quite ready to flee. I enjoyed the rush, the power of the pounding rain, the streets filling to the brim, the flashes of lightning and the rumbling thunder. It was a different kind of show from the placid sunsets. Fury and bravado. Angry gods. A part of me wished I was back in the apartment, safely watching from the sofa with the sliding doors open. But another part of me loved being in the middle of it.

I nixed the taxi idea. I would rough it. Climb the hill in a thunderstorm just to prove I could. The storm added the thrilling obstacles of water roaring down from the mountains, the danger of slipping and falling, the possibility of the electricity going out, leaving the street dark, or a tree snapping and falling on top of me. This was the new me, daring and bold, ready to face the elements.

I ventured out from the shelter, and the awning runoff immediately pounded my head and ran down my back. Before I had gone half a block, I was soaked. I put my head down, and set one foot in front of the other, staying on the sidewalk as the water in the street was a rushing river with strange substances floating on top.

I turned up my street, where a swath of light a block ahead spilled from the little store I visited earlier, both lighting up the sidewalk like a beacon and telling me the power was still on. I slowed down as I passed the store, gazing into the dryness, the coziness, the refuge, hoping the clerk would smile, beckon me in from the rain. He might wink at me and call me güero. We could banter a few minutes until the rain let up. But the man sat on a high stool, hunched over, entranced by the small screen where tiny figures ran around a green field in uniforms, kicking a ball. His face was bathed in blue light, and there was no world outside the circle of luminescence. I stood a moment at the entrance and started to raise my hand to get the man's attention but moved on instead.

From this point, the rise became steeper, and I hugged the buildings with overhangs or trees fanning out over the sidewalk to allow me a break from the heavy rain, though lightning and thunder were less frequent and farther away. No other people were out walking, and I only saw one vehicle, a Jeep climbing the hill where grooves had been etched into the pavement for such conditions.

A short distance from the entrance to my building, a rogue flash of lightning lit up the road and highlighted what looked like a marble in the gutter. I moved closer and saw the iguana just below the tree where I had seen it earlier. It lay on a bed of leaves bunched up against a fallen branch in the gutter. The water rushed by the beast as if it was enjoying a swim, though it remained still. Perhaps it didn't have the strength to move out of the strong flow and was biding its time until the rain subsided. The eyes seemed to follow my movement, making it hard for me to walk on by.

I grabbed a branch the length of a broom and put it in front of the animal's clawed feet, in hopes it might grab on so I could pull it out of the torrent. The iguana remained immobile.

"Come on, little buddy," I shouted, the rain streaming down, getting in my eyes and nearly blinding me.

I touched the branch to the clawed feet, and when there was no reaction, I nudged it. Moving closer, I poked the beast gently in its side. Nothing.

"Grab on. I'm trying to save you." I poked it again. No reaction.

With my heart pounding, I bent down close enough to touch the iguana, slowly moving my hand to the torso, ready to snap it back if there was any sign of life.

I touched the scaly skin, stroked it, running my hand along the cool body as the water rushed over it. In a desperate move, I grabbed the end of the long tail and pulled. Nada.

I fell back and sat on the pavement, putting my head on my knees, not wanting to admit that my new friend was dead. My body shook with sadness, and I sat a long time as if at a wake, the water rushing by me, tears mixing with the rain running down my face, all the loss I'd suffered in recent years overwhelming me.

I don't know how long I sat there—long enough for my backside to go numb—but I finally rose to my feet and entered the building. There was nothing more to be done.

I sloshed across the empty lobby, following a trail of towels someone had put down to absorb the water. The elevator was waiting for me, as were the mosquitoes, darting here and there in a frenzy. I danced about and left a pool of water on the elevator floor, which I felt guilty about. I paused outside my door and quickly glanced around the empty hallway, deciding to save my apartment from my drenched clothes. I took off my sandals and all my clothes, even my underwear, and bundled them in one hand as I slipped the key into the lock with the other. It felt daring and bold to be naked in the hall, the new me. A noise in the stairwell down a level made me rush inside and hurriedly close the door. After dumping my soggy clothes in the kitchen sink, I went into my bedroom, glancing at my feet covered with bits of grass, debris, and God knows what else. I turned on the shower, anxious to wash off the encounter with the iguana and the fetid water that splashed my legs.

Just as I was about to step into the stall, there was a knock on the door. My first thought was that someone had traced the puddle in the elevator to me and came to complain about it. I wrapped a towel around my waist and went to the door. It took me a second to recognize Ivan, who, instead of his daily duds of jeans and green company logo polo shirt, wore a sleeveless white T-shirt revealing nicely muscular arms. His baggy shorts showed his thin but hairy legs. The casual clothes transformed him into yet another personality, the sultry handyman appearing at my door.

"I'm so sorry about the water in the elevator," I blurted out. "I was going to clean it up."

"What?" he said. "Not about that." His piercing look ruffled me.

Relieved I wasn't facing anger about the mess I'd made, I realized how unusual it was for Ivan to be here at this hour. "Wait! What are you doing here? You already worked a full day."

"Administration ask me to go around and check all apartments for leaks. Sorry I catch you just out of the shower."

"No. I'm wet from the rain. I'm going *into* the shower now."

"I can come back." He ran a hand through his longish black hair, now curly and wild from the humidity, a nervous gesture that brought his hand to the back of his neck and exposed a tuft of thick black armpit hair.

"If you have other apartments to check..."

"Actually, yours is the last."

"Well, then, come in. I haven't noticed any leaks but really haven't had a chance to check."

He looked down at the wet footprints and drips on the wood floor. "Do you walk home in this storm, señor Dawson?" he said with a wrinkled brow.

I was tired of being addressed as señor. It made me feel old—my recent fortieth birthday had been traumatic—and it made it sound like he was subservient to me. It was his job, not his station in life.

"Yes, crazy, huh?"

"This is something to worry. Good thing you make it home okay." His eyes softened. His shoulders fell.

I was stunned by this new development, Ivan's concern for me. We stood uncomfortably in the hallway, both staring at the wet floor. It seemed he was waiting for me to say or do something.

"All right, then. I'll go take a shower, and you can check for leaks."

Under the warm and gentle water of the shower, a stark contrast from the cool pounding rain, I chuckled at how fast the sadness about the iguana had dissipated. Nothing like a sexual crackle in the air to change one's mood. When Ivan called to me, I wasn't sure if it was real or part of a fantasy.

"Señor Dawson?"

He stood in the bedroom at the threshold of the bathroom door. I had neglected to close it, when there was typically no need as I was always in the apartment alone. I opened the glass shower door and stuck my head out. "Ivan, please. No señor. Just Dawson."

He averted his eyes as if talking to someone in the bedroom. "Do you have a mop? I find some leaks by the windows in the dining room."

I rubbed a soapy hand down my torso, reveling in the fact I was naked while Ivan was just feet away. "There's one in the laundry room. Give me a minute. I'll help you."

I quickly rinsed off, exited the shower, and pulled on some gym shorts. Entering the living area, I came up behind Ivan as he mopped and gazed at his shoulder and back muscles working under his shirt. He had the calves of a long-distance runner. Up close, he gave off a tangy, musky odor from his efforts of going all over the building doing damage control on the hot, humid night.

"Ivan, you don't have to do that."

He stopped and leaned a little on the mop. "I don't mind."

I reached for the wooden handle. "You must be tired after a full day of work, and now you've checked on all the residents." At that moment, it hit me that there was no logic to leaving my apartment for last as it was in the middle of the building.

"I am fine."

I tried to pull the mop handle, but he gripped it tightly. We stood close, and he looked in my eyes for the first time since he had arrived at the door.

"Please," I said, pulling the mop toward me.

"As you wish." He let go but kept eye contact. "I should probably go and take a shower like you. I am full of sweat."

I pointed to the bedroom and the shower within. "Feel free."

"No, I mean, I'm staying in one of the empty units, so I can make the rounds again in a few hours if the storm continues."

"Why not take a shower here if you don't have to do anything for a while." I playfully swabbed the mop over his sneakers.

"I couldn't. It wouldn't be..."

"You could. What's stopping you? I can lend you a clean T-shirt and shorts." It felt daring to be insisting, and a break from my usual lack of spontaneity. Something in his eyes encouraged me.

Ivan sighed and dropped his shoulders. He let me lead him to the bathroom as if he was only following orders para servirle. I gave him a towel.

"Gracias," he said as he closed the door.

When he emerged from the bathroom, I stood at the bedroom window watching the storm still raging outside. I turned around to see he wore only a towel, my eyes going directly to a large tattoo covering his nicely formed chest. It was an eagle, symbolically drawn with a wing spread over each pec, the beak pointing up to his chin, and tail feathers expanding down over his sternum.

I stared. Of course, I did.

"What?" he said.

"The tattoo."

"I have a few, but I keep them hidden. In my last job, they wouldn't like them."

"Hidden? Like you can't show me the others?"

"No," he said firmly, but a smile tugged at his lips.

"You're full of surprises."

He nodded his head and said in a low voice, "Maybe not the surprises you want."

I huffed but let him play coy. "Would you like a beer?"

"I think is not a good idea. Actually, I'm still working."

"Or maybe it is a good idea. I'll get you one." I pointed at the clothes on the bed. "You can put those on...or not."

He waved me away with a chuckle. "Go, so I can change."

Ivan entered the living room in a pair of my favorite gym shorts and a pale blue T-shirt I had worn a hundred times. The image of him in my clothes sent a rushing nervousness coursing through me. I had never shared clothes with another person, not even my ex, Jacob, who, given the opportunity, would have been reluctant to don anything I wore.

Back in the living area, he stood shyly in the center of the room, staring at a book of Gaudi architecture on the coffee table. I handed him a beer, and his attention shifted to the bottle as if he still wasn't quite sure. I noticed an old scar above his left eyebrow, possibly from a childhood accident. I wanted to touch it, touch his past, his innocence when he was a boy.

"Salud," I said, bringing the necks of the bottles together in a clink.

We finished the first beers quickly as if quenching a great thirst. I got two more from the fridge. "Let's go out on the balcony."

It still rained hard, but we would be protected by the balcony above. As I slid the door open, we could hear noise from the rooftop pool area two floors up. Loud music. Laughing. Shouting. At least three people, maybe more. The rooftop had an infinity pool where the edge didn't feel like the edge. The pool was surrounded by lounge chairs, and the other half of the rooftop had a covered area with a bar and tables and chairs. This part of the rooftop was ringed by thick glass panels in place of a railing, also giving the illusion of infinity as if there was nothing between you and the town below all the way to the ocean and beyond.

We heard a big kerplunk like someone had cannonballed into the pool.

"Sounds like a party," I said.

"Is kind of a tradition to celebrate at the first big rain of the season. But this is too much. I should go up and tell them to quiet down."

I was afraid of losing the moment, knowing that if he left, he probably wouldn't come back. "Let them have their fun. It's not late. Anyway, you're not the on-duty manager."

"But if they go past ten… and Severino sometimes don't do his job." Severino was on the night shift from 7:00 p.m. to 7:00 a.m., but it was common knowledge that he slept through most of it.

We finished our second beers, and I went inside to get two more.

I handed him a new beer, and he shook his head. "No, I can't."

I laughed. "You can. Three beers is nothing. Drink it." He held up his bottle and looked me in the eye. He produced a quirky smile, making me think he liked me telling him what to do.

We moved closer to the railing where the rain splashed us, but it felt good on the hot night. The partiers on the roof got rowdier, singing along to the songs. Their voices had no filters in the manner of drunk people, the high-pitched voices echoing across the valley below us. I guessed it was Patrick from a neighboring unit and some of the local boys he partied with. I looked down toward the street and the cinder block houses far below. One of the houses had soggy clothes, weighing down a clothesline.

"I suppose those clothes are getting an extra rinse," he said.

I laughed nervously, feeling the usual tension with him, but it had changed in tone, now a warm buzz with a hint of possibility.

"I saw a dead iguana down on the street," I blurted.

He turned to me with a startled look. "Where?"

"Almost in front of the building." I pointed down to where I'd seen it. "I think it's the same one I saw earlier during the day perfectly fine. It made me sad. I thought it was stuck in the gutter, and I tried to move it."

"You touched it?" he said as if it was a dangerous thing.

"With a stick." I left out the part about running my hand along the skin.

"You are sure it was dead?"

"I'm afraid so."

"That is sad."

We both stared down to where I had pointed. I put my hand back on the rail, touching Ivan's. His body went rigid, but he didn't move away. He turned to look at me. I leaned in. Our lips were so close, and yet still miles apart. The shouting upstairs turned from drunken banter to angry shouting.

He pointed upward. "I really should..."

I grabbed the pointing hand, and in a crazy move, brought it to my mouth, letting my lips glide over the knuckles. A shudder seemed to pass from his hand throughout the rest of his body. His lips parted as if to say something. My other hand drifted up to the side of his face, feeling the roughness of his beard. I pulled him closer and noted the confusion in his eyes. My hand fell to his chest, and I felt his heart pounding. His lips quivered, then opened again, and I worried he was about to say no.

I kissed him.

He moved his head back, reluctant, an automatic reaction. But in the next second, he let himself go, allowing his tongue to explore with a sureness that suggested he was the one to initiate the kiss. We had crossed a line, and instead of two men with a multitude of doubts and confusions, we were two humans joining in an ancient human ritual. It felt like a beginning but also an ending, an ending to months of dancing around each other, of not knowing.

My hands slid down to his waist, pushing my thumbs under the waistband of his shorts—my shorts— searching for the prominent iliac crest I had seen above the towel he wore a few minutes before. The rain splattered our faces, and the heated voices above faded from our consciousness.

With our bodies locked tightly, my desire pushed so hard into him that he was leaning heavily against the railing, his back bending and rain collecting like jewels in his curls.

I broke the kiss and pulled him back from the edge. "Careful," I said.

He looked over my shoulder up toward the rooftop. His breathing was irregular.

"Are you okay?" I asked.

He shrugged but pulled me back into the embrace, and we kissed again. I ran a hand through his locks, shaking out the rain while he wrapped his hands around my lower back and pressed our crotches together as if he had experience with what men did together.

The beer and the excitement and the storm swirling around us made me light-headed, and I nearly lost my balance, but he held me up, his feet solidly on the ground as his tongue searched deep into my mouth. We were so lost to the world that the sudden sound of breaking glass seemed miles away. Chunks of tempered glass clattered on the wood at our feet. It was followed by a piercing scream of anguish and surprise. I opened my eyes just in time to see a large object flying through the air, like a pelican diving with its large beak into the ocean to swallow a fish. But the fall of this diving bird was not broken by the water, like the pelican, but rather hard concrete. The resulting thud was sudden and shocking.

We dropped our embrace and peered over the railing. A body tangled in clothesline and wet clothes splayed out on the concrete patio of a house below. The thumping beat of *Perdóname* by Deorro played on above, now broken by someone screaming, "No, no, no, no."

With a mix of horror and bewilderment on his face, Ivan pulled his phone out of his pocket and called 911, transitioning rapidly from intimacy to management mode while I stood transfixed in horror. He moved toward the inside. I reached out to him, laying a hand on his arm. "What are you going to do?"

He wrenched his arm away from me. "I must go up there."

"It could be dangerous. Wait for the police."

He looked at me like I was crazy. "What? No."

"I'll go with you."

"You stay here." He started to go and then turned around. "I was not here," he growled. "We were not together."

"What?"

He made a circle in the air gesturing toward the two of us. "None of this happened. You understand me?"

"Yes," I said, frightened by the intensity of his gaze. It shriveled my heart even as it still thumped with the thrill of our kiss.

He turned and left.

Three

I went to the balcony doors and took hold of the pull cords to lower the shades, anxious to block out what had happened. With the shades partway down, the two unfinished beers on the outside table came into frame. I pulled the blinds back up and stepped out to collect the bottles. The disconcerting party music still played from the rooftop, but a few seconds later, it was abruptly cut off, allowing me to hear a faint sobbing from above and the sirens in the distance.

From below, the eerie murmuring of voices drifted up, and a mother shouted at a child to go back inside. I was drawn to the edge and peeked over the railing, suffering a momentary urge to jump, that rushing high-place phenomenon, both inexplicable and powerful. The rain hit my face as I grabbed the wet railing until the urge passed, replaced by spasms in my gut at the sight of the commotion below.

Several people were gathered on the patio, where someone had draped a sheet from the clothesline over the body. I couldn't tear myself away from the horror of it, imagining that in the dark, no one would see me, until a flash of lightning lit up the sky, and I jerked back. I picked up the bottles and went inside where I closed the doors, lowered the shades, and turned on the air conditioning. At the sink, I poured the remnants of one beer down the drain but guzzled the rest of the other, wondering if the bottle I put my lips to had been the one his lips had touched.

I thought of him up on the roof dealing with the crisis, and instead of feeling sadness for the young man that had fallen, I rankled with the notion I had been robbed of a beautiful moment. In the throes of it, it had been exactly what I had come to Mexico for, to immerse myself completely in this new world, with new experiences and new people. To have that moment cut short, and more, to have Ivan reject what happened—reject me—left me feeling robbed. My hurt rose to self-righteous anger, and I made the rash decision to defy Ivan's orders and go upstairs.

I crept up the metal stairway, making as little noise as I could, and peered around the doorway to the covered area of the rooftop deck. Patrick sat in one of the lounge chairs with his head in his hands, rocking forward and back. Nearby, a skinny boy with a mop of black hair was curled up in a lounge chair in a fetal position, sobbing. Ivan stood over him, talking softly in Spanish, trying to calm him before the police came.

As Patrick was the only other gay man in the building and the only resident close to my age—all the others were well into retirement—it would seem logical we would be friendly. But, since the day we met, I'd had an uncomfortable feeling about him.

Shortly after I moved into the building, I went up to the pool and rounded the corner to see a hirsute, overweight man making out with a thin young man in the pool. I backed away and was about to return to my apartment when someone said, "Hi." A man peeked out from behind the pampas grass in the planters surrounding one of the lounge areas.

"Oh, hello. Didn't see you there," I said.

"You don't have to leave because of Patrick and his friend."

"No, I...yeah, it was awkward."

"You can sit over here." He patted the lounge chair next to him. "I just ignore them."

He looked Mexican but spoke perfect American English. He had a slim body with lots of tattoos, a ruggedly handsome face, and ridiculous eyelashes above hazel eyes.

"Are you a friend of theirs?" I asked.

"Yeah. Patrick invited me over. I don't live in the building."

"I just moved in a couple of weeks ago. I'm Dawson."

"Matthew here." He stuck out his hand, and we shook.

Patrick and the boy separated and glanced at us as if we had intruded on their private party. That was my first impression of Patrick.

"Carry on," said Matthew. "We're ignoring you."

"Bitch, you're just jealous."

"No chance of that. A little nauseated maybe."

Patrick gave him the finger.

Matthew and I fell into easy conversation, ignoring the goings-on in the pool. Matthew was born in Mexico but had gone to live with his mom in the Los Angeles area when he was seven. He moved back to Puerto Vallarta only recently. After we exchanged our stories of how we ended up in Puerto Vallarta, Matthew pointed at Patrick and his friend at the end of the pool with their backs to us, hanging on the edge and looking out at the view of the Pacific Ocean. "I'm not like that."

I had an inkling of what he meant but felt the need for clarification. "Like what?"

"Since Patrick's a friend of mine, some people think I'm like the boys he hangs out with."

"And how are the boys he hangs out with?"

"Well, look at Benny. Patrick likes young queeny types."

I let out a nervous chuckle. "Why are you telling me this?"

"I don't want you to get the wrong idea. I'm not into any of that gay shit."

"Wow. You invited me to sit with you. Have I troubled you with any of that gay shit? And how do you know I am?"

"I may not be gay, but my gaydar is on the mark."

"What the hell?" I jerked with the urge to get up and move.

Matthew put a hand on my arm. "Chill, man. I'm not homophobic. A lot of guys come on to me, and I like things to be clear from the beginning."

Before I had a chance to respond, a shadow blocked the sun, and we looked up to see Patrick standing over us. "Since Matthew has probably filled your head with all kinds of bull about me, I thought I should come over and introduce myself. You just moved in, am I right?"

"A couple weeks ago. I'm Dawson."

"Welcome."

Patrick's friend stayed in the pool while he sat down next to me. I detected an accent and asked about his Puerto Vallarta story. Patrick was Swiss German but lived in New York for the last twenty years. In telling his story, he managed to work in his real estate investments, cars he drove, people he knew, and fancy resorts he stayed at. A lot of it sounded like embellishment, and though he may not have been the vapid hedonist of my first impression, I didn't see any reason we would become friends.

Despite never feeling friendly toward Patrick, I was now moved to see him in obvious pain, rocking in his chair. In the low light, I couldn't tell if the boy speaking with Ivan was the same one Patrick had been with the day I first met him. Or was that the boy who had just fallen from the roof?

I made myself visible, and Ivan twisted his head toward me with a disturbed look.

"I heard some noise. Is everything okay?"

I didn't understand his angry eyes. I was playing dumb. Isn't that what he wanted? But he squinted and clenched his fists, looking like he wanted to come over and bust me in the jaw.

"Everything is under control. Go back to your apartment. I'm sure the police will want to talk to everyone in the building."

I surveyed the glass panels that formed a wall around the upper deck. The last time I was up here, I noticed that one of the panels had been damaged. A strip of yellow police tape had been strung across the pie-sized hole in the center and the remaining chunks of tempered glass that still held together around it. I had never felt secure when standing next to the panels even though they seemed solid to the touch. Seeing the damaged one now sent a chill through me. The ends of the yellow tape fluttered in the wind, and only a few shards of glass remained around the edges of the panel.

Patrick turned his head toward me. "He was...I don't know...he..."

"What?" I asked.

"Señor Dawson, I will explain later. Go back to your apartment," said Ivan.

"But..."

"Now!"

After returning to my apartment, I threw all the empty beer bottles in the trash. I took Ivan's dirty clothes discarded on the bathroom floor and put them in the washer. A second later, I took them out again and sniffed them, having a strange feeling it would be the closest I would be to him for a while. Maybe ever.

It was nearly eleven when two police officers, a man and a woman, got to my apartment. I spoke to the officers as best as I could in a combination of English and my limited Spanish, telling them, yes, I had been home since about eight and heard some music and then a terrible scream. The male officer walked over to the pull cord of the blinds. "Do you mind?" he said in English. Since the incident happened in a building of expats, they must have dispatched bilingual officers.

I nodded, and the man opened the wide shade dramatically, letting the tremendous view of the lights of the buildings down below and the twinkling of boats on the bay come alive. "It's strange you would keep the blinds closed with such an amazing view."

"I'm a private person. The people across the way can see right in at night."

The officer opened the siding door and went out on the balcony. The rain was now a light tapping on the railing.

"So, you didn't see anything?" said the woman officer.

"When I heard the scream, I went out on the balcony and looked down."

She went to the door and stepped out, joining her colleague. "The person would have fallen right past your balcony." She pointed out the chunks of broken glass to her fellow officer.

I joined them on the balcony and looked over the railing. "I suppose he's..."

The officer twisted his head toward me and stared. "How do you know it was a he?"

"I don't. The scream sounded male. A young man maybe?"

"A male scream?" said the woman. "Okay. You are correct. It was a young man."

"Is Patrick Schell a friend of yours?" asked the male officer.

"I have spoken to him a few times. I wouldn't say he's a friend of mine."

The officers walked back inside, and I followed them. The three of us stood awkwardly in the middle of the living room. The female officer turned to me with scrutinizing eyes. "You were home alone the whole evening?"

"Yes. Well, no. Not the whole evening. I forgot to mention that Ivan, who works in the building, stopped by to check for leaks. He helped me mop up."

"A lot of water?"

"A lot more than I would have liked."

"Of course."

"And that was before the boy fell?"

"Yes, it didn't take that long to mop."

"Do you remember what time that was?"

"It was shortly after I got home, so I suppose it was 8:15 or 8:30."

"And before the scream," asked the man, "what did you hear?"

"Loud music. It seemed like a party was going on."

"Do you know any of Mister Patrick's friends?" said the woman.

"No. Like I said, he's not really a friend."

The two officers looked at each other and nodded. "Thank you for speaking with us," said the woman.

"No problem."

At the door they said they might need to talk to me again.

After they left, I slumped in a chair, my heart pounding. My answers had been mostly truthful. They didn't need to know that the mopping was a prelude to a kiss.

I stepped back out onto the balcony and looked down. The body was gone, but there were flashing lights far below on the street. I accidentally kicked a couple of pieces of glass and watched them tumble down to the patio below, now empty of people.

After the police left the building, and the flashing lights disappeared, I knocked on the door of the apartment where Ivan was staying. I should have just left him alone, but I couldn't accept his denial of what had happened between us. And I didn't want to be alone.

"Was I not clear?" Ivan hissed. He looked up and down the hall and motioned for me to come in, closing the door quickly. No longer wearing the clothes I had given him, he grabbed a plastic bag from a table by the door and shoved it into my arms. "Here are your clothes."

I hugged the bag, the hurt flushing my face. "I put yours in the washer. I'll return them when they're clean."

He was pale and looked around the room, his eyes landing on the ceiling, the floor, everywhere but me. "It was wrong," he said in a whisper.

"What do you mean?"

"All of it. It was irresponsible. Drinking beer, not stopping the party on the roof, the other thing."

"You can't even say it? We didn't do anything wrong."

"A young man is dead," he shouted, quickly lowering his voice. "It is my job to stop it."

"No es culpa tuya. It's not your fault."

"I don't know."

"It was a tragic accident. It *was* an accident, wasn't it?"

He shrugged. "That's what Patrick and his friend say."

"Isn't there video footage of the rooftop?"

"The corner where is the broken panel, where he fall, is not in range of the camera. And the music is so loud you can't hear any argument."

"So, you watched it?"

"When Severino is talking with the police, I check it. Also, the rooftop lights are off, so it's hard to see what's going on. I don't tell nothing to the police about the angry words we hear."

"I didn't either. Just said I heard some music and a scream. I did tell the police you had stopped by to check for leaks and helped me mop."

Ivan's eyes widened. "Why did you do that?"

"They asked if I had been alone all evening. You were doing what you were supposed to do. Of course, I didn't say what happened after we mopped."

He relaxed. "It's okay. I tell them I am in the building to check for leaks and help some people mop."

"So, we're good. Can we talk about...?"

"Not now. I have too much in my head. I take a couple days off. I see you when I come back."

Home to his wife? Girlfriend? I knew so little about him, if he had a family, a dog, a life outside of work. Someone once mentioned that he was divorced.

He opened the door, and I leaned in for the hug I needed. But he took a step back.

"Okay, I get it. We'll talk in a couple days?"

But I didn't get it. Why was he being like this? He closed the door without answering.

After a sleepless night, I made the decision to go to my friend's wedding I had been ambivalent about and booked a flight to Los Angeles for the end of the week. I had two things to accomplish before I left: a talk with Ivan and a dinner with Ray and Stef.

Four

The young man's death was ruled an accident based on the statements by the two witnesses on the roof, Patrick and his friend. There was no narrative to counter the ruling since neither Ivan nor I revealed the information about an argument and shouting. Ivan most likely kept quiet in being loyal to Paradiso and its residents. It would still be a scandal in the local community, but an accidental death was a lot less traumatic than a manslaughter accusation. And local authorities were more than happy to sweep things under the rug as soon as possible, protecting the image of the town.

A couple of days after the incident, I got into the elevator where a disheveled, unshaven Patrick huddled in the corner.

"Hola," I said.

Patrick grunted, his head down, examining the rubber mat of the elevator floor.

"Are you okay?" I asked.

Patrick raised his head as if suddenly remembering I had come up to the roof that night. "Where's Ivan?" he said in a shaky voice.

"I think he's taking a little time off."

The news seemed to hit Patrick hard, and he put his hands behind him, grabbing the rail to hold himself up. Was he afraid of something?

"It was an accident, you know," Patrick mumbled.

I was having a hard time imagining how the boy had "accidentally" fallen from the exact place where a panel was broken and had tape across it. "Yes. Terrible."

We reached my floor, and I stepped out. "If you want to talk..." The doors closed before I finished the sentence.

Ivan came back to work, and when I ran into him in the lobby, his eyes were cold and distant.

"We need to talk," I said.

One of the residents, Ed, exited the elevator toward us.

In a loud voice, Ivan said, "I'll keep you informed about the repairs, señor Dawson." He excused himself and followed Ed. "Señor Ed, I have the information you ask me."

I scheduled a dinner out with Ray and Stef. I needed to decompress from the tragedy, but I particularly wanted to talk to Ray about Ivan. That first night I met Ray and Stef at the art gallery, and we went out to dinner, Ray commented, while Stef was in the bathroom, on how handsome the server was.

"Yeah, I guess," I said, twitching in my seat.

"I'm bi," Ray said matter-of-factly. "I thought you might have guessed that."

"You *were* being kind of flirty."

"You're an attractive man. I hope I didn't make you uncomfortable."

"I don't know what to say. Thanks?"

"I'm not on the down-low or anything. Stef's in the know, and we have an arrangement."

The conversation was cut short when Stef returned to the table.

After several months of spending time with Ray and Stef, I had grown used to Ray's flirty behavior and was thankful he had never crossed a line. I wouldn't have been able to face Stef if we had done something, and I couldn't afford to jeopardize our friendship as I had truly grown fond of them both. They were always there for me when I needed to talk or needed a ride somewhere or simply to have a drink together.

When I arrived at the restaurant, Ray pulled me into an embrace. Each time we hugged, I enjoyed the warmth of being in his arms but was always aware of Stef standing nearby, waiting her turn while Ray tended to drag out the hug.

As soon as we sat down at the table, Stef asked me if I was okay.

"I need a drink. Got a lot to tell you."

After downing half a glass of vodka on the rocks, I told the story in one long rambling sentence: my flirtation with Ivan, the kiss, the boy falling from the rooftop, and then Ivan's apparent denial of what had happened between us.

Ray reached over and put a hand on my arm. "My God, Dawson. What a tragedy! And at such a mindfuck time."

"Yes," said Stef. "What an awful thing to witness." She looked at her husband. "As far as Ivan, I'll let you take this one."

Ray sighed. "Mexican culture is different. I've...um..." he cleared his throat, "grown familiar with it over the years we've been here, and I suppose there are some similarities with being on the down-low in the Black community."

"It's not just the Black community," said Stef. "There are a lot of closeted white men too. My brother, for instance."

"True that," conceded Ray. "But there are some differences for white men than for men of color. Being on 'the down-low' is not just being closeted, you know? You can be closeted and not doing anything. If you're on the down-low, you be doing something. The stakes are a lot higher if you're a Black married man who is also sexually active with men, the double minority thing, Black and sexually fluid."

Stef chimed in. "When we first got together, we had a crisis. I knew what was going on and told him I wouldn't put up with the secrecy. I told him to come clean or we weren't going anywhere."

"Up to that point in my life I had dated women and felt a particularly strong emotional connection with Stef. But my attraction to men was real. Being Black and bisexual is a bitch. You get ridiculed from all sides, the Black community, the gay community, your heterosexual white friends, though they would never say it to your face."

"I never ridiculed you!" said Stef.

"That's why we're still together. When Stef accepted me for who I was, I knew she was the one I could build a life with."

"Sorry, Dawson," said Stef. "I know you're not here to listen to all our crap."

"I'm glad you feel comfortable sharing it with me," I said.

Ray nodded and put his hand on my arm again. "You are a dear friend. Though we don't hide our personal life, we don't share it with many people. And yes, I sympathize with your position. You obviously have feelings for this guy."

"Feelings? I don't know. It was just something that happened. Before that night, he was so cold. Everybody talks about how wonderful

Ivan is, how kind and friendly. He often acted as if he didn't like me, or I was a pain to deal with."

"You?" said Stef with a chuckle. "You're the nicest guy around. You've got a lot to learn about attraction. He kissed you, didn't he? From the way you described it, it wasn't a casual one. That should tell you a lot. Don't take this the wrong way, but you seem a little fixated on someone you kissed once and, it appears, someone who wants to move on."

"He can move on. That's fine. But he could at least talk to me."

"The first thing you have to get in your head is that he's not rejecting you," said Ray. "He's afraid. He's afraid for his family, his job, his life as he's known it. Trust and believe. I know."

"I think there's more to it," I said. "I think he has the boy's death and his responsibility mixed up with our kiss in his head, maybe even some kind of sick causative relationship between the events. He's dedicated to the building community and feels like he should have done something when we heard angry shouting. He wanted to leave, but I held him there."

The concern on Stef and Ray's faces shifted to something more fearful.

"That's a tough one," said Ray. "Employees like Ivan can be extremely serious about their jobs. When personal feelings get in the way, especially feelings they're not comfortable with, it becomes clear where their loyalty lies. It involves a Mexican sense of honor."

"I'm curious," said Stef. "What did you tell the police?"

"Ivan insisted we not say anything about being together at the time of the fall. Anyway, we didn't see anything that could help the investigation. I didn't exactly lie to the police, though I did withhold some information to protect Ivan's reputation."

Ray shook his head. "The poor man is screwed whatever he does. He's in a complex web of moral dilemmas."

"That's why I think we need to talk about what happened. But he won't."

"He can't," said Ray. "He's in an impossible situation. Give him time."

"I get that." I sighed. "I'm going away for a while. My best friend from grad school is getting married and my boss wants to have some meetings while I'm there. I hope she isn't going to screw up our agreement about working remotely."

"We will miss you," said Stef. "Don't stay away too long. And don't expect too much when you come back. Ivan may not be capable of whatever it is you want."

I tried to keep this advice in mind the last time I saw Ivan before I left. I told him I was going to California for a while, hoping for a reaction.

"Have a nice trip," he said with a blank face. Normally it would have been an occasion for a handshake as he was fond of doing, but he kept his hand in a fist by his side like he couldn't bear to touch me.

On my way out of the building to catch my flight, I stopped in the lobby to return Ivan's T-shirt and shorts, washed and folded in a plastic bag. He wasn't at the desk, so I put them on the counter next to the monitor showing views of the building's multiple cameras. One was focused on the pool area. And then I noticed one camera captured the hallway outside my door.

Somewhere there was a record of Ivan entering my apartment before the tragedy and leaving just after in a different set of clothes. Would someone watching the video be clever enough to catch the difference?

The pearly gray light outside the window drew my eyes open and seeped into my head fogging it up, making me unable to place myself in time or space. The objects around me had a vague familiarity, but for several long, scary moments I was suspended in the ether, not even sure who I was.

It wasn't the first time I had awakened, unsure of where I was, a consequence of jetting back and forth between two places—and two very different places, with different languages, different cultures, different climates. But something about this time was distinct, almost as if I wasn't quite sure I wanted to make it back to reality.

Here or there? I stared at the ceiling fan at rest above me, and it gave me a clue. There, the fan whirled incessantly, keeping the dense air from forming a clammy layer on my skin. There, mornings were a symphony of roosters crowing, dogs barking, and motorbikes struggling up the hill. Here, the silence was unsettling. Here, nothing happened.

I put my hands over my face, rubbed my eyes, and swung my legs out from under the covers to the side of the bed. I raked my hair back from my forehead, noting how listless it felt without the humidity to give it weight. With a grunt, I stood up and shuffled to the bathroom. *Oh yes, here, it was to the left.*

In the kitchen, I leaned over the sink, staring into the depths of the water-spotted stainless steel while inside my head the tide went in and out, making me feel like the ground was unstable under my feet. Here, back in the land of earthquakes. There, I worried about hurricanes.

I filled the electric kettle, trying to fight the images I knew were coming, images searching for a weak point to break through. They flashed like lightning in a pounding rainstorm. The memory of a kiss with its unexpected urgency filled me with warmth and the sensation of having achieved some goal I hadn't been aware of. Was a kiss on a balcony in Mexico with a man who appeared to be straight a bonus experience or a wrong turn? Wrinkling the edges of this recollection was a warbling soundtrack of dance music before it was shattered by the piercing scream and the shadow of something falling I caught out of the corner of my eye.

A truck rumbled by on the main avenue and shook me out of the memories. The water gurgled in the kettle and steam rose up. I poured the boiling water through the filter, watching the coffee grounds swell and brown foam collect around the edges, reminding me of the froth that sometimes rode up on Camarones beach with the tide. But that was there.

Out the window, the manicured lawn across the street, the foxtail palms, and the Tesla in the driveway confirmed I was in California at the Sherman Oaks house Jacob and I had acquired six years before. The last three of those years, I was alone in the house (when not in Mexico) after the "pandemic divorce," not really the fault of the pandemic and not really a divorce since we had never married. In the "settlement," Jacob, who had moved in with his new squeeze in the Hollywood hills, told me I could stay in the house as long as I wanted.

But I didn't want to be in the house or in California or in the United States of America.

It was hard to think of the pandemic as having a bright side, but it did allow me to work remotely, test the waters of moving to Puerto Vallarta, and eventually make my transition there. Buying a condo at pre-construction prices high on a hill overlooking the Pacific Ocean was central to reinventing myself. My plan was to stay in the Mexican condo as much as possible and as long as the publishing company I worked for permitted me to edit remotely. I could fly back for the occasional meeting if I had to.

The Sherman Oaks neighborhood was colorless and manicured, and I risked the disapproving eyes of the neighbors if I didn't return the garbage bins to their proper place within an acceptable amount of time after pickup. Mexico was noisy and dirty and frustrating as hell at times, but it spoke its own language that pleased my eyes and ears. A single morning on the balcony, having coffee and watching a flock of green parrots screech through the air from one jungle treetop to another could wipe out all the negatives. The sunsets, each one unique and spectacular, made me never want to leave.

The wedding I attended in California gave me a chance to distance myself from what had happened in Puerto Vallarta. It also gave me the opportunity to see my boss, Susan, who still encouraged in-person meetings as much as possible now that things had returned, for the most part, to normal.

I stayed on after the wedding, and in the two weeks since I left Mexico, I had thrown myself into current editing project in hopes of drowning out the events of that night. But I could not. They felt monumental, begging for resolution. Or, at the very least, an understanding. Why couldn't I let it go? It was, after all, an accidental death, according to the police, of someone I didn't know, a little like the time when I was ten and watched the rescuers pull a lifeless boy out of the creek near where we lived in North Carolina. It was the first dead person I'd seen. It wasn't a life-changing experience, although it did stay with me for many years. What happened in Puerto Vallarta was tangled with other things, the mysterious death of the iguana and the kiss I shared with someone I never expected to kiss, and I'm sure he wasn't expecting it either. It wasn't forced, though. Something had been brewing for months, parallel wants from very different places eventually seized in a moment when we found ourselves in the same place at the same time. Alone. In a storm.

I thought about Ivan a lot and imagined him wandering the halls of my building, checking on things, making sure everything was functioning properly, attending to his duties. When he walked by my door, I wondered what went through his head. Did he think about me and what had happened? Had the kiss meant anything to him?

I slept poorly in Sherman Oaks, the what ifs thrashing me around in bed. Maybe I did hold some responsibility for the death. Maybe Ivan was right for feeling guilty. If I had let him go up to intercede in the escalation of the argument, the young man would likely still be alive. Even if it hadn't been his responsibility, he was good at diffusing conflict. I had seen him do it once between two workers who got into a squabble.

I thought of the boy's family and how they deserved to know the truth of what really happened. I obsessed over the camera footage, the story it could tell, the withholding information from the police.

One night as I lay in bed, trying to fall asleep, my phone rang. Caller ID said Ivan. I thought for a moment it was a dream.

"Hello," I said.

There were some scratchy noises, fumbling, and then, "Uh...what?"

"You called me," I said.

"Sorry. A mistake."

"The call?"

"I mean, an accident."

"You didn't call to talk to me?"

"No. Accident. Sorry."

"Oh. Are you okay?"

"Yes. Todo bien. I must go."

"Okay."

Click.

Butt dials happened. Usually they were to someone you've spoken to recently, a call entry hanging around on your screen. Not someone you've literally never spoken to on the phone. I had to believe Ivan was reaching out to me but lost his nerve.

When I finally fell asleep, I had a nightmarish dream of being underwater, unable to fight my way to the surface. The morning brought little clarity but some resolve. I booked a return to Mexico. I would convince Ivan to talk to the police. We would come clean about what we knew, the argument that might have led to the boy's death. It would relieve both of our consciences. He wouldn't like it, and it would further complicate our interactions in the building or any possibility of a friendship, but it had to be done. I spent the three-hour flight going over it in my head.

Five

By the time I arrived at the building, I had no doubts about what I had to do. It was still the day shift, and through the glass doors I saw someone sitting at the desk with his back to me. I pushed the door open with a mix of trepidation and excitement. When the door closed, the person turned around. It was Severino.

"Where's Ivan?" I said, trying to disguise my alarm.

"He no longer works here. I work the day shift now." He wore a self-satisfied grin as if he knew something, as if he was waiting for me to ask for details.

"Oh," I said, trying to shrug it off. I sauntered to the elevator and stood in front of the doors, cursing the elevator for being so slow, all the while feeling Severino's eyes on the back of my head. The elevator looked to be stuck on the rooftop. In my state of dismay, I imagined the holdup was because of a renter, holding the door until his family could gather up all the floaty devices, sunscreen, water bottles, bags, sunglasses, and other sun paraphernalia. The full-time residents tended to blame every problem at Paradiso on the short-term renters: spills in the elevator, late-night party noise, and stains on the lounge furniture.

The elevator arrived, and I took it to my floor where I unlocked the door, detecting a faint sewage smell that sometimes arose from the drains when they hadn't been used in a while. I shoved my bags into the living room. One of them toppled over, and I didn't bother picking it up before hurrying out again. I was desperate to find Patrick, though dreading it at the same time. I didn't know where else to turn for information about Ivan. Patrick was on the HOA board and would know what happened. Why had Ivan left? Had he been fired? Had the police reopened the case?

I walked down the three floors to Patrick's apartment. As soon as I reached his floor, the sound of a sanding machine grated on my already frayed nerves. Patrick's door was open, and clouds of dust pierced by the afternoon sun made the place look like it was on fire. I stood on the threshold and waved at Sammy, one of the workers who was often on site to finish tasks in the newly constructed building. He stopped the machine and removed his headphones.

"Hola, señor Dawson," he said.

"Hi. I'm looking for Patrick."

"Señor Patrick return to his country. His place is for sale. You want to buy it?" Sammy laughed.

The news gave me that sick feeling I'd been having a lot lately. "No. One place is enough." I took a step back. "A lot of changes around here."

"You been to the rooftop yet?"

I put a hand over my nose and mouth and waved the other in front of my face. "The dust." I backed away, saying, "I've got to go."

I rushed to the rooftop, taking two stairs at a time, and saw that all the glass panels had been removed, replaced by a metal railing like I had around my balcony. No more unobstructed views, the selling point of the glass panels. I approached the area where the cordoned-off smashed panel used to be. A chill passed through me as the image of the young man falling through the air flashed in my head. With both Ivan and Patrick gone and the other young man unknown, I felt alone, the last witness. Except possibly Severino. He was working that night. Where had he been? Had he been watching the whole thing on the monitor like it was a soap opera?

I returned to the apartment to air it out and collect my thoughts. As I went around opening doors and windows, turning on ceiling fans, and checking the food supply, I couldn't get Ivan out of my head. Maybe he had left because of me, but that would be giving myself and a single kiss an importance that probably wasn't warranted. More likely it was the guilt he felt for not being able to stop the tragedy, even if it seemed to me the best way he could safeguard the building and its residents would be to stay; quitting so suddenly made it seem like something was amiss.

There was also the possibility the police had returned to question him and caught him in a lie. But that, too, seemed unlikely because the police had already closed the case in the rush to protect the reputation of the town. Severino's smug smile jumped back into my head, like he knew something. He was the only one who came out of the tragedy in a better place. And if there should have been any intervention in the rooftop quarrel, Severino was the man on duty, not Ivan.

I finished unpacking and changed into shorts, anticipating a walk down the hill to catch the sunset on the Malecón, to find peace in the chaos of a sea of humanity walking this way and that, the street entertainers eliciting smiles, and people selling their wares.

On my way out of the building, I ran into Trixie, the president of the HOA. She was the next person I had planned to contact for information about Ivan but thought she was out of the country.

"Oh, you're back," said Trixie.

"I'm surprised to see *you* here," I said. "I thought you weren't returning until late October."

"Humph. Crisis mode. Not my choice. This is normally the time Ed and I enjoy our grandbabies before they go back to school. Are you all caught up on what's happening? Wait, you were here during the…the incident."

"Yeah. Tragic."

She nodded her head in agreement, but I had a feeling tragic wasn't her sentiment. More like pain in the ass. "I'm so mad at Ivan I could spit," she said. "We left in May thinking everything was in his capable hands. He was doing such a great job. Why in the hell would he just up and quit?"

"He was traumatized by the tragedy?"

"Of course. We all were. Did you talk to him after that night? Can you give me a clue what was going on in his mind?"

Why would she think Ivan and I spoke about anything personal? "I have no idea. We talked a couple of times before I left but about other things like the leaks."

"Oh, Lord. The leaks! As if we didn't have enough to deal with. The board had no choice but to put Severino in Ivan's position, which I most certainly did not want to do. Then we had to scramble to find someone for the night shift. Ed and I felt it was best to just come down here and deal with things in person."

I tried not to stare at her dark roots and splotchy skin from too much sun. "I heard that Patrick's place is on the market."

Her eyes managed to be furious and roll at the same time. "I guess I can't blame him. On top of everything else, that leaves a hole on our board. Are you interested?"

I wasn't. "Let me think about it." I was anxious to steer the conversation back to Ivan in hopes of getting some information about his whereabouts. "In any case, I wish Ivan the best. He was very responsible."

"Aside from leaving us in the lurch, he was. I wrote him a letter of recommendation though I didn't make it as glowing as I could have."

"He has a new job already?"

"Some place in Sayulita. I think it's a new complex, Atta-something."

And there it was. I didn't even have to ask a direct question that would've sounded overly interested. "Trixie, I've got to go, but let's get together for rooftop cocktails."

"We're leaving in a couple of days. I'm working on a newsletter to go over all the changes."

"Like the new railing around the pool area?"

"Bingo. An expense we really could have done without. I guess we should be thankful. If this had been the States, we'd probably be looking at a lawsuit."

The awkward conversation with Trixie made me anxious to find my happy place on the Malecón, get lost in the crowd, take a stroll and breathe the ocean air. I tried not to think of Sayulita and Ivan, only an hour away. As I walked down the hill, everything took me back to that night: the iguana tree, the chickens pecking in the gutter, the fallen branches and leaves. But the rains that began that same night had brought the greenery back. Now an iguana could easily hide in the foliage of a tree. It could be watching me right now as I passed.

There were few people on the street until I got to the corner where the boys hung out, perched on walls, shuffling back and forth across the street, drinking beer or Coke, tank tops and baggy shorts, and always with the phone in hand like they were waiting for that one big message that would turn their lives around.

Near the bottom of the hill, the number of people on the streets increased, and when I got to the Malecón, the usual crowd of walkers and cyclists filled the wide paved area dotted with islands of plants and palm trees. Lots of Mexican families taking advantage of the last days of summer vacation snapped photos of the sculptures, their children climbing the ladder of the *In Search of Reason* sculpture to join the alien-looking creatures near the top or sitting on one of the eight high-backed, oddly shaped bronze chairs of *The Rotunda of the Sea.*

Just over the wall on the beach, palm fronds rattled with the gentle breeze while the rocks clattered together as the surf covered them and then got sucked out to sea. In one section of the beach, people had stacked the rocks on top of one another, creating gravity-defying impromptu towers. All the while the sun crept closer to the horizon, bathing everything in a rosy light.

Surrounded by so much visual stimuli, most strollers didn't notice the Huichol symbols embedded in the sidewalk with small pebbles, representing deer, corn, peyote, and other important elements in indigenous lives. I felt joy in living in a city that paid attention to art both from native and modern cultures.

Another indication of Puerto Vallarta's attention to the arts were the lines of a poem by Martín Almádez, spelled out with small pebbles embedded in the pavement in the same way as the Huichol symbols. I imagined that even fewer people looked at the words as they walked over them, but each time I reached the end of the Malecón toward the Zona Romántica, I tried to understand a new line. My Spanish was far from perfect, but even a fluent Spanish speaker might have trouble with the unusual vocabulary and ambiguous nature of poetry. I bent over, examining the words while the crowd parted and walked around me.

"Hey, there." A man who looked vaguely familiar stood in front of me, his feet planted on the line *no me hace falta,* one foot on *hace* and the other on *falta.*

"Oh, hi."

"You don't remember me, do you?"

"Uh, your face looks familiar, but..."

"I met you at the pool in your building a few months back. I'm Matthew."

Then, I had a clear memory of that day. Matthew was the flirty one but wasn't like Patrick's boys. "It's all coming back to me. I didn't recognize you with your clothes on." I could be flirty too. Until his off-putting "gay shit" comment, I had found him attractive. I'd never given Matthew a chance to explain himself. Maybe he meant he wasn't into obvious gay behavior. That didn't mean man-on-man sex was out of the question. He could have been one of those "straight-acting" men you sometimes see on dating or hookup profiles. Not that I wanted to go there. I wasn't sure why I was giving him the benefit of the doubt, though he was looking rather sexy in his tank top and tight shorts. *Somebody slap me, please.*

Matthew chuckled. "If you think you're going to get me to take them off, you're mistaken."

"I wouldn't dream of it."

"You must be the only person on the whole Malecón that would stop and read these lines of poetry. You work with words or books or something, right?"

"I'm an editor. I work for a publisher."

"Tell me your name again."

"Dawson."

"Right." He flashed a big smile and pointed at the line I was examining. "Can you understand it?"

"This one is easy. The one back there I don't get." I turned around and pointed to the previous line. We walked back to it.

"Let's have a look," he said.

"The word *enardecido.* What's that?" I asked.

"It's like when you're hot under the collar for something or someone. Passion." His eyebrows began to bounce. "Or maybe aroused."

For a person not into "gay shit," he certainly liked to flirt with men. I traced the words in the air with my finger. "This is a *pajaro enardecido.* I doubt the poet means an aroused bird."

Matthew looked me up and down with a grin and shrugged. "I'm not a poet."

"Neither am I." I liked to read poetry, although I rarely felt like I understood it. Prose, on the other hand, was my job, and I was usually able to decipher what writers were trying to say even when they did it poorly.

Matthew continued to grin and stare at me like he was high on something. "I was thinking of you the other day," he said.

"You were not."

"Seriously, that day at the pool, I meant to ask for your Instagram."

"For what?"

"Keep in touch."

Matthew drew out his phone, but I was reluctant to do the same.

"You do have Instagram, right?" asked Matthew.

"Yeah." I could have said no, but a part of me was curious. "Dawsome123. Don't ask."

Matthew chuckled and typed in the handle. "Cool. Got it."

"Soooo...Patrick?" I said.

"I was afraid you were going to bring him up."

"Did you see him before he left?"

"Once. He was in a bad way. Remember that guy he was in the pool with? Benny? That's the one who..." He lifted his right hand and made a gesture of someone falling from a high place and slapping into his left hand.

It felt like someone grabbed my insides and shook them up. It was my own fault for bringing it up.

"Were they in a relationship?" I asked. "I mean it's pretty extreme to leave the country and sell the condo."

"I don't think he was that serious about Benny, but what do I know? I don't understand..."

"I know, the gay shit."

"You're never gonna let me live that down, are you?"

"I've got to go. I'm meeting some people."

"I guess the answer is no. I was hoping we could be friends."

"Why?"

He put his hand to his chest. "Ouch! That hurts."

"I don't get you."

"You're not the only one," he mumbled, looking down at the letters on the pavement. But quickly raised his eyes framed by long lashes, a new idea clearly occurring to him. "Hey, I've got these chocolate bars with magic mushrooms in them. We could take some and hang out. I know where there are some great waterfalls."

I stared at him incredulously but had to admire his cheek. A small part of me wanted to say yes and see where it would go. But another voice in my head warned me how unlikely it would be somewhere I wanted to be. Doing mushrooms with someone I hardly knew and who made me uneasy did not fall into the repertoire of the new and adventurous me.

"I'll pass."

"You don't trust me?"

"I don't know you."

"Doing 'shrooms together is a great way to get to know someone. They open your third eye and your heart chakra."

"I don't know what that means."

He put a finger in the middle of my chest. "Your heart chakra is located around here. It governs your emotional intelligence and what you feel deep inside. If you're feeling lonely, you might want to work on your heart chakra."

"I'm good."

Matthew smiled at me like I was a lost child. "Mushrooms are also good for anxiety, depression, and breaking through denial."

"You know nothing about me."

"I don't have to know your whole life story to see something is not right with you. You're hurting. Maybe something to do with that guy dying in your building. I don't know."

I had the sensation of something creeping under my skin. Matthew couldn't possibly perceive what was going on inside me. What did he want from me? I needed to get away from him before I did something insane like agree to a date. I looked at my watch and started to back up. "My friends."

Matthew held up his phone. "I'll DM you in case you ever want to get in touch."

"Fine. Got to go."

I walked to Parque Lazaro Cárdenas, slumped onto one of the benches covered in mosaic tiles, and took out my phone. There was already an Instagram message from Matthew. **Hi. Nice running into you.**

With a need to be around real friends, I called Stef.

"Dawson, are you back?"

"I am. I know this is last minute, but would you two be available for dinner?"

"Is everything okay? You sound a little upset."

Is that how I appeared to people? A neurotic, anxious person? "Yeah, everything's fine. I was just out walking the town and thought it would be nice to see you guys."

"Why don't you come over? Ray is cooking as we speak, and he always cooks like all his crazy relatives from Texas are going to drop in unannounced, God forbid."

"I'll see you in a few."

I was in my thirties when I lost both my parents. And yes, I recognized that Ray and Stef, somewhere between fifteen and twenty years older—I had never learned their exact ages—were like surrogate parents to me, which made the attraction to Ray even more awkward. I trudged up the hill to Gringo Gulch where Stef and Ray had been able to buy a two-bedroom, traditional Mexican style apartment in a desirable neighborhood for a lot less than I paid for my one-bedroom plus a flex room. But they had made their purchase before the pandemic, before real estate prices went crazy with North Americans buying and renting everything from Merida to Oaxaca to the Bay of Banderas, driving up prices. The thing Ray and Stef didn't have, I was reminded as I climbed first the steep street, and then four flights of steps up to their door, was an elevator. I arrived in a sweaty mess, but they hugged me anyway.

In Ray's arms, I felt the warmth and love that my father's hugs had always lacked, and just as I leaned into it, I felt the spark that made me a little queasy.

"Don't smother him," said Stef to her husband.

I worked my way out of Ray's arms. "I'm all sweaty," I said as an explanation.

"We missed you," said Stef. "Can I get you a glass of wine?"

"Yes, please."

Ray took a bottle of pinot grigio out of the fridge and poured me a drink. We clinked glasses.

"To friendship," said Stef.

"Yes," I said with a smile. Perhaps I was being paranoid, but I sensed a message in Stef's toast, like she had put an extra emphasis on the *friend* part of friendship.

Ray went back to hovering over the stove while Stef and I sat on stools at the island. Their apartment was so different from mine, lots of Talavera tiles on the walls and counter, wood beams on the ceiling, and Saltillo tile on the floor. In comparison, my condo was stark, modern, stainless-steel appliances and quartz countertops, still smelling of recent construction.

"Do you see me as an anxious person?" I asked.

"No way," said Stef.

"Someone told me I needed to work on my chakras, particularly my heart chakra."

Stef rolled her eyes. "Who in the world have you been talking to?"

"This guy. He's all auras and chakras and third eye. Sounds like mumbo jumbo to me, but maybe he saw something."

Ray took a serving dish from the cabinet and scooped the veggies he had been sautéing into it. He leaned on the counter and let out a breath like he had something to say.

"What, Ray?" I said.

"I wouldn't phrase it like that, obviously. Everybody has the lingo they like to use. But you have been through some stuff lately. It shows."

Ray's comment, from someone I admired, left me deflated. I had worked so hard in recent years to become a better, stronger person. And then the muddle with Ivan and the boy's death threw everything out of whack. "I'm a mess."

Stef put a hand on my shoulder and gave Ray a hard look. "No, you're not."

"That's not what I meant," said Ray. "Of course, you're upset by what happened. Anybody would be. We're here to help."

"My question is," said Stef, "why do you care what this chakra guy said, and who is he?"

"I met Matthew the first time I met Patrick at the pool. I think I told you about him?"

"Yes, you did," said Stef.

"And who is Patrick again?" said Ray.

"Sometimes I wonder if you even listen," said Stef. "He's the guy whose friend fell off the roof. And Matthew is the guy who flirted with Dawson shamelessly while telling him he wasn't into gay shit, right? He sounds like a creep."

"That's the one," I said, although after my recent encounter with Matthew, I would describe him as weird, but not creepy. And with Ivan being a dick, maybe... *God, I am a mess. Couldn't I meet a nice man in gay-friendly Puerto Vallarta that wasn't straight, in a relationship, questioning, or a tease?*

"Sorry," said Ray. "I do listen. Sometimes I forget."

I didn't like the way Stef occasionally put Ray down. He was the sweetest man, and Stef could be hard.

"So, after Matthew's cosmic analysis of my personality, we inevitably got around to the Patrick situation. Turns out, the guy sucking face with Patrick in the pool that day was the guy who fell off the roof."

"Damn!" said Ray. "So, you had met the dead guy?"

"Patrick didn't introduce us, but it was still unnerving to learn that I'd been a few feet away from him. The second time he was a few feet away I didn't recognize him, flying through the night air. That sounds cruel, but that's what happened."

"Life's fucked up sometimes," said Ray.

I chuckled silently at how even the most intelligent, well-educated people resorted to catch-all phrases. "In other news, Patrick went back to the States, and his condo is on the market."

"I'm not surprised," said Stef.

"But wait," I said. "The breaking news keeps coming! Ivan no longer works at our building. He quit. Or was pressured to leave. I don't have any details. He screwed up my plan."

"Plan?" said Stef.

"After a number of sleepless nights back in California, I came to the conclusion that I was going to convince him to go to the police with what we knew, the shouting and argument, which could shed light on what led to the fall."

"Oh, Dawson," said Stef. "Do you really want to open that can of worms? The boy is dead. Patrick is gone. And Ivan has left his job. It's time to move on."

Ray turned off the oven and took the chicken out. He removed his oven mitt and dropped it heavily on the counter. "But don't you see, Stef? Dawson is suffering with this on his conscience."

"I'm trying to save him from making a mess a bigger mess," said Stef.

"I'm not as convinced about going to the police as I once was," I admitted. "But I still need to talk to him. We witnessed a death together. That's a bond between us even if he doesn't want to recognize it."

Stef let out a puff of air. "I'm not sure witnessing a death together bonds you for life. And is that the kind of bond you want? Let it go. I know it sounds harsh, but he's gone."

"Unless, you know where he is," said Ray.

"Why are you encouraging him?" said Stef, her voice straining.

I twisted one side of my mouth downward and said in a low voice, "I sorta do."

They both turned to me, and Stef threw up her hands.

"What do you mean?" said Ray.

"The HOA president told me Ivan asked for a letter of recommendation to manage a complex in Sayulita." Ray stood with his arms akimbo and a half-smile on his face. "Don't look at me like that. I didn't ask. She's a chatterbox."

"The food is getting cold," said Ray. "Let's continue this at the table."

We each picked up a dish and carried it to the irregular shaped parotta wood table surrounded by six Mexican equipale leather barrel chairs.

"Is everybody okay sticking to white or should we switch to red?" said Ray.

"White's fine. I'm so glad I don't have a car here." I sniggered. "No worries about driving."

"I don't mean to be insensitive," said Stef. "I care about you and want the best for you. I hope you're not planning a trip to Sayulita."

"Well..." I took the plate of vegetables Ray passed to me and put some on my plate.

Stef sighed and took the plate from me. "It seems that you're not going to let this go."

"What I was saying about not having a car isn't always convenient." My squinting eyes and frown asked the question.

"Well, we do have one and haven't been to Sayulita in a while," said Ray. "We could make a weekend of it."

Stef sighed heavily. "Ray thinks of himself as an amateur sleuth. He loves this kind of thing."

"I don't want to drag you guys into my shit."

"Just promise me one thing," said Stef. "If you can't find him or he doesn't agree with your idea about the police, and I really hope he doesn't, you'll let it go."

"I promise."

"My question is," said Ray. "Is this just an excuse to see him again? Is that what you really want?"

"No! I don't know. Maybe?"

"Remember what we told you before?" said Stef. "He may not be able to respond in the way you want."

"I'm not sure what I want. There is so much unresolved stuff. I can't believe he's not having some of the same questions."

"Maybe he is." said Stef. "But he's just handling it differently. Consider his culture, his education, his position. He's a very different person from you."

"I suppose that's part of the appeal. Opposites attract. Jacob and I were similar in many ways. We both worked in the field of writing and were well-educated. We tended to spend quiet nights at home, at least, back then. We got together young. Neither of us had been in a serious relationship."

"And then the spark went out?" asked Ray.

"I'm not sure there ever was a spark. It was a relationship that looked good on paper. We were both living in West Hollywood, and he seemed less superficial than most of the guys around. Not sure I would say that now. It was obvious it wasn't working when he went off and had an affair. I suppose it was partly my fault. Since the new boyfriend also worked in Hollywood, that scene quickly became Jacob's whole world. Studio parties and late nights on Santa Monica Boulevard."

"Likes like and opposites attract," said Ray. "You can guess where Stef and I fall in that dilemma."

"Yeah, he's all sweetness and light, and I'm the ogre," said Stef with a laugh.

"You're both sweet but in different ways."

"Precisely," said Ray.

We spent the rest of the meal planning the trip to Sayulita. As we got drunker, we argued about 80s music versus 90s.

Six

On the first half hour of the trip to Sayulita, we agreed to listen to 80s music, and on the second half, it would be 90s in a sort of battle of the decades. We left the playlists up to Spotify. We listened to "Modern Love" by David Bowie, "Private Dancer" by Tina Turner, and "Stop Making Sense" by Talking Heads. As each song came on, Ray looked over at me in the passenger seat, smiling and nodding his head. Stef insisted I sit up front, using the logic that my legs were much longer.

"Come on, man," said Ray. "Bowie. Tina. Talking Heads. And we haven't even gotten to the big ones."

"Bowie was 70s. You can't claim him. And Tina was 60s and 70s."

"Tina had her biggest hits in the 80s. *Private Dancer* was monumental."

When Prince's "When Doves Cry" came on, Ray pounded his hands on the steering wheel. "Case closed. Prince was the best and he was totally 80s."

"He made a lot of music in the 90s too."

"His biggest hits were in the 80s."

Stef perked up. "Yeah. 'Purple Rain,' 'Little Red Corvette,' 'Kiss,' '1999.'" I had almost forgotten she was in the car.

The next song was Michael Jackson's "Wanna be Startin' Somethin.'"

"I want to dance," said Stef. "This one takes me back to my disco days."

"MJ and Prince," said Ray. "The best."

"What about Fleetwood Mac? Queen. Pet Shop Boys. Eurythmics. Madonna. Pretenders," said Stef.

"You guys are ganging up on me," I said.

"Facts are facts," said Ray. "Who you got? The Spice Girls?"

"The Spice Girls were important. Stef, you should be with me on this. Girl power?"

"They were fun," said Stef.

The first song in the 90s playlist was "Smells Like Teen Spirit" by Nirvana.

"So much of 90s music was loud and angry," said Stef.

"Definitely anti-pop," said Ray. "People had a right to be angry. And then hip-hop really got going, giving Black folks in New York and LA a voice. Like it or not, it had a huge influence."

"When I was in college," I said. "I was a registered Republican and listening to Pearl Jam. I was so screwed up. That's what can happen when you have hippie parents. When I was a little kid, we actually lived on a commune in North Carolina for a couple of years. Then it was a series of intentional communities, mostly rural. I hated growing up like that and was so angry at my parents."

"Are they still around?" asked Stef.

I hung my head and took a moment to collect myself. "They both died in 2020 before the vaccines, though they probably would have been antivaxxers. Mom died directly of COVID, my father in a tragic incident a few months later."

"Is it something you can talk about?" asked Ray.

"My parents offered support to immigrants crossing the border in southern Arizona. He died in a shootout with border patrol."

"No way," said Ray.

"It was the hardest thing to wrap my head around. I saw it really more like a suicide because he couldn't stand being without my mom. I miss them a lot."

"I'm so sorry," said Ray.

"Oh, honey. I can't imagine," said Stef.

"In my twenties, I realized I was being a jerk and started spending more time with them. We became quite close, and I talked to my mom all the time by phone. They apologized for the instability of my growing up, and I apologized for voting for George Bush. I think I did it just to spite them. I later realized how many Americans vote for candidates for the wrong reasons."

"Americans are political idiots," said Stef. "I won't even mention the name that proves my point to the extreme."

R.E.M.'s "Man on the Moon" carried us into the town of Sayulita and the GPS led us to the Airbnb Stef booked. When we pulled up in front of the building, I stared out of the window in disbelief.

"No fucking way!"

"What?" said Ray.

"That's the iguana tree right in front of the building." One of Sayulita's informal tourist attractions was a huge tree where many iguanas were known to hang out. I discovered it accidentally one day on a previous trip to Sayulita.

"Yes," said Stef. "It did say something about that on the Airbnb page."

"That's cool," said Ray.

I sighed. "Yeah, I guess."

"Oh," said Stef. "I didn't think. The iguana night. Sorry."

"Don't worry about it. I'm a big boy. I'm not that easily triggered."

But I was. Everywhere I went, things brought back that night. The death of the iguana and the young man would forever be entangled in my head. And then there was the other event of that evening I couldn't get out of my head, the kiss sandwiched between the two deaths.

As we pulled our bags from the trunk of the car, a woman arrived with a pail of ripe fruit to feed the iguanas. A small crowd had already formed around the base of the tree. The woman smiled at me. "Would you like to help feed them? We need a tall person."

"No, I..." I moved toward Ray, who held the gate to the patio of the apartment building open. "I have to use the bathroom. Long drive. Maybe next time."

I hurried in the gate, and Stef punched in the code for the door.

"You okay, hon?" she asked.

"Of course. I really do have to use the bathroom."

It was a two-bedroom, two-bath apartment, and I offered Ray and Stef the bedroom with its own bath. I ducked into the other bathroom. When I came out, Ray and Stef were in their bedroom, so I went into my room and closed the door.

I lay on my bed, reminding myself why I was in Sayulita and

composing myself for it. A talk with Ivan would bring some kind of closure, if nothing else, and I felt robbed I hadn't been able to have a face-to-face with him the moment I returned to Puerto Vallarta.

Sun streamed in through yellow curtains along with the sounds of children laughing. I got up and went to the window. Drawing back the gauze curtains embroidered with flowers, I watched the parents admonishing their children to stay at a safe distance from the hungry animals. One small iguana descended all the way down to the base of the Guamuchil tree to get a morsel of mango, causing a little girl to squeal and run for her parents. I prayed that in contrast to my last encounter with an iguana that heralded a disaster, this more pleasant scene would foreshadow something positive by the end of the day. I was inclined to rush over as soon as possible to the condo complex where I hoped to find Ivan but was embarrassed that Ray and Stef would see me as overzealous and setting myself up for disappointment.

I took a long time getting dressed, emerging from my room in a pair of shorts with palm trees embroidered on them and a tank top that hugged my torso. I spent way too much time in front of the mirror, getting my dirty blond hair to look casually tousled.

Ray and Stef sat at the table making a list. Ray looked up and whistled. "Guapo."

"Aw, shucks."

"We're going shopping, but you don't have to come," said Stef. "Ray has offered to cook."

"That's not fair for you to do all the shopping *and* cook."

"Look," said Ray. "We know you're going to be unbearable until you do what you have to do. We're cool with that."

"Unbearable?"

"You know what I mean."

"At least let me give you some money."

"We'll settle later."

"I'll plan to be back for dinner. What time are you thinking?"

"After sunset," said Stef. "We're going to shop and then walk on the beach." The main beach was at the end of the street and, like everything in Sayulita, within walking distance. She accompanied me to the door and asked me again in a low voice if this was what I really wanted. I nodded.

I had a few hours before dinner and hoped to catch Ivan before his shift ended. I was making a lot of assumptions: that he worked the day shift as he had at Paradiso, that he wouldn't freak out at me coming to his work (probably not a cool thing to do), and that he would even talk to me. I was heartened by the strange phone call in the middle of the night when I was back in California that he claimed was a butt dial. I took it as a sign he was reaching out.

The condo complex, just a few blocks from our rental, looked recently finished with newly planted flowering bushes on either side of the path leading to the main glass doors embossed with the condo complex logo. The elegant lobby with polished marble floors and multi-colored, modern chandeliers was a step up from Paradiso. The automatic doors slid open, and I caught a glimpse of Ivan in his new environment, talking to a resident, totally engaged and attentive as I had seen him with the residents of Paradiso. With everyone except me. I recalled his skittish behavior and the darting eyes, particularly after the tragedy, giving me a sense of hopelessness in my mission.

I sat on a bench near a potted palm in the large lobby, but as the conversation with the resident went on, I stood up again, my heart thumping, my hands clammy. And then Ivan glanced in my direction, a brief glint before returning to the person he was talking to. There was no sign he had even noticed me except that he clenched his right hand.

His hair was shorter, and he had shaved the moustache he had started when I last saw him. He wore a black polo shirt with the company label on it. I smiled to myself, remembering what was under the shirt, the bird tattoo on his chest, soaring upward. Ivan's hand unclenched as he reached to shake the hand of the man he was talking to, ending the conversation.

I was surprised when he walked directly over to me and stuck out his hand. "Señor Dawson."

My spirit fell at his return to calling me señor. "Hola, Ivan. You don't look surprised to see me." The shake was brief, a moment of his warm hand in mine, and then it wasn't.

"I'm working," he said in a low growl, putting on a fake smile, curling his lip slightly.

"So nice you found another job after leaving us. Caused somewhat of a mess. We're stuck with Severino now." At the mention of Severino, he squinted with creases gathering at the corners of his eyes.

"I'm sure you'll do fine without me."

"Me or the building?"

"Not here." He forced his mouth into an exaggerated smile. "Meet you outside at five."

"You're not brushing me off, are you?"

"Just go. I'll be there."

I had an hour and a half to kill. I went to a coffee shop and ordered a cappuccino. I checked my email and then Instagram where Matthew had posted a reel of him playing volleyball on the beach. I watched several other reels, checked my email again, and looked at the weather forecast. I now had an hour and twenty minutes to kill.

At 4:45, I was back in front of the building where I paced and tried to stop the voice in my head. *He's not coming. He slipped out the back.* I reminded myself that Ivan might be lots of things, but he wasn't a liar.

A few minutes after five o'clock, he sauntered out.

"Sorry. Last minute issue. Let's walk." He motioned in the direction of the beach.

He walked quickly, beckoning me to follow. He had always been so hesitant or evasive with me before, but now he was taking charge. I hurried to catch up. Neither of us spoke as we walked along Pescadores Street with beautiful villas on the left and beached blue and white fishing boats on the right. In front of a boutique hotel called Villa Amor, which brought a smirk to my face, he stopped and said, "I have a daughter."

I was confused why he would open with that. "Okay. Do you need to get back to her?"

"She's with her mother this week." It seemed the divorce rumor was true.

"Oh."

"I can't lose another job." He started walking again, returning to a swift pace.

"Where are we going?"

"La playa."

I hooked my thumb over my shoulder, pointing at the main Sayulita beach we just passed. "Isn't that...?"

"Too crowded."

We came to the end of the street, passing an abandoned construction site that looked like the shell of a luxury apartment building and turned left onto a dirt road. Ahead was a brightly painted archway, covered with a Day of the Dead motif. Just on the other side of the archway was a cemetery.

We passed under the arch where, on either side of the road, tombs were festooned with multicolored banners and decorated with flowers, some fake and some real, papel picado hanging above the graves, bottles of the deceased's favorite soda, and even message balloons as if everything was prepared for a birthday party rather than death.

"Seriously?" I mumbled as I chased after him. He was too far ahead to hear me. I considered turning around at that moment and abandoning this crazy idea of making things right, if that was even possible. A young man had died. There was no changing that. But I was pulled forward by something more than my curiosity, drawn by his determined gait. If he was open to talking, as he seemed to be, I would see this through until the end.

He slowed and turned around. "It's the way to the beach," he offered as if reading my thoughts.

We turned onto a path that led down to the sand with the sound of the surf and the laughter of children getting louder. A man greeted us, asking if we wanted to rent a chair and umbrella. Ivan declined and led us toward the end of the beach to a clump of boulders in the sand. We found the flattest ones we could and sat down on separate rocks, facing out to sea.

The sound of the waves and the calming beach air began the process of eroding my anxiety. "Nice beach," I said. "So much calmer than the main one."

"Hm," he said, falling silent as if he too was letting the atmosphere roll over him, relaxing him. He put his feet on a lower rock and rested his hands on his knees. I stared at the lightly hairy arms that had been wrapped around me that night and the beautiful hands that had pulled me close. It felt like a dream, that brief moment when we had found pleasure in an embrace, a kiss.

"How's the new job?" I asked.

"Good. The people are nice." He adjusted his position again, still staring out to sea. "Your trip back to California is okay?"

"For the most part. Went to a wedding and met with my boss a couple of times. Spent a lot of time worrying about things."

He nodded while he made circles on the knee of his jeans with his finger.

"You're not going to ask why?" I said.

He took a big breath and let it out. "I think you are going to tell me."

"I've been feeling this guilt. We have information the police should know. If it wasn't exactly an accident, there should be some justice for the family. Truth matters."

He produced a sound that was half-groan, half-laugh. "Do you realize how American you sound right now? Talking about truth and justice? You come here to our country and tell us how to do things. It's so...ingenuo, what's the word...like simple. You are ready to ruin other lives, so you can settle your own conscience."

"But you must feel it too if you quit your job and left town."

He lifted his hands and let them fall back onto his knees. "Not my choice," he growled.

"You got fired?"

"No." He closed his eyes, and his face tightened as if he shouldn't say anymore. "I don't tell anyone this."

"What?"

"It was chantaje."

"Someone is blackmailing you? Who? Why?"

"Think who is to benefit with me gone."

I pictured Severino sitting in Ivan's chair at the front desk with a satisfied smile on his lips. The monitors. The story they told of Ivan entering my apartment. "Severino?"

"Sí."

"The surveillance video?"

He nodded.

"But you were supposed to be checking the apartments. You were doing your job."

"It is not only the video. When I am in your apartment longer time than maybe necessary, he go to an apartment where the owners are out of town and from the balcony take pictures of us."

"That's sick."

"He wanted my job. Always wanted my job. He is so angry he don't get the day shift since working nights from the beginning. The day is better hours, more responsibility, so more pay. He have six kids."

"That's fucked up. And he wasn't doing his job. He should have been monitoring what was happening on the roof, not playing private detective. What about the video proving that the rooftop situation was out of hand, and he did nothing?"

"The video is fuzzy, and the lights are low. Because of the loud music, you can't hear nothing."

"Did the police even ask for it?"

"The police want to believe in the accident theory. Better for them."

"I'm so sorry." I laid a hand on his arm.

He stared at my hand, and I quickly removed it. "I'm thinking of many things since you left. I think you go back to States because of me. I was very hard with you."

Amid the tension, I felt a sense of relief that he had admitted being unkind, but his remark that I was being a typical American hit its mark, especially when I didn't consider myself one at all. Ivan was right. In my plan to go to the police, I had only been thinking of myself and what would make me feel better. I hadn't considered how much I might screw up his life and maybe others. "I'm sorry."

"Stop saying you're sorry. You didn't force me."

"It was the beer," I said, trying to lighten the mood.

"Hah! You make a joke. It was all a joke for you?"

I wiped my sweaty palms on my shorts. "I can't stop thinking about it actually. Us."

He hesitated but finally let his words out in a low voice, his eyes lost in a memory. "One moment I enjoy. And the next, I am in shock."

"Me too. I thought you regretted it."

"At first, yes. So many bad things happen. I am confused. And then the Severino thing. God is punishing me. But sometimes in bed before I go to sleep, I remember what we do."

"You liked it?"

He turned his head slowly to meet my eyes. "Maybe."

Though our eyes met only for a moment, I had a strong feeling it wasn't the end. There would be no clean break and moving on. I turned to stare at the ocean, watching the seagulls skim the waves. "Do you want a beer?"

He shook his head. "You are crazy."

"It's not a joke. There's a palapa over there. Just one beer."

"Hm. I hear this before."

We sat on rusty metal chairs at a rough, sun-bleached table. Ivan ordered Modelos, and we touched bottles as we had that night. I took a sip and looked at my watch.

"Somebody waiting for you?" he asked with one eye half-closed.

"My friends are cooking dinner. You could join us."

"Oh, you are not here alone."

"I'm with Stef and Ray, my best friends in Vallarta. I want you to meet them."

"Thank you, but no. You are very nice guy. But we are from different worlds. You want to take me into your world for what? Introduce me to your dear friends for what?"

"Different worlds? That's bullshit. Because we grew up speaking different languages in different countries, we can't be friends?"

"I'm not gay, Dawson."

The words hit me and then hung in the air. But I felt some solace that he had used my name without señor. "There's an app for that."

"Very funny."

"You never kissed a guy before?"

He looked around. "Por Dios," he hissed. "I can't talk about this things. Not here."

I lowered my voice. "Then come to the place where I'm staying. Ray and Stef are married, but Ray is..." I stopped, thinking I didn't have the right to reveal personal information about Ray.

"Everything is so simple for you." He narrowed his eyes. "Wait, you have some three-way thing with them?"

"No way. They are my friends, and I think you would like them."

"You told them about me?"

"I had to talk to someone. You wouldn't talk to me."

His lips twitched, and he looked toward the sky. "I met the boy's parents."

"What? No. How?"

"When they come to Vallarta for the body, they want to see where it happen. They are simple people from a pueblo in Nayarit. I meet them and show them the building, the rooftop. Very strange. They are humble people. Ask me no questions."

"Do they know about their son?"

"I don't know, but I'm sure they don't want to talk about it. In most Mexican families, they don't talk about such things."

"It's the same in the States for a lot of people. Kids getting thrown out by their parents."

"It was difficult for you?"

"I suppose it was easier for me than most." In truth, I had always been harder on myself than my parents were. They started educating me about sex at an early age and later gave me the lecture about condoms with "whoever you end up having sex with," which made me more upset as it seemed they might have detected my feelings for boys. I blamed them at one point for putting ideas in my head.

I checked the time again. "I have to go. Are you sure you don't want to come with me? I would like to continue this conversation."

"I walk you back, but I don't come in."

As we kicked up sand on the path back to the road, I looked over my shoulder at the sun painting the sky yellow and orange and rose. I stopped and turned around. He stood beside me, and as we watched the glowing ball disappear below the horizon, we were taken, for a moment, out of the things that confused and unsettled us.

At the gate to the Airbnb, I promised him I wouldn't say anything to the police. "I understand your point of view. I mostly wanted to talk to you and...you know...see you. Can I see you again before we leave?"

He sighed and stared at the ground. "I don't think this is good idea."

"Just have a beer and talk," I said, raising my voice slightly. "I don't understand what the problem is."

"You are the problem. You won't let things go."

Ray opened the door and poked his head out. "Everything okay?"

"I'll be right in."

Ray stood a moment, staring at us.

"Really. It's okay," I said. "I'll be there in a minute."

Ray made a half-smile and closed the door.

"This is your friend?" he asked.

"That's Ray."

"Don't be angry with me," he said. "You will thank me. I want you have a good life."

He turned and walked down the street, glancing up at the iguana tree but not looking back at me. I stood a moment, watching him fade away with an emptiness in my chest.

Seven

I lay in bed, restless, my mind spinning from the several beers we'd had with dinner, the day strange and at times wonderful though ultimately disappointing in the meeting I'd had with Ivan. As everyone asked me, including my internal voice: what did I expect? But the even bigger question loomed: what did I want?

In the years before I met Jacob, I kept falling for guys who were unattainable, either not open to relationships or already in one. I knew I had to be careful, although being careful got me the relationship I had with Jacob. I was in Mexico for something different though I still didn't know what that was. I tried to focus on the positives of my encounter with Ivan. He didn't hate the kiss and came close to admitting he liked it, or, at least, thought about it later, and it seemed more than once. He also made me realize some things concerning the death of the boy and life in Mexico, my obtuse attitude as an American, trying to impose my sense of justice and truth on another culture. And even though Ivan insisted there was no reason to get together again or continue a friendship, his eyes and body language hinted at something else. When we were sitting at the little table on the beach drinking beers, our knees bumped and feet touched, but instead of moving away, he allowed the contact to continue. I tested it by nudging my knee a little closer, my foot lined side by side with his. He didn't budge.

When he asked if coming out to my parents had been hard, he put his hand on my arm for a pair of seconds with a concerned look in his eye. And several times, I caught him looking at me with something more than casual curiosity. The signs were subtle, and I admitted, they could have been imagined, wishful thinking. I had hoped that confronting him would be closure, a resolution, a chance to see that it had only been a furtive kiss with someone I had little interest in. The reality was the exact opposite. I was intrigued more than ever, different worlds be damned. When I closed my eyes, I saw his face and remembered what it had felt like being in his arms. As much as he tried to hide it on the surface, I knew that deep within Ivan was a passionate person. And in the right circumstances, he was brave enough to follow that passion.

At dinner, Stef and Ray had pumped me for information about my time with Ivan while I kept shifting the conversation back to the new information of him being blackmailed. Stef and Ray were troubled by the way Ivan had been treated but could offer no advice on how he could get his job back without a lot of awkward revelations.

"I only got a glimpse of him," said Ray with a smile, "but I see the attraction, at least the physical aspect of it. Were you having an argument?"

"He doesn't want to see me again, even as friends. I thought things were going well. He seemed relaxed and admitted he thought about our kiss sometimes. But we're from different worlds, he said, as if there was no space where our lives could overlap."

"Perhaps it's for the best," said Stef. "Good thing he's not still working in your building. It would be awkward."

With all the thoughts of the day in my head, I tossed and turned, and then rolled over on my back, staring at another ceiling fan in another place, spinning like my brain. A stripe of light coming in under the door meant Ray was probably still up. Stef said he often stayed up long after she went to bed. I felt a twinge of loneliness and guessed that Ray did too. I could imagine cuddling up with Ray and the book he was reading on the couch but kept it as a fantasy. I knew it was better that way.

I had reached a groggy state of almost asleep when I heard voices at the front door next to my window. My phone told me it was 11:30. Two male voices. One was clearly Ray, and it took me a minute to realize the other was Ivan. In my foggy brain, it made no sense. I sat up and slapped myself awake.

"He's asleep," Ray said. "Can I give him a message?"

"Tomorrow is my day off and maybe if he's not too busy…"

I jumped out of bed and opened the bedroom door, walking out in my underwear and a tank top.

"I heard voices," I said.

Ray winked at me. "I guess I'm no longer needed as the messenger. I'll let you take over."

Ivan was still outside the door in shadow. Norteño music pulsed from a bar nearby. I stared over his shoulder at the iguana tree but didn't spot any iguanas.

"Sorry to wake you," he said.

"What are you doing? I thought…"

"Invite the man in, Dawson," Ray said on the way to his bedroom.

I let my eyes fall on Ivan's anxious face. The seconds ticked by.

"It's okay. I can go," he said.

"No, you can't." I grabbed his arm and pulled him inside. "You're letting the mosquitoes in."

"You maybe think I'm crazy."

"You said I was crazy earlier, so I guess that makes two of us. Have a seat. Can I get you anything?"

"No, thanks." He sat gingerly on the edge of the sofa, right in the middle. He looked around and scratched the back of his head like I'd seen him do before. Then he stood up rapidly. "I should go."

I moved in front of him, put a finger in the middle of his chest, and pushed gently until he was sitting again. The alcohol in my veins helped me take charge. "No. You knocked on my door. You're not leaving until you tell me why you're here."

"No sé."

"Great. You don't know."

"It was not polite the way I leave this afternoon."

I sat down next to him. "You got that right."

He bounced his leg, and I put my hand on his knee. "Is something wrong?"

"You make me…nervioso."

"You make *me* nervous."

"I do? Since when?"

"Since always."

"After I leave you here, I go back to my room, have dinner, and try to sleep. I think of…"

"The kiss?"

"I was married. I have a daughter," he said in almost a whimper.

"But you liked it." I leaned toward him and pecked him on the lips. He smelled of toothpaste and soap like he was freshly showered.

"I thought a man's lips would be rough. But they are not. Yours are not."

I stood up. "Come to my room."

"No!"

I pulled him up, so we were face to face again. He opened his eyes wide. "Come to my room," I said more forcefully.

"I can't."

"Stop saying you can't. Just do what you want to do, por Dios."

He laughed and some of the tension left his face. "I forget you speak Spanish."

"Vamos," I said, taking his hand, pulling him toward the bedroom. "We don't have to do anything. We can talk or not talk. Sleep or not sleep. Whatever you want."

We entered the dark bedroom with a yellow glow coming in from the street, and I closed the door with one hand while still holding his hand in the other.

He pulled his hand away. "I can't see."

I turned on a bedside lamp and smoothed out the sheets that were still warm from when I left them. "Have a seat."

Instead of sitting down, he pulled his T-shirt over his head and dropped it on the floor. He kicked off his boots and dropped his jeans before crawling under the sheet in his boxers and socks.

"What are you doing?" I said.

"Is this not what you want?"

"Take off your socks."

"Why?"

"I just have this thing about socks in bed."

"I take off my clothes and put myself in your bed, and you are worried about my socks?"

"How can I suck your toes with your socks on?"

He scrunched his face into a look of disgust. "Is this a required activity for you guys?"

"Us guys? You mean the gays? It was a joke."

"I know. But I take them off just in case." He took off his socks, balled them up, and threw them at me while I stood by the side of the bed in a state of shock. They bounced off my chest and fell to the floor. "Come on," he said. "What are you waiting for?"

I removed my tank top and slid under the sheets. "Is this like an experiment for you? Will you sneak away in the middle of the night, feeling guilty and never talk to me again?"

"That is the risk you take."

"Fuck you."

He rose up on his elbow and stared at me while I stared at the ceiling fan going round and round. "I think you are not really angry. I think you are happy I'm here."

"Más o menos."

I pushed him onto his back and got on top of him. "I could strangle you right now."

"This is something else you guys like, the physical abuse?"

I leaned down to kiss him but then pulled back. "It couldn't be worse than the psychological torture you have put me through."

"Talk. Talk. Talk. Cállate." He put his hands behind my head and brought our lips together.

I broke the kiss. "Are my lips soft enough for you?"

"Shut up!" He rolled me onto my back and pressed our lips together again, slipping his tongue in.

He had succeeded in getting me to shut my mouth but not my thoughts, which were spinning faster than the ceiling fan. As much as I wanted to sit back and enjoy the weird and wacky moment the last half hour had given me, one of those times in life where something happened that didn't begin to make sense, I couldn't stop my now sobering brain from reminding me I was dealing with two completely distinct people in Ivan, someone who could run away from me and run toward me within the same fervor within a few hours. It was way more than I bargained for. And yet, I had put myself in this position.

He stopped the tongue action and pulled back. "What's wrong?"

"Nada."

"Bullshit. You are afraid I am going to jump up and run away."

"Didn't you make it clear you're not gay?"

"You can't only enjoy what we do? This maybe sound funny, but I want to make you happy. I don't know why."

"That's why you're here? To make me happy?"

"And maybe to make myself a little happy too. Things have not been good for me for a long time."

"I've got an idea what could make you happy."

I slid down so that my face was level with his crotch. I hoped it would give me something to focus on and stop my meandering brain.

He tensed and let out a long "Oh."

I pulled the waistband of his underwear down, wiggling the elastic back and forth until it was down to his knees. "Hello," I said. He needed nothing more than mere suggestion to get things going. I peeled back the skin and touched the tip of my tongue to him, causing him to jump like he'd been hit with a bolt of lightning.

I didn't fully get to exercise my skills before there was a moan, another jolt, a shout, and it was over except for a few aftershocks. When he had caught his breath, he reached down and pulled me up, smothering his face in the crook of my neck as his body settled.

"Are you gay yet?" I asked.

He slapped me on the butt. "Pendejo!"

"Alright. Slap on the butt. You're getting it!"

"Can we have a little quiet? I'm so...so relaxed." He pulled me closer and wrapped his arms around me.

I was *not* relaxed but forced myself to be, always reminding myself to be grateful for life's little blessings. I took a few deep breaths, enjoying the fit of our bodies together. I ran a finger along his jaw, feeling the stubble that sent little sparks through my finger, my hand, my arm, all the way to my heart. *Damn it!*

The morning brought miracles. We had shifted position, me now embracing him from behind, my chin on his shoulder, a wisp of his hair tickling my nose. The first miracle was that he was still there. Within seconds, I had an erection very close to his ass. I backed away a few inches out of respect, not wanting to scare the bejesus out of this rookie in the land of male-male sex. He rolled over and looked at me, tilted his head with eyes struggling to open.

The second miracle was his smile.

"Can I do something for you?" he said.

"No, I'm good."

"Liar. You almost break out of your shorts."

I put my hands over my face.

He sighed. "I can't, you know, do what you did...maybe someday... but something else?"

"If you touch it, I'll probably explode like you did."

"Sorry for that."

"I'm glad I gave you some pleasure. It was pleasurable, right?"

"Muy."

I slid my underwear down and finished pushing them down with my feet until I was naked. "I can do myself if you don't want to touch it."

"Be patient with me. Tell me what to do."

I got on my knees. "Get behind me and put your arms around me. Kiss my neck and whisper in my ear. Are you comfortable with that?"

"Sure." He did as he was told, moving his hands up and down my torso, nibbling on my neck, whispering nonsense in Spanish in my ear. The hot breath nearly sent me over the edge.

I stopped pumping myself. "What the hell is going on back there?"

"I think I'm excited."

"You think?"

In my mind's eye, I saw the eagle tattooed on his chest and imagined I was in the talons of the bird, being carried away, flying through the air. I reached back and pulled him out of his underwear.

He moved his curious hands down to my pubic hair and tugged it gently. He cupped my hands, sliding with me while pressing against my butt. "Vamos, chico. Tú puedes," he whispered directly into my ear. And that was all it took.

Feeling spent, my head light and my heart settled, I leaned back into him. We fell like China dolls onto our sides, laughing. He continued to hold me. "Do you need...?" I asked.

"What I need is to use the bathroom."

"If you go in the hall, it's the first door on the right. Ray and Stef have their own ensuite bathroom."

He got out of bed and pulled on his boxers. "Can I go like this?"

"Wait. You never showed me your other tattoos."

He lifted the legs of his underwear, revealing a stylized jaguar head on each upper thigh.

"Why two?"

"Uh...I have two legs?"

"Nice ones, too."

"Thanks."

"You have something crusty on the face of the right jaguar."

He rolled his eyes up toward the ceiling. "I think I need a shower."

"Me too."

He grabbed his crotch. "Can I go pee now?"

"Go."

A few minutes later I heard the shower running and knocked on the door. "Sorry. Have to pee." I stood at the toilet and looked at this beautiful stranger in the shower, soaping his crotch, getting rid of the evidence, ignoring me like he was in another world.

I leaned on the wall next to the shower door. "Would it be weird if I joined you?"

He looked up and shrugged. "As you wish, señor Dawson."

"Yes, I wish."

It was a tight fit. I rested my head in the groove of his upper back, between his shoulder blades, feeling the water splatter my face, taking me back to the rainy night when we kissed on the balcony. I turned him around and kissed him under the water.

"Señor Dawson, what are you doing?" Señor had started as a sign of respect and then turned cruel when he tried to ignore me. Now it was playful.

"I don't know what comes next, but I just wanted to say..."

He put his hand over my mouth. "Cállate and wash my back?"

"I will shut up for now and happily wash your back, but..."

He held up his index finger in warning, handed me the soap, and turned around.

Eight

Ray kept smiling at me from across the table while Stef was more discreet, bringing up topics of conversation that did not relate to the night before. I was willing to talk about anything else, but not anxious to share my thoughts about Ivan spending the night. The feelings were still new and undefined. We were at a crowded breakfast spot on Sayulita's square called ChocoBanana that despite its name served everything from waffles to breakfast burritos to chicken burgers. When I ordered the Big Boy Breakfast, Ray howled with laughter.

"Didn't you already have your big boy breakfast?"

"Leave the man alone," said Stef though she was also choking back a giggle.

"At least I didn't order the ChocoBanana," I said with a smirk.

"So, you're not going to tell us anything?" said Ray.

I was glad I saved Ivan the morning scrutiny, though, in truth, it had been his decision, saying he wasn't quite ready to meet Ray and Stef. He hurried out after our shower with the excuse that he had things to do, which he could only do on his day off. We made no plan to see each other later or ever.

In the early morning, when the sun had not yet peeked over the mountains, we stood at the door of the rental unit. "Can you at least give me your phone number?" I said, forgetting the accidental call when I was in the States.

"You have my number. WhatsApp. The messages I used to send you about packages."

"Oh, the packages I didn't get until a few days after they were delivered to the building?"

"What are you talking about? Now you're accusing me of not doing my job?"

Separation anxiety was making me bring up stupid shit. "Never mind."

"Never mind, nothing. Tell me what you mean."

I motioned for him to keep his voice down. "It just seemed like other people got their packages right away, and I didn't."

He mouthed an "oh." After staring at me a minute, his eyes still hot, he looked away and sighed. "It maybe happen once or twice."

"Why would it happen at all?" My voice had turned from an accusation into a plea.

"One time I wait until I know you are home to deliver it in person," he said in a soft voice, his eyes focused on a cactus in a pot by the door.

My jaw fell, at a loss for what to do with that information. I took a couple of shallow breaths. "That's water under the bridge as they say. We're here now in a different reality."

He let his eyes swivel to slowly meet mine. "Not sure what that means. You need to be more patient."

"You keep saying that. I'm going back to Vallarta in a couple days, and you're here. You say we live in different worlds. It does feel like that sometimes." I felt tears in my eyes and knew it was the exact wrong thing to do, getting all weepy after our second "date." I saw fear creeping into his face. "Sorry. Go do what you have to do. I'll text you later."

"Okay. Bye." He turned and left. Again. Without looking back.

"Dawson," said Ray, breaking into my thoughts. "You haven't touched your Big Boy breakfast."

"Okay. This is all I'm going to say. It was a nice night...and morning...and..."

"And shower?" Ray had seen us come out of the bathroom together with towels wrapped around our waists.

"And then he left in an awkward goodbye."

"Oh, honey," said Stef. "I told you to be careful. You've got too big of a heart."

"Moving on," I said. "What should we do today? Ivan showed me a cool beach. Much quieter than the main one. The waves are gentler too. But you have to walk through a graveyard to get there."

Before we left for the beach, I sent Ivan a text. **We're going to Playa de los Muertos this afternoon.** It wasn't exactly an invitation. I didn't say how long we would be there. I left it as is. A statement of fact. If he wanted more information, he'd have to ask for it.

We rented beach chairs under an umbrella in the middle of the curved line of chairs that followed the shoreline of the small bay. Stef headed for the water barely minutes after we arrived. Ray ordered mojitos for the two of us.

"And Stef?" I said.

"She's a little hung over. I told her hair of the dog and all that, but she's sticking with ice water. She brought this big-ass thermos full of ice."

I leaned back in the chair and closed my eyes.

"So, there's nothing you want to talk about?" said Ray.

"Nope."

"Come on. You're killing me. Gimme something. What a tease to see you guys half naked, leaving the bathroom!"

I opened one eye. "Ray," I said like an admonishment.

"I know. None of my business. I just want you to be happy."

"I think I want that too. Seems like I have a peculiar way of going about it."

Stef came back quickly from her dip as if she knew Ray would be badgering me for details. "The water is great, and you were right, the waves are calmer."

"I'll try it out in a minute," said Ray.

I checked my phone. No response.

Ray noticed it and seemed about to say something, but I cut him off. "Ray, I've been meaning to ask you something."

"Uh-oh."

"How autobiographical is *Night Dancer?*"

Despite the many conversations we'd had from everything about life in Mexico to good books we'd read to writing in general, I had been reluctant to ask that burning question about his work. It felt so cliché for a reader to want to know how much of a novel comes from a writer's real life.

Stef had just taken a drink of water, and she ended up spraying it out.

"What?" I said. "Was that one of those questions you're never supposed to ask a writer?"

"Of course, people want to know," said Ray. "I'll tell you one thing. I was not the dancer."

"He could have been," said Stef, "with that body."

"You don't have to go into it," I said. "I should have known better than to ask."

"Frankly, I'm surprised you've waited this long. We've known each other a minute. It gets a little annoying at cocktail parties, but you're one person I don't mind telling my story." The server arrived with the mojitos and set them on the rough wooden table in front of us. "Are you sure you don't want something, hon?"

"No, thank you," said Stef.

"In the story, the bouncer at the club was more or less me. I played football back in Illinois at Peoria High, like the bouncer in the book, not because I wanted to, but I was big for my age and athletic and Black. What choice did I have? All I wanted to do was hang out behind the school with the dopers and freaks. I tried one time, and they treated me like I was a narc. Anyway, I got a scholarship to the University of Illinois in Champaign-Urbana and majored in English. I graduated with no fucking idea what I was going to do. My parents freaked out when I told them I was taking a year off and moving to Chicago. Good Christian people as they were, they thought I was jumping into the devil's den, which wasn't too far from the truth, and more than that, they worried about how I would support myself. But I got a job as a bouncer at a club in Boystown, and like Sam in the novel, I tried to protect the dancers from harm, mostly the harm they brought on themselves. I got very close to one dancer, Alex. Not romantically. He was a sweet guy but tragic. His parents brought him over from Cuba when he was twelve, and he never really fit in. He wasn't Black enough for the Blacks and the Latinos looked at him suspiciously. And then he was gay, which, where he grew up on the South Side, was asking for trouble."

"In the book, he was Puerto Rican, right?"

"And I gave him the name of Oscar. Who was I fooling? Anybody who knew my life around that time could figure out who was who."

"Did Alex die the way Oscar did in the book?"

"Not exactly. I didn't find him in an alley, stabbed to death, like Sam found Oscar. Alex took home the wrong guy who stabbed him and left him to die. But the emotions Sam felt after his death were so real because I lived them." Ray took a moment to catch his breath. "Even now I get choked up."

Stef stepped in. "I had read his book, so when I saw he was teaching a seminar in creative writing, I jumped at the chance."

"After the book took off, I went from a nobody to a somebody overnight. It was completely unexpected and scary. I was this Black ex-jock that was lucky enough to go to college. All of a sudden, everybody wanted me. When something so monumental happens like that, your choices hardly seem your own. I got into DePaul to go for a Masters. I was teaching classes to students who were bright and committed and talented writers. Like this woman right here."

"I remember now you said Stef was a student of yours."

"She's a brilliant writer. I bet you didn't know that."

"Was," said Stef. "I had a brilliant teacher. And everybody in that class pushed each other to be better. We were all dizzy with the atmosphere of creativity. And of course, everyone in that seminar was in love with Ray Burnside."

"She's exaggerating."

"No, I'm not. He created an environment of support and, yes, love that we were allowed to swim around in. There were no sharks, only lovely sleek dolphins. We were soon to find out that it was not the real world, not even the academic world. I never had another class like that."

"Stef and I didn't get together then, so don't be thinking there was any teacher-student hanky-panky going on."

I sat up straight. A young man who looked like Ivan was walking toward us. I rose to my feet, but as the young man got closer, I saw he had no tattoo on his chest.

"Down, boy," said Ray. "You got it bad."

"No. I don't," I stuttered. "I sent him a message that we were here. I thought it might be him."

"Hey, let's go in the water," said Ray. "You need to cool down."

"I'll stay here," said Stef.

"I want to hear the rest of your story as well." I pointed at Stef. "I have questions."

Though I was focused on the person I had woken up with my arms around that morning and anyone on the beach that looked vaguely like him, it wasn't lost on me that Ray still had the bod, and I could imagine the impression he must have made when he was young. At fifty-eight—I was shocked when he'd told me his age—Ray was still fit, and as I watched him dive into an oncoming wave, I was inspired to stay in shape like him. As we played in the waves, a big one knocked me into Ray, and he grabbed me, holding me up. For a moment, we were eye to eye. The possibility of a kiss hung in the air between us and then flew away. We separated, and I panicked that Stef might have been watching. Ray didn't seem to care in the least.

We left the water and came back to Stef, who appeared to be reading a book, but behind her dark glasses, she could also have been sound asleep or plotting murder. We shook our hair and bodies like dogs, sending droplets of water in all directions.

"Stop it," said Stef. "You're getting my book wet."

"You never thought of writing one of those?" I said, indicating the book in her hand. "Or maybe you did. I shouldn't assume."

"Thought is the operative word. I point to two things that made me crumble under the idea. When we first started living together, Ray's second book had just come out. It was a brutal time, and I saw how it affected him. Every review began the same way. 'It was no *Night Dancer*.'"

"When you reach the top, there's only one way to go," said Ray.

Stef sighed. "I told Ray not to read the reviews, but he did, of course. He had already started on the third one, and I begged him to focus on that. What he was going through put a strain on our relationship. A couple of my girlfriends were going to Cuba, so I tagged along, thinking Ray needed the space."

"She up and abandoned me in my misery," Ray whined.

"What a drama queen! We talked about it, and you told me to go."

I intervened in the teasing to get us back on track. "You said there were two things that turned you away from writing?"

"In Cuba we went on a Hemingway tour, visiting all his old haunts like El Floridita bar, Hotel Ambos Mundos, and the house, Finca La

Vigía, where he lived off and on for over twenty years. I invited Maribel, the woman who rented us rooms, to go with us. She had lived in Havana her whole life but had never been to Hemingway's home. The house is kept as a museum and set up with his belongings, but a museum you couldn't enter. All we could do was look in the windows and see his slippers under the bed, his typewriter on the desk. As we walked around the grounds where there was a large swimming pool and Hemingway's yacht, El Pilar, displayed on blocks, I mentioned to Maribel how sad it was that the writer had committed suicide. She was shocked. Most Cubans live a rather hand-to-mouth existence, and it seemed beyond her comprehension that someone who had so much, a famous writer, would kill himself. Her reaction really hit me, and I started thinking about all the other writers who had killed themselves: Virginia Woolf, Sylvia Plath, Yukio Mishima, Jack London, the list goes on and on. I began to obsess over the idea that Ray might do something crazy like that, and I was desperate to get back home and be there for him."

"I had some dark moments," said Ray, "where offing myself entered my thoughts. But it was my students who kept me going. I loved teaching. When my third novel got run through the mill of vicious reviewers, I devoted my energy to teaching. I published some academic articles to keep my status at the university, but that was it."

"And I went into tech," said Stef. "I figured the best thing I could do for us was to provide stability and a steady income. Ray was able to take an early retirement. And here we are."

"Working with writers the way I do, I know it can be a bumpy road," I said. "But there must be something wonderful about connecting with readers, having your words dance around in their heads, bringing laughter and tears."

"It's not fair that the writer gets all the credit and the editor almost none," said Ray. "I'm sure you must get some works with potential but in bad shape. You're the one that makes the magic."

"You wouldn't believe some of the stuff our acquisitions department takes on because they think it will be a commercial success. If you are famous for whatever good or bad reason, regardless of your ability to write, you are almost guaranteed a contract at some publishing house. I find it fun and challenging to make it readable."

Stef got up to go in the water again. I thought it strange that it was almost as if Ray and I were a couple at the beach, and Stef was the third wheel. I watched her head to the water.

"She's in great shape," I said. "She must exercise."

"Pilates. She's been doing it for years. We both swim and walk a lot."

"You guys are an inspiration."

"You probably think it's weird that Stef and I stay together."

"No. She's great."

A couple of young men were playing frisbee nearby. A wild throw landed at the foot of Ray's chair. He leaned over to pick it up but held onto it until one of them ran over.

"Sorry, sir," said the young man with a six pack and shoulder length hair.

"No problem," Ray said, looking the man up and down. "Enjoy your game." He zeroed in on the man's ass as he ran back to his friend.

I checked my phone. Still nothing.

"And you probably think it's weird that I care about this guy who's probably never going to respond," I said.

"Not weird at all. Stef wouldn't agree with me, but go for it. So many motherfuckers in this world have no chance to feel anything or have a moment of pleasure. If you enjoy being with him, ride it as long as you can." He laughed. "I didn't mean it like that unless, of course, that's what you like."

"Okay. I have to ask, but tell me if it's none of my business. I saw the way you looked at that guy. Do you ever...?"

"Fuck around? Not as much as I used to. Hate to tell you this, but with each decade the opportunities decrease exponentially."

"Come on. You're a hot man. I bet you have no problem hooking up."

"You're a dear to say that. You are, too, by the way."

I laughed. "Maybe in another universe we..."

"As I mentioned before, Stef and I have an arrangement. I go to Mexico City on my own from time to time. I've been to Zipolite in Oaxaca a couple of times."

"Is she really cool with it?"

"She knows I'm going to do it anyway, so it works best to have rules. Like she says, she can't tolerate the down-low stuff."

"If it ever got to that point with Ivan, I don't think I could handle him going off and being with a woman."

"What about another man?"

"Meaning?"

"When you and Jacob were together, were you monogamous?"

"We tried."

Ray threw up his hands. "That's just it! You tried."

"It seems pretty stupid to me to be in a relationship and be out fucking around all the time."

"Who's talking about all the time? People have needs outside the relationship. It doesn't have to be all the time."

"There are no degrees of fidelity. Either you are or you aren't."

"Enjoy your life, Dawson! Are you seriously worrying about whether Ivan would be faithful to you after you spent one night together? No wonder he ran away."

"Stop trying to manage my life." I was irked and jumped up. "I'm going for a walk."

"Whoa...I'm not...Dawson, come on. I'm trying to help you."

I ignored him and kept walking toward the shoreline. I met Stef on the way back from the water. I had been in such a huff, I'd forgotten my hat and sunglasses, which I needed to hide behind as she scrutinized me.

"What's wrong?" said Stef.

"Nothing. Just going for a walk."

"You look like you're about ready to kill someone. Don't let Ray put ideas in your head. You know what's best for you."

"Really, Stef. I'm fine. Tell Ray to order a couple more mojitos. See you in a few minutes."

I walked to the rocks at the end of the beach where Ivan and I had been the day before as if returning to the spot could conjure up the guy who was in my head and wouldn't leave. Ray was right about one thing. It was completely ridiculous to put Ivan and fidelity in the same sentence after one night together, especially since we hadn't consummated what a lot of people would consider sex, as in peg-in-the-hole sex. But the fact that he had allowed himself to be held all night by another man had to count for something. Erotic touch had to count for something. Kissing had to count for something. Coming to my door in the fucking middle of the night had to count for something.

Nine

I returned to Ray and Stef feeling contrite for going off in a mood. My mojito in a plastic cup sat on the little table. Stef was deep in a book, and Ray discreetly mouthed, "Sorry." I shook my head and smiled. I sat and we touched plastic glasses.

I spent the rest of the afternoon and evening trying not to look at my phone for messages. As we left the apartment to go out to dinner, we heard music in the square and the side streets were lined with horse trailers. The street by the square had been blocked off and a crowd had formed around Mexican cowboys on horses though whatever show was going to happen hadn't started yet. We decided to go to dinner and see what was happening on our way back.

An hour later things were in full swing with horses dancing to the music on the cobblestone street, prancing up and down, doing a side-step. One rider in particular caught my eye, and most likely Ray's, a handsome young man in a cowboy hat, riding boots up to his knees over tight jeans, and a blue jean shirt with pearl snaps. He rode a large black horse with a bushy mane and tail that swished with the music as it gingerly stomped up and down. It had feathering on the lower legs, long black hair that almost covered the hooves and swayed as it danced.

As the five or six horses moved to the edge of the crowd, an animador came into the middle of the street with a microphone, encouraging people to dance but joking that the horses were a hard act to follow and that stomping wasn't necessary. When people were reluctant, he got a few of them to form a line, which circled around the wide street, gaining more participants. I kept looking for Ivan in the crowd. My fantasy brain took off, imagining him riding up on a horse in boots and cowboy hat, pulling me up to sit behind him and encouraging me to wrap my arms around him.

"Earth to Dawson!" said Ray. "Let's join in."

Ray, Stef, and I shuffled into the line along with a few other foreigners in the mostly Mexican gathering.

"How do you dance to this?" I said.

"You just kind of bounce," said Stef. "It's all in the knees. Oompa. Oompa."

"It's not an accident that it sounds like a polka," said Ray. "Polish and German immigrants brought over brass instruments in the nineteenth century, and it all got mixed with Mexican traditional music."

One of the things I loved about Mexico was the number of festivities that brought people together, out into the streets, with music and dancing. Little children and grandmas, teenagers and parents, all staying out late and being part of something. People in the States tended to socialize at home. Mexicans took to the streets. The three of us felt comfortable in the mix, welcomed, and we stayed, laughing and dancing until after eleven. I even managed to not check my phone for a couple of hours.

The next day we drove fifteen minutes north to San Francisco, Nayarit, commonly known as San Pancho. It had a small walking bridge from one side of a drainage ditch to the other, gaily painted with the letters San Francisco Golden Gate. There were lots of restaurants and cafes, multicolored papel picado hanging over the streets, and a more relaxed beach than Sayulita. An open-air yoga class was going on in the central square when we arrived. Like Sayulita, San Pancho had a lot of foreigners, while at the same time remained very Mexican. The foreigners who came to Sayulita and San Pancho didn't try to create enclaves of exclusivity like they did in other parts of Mexico, making "safe" communities or resorts separated from Mexican culture. I worried that the North American invasion would cut into the colorful fabric of Mexico and tailor it to something with clean lines, coordinating colors, and a veneer of respectability.

"What do you like about Mexico?" I asked Stef and Ray as we sat at a beachfront café, having cocktails.

Ray sat up and answered without having to think about it. "I love that it's messy and unpredictable. I love not knowing what's around every corner. It could be a hidden treasure like a fantastic mural or something disgusting like a vacant lot with rotting garbage. It's all so alive."

"I love the kaleidoscope of color," said Stef. "When I go back home, everything seems so drab."

"This is *home*," said Ray.

"I've got to stop saying that. Believe me, this is a lot more of a home than Chicago ever was. When Ray wanted to move here, I had my doubts. Now, I couldn't be happier."

"Can I get another round of cocktails?" I said.

"Let's get some lunch to soak up some of this alcohol," said Stef. "Ask for a menu on the way back."

After lunch, we ambled down to the water and hired chairs with a rainbow-colored umbrella just a few feet from where the waves hit the beach. I watched pelicans flying overhead until one of them broke formation and dove straight down into the water with the speed of a jet where the pilot had lost control. I closed my eyes, and there was the boy again, flying through the air. With another drink, I eventually fell into a gentle slumber to the sound of the surf pounding the shore.

We went back to Sayulita and had leftovers for dinner because none of us had the energy to go out. We were pleasantly exhausted from the sun and salty air at the beach, and the number of cocktails we had lost track of.

Stef went to bed early, and I was headed in the same direction. I was in the bathroom brushing my teeth when a text pinged on my phone. **Come out.**

For two seconds, I decided I was going to ignore it. In the next two seconds, I thought I would answer but say I was already in bed and half asleep. Fuck! Okay, I would go and say goodbye. Thank him for coming by.

I spit out the toothpaste and growled. I tossed my toothbrush into a cup. It missed and landed on the floor. "Fuck!" I picked it up and rinsed it off. I slapped on some deodorant and splashed water on my face. "Fuck!" I exited the bathroom, holding the phone aloft.

Ray sat in the living room, reading Luis Alberto Urrea's *The House of Broken Angels.*

"You look like Moses who just got the Ten Commandments from God," said Ray.

"Just a text from nobody."

Ray looked out over his reading glasses. "So, what was all the noise about?"

I pointed at his book. "I met him once, Urrea. At a writing conference. We were presenting a new book by one of our Latino authors who happened to be a friend of his."

"Are you going out?"

"He's outside apparently."

"Have fun."

"I'll probably be back in two minutes."

I didn't see anybody in front of the apartment. From being reluctant at first, I fell into a panic that he had already left. To act nonchalant in case he was hiding somewhere nearby, I walked over to the sign near the iguana tree and read that the iguanas in this location were green iguanas, and they were an endangered species.

I'm in the truck right next to you.

An older model small blue Toyota pickup was parked at the curb. I opened the door. "Hey."

"Get in."

I sighed but was more than willing to comply. "You are full of surprises."

"You said that before like maybe a hundred times," he said with a smile. "I remember what happen the last time you said that."

"It was good for you?"

"Sorry. I was busy yesterday. And today I work."

"I leave tomorrow."

"That's why I pick you up."

"Okay," I said, dragging out the word as if it contained multiple messages.

"What okay? You are not happy to see me?"

"Meh," I said, tilting my hand back and forth in the air.

"Cabrón."

We drove along the road that led to Playa de Los Muertos, through the archway, past the cemetery and past the entrance to the beach.

"Where are we going?"

"I'm taking you to the moon."

"That's a big promise."

"You gonna see and believe."

With the window down, I leaned out, staring at the dark wall of trees, wondering if there were any iguanas in them.

"Why you hug the door?" he said, reaching over and putting his hand on my knee.

"Two hands on the wheel."

As the headlights stabbed the darkness, he drove faster than he should have on the narrow road but removed his hand to make a turn onto an even narrower and curvier road where no other cars ventured. "Don't be afraid. You are in good hands."

Right. Why should I be afraid? I was on a dark, bumpy, twisty road with an almost stranger who was driving too fast and taking me to an unknown destination deep in the woods.

He slowed and the trees broke as he pulled into a lookout point over the pacific with the rising full moon hanging above the horizon like a giant peach.

He turned off the engine and pointed. "I told you."

"Don't point at the moon. It's bad luck."

"Who told you that?"

"My grandma. She was from Romania."

"You could be a werewolf or something."

"It's the full moon. You'd know by now."

"I always wondered about your name, Wozniak."

"It's Polish. Most of my ancestors came from Poland but a long time ago."

He patted the seat next to him. "You are so far away. Acércate."

I slid over, and he draped an arm over my shoulder. "Is this some kind of lover's lane?" I asked.

"I don't know what that is."

"In high school, there was this narrow turnoff near the ocean where teenagers used to go and make out."

"And other things?"

"Sometimes in the backseat." I looked over my shoulder. "No back-seat. What a shame."

"Hmm." He rubbed his index finger along my neck and then along my collarbone, quietly, absentmindedly. The surf pounded far below echoing the sound in my head. The air was heavy and smelled of salt-water and seaweed. He moved closer. I leaned my head on his shoulder, dropped a hand onto his thigh. The moon climbed in the night sky, getting smaller and paler, allowing the stars and planets to shine brighter.

His hand slipped under the collar of my T-shirt and began sliding back and forth over my upper chest. Down it crept until it touched my right nipple. He tweaked it gently, and I bolted upright.

"Shit. Sorry. I thought maybe you like this."

"I do. But it unlocks a beast in me and makes me do bad things."

"And there's no backseat."

"And there's no backseat," I repeated.

"But there is a trail down to the beach."

"You are full of…"

"I know. Surprises."

"Where did you get the idea that I might like nipple play?"

"I can't tell you." He pulled me back to the previous position and put his hand down my shirt again."

"Did someone do it to you?"

"So many questions."

"A lot of gay guys like it, but I don't know about straight guys."

He closed his eyes and nuzzled my head with his forehead. "Okay. I see it in a video."

I sat up again. "You watch gay porn?"

"No way. One time there is two men and one woman. They take turns with the woman. Then something happen. The two men start kissing while one is doing the woman. I almost turn it off. But I want to see what happen. One man begin to play with tetilla of other, and he like it a lot. Then they change, and the man start fucking the other man."

"And then you turned it off, right?"

"No," he said almost sadly. "I think maybe I try that one day."

"Now, if you could just find someone crazy enough to do that."

His hand was back on my nipple, grazing over it ever so gently. I turned my head to look up at him. Our lips met.

He broke the kiss, pulled my shirt over my head, and began rubbing my stomach.

"Your skin is like milk in the moonlight." He let his hand slip below the waistband of my shorts.

"What are you doing?"

"Come with me," he said as he opened his door, casting a rude light on our surroundings. In the light, he glanced at my hard-on pushing against my shorts.

"Give me a sec," I laughed.

While I calmed myself, he grabbed something out of the back.

We closed the car doors and were again bathed in the much softer light of the moon. But when we got into the woods, we used our phone flashlights, stepping carefully down the path with the moon guiding us as it peeked in and out of tree branches. My heart was thumping in my chest with the anticipation of where this was leading while noises of night animals all around us added to my jumpiness. In the distance, waves pounded the shore.

"Be careful," he said. "Sometimes iguanas fall from the trees."

"Shut up."

"It's a thing."

"It's not a thing."

"It is. But not usually here. Only in cold places where the temperature falls. Here it would probably be just a snake."

"Just a snake? No problem."

When I got home, Ray was still awake, like a dad waiting for his son to get home safely, reading his book. I wanted to tell him how Ivan had mysteriously produced a blanket from the box in the bed of his truck and a condom from his pocket. How we had traversed the trail lit by the moon like Balboa and his men who "discovered" the Pacific Ocean. How we peeled off our clothes in the haste of the moment. How his curious eyes monitored the various pain-pleasure expressions on my face. How he was gentle up to a point. How it felt normal and exhilarating at the same time. How the moon formed a halo behind his head. How we lay under the stars for a long time afterward, listening to the waves without saying a word. How the breeze off the ocean swept over our naked skin and fluttered the hair on our legs. How even Leonardo da Vinci couldn't capture the enigmatic smile on his face. How our hands found each other. How he helped me up the trail when my legs were a little wobbly, joking about how I was getting old.

Ray splayed his book over the armrest and looked up. In his eyes, I could see how much he wanted to hear every detail, but I couldn't talk about it. And like my dad would say when I used to come home as a teenager, he asked, "Everything okay?"

"Sure. Little tired. Going to bed. You good?"

"About to go to bed myself."

"Sleep well."

"You too."

I felt his eyes on me as I walked toward the bedroom door, giving me the urge to turn around and give him a powerful hug and tell him how happy I was to have him as a friend. I couldn't do that either.

When Ivan had dropped me off, there had been no promises and certainly no declarations of love. As we sat in his truck parked next to the iguana tree, he mentioned, gazing straight ahead, that he came to Vallarta every week to see his daughter.

"You could come and visit me."

He snorted. "You know I can't come to the building."

"I guess not."

"Maybe we go to no-tell motel."

"That sounds creepy."

"I was joking, but..."

He turned to look at me and the warm glow from the streetlight softened his face. The spark of desire in his eyes was undeniable no matter how much he tried to play it down. Joking? Maybe. But there was something real behind the joke.

Ten

Back in Puerto Vallarta, I threw myself into work. I hadn't looked at my email all weekend because I knew there would be snarky messages from Susan asking if I'd gotten lost in the jungle, her favorite expression since I'd started editing a manuscript about a group of teenagers on a trek through the jungle in Costa Rica. The youths discovered a magical garden where they ate the fruit, giving them superpowers and knowledge about everything except how to leave the garden. The author was an expert in world building, but the writing was often unclear. I found the book annoying, but it was not my job to like or dislike. I was to take the awkward and convoluted sentences and make them, if not beautiful, at least readable. And I was a little pissed off at my boss for assigning me another speculative fiction book, my least favorite genre to work in. I wanted to remind her about the original goals of the company she had talked about at my first interview, the focus on literary and historical, but the marketing department kept saying genre fiction was what sold.

When I hit a particularly obstinate sentence in a crucial segment of the book, my mind drifted to the discussion with Ray and Stef at the beach, particularly Ray's second and third books. They were beautifully written and had something to say but never got off the ground. It was mind-boggling to think of the big picture of publishing, how good books were pushed aside or not promoted for works that targeted a particular genre audience. I realized that publishers, especially small ones, had to make business decisions that allowed to them to survive and, I reminded myself, pay my salary.

After working the rest of the morning on the manuscript and answering emails to the senior editor where I told the big lie that I was nearly finished with the book, I decided to go for a swim to clear my mind. I ran into Trixie at the pool. Though I was inclined to take one of the lounges far away from her, I didn't want to appear antisocial. I took a chair one over from hers.

"Hi, Trixie. I thought you'd be back in…" It was hard to keep track of all the various northern locations Paradiso residents were from.

"Minnesota. Leaving tomorrow. Catching the last rays before I go. Ed is already back home, but there were still some loose ends to tie up."

Based on what I had learned from Ivan over the weekend, she had no idea how many loose ends there were. "Are you pleased with the way Severino is working out?"

"I guess. But there is this weird rumor going around, and I have a feeling it came from him."

"What kind of rumor?"

Trixie leaned forward, tightened her jaw, which accentuated her wrinkles, and whispered in her gossip voice. "That Ivan was involved in some kind of love triangle with Patrick and the young man who died."

"That's ridiculous," I said, perhaps a little too loud and showing too much emotion.

With a French tip fingernail, Trixie pushed her sunglasses down her nose and stared at me over the top of them. "Look, I don't care if Ivan is gay or bi or trans as long as he does his job."

"Uh…trans is not a sexual preference."

"Whatever. I thought it sounded ridiculous, but we have to check things like that out. Employees can't be involved with residents, period."

My stomach did a little flip, but I tried to calm my speech. "I can't believe you'd even consider something so ludicrous."

"When Ed heard it, he said he wasn't surprised. He always had a feeling that Ivan was gay."

I suppressed a chuckle. I had pegged Ed as a closet case who projected his internalized homophobia on others. He had probably fantasized about Ivan since day one. He'd also stared at me coming out of the pool on several occasions. "I may not have the best gaydar in the world, but I got nothing from Ivan." *Now, your husband on the other hand…*

"I'll be the first to say it. My husband can be an idiot. He's the only one around here who really likes Severino. He fixed our car one time and didn't charge us a dime. Ever since, Ed has worshipped the ground he walks on."

I had seen the way Severino sucked up to Ed and some of the others, especially after he had applied for the day job. Severino could be mildly charming in a cloying kind of way, though I had never fallen for it. I was sure he had been on a campaign to get rid of Ivan since his first day on the job. With the nasty rumor about Ivan and the fact that Severino now had something on him, Severino had risen to the top of my shitlist. And the package thing! Severino was the person who put the idea in my head that Ivan was lazy about delivering packages, feeding into the uncomfortable feeling I already had about him. Severino was a clever bastard.

"He's had a grudge against Ivan since he was passed over for the day job," I said. "You know that."

"But Ivan *was* up on the roof that night. I just wonder..."

"Who told you that?"

"I guess I heard it from Severino."

"Really, Trixie? He was *not* there when it happened. He went up right after."

"How do you know that?"

I hesitated but had already gone too far to back out now. "Because he was with me."

This time she took her glasses completely off and leaned toward me. "What do you mean *with* you?"

"With me as in my presence. What your husband said has gone to your head. He was doing what he was told to do, checking the apartments for leaks. Since mine was the last one, I invited him to have a beer, which I probably shouldn't have done. But technically he was off work. We heard the commotion upstairs followed by the terrible scream. He rushed up to the roof. If you're going to be suspicious of anybody, you might wonder what Severino was doing when he should have been monitoring the rooftop situation. They were swimming in the middle of an electrical storm and playing loud music."

Trixie fell back in her chair and groaned. "So, what do I do?"

"You could start by squashing the rumor about Ivan every time it comes up. Put something in the newsletter."

"I trust you on this, and I will."

I got up and jumped into the pool to drown the sordid conversation. I had denied that Ivan was gay less than twenty-four hours after we'd screwed on the beach. Or made love? I still wasn't sure how to phrase it in my mind. I dove under the water and came up at the end of the pool where I leaned on the edge and looked out over the Bay of Banderas.

The next two days, I worked on the manuscript and managed to finish it only two weeks behind schedule. I avoided Severino as much as I could and heard nothing from Ivan despite my reaching out, limiting myself to one text a day, mundane comments like: **I'm still finding sand everywhere**; or **On my walk down the hill I heard something fall from the trees. It wasn't an iguana**; or **Is it possible to moon the moon?** The last one would need some explanation, but since he didn't respond to the other messages, I didn't bother.

I got a message from Stef on Thursday asking if I was free for dinner on Friday. They were going out to Bonita Kitchen with a friend they wanted me to meet. I was sure it was the architect from Guadalajara they had mentioned before. I couldn't count the number of times coupled up straight friends—and whatever Stef and Ray were—had tried to set me up. It never worked out. Always the same scenario. They have two friends who are gay who they really like. Ergo, the two men should like each other, right? I agreed to the dinner even though it meant I wouldn't be able to discuss Ivan out of courtesy to Ricardo or Roberto or whatever his name was. Now that I had some distance from the weekend, I was ready to talk about it, but realized at the same time it would probably be a lot of whining. Perhaps Stef and Ray knew that too, and this was their plan to distract me.

As I was shy about meeting new people, I bumped myself up with a couple of shots of tequila before heading out to the dinner, which I planned to enjoy even if the guy was a total troll. It would be obvious we weren't a match, and I could put an end to Stef and Ray playing matchmaker.

I stood outside my building, waiting for the rideshare I had ordered, when Severino walked out after his shift.

"Hola, señor Dawson."

"Hey, Severino."

"Going out to party?"

Yeah, cause that's what we gay boys do, that and push each other off rooftops, and pose for snoops taking secret photos. "No, I'm going out to dinner with friends."

"Great. You guys always seem to enjoy life."

Really, Severino. Us guys? "I ran into Ivan. He's got a great new job, and the staff there are really nice and respectful. Better salary too."

He was stunned for a second but recovered quickly. "Cool. Where is he working?"

No way I'm going to tell you, asshole. "I don't remember the name of the place. Some fancy new complex."

My car pulled up. "See ya," I said and jumped in the car.

Ray, Stef, and the potential boyfriend were already seated. I looked at my watch as I walked in the restaurant and felt bad about my tardiness. I'd had to wait a long time for the car. When Ray hugged me, he whispered in my ear, "Not my idea."

"Dawson," said Stef, "I'd like you to meet our dear friend Rafael." She laughed. "Well, you're both dear friends."

"Mucho gusto," I said.

"Qué chévere. You speak Spanish?"

"I'm working on it."

Rafael spoke excellent English and was a good conversationalist, nice looking with curly dark hair and designer glasses. He was also a snappy dresser though his suit jacket and button-down shirt seemed too formal for the situation unless he was going to propose on the spot.

The menu highlighted cuisine from various Asian countries, and we shared plates of potstickers, dumplings, kimchi, samosas, spicy wings, and Japanese friend chicken. I drained my glass of wine and reached for the bottle for the third time, offering to fill everyone else's glass first, until I realized they still had half full glasses. I felt a tinge of embarrassment but continued with the pour.

"Rafa, you're not drinking. Can I call you Rafa?"

"A lot of my friends do. I'm a cheap drunk," he said with a laugh. "Don't want to end up dancing on top of the table."

"I would love to see that," I said, resting my hand on Rafael's thigh.

Stef had a satisfied smile on her face. Ray's was more of a suspicious grin.

The drunker I got, the more charming Rafael appeared, though his leg twitched, and I removed my hand.

"I heard that the handsomest men in Mexico are from Guadalajara," I said.

"That would seem to be the case," said Stef in a giddy voice.

"Oh, come on, guys," said Rafael.

"You're cute when you're embarrassed," I said. I filled my glass again.

Ray's doubtful grin seemed to be frozen on his face.

Rafael perked up as if he had accepted a challenge. "Well, I heard that Polish boys have the creamiest skin."

People didn't often refer to me as Polish since I was a third generation American, but I was willing to go with it. It might get me laid. "Guess you'll just have to find out."

The server came to clear the plates and gave us dessert menus. I stood up awkwardly. "Excuse me. Have to use the facilities." I weaved between the now mostly empty tables, reaching out once to steady myself with a hand on the back of a chair. I hoped they weren't watching.

I planted myself at the urinal, a little unsteady on my feet and my vision blurry. "He's nice," I said out loud. "Cute, really. Not as nerdy as I thought at first. Should I make a move? God, I'm drunk."

A toilet flushed and a stall door swung open. "Oh, shit," I mumbled. It was a kitchen worker. At least he probably wouldn't understand my babble.

I stayed at the urinal until the worker had finished washing his hands. I glanced over my shoulder and caught the man's eyes in the mirror. "Go for it, man," he said.

I groaned. How many embarrassing moments could I have in one evening? The night was young. I smiled grimly at the worker and gave him a thumbs up.

At the sink I splashed water on my face, trying to sober up before I went back to the table. My phone buzzed in my pocket. Probably a message from the publisher about some detail with the manuscript. Did she ever stop working? I could ignore it. But what if it was an emergency? I had to stay in her good graces and took the phone out of my pocket to read the text.

I will be in Vallarta tomorrow.

What? The publisher was coming to Puerto Vallarta. *No, wait.* Fuck! It was from Ivan. What would be a proper response? No response? My brain was cloudy.

Me too.

Did my response sound snarky enough? It was better than the "Fuck you" I wanted to write. I hadn't heard from him all week, and just when I was about to jump into bed with another guy, he reminded me of his existence, and that he was going to be in town and was probably at that moment sitting on his bed waiting for me to respond with a message that I was dying to see him. Bastard.

I pick up my daughter around noon. I can come early and meet you some place.

Oh, right. He has a daughter and a wife and maybe wants a quick blow job in his truck so he can pick up his daughter with a smile on his face. In the next room was a handsome, successful man who I guessed didn't have a wife and a daughter but probably a nice apartment where we could go and have sex in a bed with 400 thread count cotton sheets and coffee in the morning.

My fingers started working while my mind was still in an angry jumble. **Text me when you get here.**

I shoved the phone back into my pocket and returned to the table. They were all laughing about something, and I hoped it wasn't me.

"We thought you got lost," said Ray.

I picked up my glass and downed what was left. I stared at the empty bottle. "Should we order another one?"

"I think they want to close up," said Stef. "Hope you didn't want dessert because we all declined."

"God, no," I said. I looked around and saw the staff discreetly waiting for us to leave. "I should go home." I felt Rafael's eyes on me.

My stomach churned as if I might vomit. Painful tears formed in my eyes.

Ray insisted on picking up the bill. We stood, and I, still wobbly and dizzy, put a hand on the table for support. Rafael took my arm, but I shrugged him off. Outside, the dense tropical air hit us hard after the air conditioning. Across the street a lone taxi sat under a giant tree.

"You take that one," said Ray. "We're going to walk."

"Good night," I muttered and staggered across the cobblestones. I got in the backseat, but before I could close the door, Rafael slid in next to me.

"I'm going to make sure you get home alright. You don't look so good."

"No es nece…nece…necessary." With a little wine my Spanish got better. With a lot, I stumbled in any language.

"What's your address?"

I told him, and Rafael told the driver. I slumped against the window and closed my eyes but opened them right away because the car was spinning. I really didn't want spray the lovely Asian dinner all over the seat and possibly Rafael. "Sorry."

"No worries."

Eleven

I awoke unnerved from a dream about an editor's meeting I had to attend. I was late and things kept getting in my way. The elevator in my building didn't work. My car wouldn't start. I went to the wrong location. When I arrived in the glass-walled room with skyscrapers outside the windows, they all sat with glum faces around a table that later morphed into a piano. Stef and Ray were two of my fellow editors, and Ray was stretched out on top of the piano like a cabaret singer. A copy of my recent edits on the Garden of Eden teen fantasy book sat on the music stand. Ray said, "I'm so disappointed in you. This is terrible work. I know you're distracted, but this can't continue."

The pounding in my brain brought me to reality as I forced my eyes open. Thank God for blackout shades. I breathed a sigh of relief when I realized I was alone in the bed. I checked my messages, but there was nothing from Susan. I saw a new one from Ivan and the previous evening tramped through my fragile head, leaving me with a queasy stomach. I had vague memories of Rafael helping me out of the taxi and into the building; fishing the keys out of my pocket and opening the door; helping me out of my clothes and into bed; putting a glass of water on the bedside table. I was almost certain nothing else happened.

Next to my phone and the glass of water on the bedside table was a Post-it. "I hope you awake without too much of a hangover." Signed, Rafa, with his phone number. Everything had been going so well the night before (except that I had been guzzling wine) until I got the text from Ivan. The flirtation with Rafael stopped cold. I hadn't properly said goodnight to Stef and Ray. I had walked to the taxi without saying anything to Rafael. And still, Rafa got me home safe and tucked me into bed, someone who I'd only known a couple of hours. Had I thanked him at any point during the time he took care of me?

My phone rang. It was Ivan.

"Hola," I said, my voice groggy and echoing painfully in my head.

"Why you didn't answer my text? I'm waiting at the bottom of the hill." He was angry.

"Hill? What? Sorry. I'm just waking up. Had too much to drink. Didn't see your text. Where?"

"My message say I wait you at the bottom of the hill of your street at 10 o'clock. It's 10:15. I don't have much time."

"Okay. Drive up to the corner store where the boys hang out. I'll be there at 10:30. Promise."

"10:30. No later." He hung up.

I jumped in the shower and let the warm water pour over my head. I could have stayed there for hours, but I forced myself out and threw on a tank top, shorts, and sandals. No time for coffee. I would have killed for a cup of coffee. Maybe we could go to the patchouli place where I bought the beans from Nayarit. They had an espresso machine with a window to the street. But the patchouli smell would put me over the edge. Perhaps I should adopt the Mexican Coke habit and run in the corner store and get a liter bottle of it.

I ran down the hill though it nearly killed me; my feet pounding on the pavement sent shockwaves to my brain. Ivan's truck was parked on a side street, and I got in.

"I'm so, so sorry."

"You look terrible."

"Thank you. You look very handsome today."

"I just mean you look not well or something."

I pointed to my head. "Resaca. What do you guys say?"

"La cruda."

"So crude. Take me to coffee, please."

He started the truck. "There's a place near."

We pulled in front of an Italian café near the Malecón that I always thought looked a little too fancy for the area.

"Do you want anything?" I asked.

"No, gracias." He waited in the truck while I went in for my double cappuccino.

I got back in the truck with the awareness we hadn't touched or hugged or anything. I had given it all to him on the beach. Didn't I deserve, at the very least, a pat on the leg. Despite my hangover, I felt turned on as I glanced at his legs in shorts, and all the memories of our beach sex washed over me like the tide. We both started to speak at the same time.

"Go ahead," he said.

"No, you."

"I have very busy at work this week."

"Me too. You could have responded to at least one of my texts so I would know you're still alive."

"I didn't know what to say."

"You could try hello, hi, hola, anything."

"Easy for you."

I had no idea why a simple greeting would be easier for me, but I let it go. "Do you know anyplace we could go? Like a hidden place?" I jiggled my eyebrows at his crotch.

"Chingada madre! You think I come see you for this?"

"That's what we do, isn't it?"

"We do something then immediately after I go see my daughter? This what you think of me?"

"I was kidding."

"I don't think so."

I was not used to fighting with partners or potential boyfriends or whatever Ivan was. Since I met him, it seemed like that's all we did. Instead of calming the waters, I made more waves, things coming out of my mouth that I had no power to stop.

"When you see your daughter, do you see your wife too?"

"None of your business," he spit out.

A voice in my head told me to stop. But I couldn't. "Do you still have sex with her?"

"None. Of. Your. Fucking. Business." His face was now red.

"You're right. Sorry."

"I don't have time for this. You should get out."

"I get it. It's none of my business."

"I mean it. Get out."

"You're actually kicking me out of your car?"

"Yes. Go."

I opened the door and stepped out. I closed the door quietly, and in backing away from the truck, I ran into a woman with a baby stroller. She screamed. I managed to avoid crushing the baby, but my coffee slipped out of my hands and splattered on the sidewalk.

"Lo siento," I said to the woman, but she had moved on down the street. I looked at the empty space where Ivan's truck had been. It was about to turn the corner up the block. I lifted my hand in a sorry attempt at a wave, which I was sure he didn't see. I felt like sitting on the curb and bawling my eyes out, but that was the old me. The new me said, "Fine. It's over. What a relief!"

I marched into the café and ordered another cappuccino. The manager had seen what happened with my coffee and told the girl at the counter not to charge me. I nodded thanks to the manager and walked the half block down to the Malecón where I found an empty bench. I sipped my coffee and watched the people strolling by, sweaty joggers braving the heat, and a few cyclists riding too fast around people walking in the bike lane.

Though my Malecón therapy calmed me, an unsettling feeling deep inside kept raising its hand, wanting to be called on. Was there something wrong with me? Why was I pursuing a man that seemed unattainable? In moments of self-doubt, I used to call my mom who always made me feel better. It made me heartsick I couldn't.

One Saturday in June of 2020, I called to check in with my parents. My mom said she had a bug that she couldn't shake. Probably the flu.

"You need to go to a doctor, Mom."

"I did. Well, I talked to my naturopath, and she prescribed some herbs. They need time to work."

"A real doctor, please."

I was surprised she didn't argue with me as she usually did about matters of health and standard medical treatment. She didn't seem to have the energy and rang off soon after. In my busy week, I had called a couple of times, but no one answered. I finally got through a week after I had last talked to them. My father told me Mom couldn't talk because she was short of breath. I begged Dad to take her to the doctor as I feared it could be COVID.

"You know how stubborn your mother is. She won't go. Anyway, there are hardly any cases of COVID around here."

"Dad, take her to the doctor, or I'll come there and do it myself."

"Your mother is strong. She'll beat this."

The next day I packed a bag with a few clothes and lots of masks and antibacterial gel and got in my car to drive the six hours to my parents' house on the edge of the Sonoran Desert north of Lukeville, Arizona. Nobody was flying in those days. By the time I arrived, she was in the hospital. They didn't allow visitors. Two days later she was gone. I wanted to scream at my dad for not taking her to the hospital sooner, but the devastation on his face was so vast, all I could do was fall into his arms and weep. The next morning, I woke up after a mostly sleepless night—my mom's death, the howling coyotes, the dry air—to noise in the kitchen of the little adobe house.

I stumbled into the kitchen and found my father leaning against the counter, dressed in tactical pants, sweatshirt, and boonie hat, staring into his coffee. "What are you doing?" I asked.

"Got to check the water stations." My parents had devoted the last ten years to the migrant population on the border. My mom had gone back to school and gotten a paralegal degree so she could help migrants file for asylum. One of the things they did on a daily basis was go out into the desert and maintain water stations, usually just plastic jugs of water hidden among rocks, along migration routes from Mexico.

"You can surely take a break from that for a couple days," I said.

"Those people need me. Life goes on."

"Dad, I hate to leave you, but I have to go back to Los Angeles." I had an editing deadline, plus I had already detected signs that Jacob was having an affair.

"Don't worry about me. Your sister is coming tomorrow."

"That's good." She would take care of picking up Mom's ashes. At a later date we would scatter them in the desert she loved so much.

He cleared his throat and took a sip of coffee. "I wish you and Nell were..."

"We're good," I said.

"I don't know what's going on with you two, but you need to fix it. Do it for your mother."

"I will." And I fully intended to mend the rift between us, and hopefully Mom's death would be the catalyst.

I was also pleased that Dad was taking what appeared to be a healthy survivor's attitude, though I knew that in his heart, life had stopped. A few months later, my father was out in the desert and came upon a dehydrated and bedraggled group on their way north. He gave them water and food from the back of his jeep.

Tucked into the back of his trousers was a gun he had bought to defend himself against border vigilantes who patrolled the desert, threatening migrants and shooting holes in the plastic jugs they discovered, sending the life-saving water onto the parched earth. His stance on nonviolence had taken a hit in recent years as he witnessed firsthand the cruelties of the world. Before he had a chance to shoo the migrants on their way, a border patrol car sped toward them, a vehicle moving along the horizon in a cloud of dust. When they tried to round up the people he was helping, he pulled out his gun and told the officers to let them go.

He died in a blaze of gunfire, doing what he believed in. The officers and body cameras confirmed that he shot first, injuring one of the officers. I didn't want to call it suicide by cop. I don't believe he set out to die that way, but his despondency at losing my mother must have been a factor in his making a fatal decision.

In a period of a few months, I lost both my parents in tragic ways. In that same year, my boyfriend left me for another guy, a Black bear type who was both physically and personality-wise the exact opposite of me. I wondered what I had done to make him dissatisfied with me and seek a new partner. What got me out of the funk of losing my parents and of being dumped was my first trip to Puerto Vallarta, prompted by some photos I had found in a box in my parents' house of their honeymoon in Puerto Vallarta. One of the photos was of my parents, a young and innocent Tess and Stan, standing in front of the Hotel Rosita at the end of the Malecón just a couple blocks from where I now sat on a bench.

That first time I rode in the taxi on the cobblestone streets, along the Malecón and past the church with the crown—all part of the stories my parents had told me—I felt the presence of my mom and dad, so much in love, and it soothed me. Doing a little math, I guessed that my life began shortly before or soon after someone snapped that picture at the Hotel Rosita.

On that first trip to Puerto Vallarta, and every other, the letter my mother wrote a few days before she died traveled with me. When I went to collect her things at the hospital, a kind nurse told me that my mother had dictated the letter to her soon after entering the hospital. She must have had a feeling about what was coming, and it pained me to think of her in that state and all alone. I had read the letter so many times, I had it memorized.

My dear son,

I'm writing down a few things I wanted to tell you because I'm not sure I'll have the chance to tell you in person. First and foremost, I love you more than you can imagine. You are my darling boy, and yes, I know you are a man, but to me you will always be that sweet, funny boy with tousled blond hair who brought such joy to my heart. My awesome Dawson. I know you hated it when you would ask how we had come up with your weird name, which isn't weird at all, and I would always laugh and say it was because it rhymed with awesome.

My dearest, I think it is time I tell you the real story. My best friend in high school was named Dawson Clark. He was a boy I loved, but in a different way and long before your father. I was drawn to him because he had the most beautiful soul, and he was drawn to me because I gave him a safe space to be the person he was. His life at home was horrible, a father who disapproved of every single thing he did or said and a mother who was sympathetic but didn't have the strength to stand up to his father. He was an all-around beautiful person inside and out, like you, and I loved him deeply as I do you. He started taking whatever drugs he could get his hands on to escape the pain at home. He overdosed at seventeen, and I was devastated. I realized years later that he was probably gay. I never told you the story because I didn't want you to feel strange I had given you the name of someone who had overdosed on drugs, probably deliberately, and was miserable about his homosexual feelings. In more recent years, I'm sure you could have handled it, but I never got around to telling you. But giving you his name reminded me every day of the person who taught me about love and friendship, so that when I met your father, I was ready.

That day you came home to us after years of almost no communication, the day we jokingly dubbed "the day of grand reconciliation," was one of the happiest days of my life. You told us you had realized some things about yourself, about us, and the world in general. When you told us you were gay (we already had a pretty good idea), my heart swelled because you felt comfortable telling us and it meant that we had done something right. We laughed and cried and drank wine, and you even shared a joint with us. You swore you would never ever vote for a Republican again. I laughed so hard I thought I would burst.

I am so proud of you, my son. If your childhood was lacking in any way (I know, stability) I apologize from the bottom of my heart. Maybe it wasn't right to push so hard for you to see another side of life, another way to live. But you developed into a loving, smart, and yes, awesome human being that any mother would be proud of. Know that I will always be with you, and I hope you will carry me in your heart as I have carried you in mine all these years.

One last thing. Take care of your father. He's a stubborn old coot, but he loves you as dearly as I do, well, maybe a tiny bit less, since I am and will always be your mother.

All my love.

Mom

Twelve

I had been strong enough not to dissolve into tears when Ivan had kicked me out of the car, signaling the end of whatever that involvement was. But thinking about my mother's letter there on the Malecón in sight of the Hotel Rosita sent me over the edge. I wondered if she would still think of me as awesome if she knew about Ivan and my unawesome involvement.

For once it felt good to be alone in a crowd with no one noticing my sniffles or the tears streaming down my face. A good cry was what I needed. I set my coffee cup on the ground and lifted the body of my T-shirt to wipe my eyes. And just as I had grown comfortable in my misery, thinking no one noticed, I sensed someone in front of me, blocking the light of the sun.

"Nice abs."

I dropped my shirt and raised my eyes. "Hey, Matthew. Are you stalking me?"

"Ha ha. Are you okay, man?"

"Fine."

"Obviously not. Can I sit?"

I motioned to the empty space on the bench. "And you're like a ghost that appears out of nowhere at the strangest times."

"I'm like a panther. You don't see me until you see me. And then it's too late."

Two people could play the flirty game. "Are you going to pounce on me and drag me into the jungle?"

"Seriously. No one sits on a bench on the Malecón, crying his eyes out unless something's going on."

"I was thinking about my mom and a letter she wrote me before she died."

"Was that recent?"

"She died of COVID a few years ago."

"Bummer. Can I give you a hug?"

"Why not?"

Matthew put his arm around my shoulder and leaned in for an awkward hug. As he retrieved his arm, he gave me a nice hetero pat on the back lest I think there were anything gay about it. We sat a moment in silence.

He turned to me. "Do you like massage?"

"I've only had a few. One good one and a couple of uncomfortable ones."

"I started massage training a few weeks ago. I need people to practice on. It's free, and my teacher says I very good and intuitive."

"Is that what you're doing? Trawling the boardwalk looking for la proxima victima?"

"You're funny. Just give it a try. If you don't love it, I'll..." he rubbed his forehead trying to think of something.

"What?"

"Clean your apartment for a month?"

It was a ridiculous proposal I knew was never going to happen, but what the hell? "Fair enough. When?"

"Right now. I don't live far away."

The last twenty-four hours had been so insane that a massage from flirty, no-gay-shit Matthew sounded like the perfect thing to finish out the cycle. On the way to his apartment through the noisy streets of Centro, he brought up the subject of mushrooms again.

"I like to recommend at least a small dose of shrooms before a massage to get the full effects."

"You mean, like a microdose? I've read about microdosing."

His eyes lit up. "Microdosing is awesome but more of a gradual process over a period of time to improve well-being and mental function. What I recommend is about double a microdose that you will barely feel, but it will unblock and help clean your chakras. It's like a tune-up."

I was uncomfortable with all the chakra talk, but as Ray said, everybody had their lingo for expressing what they observed, and even Ray had implied I had things I needed to work on. If the last twenty-four hours were any indication, I didn't only need a tune-up but was due for a complete overhaul. I had gotten uncharacteristically smashed, flirted shamelessly with and then promptly rejected a nice guy, provoked a fight with Ivan, and ended up breaking down in public. I had never discussed chakras and mushrooms and auras with my mom, but I had a feeling it was language she would have been comfortable with. In my head, I heard her voice, "Give it a try."

Matthew flipped on the kitchen light and took a chocolate bar out of the refrigerator. He broke off two little squares.

"One you don't even feel. Two is like a mood enhancer. That should be perfect."

"So, I'm not going to end up running through the jungle naked and finding God?"

He laughed and held out the rest of the bar. "If you want that, I suggest taking the whole thing."

I took the two squares and popped them into my mouth, chewing them slowly. "This should be good."

"Have you eaten anything today?"

"Nope."

"Perfect. It works better on an empty stomach."

We went into his small but neat bedroom with colorful psychedelic posters on the walls. I stared at the mattress on the floor.

"Don't worry," he said. "I have a massage table." He lifted the mattress on its side and leaned it against the wall to make room before pulling the table out of a closet and setting it up. He spread a clean sheet over it.

"I'm gonna leave you alone to get undressed to the level you're comfortable with. I prefer to work on a naked body, but that's up to you. I will drape a towel over your privates." He turned off the overhead light and switched on a Himalayan salt lamp that gave the room a warm pink glow.

When he came back in, I was face down on the table. He lay a towel over my ass and searched for music on his phone. I recognized the relaxing ambient chillout music coming out of the small Bluetooth speaker as Arno Elias from the Buddha Bar CD. I had heard it at my parent's house. A stream of emotion flowed through me from head to toe, a connection to my mom and dad as if they would be with me on this journey. I felt all fuzzy but couldn't imagine I was feeling the effects of the chocolate already.

"Turn over," he said in a soft voice. "I want to work on your chakras for a few minutes before we start the massage."

He placed the palm of his hand on my lower abdomen, just above the pelvis. I jumped.

"Tranquilo. This is your root chakra." He pressed the heel of his palm gently on the spot and rocked it back and forth. "It is the energy center of your physical body and security. The color associated with it is red."

He used the same gentle rocking motion over the next five chakras, and then for the seventh one, the crown chakra, he simply swayed his hands above my head. He described each chakra, its meaning, and associated color. I had a hard time following the jargon, but I found his voice hypnotizing and had a moment of panic that he was taking control of my body and mind. Again, I heard my mother's voice, telling me to let go.

Next, he instructed me to move back onto my stomach. I opened my eyes and saw the ceiling fan spinning one way and then the other. I kept staring at the fan wondering if it was possible for it to spin two directions at the same time.

"Hello, Dawson. Onto your stomach."

I was surprised by the voice, having forgotten for a moment that someone else was in the room.

He began massaging my feet and worked his way up, his hands warm and electric. The touch alternated between deep, painful digs into my muscles and sensual strokes that made my skin tingle. I yelped when he worked on my calves and moaned as his oily hands slid up and down my back. I had the sensation that he was taking me apart and putting me back together.

"Are you feeling something?" he asked.

"I'm feeling everything. Your hands. The music. The room. The fan." With my eyes closed, the music orchestrated colorful, constantly shifting geometric patterns on my eyelids. The warm, moist air of the room and the rosy light made me feel like I was back in the womb. "Are you sure two was the right dose?"

"Hmm. It seems you are quite sensitive to the mushrooms." He moved to the front of the table and laid his hands on my head. "Take deep breaths."

In a few minutes of breathing in and out at his command, my mind slowed and drifted.

"Feeling better?"

"Uh-huh."

I floated a minute until I heard the creak of the wood table and the pressure of another body getting on top of it. Matthew, wearing only gym shorts, stretched out on top of me. I felt every inch of his skin in places where bare skin touched, and even through the layers of the towel and his shorts, I noted the presence of his dick nestled in the crevice of my ass. He slid his arms along mine that hung over the edge of the table and interlaced our fingers. Sweat began to accumulate where his naked upper torso was pressed to my back. He remained still as if allowing our individual skin cells to merge and make our two bodies like conjoined twins.

"Matthew, I don't want to have sex," I whispered.

"Shhhh." The rushing sound snaked through my brain. "It's not about sex. It's connecting our energies. Relájate."

I relaxed and tried to tamp down any sexual feelings, experiencing it as a complete hug plus the security of being protected. "My root chakra is so happy right now."

"See, you're getting it."

Suddenly, I felt tears running down my face. I didn't feel sad in the moment, but the sadness of years, of losses, of loneliness flowed out of me like water coming down the mountain after a big rain. "Sorry," I sniffled.

"No. It's perfect. Let it go."

I sobbed for a good five minutes before it, too, suddenly shifted to happiness, all the while Matthew holding me.

He kissed me on the back of my head and got up. "Take your time," he said as he left the room.

The sensation of having my security blanket peeled off of me was daunting. Oh, right, I thought, all good things come to an end or is it a new beginning or is it just a change? Things change. Nothing stays the same.

I dressed and went out into the living room, where he sat yogi style on the sofa, thumbing through his phone.

"Can you get home by yourself, or do you want me to take you?" he asked.

We had quickly moved from mind-blowing intimate connection to practical considerations. "I'm good."

He looked up from his phone. "You look good. Different."

"Thank you. I mean, for everything. Thank you seems so inadequate. It was..."

"It's okay. I get it. It was my pleasure. Seriously."

We hugged at the door.

I stood inside the street door of Matthew's building with a sense of trepidation, unsure of what I would find on the other side, how my neighborhood and my town would measure up in my heightened reality. The intensity of the drug had worn off some but still toyed with my vision and hearing, distorting the muffled talking and traffic noises on the other side of the door.

When I got the courage to open it, bright light, filled with the heat of the afternoon, blasted into the dim hallway and wrapped around me. On the sidewalk of the busy street, I turned in the direction of my home, walking side by side with the clopping of tires on cobblestones, sounding like the garble of aliens who had just landed. I paused in front of the huge windows of an art gallery where the colors of the paintings on the walls appeared so vibrant the figures nearly jumped off the canvases. Two squares of chocolate was a mood enhancer, huh? A woman in the gallery walked toward the window and beckoned me in, but I gave her a small wave and walked on.

I got to my street and my head automatically turned toward the left, searching for the café where I had last seen Ivan. The memory, only hours before but seeming like weeks, cut momentarily into my well-being until I forced my legs toward the right, beginning my trek up the hill toward home.

Walking by the grocer, I waved, and the man answered with, "Hola, güero." Afraid I would make a fool of myself if I entered the store and tried to make conversation, I trudged on. The corner boys were out in force, and one of them, with his T-shirt tied around his head and a skinny torso with multiple tattoos, put his finger to his forehead and flicked it like a tiny salute, staring at me as if he saw something different, an energy field surrounding me. The gesture and look might have been my overactive imagination, but I smiled in response and said, "Hola."

As I continued up the street, I was so entertained by chickens running wild, stray dogs lounging on the sidewalk and barely raising their eyelids when I passed, multiple colors of bougainvillea tumbling like a colorful rivers down the front of houses, and roosters crowing in the middle of the afternoon, I barely noticed the climb. After a brief pause at the tree where I had seen the iguana, causing a chill to flash through me, I arrived at the entrance to my building, astonished at how quickly the ascent had been.

Please don't let Severino be at the desk. I can't face him right now.

Through the glass door, I saw that he was not there, so I entered the lobby and dashed to the elevator. In my apartment, I drank a large glass of water, put on my swimming suit, grabbed my sunglasses, and went directly to the pool, which was gloriously free of other guests. The last thing I wanted to do was to make small talk.

The water felt like liquid silk, and it cooled my body radiating heat from the walk up the hill. I dove under, swimming to the bottom with a transitory anxiety I would never resurface. But resurface I did, bursting out of the water like a whale and diving back under to swim to the end of the pool. On the edge, I rested my chin on my arms as I gazed at the view that seemed more like a backdrop to a show than something real. The blazing sun, like a mechanical prop, played hide and seek with the clouds.

I felt a tiny spasm in my shoulder muscle where Matthew had dug in deep, and the massage experience came rushing back to me, the skin-on-skin contact, the chakra cleanse, the music rocking the massage table without moving it at all, and the smell of sweat, not unpleasant but earthy, human, and sensual. Matthew had amazed me with an encounter that was profoundly moving, both distracting me from my anxieties and changing my attitude about Matthew as a person. I was also relieved there hadn't been anything sexual. Matthew appeared to have a handle on the difference between flirtation and follow-through when it came to men. Ivan, on the other hand, wallowed in the tides of his attraction, at times letting it carry him onto the beach and at others drifting back out to sea. Why was I thinking about Ivan at all? It seemed that in the chakra cleanse, Matthew had missed the dust particles of Ivan floating around in my sacral chakra, governing my sexual flow. The color of the sacral chakra was orange, and I saw the sun beginning to tinge orange. *My, my, my, this chakra business is going to my head and I'm starting to use the lingo. What's next? Jetting off to India and joining an ashram?*

My wrinkly fingers told me I had been in the pool a long time. I climbed out of the water and stretched out on a lounge chair to watch the sunset. When it was no more spectacular than the ones I'd watched in recent days, I acknowledged, a bit sadly, that I had returned to reality. My stomach growled from not having eaten all day.

On the way down to my apartment I questioned what I should feed a body after having been kneaded, prodded, cleansed, and delightfully covered with a human blanket. Tacos or a hamburger and fries from Uber Eats just wouldn't cut it. It was time to try the Indian restaurant I'd heard about—a better option than jetting off to India itself—and I ordered a couple of vegetarian dishes with naan to be delivered.

By the time the food arrived, I was so famished that I wolfed it down with a Modelo Negra. I burped loudly and felt slightly nauseous. I burped again and tasted a bile-y version of the Channa Masala sauce rise in my throat. I had to lie down.

Before I could fall onto the bed, the Post-it note from Rafael grabbed my attention, the words and number jumping off the paper and hitting me with a sense of guilt. Oh, I was definitely back in realityland.

I entered Rafael's number into my contacts and sent him a message, thanking him for his kindness the previous evening. Ten minutes later Rafael responded with a suggestion we go out to dinner later in the week. I answered that Rafael should pick the restaurant, and I would pay in gratitude for him being a decent human being when I hadn't been.

I was about to put my phone away for the evening when I noticed an email from Susan with the subject: next editing job. She suggested I would be pleased as it was a literary novel about two men who met just before the pandemic lockdown and circumstances didn't allow them to continue seeing each other in person. They decide to write letters, real letters on paper through the mail, telling things about themselves they would normally do in person at the beginning of a relationship. The working title was *Between the Lines.*

"We probably won't make any money on it, but it's very good," she said. I was compelled to open the file and read the first paragraph, which would tell me a lot about how pleased I was going to be. It had a strong start, but in the few minutes I read, a couple of tweaks came to mind.

Before I went to sleep, I sent a message to Stef and Ray, apologizing for my behavior the previous night. I said that Rafael had been sweet to see me home and that we had a date for later in the week.

As I entered the foothills of sleep, I felt mildly excited about my upcoming date with Rafael and strong enough that I could leave his infatuation with Ivan behind. I planned to get up early in the morning to start my new editing project. And just before I drifted off, I sensed my life was back on track.

In the middle of the night, a text notification roused me to a half-awake state, but my exhaustion from the previous day's events pulled me back under. In the morning, I had forgotten about the text and got up without looking at my phone.

With my morning coffee, I sat out on the balcony, reveling anew in the beauty of the surroundings. The flock of parrots screeching across my line of sight brought a smile to my lips, and the chickens' clucking from the branches of a tree down below was like a little song to my ears. Far out at sea, a cruise ship made its way into the bay, seeming to move as leisurely as a toy boat in a bathtub.

After a light breakfast, I went to my desk and opened the manuscript file on my laptop. I was anxious to get to work, but the middle-of-the-night text popped into my head, reminding me I had left my phone on the nightstand in the bedroom. Perhaps, Rafa had been feeling frisky in anticipation of our date and sent me a sexy photo. I tried to put it out of my mind and get to work, but a curious mind was dying to know.

I retrieved the phone and opened the message app. "Fuck no!" I shouted. It was from Ivan.

Hello, hi, hola.

Thanks, Ivan, for fucking up my day.

Now I was the one who didn't know what to say or if anything needed to be said at all. "Work," I shouted. "I've got to work."

Back at my desk, I had difficulty concentrating. I kept hearing the words "Hello, hi, hola" in Ivan's voice, and they didn't sound cute but rather sinister. Ivan was on a mission to torture me, and I wouldn't stand for it.

Thirteen

I went through several changes of clothes in preparation for the date with Rafael, ending up with some navy-blue Mack Weldon shorts, showing I had an appreciation for designer brands, and a vintage Hawaiian shirt as a nod to the past when my mom bought all my clothes at Goodwill. When Jacob and I first got together, I didn't have a single designer-label article of clothing in my closet. I often bought clothes at Target and furniture, what little I had, from Ikea. I drove a Toyota Matrix and ate a lot of fast food. Jacob had a sense of style and had grown up with a mother who was an interior decorator. He was constantly on my case to step it up. He taught me about food and clothes and how to set a table for a party.

When we moved in together, we bought nice furniture, even though the price often horrified me. I initially resisted Jacob's push to bring my clothing into the world of design and style. I kept hearing my father's voice in my head saying, "The clothes don't make the man, and driving a fancy car doesn't make you a better person." But one excruciating dinner party with Jacob's friends made me realize that if Jacob and I were going to stay together, I had to make some changes to keep the peace if nothing else. At the table I sipped my wine before the host made a toast, picked at my food before everyone was served, argued with the person sitting next to me that Sketchers were just as good as Hokas, and revealed I had never been to New York City and thought it was over-rated. During the long drive home from the party, Jacob sat in angry silence.

With time, I accepted that quality things were not just expensive so the fat cats could make more money, like my father told me, but because they were better made, lasted longer, and had an esthetic appeal. When Jacob and I took our first trip to New York, I fell in love with it, making me cringe every time I thought about what I'd said at the dinner party.

Standing in front of the mirror before my date with the stylish

Rafael, I scrutinized my appearance. I was unsure about my new trendy haircut I got in Zona Romántica. It was very short on the sides, making my ears look bigger, and long on the top, maintaining the sun-streaked locks I'd achieved since living in Puerto Vallarta. The barber sold me an expensive Swedish hair product that smelled of vanilla and tobacco and showed me how to tousle my hair to enhance the thickness due to the humidity, and at the same time give it an unkempt look. Maybe there were times expensive things didn't make sense, like buying an overpriced hair gel to arrive at a hairdo that a homeless person got naturally.

I had agreed to meet Rafael at La Capella bar, attached to the well-known restaurant where we could watch the sun go down behind Our Lady of Guadalupe church, coloring its towers and cupola with golden light. The main bell tower, with its elaborate crown held up by eight angels, felt so close you could reach out and touch the angels' wings.

Rafael was sitting at a high top, bathed in the same golden light when I arrived. He stood up to hug me, and I noticed the similarities to Jacob that I ignored in my haste to get drunk at our previous encounter. Rafa and Jacob were of similar stature and build, and they both wore designer glasses and had curly black hair. I also had a feeling that Rafael had grown up with money as Jacob had. In a starched button-down shirt, chinos, and loafers with a buckle across the instep that I was not fond of, Rafael again seemed overdressed for the town's mostly casual and bohemian ambience. But he did have a beautiful smile and inquisitive brown eyes. The strength of his hug felt genuine.

"Sorry I'm late," I said. "I walked."

"No biggie. You're not that late."

"I have to ask. Did you live in the States for a while? Your English is not only perfect but colloquial."

"I went to university in North Carolina. We talked about that the other night."

"Oops. Once again, you have to forgive me. The person you met the other night was not me. If I start to ask you another question we talked about that night, just hold up a finger and save me the embarrassment."

"I guess it wasn't that bad because I'm here. Ray said you've been under a lot of stress lately."

"He did? Did he say anything about the nature of that stress?"

"He did not. I think he just wanted me to know it wasn't your normal behavior, which I had already surmised. Anyway, you had your moments." Rafa smiled demurely.

"I think I might have gotten a little too familiar, like grabbing your leg under the table. Living up to the crass image of an American."

"Remember I lived there. In North Carolina of all places. I've seen it all."

"One thing I'm sure I didn't tell you the other night is that I also lived in North Carolina for a while when I was a kid. We lived in a community...okay, I should call it what it was, a commune. I actually lived in a yurt for two whole years. I'll understand if you want to get up and walk out right now."

Rafael laughed. "I love your sense of humor. We all have deep dark secrets in our past," he said in a mysterious voice.

"I can't imagine you having a lot."

"I might surprise you."

I enjoyed our conversation, and though Rafael's English was nearly perfect, there was just enough of an accent to give his masculine voice a sexy twist. I imagined getting Rafa to relax and kick off those awful shoes.

"Do you own a pair of shorts?" I asked.

"Of course, I do. Were you hoping to get a look at my legs?"

"I do like legs. I don't think I've worn a pair of long pants since I moved here."

"And yes, I might also have a T-shirt stuffed away in a drawer." He stuck out his tongue at me. "Now, are you hungry?"

"Are we going to eat here?"

"I have another place I want to take you. It's in Versalles. I brought my car this time."

We paid for the drinks and walked to Rafa's car. I could only smirk when I saw it. A BMW. A quality person who liked the finer things in life. Like Jacob.

Oh, shut up, brain.

Rafa also proved himself again in the choice of the restaurant, Homún, a classy little place with great food at reasonable prices. Not one of the snobby places people always talked about as the best restaurants in Puerto Vallarta that overcharged for mediocre meals. We shared a fried artichoke salad and a pizza to start, followed by a risotto of seasonal mushrooms and roasted chicken. I asked the appropriate questions about the menu and tried to remember all the manners I adopted in my adult years with Jacob. It was, after all, a first date. Rafael continued to be all the things one was supposed to be on a first time out: funny, charming, and serious at the proper times.

He drove me home and the moment came when it might be expected to invite a date in for a nightcap. He probably sensed my hesitation to do so and stepped in to be the perfect gentleman. "I have to get up early for work, so I'm going to head home. I had a fabulous time."

"Me too. As you saw, I don't have to be drunk to enjoy myself."

He put his hand on my leg and leaned in for a kiss. He had full kissable lips and a hint of beard that tickled my chin. It was a bit more than a goodnight kiss and considerably less than a let's-go-fuck kiss.

"Hey, good kisser too," I said.

"Would love to do it again."

"Kiss?"

"All of it."

"Cool."

Early the next morning I was at my desk with the *Between the Lines* manuscript in front of me, trying to purge thoughts of Ivan who I pretended to know but didn't, as well as Rafael who I felt like I knew only too well. For good measure, Matthew's body lying on top of me, crotch to butt, popped into my head. Rafael's kiss. Ivan's text. Matthew's chest on my back. Ivan holding my hand at the beach under the moon. Rafael's hand on my thigh. Matthew kissing the back of my head. Ivan kissing me on the balcony. Rafael putting me to bed. And, if all that wasn't enough, I thought of the last time I hugged Ray, and he whispered in my ear, "How ya doin', baby?" It was like my brain was a factory churning out new products and new versions of products that I didn't need but couldn't stop buying. *Jesus, it's not easy being a homosexual.*

I forced myself away from my own jumbled reality and back into the love lives of the fictional characters. I began a quick readthrough to get the scope of the novel, leaving the track changes mode off so as not to get bogged down in the micro level, the particles that made up the whole. I soon learned that the two protagonists, Julian and Edgar, were in their late twenties and grew up in a time when no one handwrote and mailed letters. Edgar lived in Chicago and Julian in Toronto. They both worked for solar panel companies, starting as technicians but had moved up to mid management. Their everyday language was kilowatt hours, photovoltaic systems, and feed-in tariffs. Neither of them had ever written a personal letter. Soon after their chance meeting at a solar panel tech conference in Tampa, the pandemic lockdown happened in their respective cities, made worse by the fact that they lived in different countries. They vowed to only communicate in handwritten letters, bringing back the lost art. No abbreviations were allowed like BTW or LMAO. In the early letters, they both revealed they were in heterosexual relationships, one married, the other with a girlfriend. Neither was happy. They wrote about their lives and intimate feelings. They wrote about their childhoods. They wrote about their parents and siblings, telling each other things they had never revealed to anyone, things that would have been hard to say in person.

It wasn't until about a quarter of the way through the book that the circumstances of their meeting were revealed. One night at the conference hotel, neither man could sleep and, by chance, went up to the rooftop at the same time. They struck up a conversation at the railing, looking out over the city of Tampa. Their hands touched. They shared a secret kiss. Reading their encounter, I felt a bizarre tingling under my skin.

A couple of days after their first kiss, the two men went to an isolated beach and made love under the moonlight. I jumped up from my chair and paced the room. Were my eyes playing tricks on me? Was I having a drug-induced flashback and somehow editing in my own ideas? Did I have an alter ego where one Dawson got up in the middle of the night and wrote a novel that the other Dawson didn't know about?

I took several deep breaths and sat back down to continue reading. Some of the letters brought me to tears. It seemed that both men had spent their lives unable to really open up to another person, and through letter-writing they found their ideal means of communication.

After several hours, I put the manuscript aside. It was the best thing I had ever worked on. I was afraid to read the ending, afraid that it wouldn't—couldn't—be a happy one. As the day went on, the images of Rafael and Matthew faded, but the text from Ivan stuck in my head like the fly that refused to exit the open window. In the late afternoon, I went out on the balcony. I spotted something shiny in the gap between the wood slats of the deck. I reached down and extracted a small chunk of glass. The scream and the falling body flashed in my head, more intense since I'd had my little mushroom adventure. How long would it take before I could enjoy my balcony without being reminded of that night?

I went back inside and slumped onto the sofa. A minute later I got up to get a beer, done with work for the day. The editing would begin the following day without knowing the ending of the book. I made a toast to an imaginary Ivan, standing in front of me in shorts and a sleeveless T-shirt, clothes Rafa wouldn't have been caught dead in. We clinked bottles, and Ivan smiled. With phone in hand, I returned to the sofa and started several texts to Ivan, erasing each one.

"Frickin' texts," I said. "Maybe I should write a letter." I laughed. How long would a letter take to arrive the few miles to Sayulita? A month if it arrived at all? I pulled up his profile and punched the call symbol.

"Bueno," he answered with rising intonation.

"Hello, hi, hola."

"Ha! You give me problem about no answer to your text. Then you do the same."

"I didn't know what to say."

"Anything."

"You threw me out of your car! That hurt."

"Truck."

"Excuuuse me. Truck."

"You hurt me with your questions."

"I apologized."

He sighed and his voice softened. "My daughter say I look sad."

It wasn't exactly an apology, but his words contained a sense of regret, prompted by his daughter. Out of the mouth of babes. Silence reigned.

Then, in barely more than a whisper, "I'm sorry." The tone of his voice healed all my wounds past, present, and future.

"What's your daughter's name?"

"Isa. Isabela."

"Beautiful name."

Another long silence. I looked at the screen to see if there was a dropped connection. I couldn't hear breathing but sensed life at the other end, a confusing jumble of thoughts and emotions. Out the window the sky was orange and red, the colors of my sacral and root chakras.

"And I *don't* have sex with Isa's mother."

"It's none of my business."

"Then why you want to know?"

The sun went behind a cloud. "I know this is stupid, but that night on the beach, I felt for a moment that you were mine."

"Is not stupid."

"What is it?"

"Nice."

"Nice? That's all?"

"Okay. Something I have no word for."

"Try one."

"Bello?"

"I'll take that. Is there mail service in Sayulita?"

"You want to write me a letter?"

"I sometimes think we don't say the right thing in texts, or on the phone, or even in person."

"That happens with time, no?"

"Do we have time?"

"Is not easy, but I'm thinking we can make time."

My heart thumped wildly. It was insane that he teased me with a future. What kind of future could we have? "Are you coming to Vallarta this weekend?"

"No. Isa is going to her maternal grandparents. Is the birthday of her abuela."

"And you're not invited?"

He snickered. "No way. Nobody want to see me."

"I do."

"Hmm. Only possible if you promise to no ask silly questions?"

"Like what is your sun sign?"

"You know what I mean."

"I can come to Sayulita. Rent an Airbnb. Maybe one that doesn't have a mess of iguanas out front."

"Is better I think San Pancho."

"Más discreto?"

"Sí."

On Friday, I received messages from both Stef and Rafael, asking about my plans for the weekend. I lied. I said I had a Monday deadline for an editing project and would need to spend the whole weekend working. I booked a casita on the edge of San Pancho, a five-minute walk to the beach and the center. I stopped working in the early afternoon and took the bus to Sayulita, and then a taxi to San Pancho. If I was doing a bad thing, I was determined to own it. I texted Ivan the address, and he promised to come soon after he finished work. I walked to the market and bought enough food and beer that we wouldn't have to leave the house if he didn't want to be seen in public. For now, I could enjoy the secrecy of it, the excitement of a clandestine affair. But who were we hiding from? *He is divorced, even if it's easy to forget, and I truly am a free agent.*

He hadn't said a specific time, but by eight p.m. a sense of doom began to creep in. I couldn't stand it any longer and sent a text.

The beer is cold.

On my way.

Those were the three most beautiful words I had heard all day. I thought how lucky I was in comparison to Julian and Edgar, the main characters from my latest manuscript. They could never send a text message that they were on their way. It would have to be something like, "my letter is on the way," if they sent messages at all, which they had vowed not to do.

From my position in an armchair, pretending to read a book, the lights pulling into the driveway struck me in the chest, startling me and warming me at the same time. I was glad I hadn't been caught at the window, which I had been to many times.

He arrived with a backpack.

"Hello, hi, hola," he sang at the door.

"Hello, young man. Are you lost? Do you need refuge for the night?"

"What do you offer?"

"Food and beer and...me."

"Que bobo! Invite me in."

I waved him in, and he put his backpack on a chair. He opened his arms in half shrug half invitation to hug. I dove in like I was going underwater. I nuzzled his neck and took a little nibble.

"Hey, save a little of that passion for later and get me a beer."

Ah, yes. A realizable task. "Are you hungry?"

"I ate lunch very late. I kept getting sidetracked."

We clinked beer bottles and took a sip, standing in the middle of the living room.

"Wait," he said. He put his beer on the coffee table, grabbed my face in his two hands and kissed me, an exploratory kiss, taking me by surprise. He stopped and nodded his head. "Yes, still good."

"Thank God. I wouldn't want this Airbnb to go to waste. I almost..." I stopped. *I can't show any of the desperation I feel.*

"You think I'm not coming, verdad?"

"No. I know you are a man of your word. And I think we both want... a repeat of bello?"

"No sand this time. Hey, you never tell me where you find sand?"

"What?"

"Your text."

"Oh, you read it."

"I try to imagine all the places."

"Like shoes, socks, floor."

He lifted my shirt. "Or here in this little hole. What is it called?"

"Belly button."

"I like your belly button. The soft hair here." He circled my navel with his finger, and then very gently inserted it as far as it would go.

"You are the first person who has penetrated my hole."

"I doubt it."

"This one."

"Are you trying to excite me?"

"You started it."

"And I plan to finish, but first we drink the beer. Let me sit down. I am on my feet all day."

We sat close on the sofa, sipping our beers.

"Nice haircut," he said. "I don't tell you."

"Thanks."

"Tell me something. You have a good day?"

I told him about the book I was working on, the two men, how they wrote letters to each other and how they met.

"You invent this story."

"I swear I didn't. Almost their whole relationship was through the mail."

"That's why you ask me about mail service in Mexico. You want this kind of relationship? No touching?" He ran his finger along my arm, through the fine hair like a breeze through a field of wheat. "No kissing?" He moved his lips very close to mine without touching them.

I turned my head. "Nope. The descriptions in the letters of their kiss is so powerful."

He used his hand to bring my face back into position. "I prefer this." He joined our lips and let his tongue explore.

Fourteen

"Aún más bello," I whispered as my head lay on Ivan's sweaty chest in a dark room.

"Shh." He ran his hand through my hair. "Listen."

The wind had picked up and rattled the palm trees in the yard. If we listened closely, we could hear the waves hitting the shore.

"I want to go to the beach," he said.

"Nooo. We would have to put our clothes on and...and...the sand."

He pushed me off his chest. "Come on, niño. We don't even take shower. Go as we are. I mean, with clothes but wearing the smells of you and me."

"Lovely!"

"Come on. Vamos."

His boyish enthusiasm was too contagious to avoid. It felt like one of those quirky, spontaneous times at the beginning of something that you look back on later and sigh.

We threw on swim shorts, tank tops, flip-flops—the bare minimum —and headed out into the warm night and quiet streets. The sounds of the ocean got louder as I hurried to catch up with his excitement.

Only a few people were at the beach close to the center: people walking dogs, a couple of teenagers entangled and making out on the sand, two guys hopping waves in the water. We hurried past them toward the end of the beach where an outcrop of rock too high to climb over blocked our passage like a palace guard stopping us from reaching a secret place. A new moon hung out over the water, making it so much darker than the last time at the beach, the night of the full moon.

"This is good," he said, pointing at the sand around us.

"For what?"

"Don't worry. I have nothing bad in my head."

"Qué pena!" I said with an exaggerated pout.

"And you are sinvergüenza. I must teach you to be a good boy." He grabbed my hand and pulled me toward the sea. "First, we must clean your body."

We kicked off our flip-flops, pulled our shirts over our heads, and let them fall to the sand. He waded in first before diving in. He came up, hair plastered to his face, his body glistening like a sea god. I went under the water and swam in the scary darkness until I bumped into his legs. I rose out of the water, and we were face to face. He stared at me, tilting his head this way and that as if he were trying to decide on a purchase.

"I think you're supposed to kiss me now," I said. "Not look at me like I'm a piece of driftwood."

"If that is the only way to make you shut up…"

He brought his lips to mine briefly, and then he pushed me away before diving back under the water. We played in the waves and splashed each other like teenagers, not two adult men who had responsibilities, not two men unsure of what they were doing with each other, not two men bound by the painful ties of having witnessed the death of a young man.

He swam out to deeper water past where the waves were breaking as if feeling the need to get away from this thing he didn't yet understand, or perhaps he wanted to show he was a man unafraid of danger, at least the physical kind. I stayed where my feet could still touch the bottom and watched him go under, losing sight of him long enough for a fearful shiver to snake through me.

"Come back," I shouted when his head resurfaced.

He dove under again, moving like a shark in the dark water until he reached me, grabbing me around the legs and pulling me under. We came back up, and I pushed him in feigned anger.

"Thanks a lot," I said, coughing and spitting out the salt water.

"Sorry. You okay?" He raised his hand to touch my shoulder. His shorts were dangling from his wrist.

"What is this?" I said, touching the fabric of the trunks he had taken off.

He raised his hands in the air, water streaming down from his shorts. "I am free."

I snatched the shorts off his wrist and ran toward the beach somewhat awkwardly against the tide going out and with pebbles under my feet.

"Te voy a matar!" he said, running after me.

"Don't kill me, please," I shouted over my shoulder.

He caught up and tackled me, sending me tumbling onto the sand with him on top. I tossed his shorts away.

"I don't care. I'm naked. So what?" He held my arms above my head.

"Okay, naked man. What are you going to do now?"

He let go of one hand and grabbed a fistful of sand, which he poured down the middle of my torso. "I know how you love the sand."

"I hate you." I tried to buck him off.

"Ooh, you have the fire in the belly. I want to take you home."

"I respond to kindness. Not torture."

"I can be kind, or do you not remember?"

On the walk back, joyful thoughts swam through my head. *This is me. This is the kind of person I want to be.* The thrill of going to the beach late at night. Playing in the waves under the stars with a person who wasn't an open book. I would gladly take the mystery despite the frustration at times. I thought of my date with Rafael and the possibilities he offered: a gentle life with trappings of nice restaurants, fancy cars, and designer clothes, the life I had left behind in Los Angeles, the life I'd had with Jacob.

"Hey, Dawson. Dónde estás?" He threw an arm around my shoulders. We were now on the main part of the beach where there were other people, and he didn't seem to care that others saw us being affectionate.

"What? Sorry." I leaned in and bumped my hip against his.

As we approached the casita, I imagined it was ours, and we were going home to brush our teeth side by side and crawl in bed. He would get up and go to work, and I would spend the day editing. I would be waiting when he came home. I knew it was a ridiculous fantasy, and maybe not a healthy one. Instead of enjoying the walk back, feeling the night breeze off the ocean, smelling the seaweed, relishing in the fact that he was so close that all I had to do was extend my hand and touch him, I began obsessing over whether he would spend the night, expecting any moment for him to say he had to go back to Sayulita, that he had things to do in the morning, that it was difficult for him to sleep in the same bed with another person, that he didn't bring a toothbrush.

I pointed at the outdoor shower. "We should get the sand off." I turned on the water and rinsed my feet. "You go ahead. I'll get some towels."

When I came back out, I tripped a sensor, lighting up the contours of his back as he stood under the shower, eyes closed and the water beating down on his head.

"Don't fall asleep," I said.

He looked over his shoulder. "Come."

I slipped off my trunks and joined him. A dog started barking next door, and a light went on in the neighbor's yard. We were screened from view by a partition but still felt the excitement of being outside nude, our bodies touching. I kissed the back of his neck. "This is fun."

"Shh," he said.

With towels wrapped around us, we went inside and sat on the sofa.

"Do you want to watch a movie?" I asked. The house had a DVD player and a stack of old movies.

"Sure."

I flipped through the collection and pulled one out. "You're not going to believe this." I held up *Moonstruck*. "I love this movie. Cher won an Oscar."

"Okay." His eyes drooped. And then he got it. "Moonstruck like you."

"Do you understand what it means?"

"I suppose is like the moon hit you and make you feel things."

"Well, there is no moon tonight, so I feel nothing."

"Whatever you say, señor Dawson."

"Don't call me that."

He laughed. "Put the movie."

We sat close on the sofa, feet up on the coffee table. In five minutes, his chin fell to his chest, and I pulled his mop of curls into my lap and let him draw his feet up on the end of the sofa. I played with his hair as he drifted into sleep. Halfway through the movie, I began nodding off too. We got up, staggered to the bedroom, dropped our towels, and fell into bed.

I had nearly fallen asleep on the sofa, but now my mind wandered. The normalcy of our evening frightened me, that it could be like this, that he seemed into it as much as I was. But the number of things against any kind of long-term normalcy started marching through my head. I moved close to him and wrapped my arm around him. "Be here now," I whispered in an echo of my mom's voice.

When I was little, that frequent refrain from my mother didn't mean much to me. If anything, I thought it was funny. Of course I was here now. In college, I saw it as my parents' philosophy that kept them from establishing stability in our lives, being "here now" all over the country, the mantra taking them wherever they fancied and getting them involved in movements that were trending at the time. Starting in my teenage years, I argued with them all the time about it, and for a while hardly spoke to them. In my late twenties, the angst and unrest of my youth had softened, and I was more willing to listen to what they had to say, though I still had a problem with their insistence of living in the moment. And even into my thirties, after accepting my parents for who they were, we had discussions about life.

"Your dad and I are happy," my mom said to me once. "Are you?"

"I'm in a relationship. Jacob and I have a good life. I have a job that I like."

"That's not an answer to my question." She touched the hem of my John Varvatos shirt. "Beautiful shirt. Does it make you happy?"

The truth was, at the time she asked the question, I wasn't very happy. My relationship with Jacob was beginning to unravel, partly because we were so obsessed about the future, we didn't have time to live in the present. But *here, now*, as I draped my arm over Ivan, my mother's words made more sense than they ever had. I was happy at that moment and wanted to cherish it, knowing that it could be gone in a flash.

In the morning, still floating in that half-awake dreaminess, eyes closed, I felt the warmth of the sun streaming in the window. Another presence was radiating heat, and on that heat rode the unfamiliar smells of the rental's soap and shampoo, but the finish was all Ivan, earthy undertones of tobacco before it's burned and the tiniest hint of cinnamon. I opened my eyes to see a broad back and a muscled shoulder pointing up. Sometime during the night, he had gone from holding me to facing the other way.

The shoulder began to rotate, and a profile was revealed as if I was approaching a statue in a museum from behind, a profile I was beginning to know, although never before in this light or from this exact angle. And then his eyes fell on me, the deep brown freckled with wonder, followed by a grin of acceptance.

"Hello," he said.

"Hi."

"Hola."

We were starting to bank shared memories and catchphrases, and with it came the comfort of having funds to fall back on.

"Do you like coffee in the morning?" I asked.

His hand slid over and landed, almost as if by accident, on my crotch. "Yes, but I maybe like another thing first." He cupped my cock in his hand and squeezed gently. The reaction was instant.

"Oh."

We sat at a small table in the shade of an umbrella at the back of the house, drinking coffee and eating pan dulce I had picked up in the market the previous evening, not knowing but hoping I would be sharing them. Every new thing we did together felt like a hard-won victory, beating the odds.

Despite the serenity of the morning with the sun peeking through the thick leaves of the Ficus trees and the sound of the surf in the distance, I felt the need to clarify something. "I'm not still thinking about going to the police."

Concern pinched his face. "Good. I think the police is not interested. The family of the boy is not interested. Patrick for sure is not interested. Same for the other boy who must live with some torture."

"We do know something."

"We know nothing for sure. Only Patrick and the other boy."

At that moment, it was hard to believe I had considered doing something that might have hurt this man who I had shared my body with and held during the night. Before leaving for the States, still traumatized by the death, I had been so angry when he rejected me. That anger clouded my thoughts.

"You're right," I said. "We need to try and forget about it."

Some of the tension left his face, but I was reminded of the rumor Severino had started that Ivan was somehow involved, that he was on the roof at the time. I wanted to tell him, but if I didn't stir things up, it might fade away. We were already walking a tightrope in this new thing between us. Why upset the balance?

"Let's go for a drive up the coast," he said.

We went to Lo de Marcos, a small town to the north that was attracting foreigners but had not reached the level of "gringo invasion" like San Pancho and certainly not Sayulita. We parked in the center and hiked along the water to Atracadero beach where we spent the day and ate lunch at Restaurante Olivia. As we lay on the beach after lunch, I turned to him, shielding my eyes from the sun.

"Can I ask you something?"

"Is this going to be a silly question?"

"I'm just curious if you ever thought about doing something with men or if it was spontaneous."

"You mean like I never think about it and suddenly I meet someone like you who I cannot resist?"

"Well, I have been told..."

"Dream on." He laughed. "Okay. I can say I never have problem with sex with women, but sometimes...I don't know...I am curious. Then I see men like Patrick and the friends he bring over and that husband of Trixie who look at me and give me like bumpy skin, you know, piel de gallina."

"Goosebumps."

"Yes, and not in a good way. This guy is weird. He is married, but his eyes like take my clothes off." He shook his head. "And then I meet you. You are nice guy, quiet and normal."

"You make me sound boring."

"Those are the dangerous ones. In bed they become animals like this morning."

"Thank you, I guess?"

"En serio, I never imagine doing anything like that until I meet you."

"Thank you, I guess?" I pinched his thigh.

"Ay!" He grabbed a handful of sand. "Do you want the sand treatment again?"

"No, please!"

"My brother tell me sometimes I'm like the gays. He believe everything the church tell him, very religious. He say I should not have tattoos, not wear shorts and shirts with no sleeves, not spend so much time making my body look good."

"You think your body looks good?"

"Here comes the sand." He covered my chest with a handful.

"I hate you, again." I jumped up and ran to the water to wash myself off.

Fifteen

The time of separation that I had dreaded arrived with telltale signs. Ivan was quiet when we got back from the beach, fidgety and uncertain. He went into the bathroom and closed the door to take a shower. The gods gifted us a second night together, but I couldn't expect more.

After his shower, he began to stuff things in his backpack. "I must get up early tomorrow. Workday."

"I have to go back to Vallarta," I said.

"Tonight?"

"No, tomorrow. Also have work to do."

"The book about the moonstruck guys, huh?"

"Maybe I'll suggest that as a new title. *Moonstruck Guys*."

"You seem sad."

"Me? No way. I need my alone time. Not used to spending so much time with another person."

"Oh, that's it. You are tired of me." He pulled me into an embrace.

"You can be annoying with your sand treatment and all that." I buried my face in the crook of his neck.

"Dawson, look at me. It was good, no?"

I raised my eyes and shrugged.

"Mira, niño. We can do again."

"Sure."

"Okay. I go, but I leave you with un beso to remember me."

I stood at the door and watched him go. *Parting is such sweet sorrow.* Thanks, Will, for sticking this maudlin phrase in our heads for the last few centuries.

❧

"I really need to talk to you," I said when Ray answered my call.

"Stef is at her yoga class, but I'm sure…"

"I'd rather it's just you. I'm not sure she would understand."

"Okay. Got it. Let's meet for coffee."

Our conversation began with my downcast eyes and a confession. "I lied to you guys. I hate doing that. I wasn't working all weekend like I said. I was out of town."

Ray chuckled. "Let me guess. You were in Sayulita."

"San Pancho. He thought it would be more discreet."

Ray raised his eyebrows. "Was it everything your sweet little heart desired?"

"I was trying not to hope for anything. I wasn't sure he would show up at the house I rented."

"But he did."

"Not only did he, it was the full spectrum boyfriend experience with an overnight, coffee in the morning, and a day at the beach in Lo de Marcos."

"Then what are you upset about?"

"I'm not upset."

"Your hands are shaking."

"Too much coffee." I drummed my fingers on the surface of the table. "I think I'm falling for the jerk."

"I guess you're not interested in pursuing anything with Rafa. You need to tell him."

"I'm not sure I'm not."

"You can't keep him in the wings. That's not fair. I think he really likes you."

"That's why I didn't want Stef here. She seemed so excited that Rafa and I were getting together."

"Your date with Rafa didn't go well?"

"It was fine. Perfect, really. We had drinks, a nice dinner, and a kiss at the door. He's a great guy." I paused and scrunched my face. "He really likes me after one kiss?"

Ray chuckled. "I remember when you and Ivan only had one kiss, and you were frickin' howling at the moon."

"But that was a monumental kiss, a kiss in chaos, surrounded by tragedy. Maybe that's why it got blown out of proportion and took on a life of its own."

"Bullshit. It took on a life of its own because you were dancing around each other for weeks just waiting for the moment."

"How do you know that?"

"I'm a writer, remember? Or used to be. I see these things. You couldn't stop talking about him, just normal things like running into him in the elevator or the embarrassing time you were up by the pool scrolling through pics of the hottest men of the year, and he came up behind you. Every time you mentioned him, you had a dumbass look on your face and a sparkle in your eyes. That guy is in your head and ain't leaving anytime soon."

"Now you're blowing things out of proportion."

"I think not."

"Okay, I admit there is a particular kind of trigger when a person who isn't sure about himself loses control with someone who is sure about himself but unsure about with whom."

Ray lowered his chin and moved his head back. "Do you think I'm unsure about myself?"

"I wasn't going there at all, Ray. Anyway, we're not talking about you."

"It looks like Ivan is discovering something about himself. What an exciting time for him. And torturous."

"There was no time in our twenty-four plus hours together that he appeared uncomfortable or *tortured*, as you say."

"That comes later. Lying in bed tonight, trying to go to sleep."

"That's not helpful."

"I just want you to be aware of the reality of what you're involved in. I'm not trying to discourage you. Ride the highs, but be prepared for the lows."

"I'm not sure how one prepares, but thanks."

Ray looked around the room and blew out a long puff of air through his lips. "We haven't been completely honest with you either. I have a boyfriend in Mexico City. Stef knows about it."

I winced. It was information I didn't want to possess. "That's great. If you and Stef are cool with it, what can I say?"

"You could say you're happy for me."

"I am."

"That was convincing."

"It can't be easy for Stef."

"Life is not easy, Dawson. Stef and I always promised to tell each other about any outside involvement."

"You don't have a clause about emotional attachment? If you're calling him your boyfriend, it sounds like more than a fuck buddy."

"Boyfriend," Ray snarked. "I mean, we've seen each other a few times. I suppose the whole thing will fizzle out under the pressure, what with him being on the down-low and all. I like him, but I'm not throwing away a twenty-five-year relationship."

I shook my head. "I don't get it."

"It's not yours to get. It's my life."

"You're right."

"Let me explain it in the best way I can."

"You don't have to."

"I want to. It's important to me that you understand." He steepled his hands under his chin and spoke in a slow deliberate way like he was my professor. "I dated women in high school and college. I always imagined I would share my life with a woman. In Chicago, this whole new world of sex with men opened up. Who knows? Maybe when I took that job in Boystown, there was something going on in the back of my mind, pushing me that way. The first time with a guy, I felt no trauma, no guilt, just a little silly that I had been denying a part of me that was probably always there. I went through a time of dating women and having man sex on the side. And then I met Stef. I was completely honest with her. She got it. It hasn't always been easy, but we're committed to each other. We find a way forward. I agreed not to see other women but continued having casual sex with men. Hard sex. Rough sex. Mind-blowing sex. And then it's done. I'm good for a while."

I must have looked shocked. I didn't mean to.

"Too much info?"

"Has Stef ever...? Tell me if it's none of my business."

"Her yoga instructor. Classic. Not the one she's in class with right now."

"That would be weird. Did it bother you?"

"To be honest, it took some of the pressure off. It sounds trite to say what's good for the goose is good for the gander, but it's true, at least for us. I honestly don't know how traditional marriages survive."

"A good half of them don't."

"And the other half turns a blind eye when the partner wanders."

"That's pretty cynical."

"My parents were together for sixty-seven years in what for all appearances was a happy marriage. I always assumed there was no cheating. Good people. Deacons in their church. After my father died, my mother admitted that he'd had several affairs over the time of their marriage. All those statistics you read about, high percentages of married couples being faithful, are based on self-reporting. What a joke. Men deny it even when their wives confront them after finding lipstick on their collars and panties in their coat pockets. Deny. Deny. Deny. That's the name of the game."

"I think my parents were faithful."

"Are you one hundred percent certain?"

"Let me have my illusion."

"Who knows? They could have been one of the few."

"I should probably tell Stef about Rafa."

"First, you should tell Rafa about Rafa."

I approached my building with the dread of seeing Severino in the lobby. I had to find a way of dealing with my anger because it looked like he was there to stay.

He looked up from the monitors with the same lopsided smile that made me want to slap him every time I saw him. "Hola, señor Dawson," he said with a sing-song tone and dubious intent.

I didn't have the energy to force a smile and stared at him blank-faced. The more I had feelings for Ivan, the more I had contempt for this man. "How are you doing, Severino?"

"Can't complain. Things are good."

"Glad to hear it." I was almost past the desk, inching toward the elevator.

"How's your friend, Ivan? Give him my regards if you see him."

Severino couldn't know that I had spent the weekend with him. He was taunting me, and I tried my best not to fall into the trap, to keep walking, but rage took control of my legs, forcing me to turn around. I marched back to the desk and leaned over it, staring at him, that annoying face with a mole on its cheek and ugly hair growing out of it.

"Do you like your job here?"

"Yes, of course. *Most* of the people are very nice."

"Stop spreading rumors. You know they are lies."

"I don't know what you are talking about."

"I'm sure you do."

He stared at the monitors as if something interesting was happening in one of the squares. "I like my job here," he said casually, hitting a key that changed the view to a different space. "And I'm sure señor Ivan likes his job in Sayulita. It would be terrible if the management found out that he has a history of getting involved with residents." He swept his eyes to me and angled his head.

I leaned back on my side of the counter. It seemed he knew where Ivan worked, and he was prepared to make trouble. Why was he continuing to meddle? He had gotten the job he wanted, but I supposed he wanted a guarantee that he would keep it. As much as I hated it, I had to back down for Ivan's sake. "Yes, I think it's important that everyone keeps their jobs. I'll be reasonable if you will."

"Of course, señor Dawson. Have a good evening."

I was shaking when I got back to the apartment. It took a couple of vodkas and a joint to calm down. Before I went to bed, I sent Ivan a text. **Thinking of you.**

A few minutes later, a reply. **Me too. Sweet dreams**.

I went into the bathroom to brush my teeth and heard my phone ring. I rushed back to the bedroom with the excitement that Ivan was calling. I would lie on my bed, and we would talk about what we had done that day. We would plan our next meeting. We would sign off with besos.

Instead, the caller ID said Rafael, and I chose not to pick up. I wasn't in the mood to be nice, let him down gently if he wanted to make a date. I sat on the edge of the bed, put my hands over my face, and snarled in frustration. Lightning flashed over the mountains outside my bedroom window, followed by fat raindrops tapping the glass. In seconds, the rain became a powerful force, taking me back to the night when Ivan had come around to check for leaks. I stood up and went to the window, staring out at the world distorted by the water streaming down the glass. How had life gotten so complicated? I came to Mexico to chill. Life's a beach and all that.

I needed to concentrate on work. Work would take my mind off my predicament, and I vowed to spend the rest of the week concentrating on the manuscript, working all morning, swimming in the pool in the afternoon. Maybe I would meet Stef and Ray for a walk on the Malecón one evening.

Focusing on the manuscript got me through the week. In my comments, I agreed with the author's delay in revealing the circumstance of Julian and Edgar's meeting, letting the readers get to know them first through their letters. But I suggested the meeting could be brought up earlier because readers would be hungry to know. Give people a little juicy stuff to keep their interest.

I did my utmost to be cordial with Severino as I went in and out of the building. Our exchanges were limited to standard greetings. I sent an email to Trixie that I was interested in Patrick's position on the board.

On Wednesday, I met with Rafael for drinks at a beachside bar in the Zona Romántica. We hugged and sat down to order cocktails. The hope in his demeanor gave me a queasiness in my gut. Halfway through the drink, I blurted out the it's-not-you-it's-me speech, looking at his sweet face and into his deep brown eyes, wondering if I was doing the right thing.

"Is there someone else?" he asked.

"No. Well, yes, but it probably won't go anywhere. I hope you and I can still be friends."

Rafael blinked a couple of times. "I have lots of friends, Dawson."

"Oh, yeah. Okay. I'm sorry. My behavior has been confusing at best."

"You need to figure things out." He didn't say it as an insult, but it hit me like one.

"I know."

I didn't feel particularly good about casting Rafael aside after having one romantic weekend with Ivan, but that was the path I had chosen. Since our weekend, I had limited my texts to Ivan to one in the morning and another at night, short messages that said nothing of consequence. Ivan responded, usually within a few minutes. On Friday morning, I upped the ante by asking if he would be coming to Vallarta on Saturday to see his daughter. The day passed without an answer. On Friday night I sent another, saying that if he was coming to town, maybe we could have a beer after his time with his daughter. Again, no response.

On Saturday morning, I made a withdrawal from the bank of our personal catchphrases. **Hello, hi, hola.** When there was no response, I refused to panic. I went back to the last text Ivan had sent a couple nights before. **Buenas noches, blue eyes.** It was hardly a sign that anything was amiss. I thought back to my conversation with Ray and imagined how Ivan might have been lying in bed one night, possibly after the blue-eyes text, when the reality of what we were doing crushed him. When Sunday arrived without a response, the panic did creep in. These were the lows Ray warned me about. I bucked myself up with confidence it would pass.

Sixteen

On Sunday, I plunged into editing in hopes of quieting the screaming in my head. I had found Julian's and Edgar's letters up to that point to be endearing, romantic, and honest. Now, I came upon passages that were over the top, too flowery by half, and I marked them so. Always careful to confirm my comments with second and third reads, the thought crawled into my brain that I was being too harsh. I knew the dangers of letting what was going on in my personal life influence my edits and went back to read some of the early letters, making sure there was a natural progression of style for two people who admittedly had never written a personal letter in their lives.

Julian and Edgar surmised early on that in order to learn how to write each other, they would study famous letters from history. Despite being techies, they both were well educated in literature and history. Julian studied English literature in college before he realized how difficult it would be to make a living with it. He shared with Edgar a quote from Jane Austen's final novel, *Persuasion,* where the character Frederick Wentworth writes to Anne Elliot: "I can listen no longer in silence. I must speak to you by such means as are within my reach."

The two men periodically renewed their excitement about not using any form of technology and joked about the irony that they were solar technicians who dealt with technology every day.

Edgar wrote that he wasn't nearly so classically well read as Julian, but he did find something interesting from Vita Sackville-West to Virginia Woolf: "I just miss you, in a quite simple desperate human way. You, with all your un-dumb letters, would never write so elementary a phrase as that; perhaps you wouldn't even feel it."

As time went on, Edgar emerged as the one more willing to delve into matters of sex. He asked Julian to indulge him but couldn't resist sharing a letter from James Joyce to his wife, Nora: "...I did as you told me, you dirty little girl, and pulled myself off twice when I read your letter. I am delighted to see that you do like being fucked arseways."

The two men found dozens of quotes that reflected their feelings, but with time, they agreed they should stop using quotes and focus on their own words. As the letters progressed, each writer clearly showed a unique and developing style.

I took a break to do some stretching, and when I went back to where I had left off, softened a few of my comments, completely deleting others. Perhaps the passion the two men felt for each other was based in fantasy—they had only shared a kiss and later had sex once—but that fantasy resulted in a living, breathing entity created with words. What the writer had done was brilliant. Who was I, Dawson Wozniak, a mere editor, to check that?

I looked at the time and saw that several hours had passed without once thinking of Ivan. When I broke for lunch, I checked my messages again. I concluded that it wasn't the pain of being ghosted, but a true concern that something might have happened to him. There was no way for me to know. In the evening, I called instead of texting. No answer. I left a message that I wanted to make sure he was okay.

At the beginning of the week, I resolved not to send any more messages. If it was over, it was over. If he wanted to contact me, he knew how. By mid-week, I got to the part in the book where Julian has stopped writing, and Edgar is losing his mind because he has broken up with his girlfriend due to his feelings for Julian and feels betrayed. But the only thing he knows to do is keep writing, keep expressing his thoughts and feelings whether he gets a response or not. One of Edgar's heartbreaking letters made me cry.

"I have to do something," I shouted at the computer screen.

On Thursday afternoon, I was on a bus to Sayulita. I didn't message Ivan for fear he would refuse to see me. If I was already in town, a few blocks away, it would be harder for him to decline to see me, or so I reasoned. Once in Sayulita, I sent a message that I was in town and would wait outside the building at the time he got off work. This time the response was almost immediate. **Do not come to my work. Please. Go to the cemetery by the beach.**

How appropriate! Our relationship began with death—two if you count the iguana—and it would end surrounded by it. The rejected person never wants to go quietly, always wants to know why, and I deserved to know why. I deserved a face-to-face why.

Just beyond the arch entrance to the cemetery, I found a low wall to sit on and wait. Finally, Ivan walked toward me with a determined gait, showing confidence in his decision. What tiny hope I still carried in my heart withered. As he got closer, his eyes looked a little less sure. He was human after all.

"Let's walk," he said, barely slowing down. "To the rocks." No greeting. No handshake. Not even a meeting of eyes.

I followed him down the path, across the beach, and to the rocks where we had talked before. He motioned for me to sit, but he remained standing as if he was going to give a lecture. He began what sounded like a prepared speech. "I know you are angry with me. Please understand. This can't continue."

I stood up, not wanting to be in a lower position, the position of a supplicant. We were about the same height when standing. "I'm not angry. But I believe I deserve to know why."

"I don't want to go back and forth with the whys. In the end, it doesn't matter why. It must stop."

"You're not making sense. Don't tell me you didn't feel something. Don't tell me you didn't enjoy our time together. What made you come to this decision? Did I do something?"

"Nothing. Everything. I can't live this life."

"You prefer to be a divorced man who sees his daughter maybe once a week and spends all his time at work because he has nothing to go home to? And I'm sure you will find women to have sex with, but in the corner of your mind you will still have that curiosity and know that you shared something beautiful with a man who can't stop thinking about you. Of course, it's easier to run away because loving someone is hard." I hadn't planned on bringing up love. My emotions took me there. I was determined not to cry, though I was so close I could feel water pooling in my eyes.

He took a step back and winced like I had punched him. He put a hand to his forehead and looked out to sea. Not far away, a wave knocked a boy off his boogie board, and he yelped as he tumbled in the water. "I'm not running away. I have no choice."

"Of course, you have a choice."

"You don't understand."

"Then help me."

He sat on a rock and stared at the sand between his feet. He picked up a stone and cast it aside. "My boss called me into her office," he said in a voice barely above a whisper. "She receive a message from someone who say I can't be trusted because I get in bad situations with residents. That's why I leave my job before. She don't say who it was. Sure, we know. I tell her it is not true, and this person has like a vendetta against me. She agree to let me keep my job, but now she is suspicious."

"That motherfucker. He promised not to do that."

"What? He tell you he's going to do this."

"He threatened to do it when I told him his job was in danger."

"You threaten him, and then he come after me?" He slumped to the ground, sitting on the sand. "Dios mio! You are in the middle of all these bad things. Everything begin that night. You did this. You want why?" he yelled. "This is why."

I felt battered by the turn of events. This had gone far beyond simple rejection. This was about slander and job security and the guilt Ivan still felt about his homosexual feelings getting mixed up in his head with bad things that happened. And Severino knew exactly what he was doing. Another big why. Why was Severino going after Ivan so viciously? But for now, I had to make Ivan realize what was happening. I sat on the ground in front of him.

"I have to explain some things," I said.

"Forget it. The damage is done. I'm fucked."

"First, the problem is not you or me or us."

"There is no us."

"Shut up for a minute. The problem is Severino. I didn't want to tell you before, but he has been spreading rumors about you, crazy things like you were involved with Patrick and the boy who died. He said you were on the roof when it happened. I told Trixie it was a big lie. I told her you were with me."

Ivan looked up in shock. "Nooo," he moaned. He rounded his

shoulders and hugged his knees like a child, trying to protect himself from abuse.

"Wait. I said you were only in my apartment to check for leaks and went to the roof after it happened. Trixie didn't believe the rumors and thought the whole thing about you was absurd. I reminded her that Severino was angry he wasn't hired for your position originally. Which brings me to my next point. Severino was out to hurt you. If it didn't happen as result of that night, he would have found another way. You have to get it out of your head that we did something bad. You felt something. I felt something. We acted on it. Yes, the timing was dreadful. And Severino jumped on it. But he was the man on duty that night. It was his job to monitor the situation. Where was he? Taking pictures of us. He's evil. I want to hurt that fucker. I want to smash his face in."

In his agony, a slight grin emerged on his face. "Señor Dawson! I never hear you speak this way. With violence."

"I would fight for you. You don't deserve this. Nothing is your fault. And it hurts me that you think it's all my fault." I choked up. I squeezed the bridge of my nose, trying to stop the tears.

"Don't, please. I understand what you say. Just when I am beginning to feel good about things, this happen at work. I'm scared. I can't lose my job. I must take care of my daughter. She is everything to me."

I wiped my eyes and sniffled. "I can go to your boss and tell her exactly what a sniveling little backstabbing prick Severino is."

"No, please don't. He has the pictures."

"I bet someone would have a hard time identifying us in those pics. It was night with little light, and they were taken from a distance. And Severino forgot one thing. He can't say you were on my balcony and the roof at the same time."

"I suppose, but all he has to do is to make some doubt to ruin me."

"I care about you, Ivan, more than I have cared about anyone in a long time."

"We are not good for each other. We are like a disaster."

I reached out and put a hand on his knee. "Yes, things are fucked. But you make me feel something and I think I make you feel something. Am I wrong?"

"I can't lose my job," he groaned.

"I will do everything in my power to make this right. But I'm afraid we are dealing with someone who is a little insane."

He snorted. "You mean you?"

"Very funny. But yes, I am a little insane to want to be with you. I guess I got that from my parents. Never do anything the normal way." I didn't mean it the way it came out.

"Uh, you are making it worse," he said, dropping his head onto his arms. It killed me to see him so distraught. I reached up to rake my hand through his thick hair and began massaging the back of his head.

"Your hand has some energy like it can make everything okay. But everything is not okay."

"When I was a kid, I sometimes complained to my parents. Why don't we have a nicer house? Why do we move all the time? Why can't I have cool sneakers like the other kids at school? My mother would smile and ask me, 'Do you have food on the table, a bed to sleep in? Do you have people around you who love you and take care of you? What more do you need?'"

He shifted his position, moving his head away from my hand. "It feels nice, but I can't think. You make me a zombie."

"You're not in this alone. Even if you decide we can't continue, I will help you with the Severino situation. I feel responsible."

"Remember I tell you Isa say I look sad the day of our fight? Last week I talk to her on the phone after our weekend. She say, Daddy, you sound happy today. These are simple things, but Isa can see my moods." He stretched out his legs, crossed his arms, and leaned against a rock.

I moved next to him and leaned back against the same rock, our shoulders touching. "We must find a way to keep you happy, then, so Isa doesn't see you sad."

"On Saturday I come to see her, and we usually go to Conchas Chinas beach. Then we go to the restaurant there, La Playita. I take her home around 6:00. Before you ask me about have a beer after. We can do that."

"Are you sure? No pressure."

"I am sure of nothing these days. But you are my friend, and I want to see you."

I balked at the word friend, but I would take it. "I hope I can meet Isa one day."

"I hope too."

In silence we watched the sun go down. I discreetly put my hand under his thigh and kept it there, feeling the heat. Turning my head slightly, I caught the way golden light caressed his face and shone in his curls. A grin of contentment turned the edges of his lips slightly up and spread lines out from the corner of his eyes.

When the sun had gone below the horizon, I moved my hand from under his thigh. "I need to go back to Vallarta. Not sure about the bus schedule."

"I walk you to the station."

"It's not necessary. I know you're worried about appearances. This is a small town."

"Fuck it. Can I not walk down the street with my friend?"

"Okay, amigo. Let's go."

"Don't be silly. I mean friend in the best way."

Seventeen

S tef and Ray agreed to meet me on the Malecón halfway between my house and theirs. Then we would walk to Zona Romántica and have dinner where I planned to tell them the latest developments in my soap opera life. I also needed their advice.

"This guy is putting an awful lot of energy into being hateful," said Stef after the server had brought our wine. "I get it that he was passed over for a job he wanted and thought he deserved, but to go to such extremes?"

"Here's what I think," said Ray. "He was all set up in the building, been there from the beginning. Along comes Ivan who steals the job he felt entitled to. Ivan is everything Severino is not—good-looking, personable—and he even got you."

"What? No," I said. "You think Severino is a repressed homosexual that had the hots for me? He's jealous of Ivan and me? That creeps me out."

"When he saw you together, it must have added one more log to the raging fire inside him. He had the opportunity to take you both down. He got Ivan to quit, removing him from the picture. When you came back to town, Severino must have delighted in the look on your face when he told you Ivan was gone. My dear, you would be a terrible poker player. I can imagine the panic on your face. But our bold Sir Dawson is undaunted and continues the pursuit. Somehow, Severino found out you two were still seeing each other and took it to the next level with the rumors and threats."

"This all sounds so Shakespearean," said Stef.

"And the plot thickens. 'O beware, my lord, of jealousy; it is the green-eyed monster which doth mock the meat it feeds on.'"

Stef nodded. "*Othello.*"

"Bingo. So, Severino makes a pact with Sir Dawson, but he can't help himself. He breaks the pact and plays his next card, throwing Ivan's livelihood in danger, knowing it will cause a rift between the gallant Ivan and his heartsick paramour Sir Dawson."

"Stop," I said, giggling and traumatized at the same time. "You're killing me."

"The villain Iago, I mean, Severino, has one more play, the photos that prove that lusty Ivan can't keep his hands off the residents he's supposed to be working for. Or is it just one in particular that has brought fire to his loins? The pure of heart and much desired Sir Dawson."

I shook my head. "I feel like applause is in order. You rival the bard himself. But can you give me a clue as to what is next?"

"It depends on how much you want this," said Ray.

"I don't even know what 'this' is. In a best-case scenario, is a relationship even possible?"

"I tried to warn you," said Stef.

"What I do know is that I am at least partially responsible for Ivan being in this mess. And I feel like I have some power in getting Severino to stop this nonsense."

"Like what?"

"I'm going to get on the HOA board. I'm going to let other members know what he's been up to. If he doesn't stop with his meddling, we can fire his ass."

"And how did your threats work out for you last time?" said Ray.

"That's not helping, Ray. I'm desperate. I don't know what to do. I already tried reasoning with him, but hiring a hit man might be a little extreme."

"Sorry. I wish I had good advice for you. Even if you get Severino fired, it might cause him to go full-on revenge."

"I forget. What happens to Iago in the end?" I asked.

"Oh, it's a big bloodbath," said Stef. "Iago kills his wife for revealing his scheme. He's arrested and tortured. And Othello commits suicide after killing his own wife."

"Lovely."

Saturday came, and I spent the morning and early afternoon working on the manuscript, trying to keep the promised evening meetup with Ivan for beers out of my head. After finishing several chapters of editing, I went for a swim to relax. I got out of the pool and saw there was a message from Ivan. My gut twisted in fear he was cancelling.

Come to beach near La Playita restaurant. I'm here with Isa.

It was a change in plans, another swing in Ivan's moods. The thought of meeting Isa, something I'd hoped for, now gave me the jitters. What if she didn't like me? That would put an end to things much quicker than any of Severino's machinations.

I took a taxi to the beach and walked down the long stairway, scanning the beach for Ivan and Isa. When I spotted a father and young daughter spread out on a blanket, I headed in their direction, unsure if I was supposed to act like it was a chance meeting or something planned.

As I came close to them, I shaded my eyes and decided to act surprised.

"Ivan, is that you?"

He went along with the chance meeting ruse and introduced me to Isa as a friend. He patted a place next to him on the blanket, a blanket I recognized—I hoped he had washed it—throwing me back to the night on the beach in the moonlight. I examined the surface of the blanket before sitting down.

"It's clean," he said, shaking his head.

I leaned forward and spoke to Isa in Spanish. She had curly black hair like her father, gathered on top of her head, and stared at her lap like Ivan sometimes did when he didn't know what to say, shy as any eight-year-old would be, meeting not only a stranger but a foreigner.

"Speak to her in English," said Ivan. "She study English in school and need to practice."

"Stud*ies*," said Isa quietly.

"What?"

"It's stud*ies*, Papi. I study, she studies."

"See how smart she is? She corrects her daddy's bad English."

I tried a few questions in English, asking her age, what she liked to do. Her answers were short and in Spanish. Ivan encouraged her to practice her English, telling her what a great opportunity it was, but she appeared uncomfortable, looking away or at the hands in her lap.

"Don't push her," I said. "She'll speak when she's ready."

Isa pointed at the sea. "Water. Swimming," she said in hesitant English. He shrugged and grinned at me. Taking his daughter's hand, they walked toward the water. It warmed me to see how loving he was with her, how protective when a wave rolled in. I was mesmerized with the father-daughter silhouette with the sun behind them, making me infinitely more attracted to him, while at the same time bringing into question how attainable this man was, as if anyone could break into the father-daughter universe of two.

They returned to the blanket, and he buried Isa in a towel, his eyes flickering with affection as he dried her hair, now hanging down loose.

I was stretched out, leaning on an elbow, head resting on my palm, watching the sea water drip from his shorts onto the sand. Though I thought my staring behind the sunglasses was subtle, Ivan looked at me over Isa's shoulder with a smile tugging at his lips.

"Are you hungry?" he said. "We're going to eat something." He pointed to the restaurant down the beach. "Want to join us?"

I sat up as if I had been summoned. What an extraordinary miracle this was, Ivan including me in his weekly ritual with his beloved daughter.

At the restaurant, Isa leaned close to her father and whispered in his ear. He laughed.

"What did she say?" I asked.

"No, Papi," she squealed, playfully slapping his arm.

"She thinks your Spanish is funny."

"I know," I said, ducking to be at her eye level. "Maybe you can help me. Why don't we have an intercambio, half in English, half in Spanish, okay?"

She looked at her dad with reddened cheeks. He nodded.

She tucked her chin into her chest and giggled. "Sí."

After the meal, Ivan announced it was time to take her home, causing her mouth to turn down in an exaggerated frown and water to well in her eyes. "No, Papi," she whined. She glared at me like it was my fault.

"Sí, hija."

We entered a part of the 5 de diciembre neighborhood I was unfamiliar with, and Ivan pulled into a space across from a small, plain, white house with a chain link fence around it. Ivan and Isa got out of the car.

"Adiós, Isa," I said. She flipped her hair back with her hand, ignoring me.

Ivan chided her for not saying goodbye. She turned for a moment and gave me a half wave.

He unlocked the gate, and at the same moment, the door opened. A pretty, petite woman with dyed blond hair stood in the doorway. I scrunched down in my seat in hopes of not being detected but still wanted to be able to see over the dashboard. I was curious to know if they would kiss. They didn't. It was a brief handover. Isa gave her daddy one last desperate hug, and her mother ushered her into the house, closing the door.

He returned to the truck with an irritated gait and sweat gathering in the troughs of his forehead. He got in the truck and grabbed the steering wheel firmly, staring at the house. "I build this house, and I can't even live in it."

"Really? You built it?"

"You doubt me?"

"Never."

"My parents buy the lot many years ago. It is empty for a long time. Then, after I marry, I start and do much of the work myself. I get help with plumbing and electricity."

I wanted to joke that maybe he would build us a house one day, but he clearly wasn't in the mood for a joke based on my fantasy.

He started the car. "I know a place."

"What kind of place?"

He turned to me with a look I had seen him give Isa earlier when she was being silly. "You know. Little hotel. Not expensive. Clean."

"Oh. You don't have to go back to Sayulita?"

"I can go right now if you want."

"That's not what I meant. I'm just surprised. Of course, I want to spend more time with you."

"I can get up very early and drive back."

When we got to the small hotel, I felt some relief that, at least, it wasn't a by-the-hour place. It was a step up from a transient hotel, but the payment was done through a window, which gave me a queasy feeling as I wondered if he had taken women there. The heavy man with rheumy eyes on the other side of the glass showed no recognition, but I supposed it was part of his job to be as discreet as possible.

As we entered the room, Ivan flipped a switch to the right of the door and a fluorescent lamp flickered on, casting a stark light on the pale green walls. It had a double bed, one bedside table with a lamp, a desk with a chair by a single window. Over the bed was a faded painting of Puerto Vallarta's main church with its distinctive crown on the bell tower. The smell of disinfectant was nauseating.

He set the beers we had stopped to get on the desk and switched on the bedside lamp. He motioned for me to turn off the other light.

"It's ridiculous we can't just go to my place," I said. "Fucking Severino!"

"Is not only Severino. Imagine we go in elevator and Trixie and Ed is there. Super incomodo." He let out a half-hearted laugh.

"Right. I suppose if we ran into anyone in the building, we would have to invent an explanation."

"I think there is none that make sense."

I walked around the room and then into the bathroom. Everything was clean as he had promised. "I don't have a toothbrush."

"I have mine," said Ivan.

"You planned this?"

He gave me a sheepish grin. For the last two hours, I had been dying to touch him, but couldn't in front of Isa. Now that we were alone, in our private world with no one watching, we still hadn't touched.

"If you have toothpaste, I can do a finger brush."

"This is what you worry about? The brushing of teeth?" he said. He opened a beer and handed it to me.

I really needed not to be sober. The sleaze factor of the room played with my head. "Be here now," my mom's voice reminded me.

"I'm trying," I said out loud.

"What? You okay." He got a beer for himself, and we bumped the bottles together.

"I will be."

He put a hand on my shoulder. Ah, finally a touch. It went a long way in breaking the awkwardness. "I think Isa liked you."

"Even with my funny Spanish and that certain way I was looking at you, which she caught me doing several times."

"What way?"

"Like I couldn't wait to be alone with you."

"Here we are, and now you have the trouble to look at me."

"The smell is driving me crazy. Can we open the window? It's also hot as fuck in here."

Again, he had the exhausted look like he was dealing with his daughter's poutiness. He turned on the ceiling fan and opened the window wide, letting in the noise of traffic from the street.

I sat on the bed, and he turned the desk chair around, facing me. "I'm sorry you don't like this place."

I was on the verge of ruining what had been a perfect afternoon. I took a big swallow of beer and imagined kicking myself in the ass. "It's not so bad. You're here. We're alone together. That's nice. Come over here."

"I am thinking you never going to ask."

"Your daughter is so beautiful...like you, with your eyes."

"Oh, now with the flatter. I think you want something." He set his beer on the nightstand. He put his hand behind my head and pulled me in for a kiss.

"Beer kiss," I said as I licked my lips of the cool yeasty taste.

"You complaining?"

"Seriously, thank you for inviting me to meet Isa. It meant a lot to me."

"To me too. You are special to me."

I leaned back and gawked at him.

"What?" said Ivan.

"You never said that before."

"Come on. You must know. I have been with no one since my wife.

Okay, one time. It was nothing. This is new and strange to me, but same time is great. It is something. Something I need."

It felt good to be needed and to need someone in return. If only it was that simple.

Eighteen

The sex was rougher than it had been as if the stark walls and all the tales they had to tell demanded it. As our hearts settled, our breathing slowed, and the sweat on our bodies began to dry, Ivan was extra gentle, holding me tightly, running a finger along the ridge of my ear, my cheeks, nose, and lips like he wanted to memorize them, or along the contours of my face and the pores of my skin like they held a message in Braille.

It was still early and neither of us were tired. We sat up, backs against the headboard, drinking the beer that was now warm.

"I saw your wife at the door," I began, observing his face for a reaction in case I needed to stop. "She's very pretty."

"Ex."

"Right. Can I ask you something?"

"Silly question?"

"You can always tell me to mind my own business."

He dropped his shoulders and let out a puff of air. "Go ahead."

"What happened?"

"Oof! You want to know the story of my life? I am not so good talking about such things, but I try." He adjusted the pillow behind his head and crossed his arms over his chest. "Sara and me are high school sweethearts, but after graduation she goes to Los Angeles to work in her father's restaurant. She is actually born over there but return here with her mother when she is like three years old."

"She has a U.S. passport?"

"Yep. I begin work in construction after high school. Sara come back after six years, and we start seeing each other again. In those years of separation, we become different people, but everyone expect us to marry. So, we do. She wants a child, but I am not sure. The moment I see Isa's little hands and feet, I feel pure love. I hold her against my chest and I am crazy with love."

The emotion in his voice brought tears to my eyes and I wondered what it would feel like to have a child. "That's so sweet," I said.

"I want to give her everything. I get a better job as a crew manager. I work twelve-hour days. On days off I work on the house. My little free time I spend with Isa. Sara feels like abandonada. I know it's not fair. My brother tell me he see her with another man, a neighbor who is divorced. He say I am not a man to allow this. Sara and I fight. In the end, we divorce. I move to a rented room nearby where I can see Isa frequently. When I start work in Sayulita, I have only Saturdays with Isa. And that's my story. Are you still awake?"

"You left out the part about meeting a handsome prince and living happily ever after."

He laughed out loud. "I think you read too many books. But in case you know a handsome prince or a beautiful princess who is free maybe…"

I rolled over, rested my arm on Ivan's chest and looked him in the eye. "I may not be a prince, but my intentions are honorable."

"You are not honorable a little while ago to make me do these terrible things."

I smacked him lightly on the cheek. "And you, sir, were a ruffian, taking me to your dungeon and having your way we me."

He pushed me back and got on top of me. "You can leave any time."

"From this position, it's a little difficult to go anywhere."

He kissed me and rolled onto his back. Then he picked up his phone from the nightstand, checked the time, and set the alarm. "It is late. We need to sleep."

"Okay, mi príncipe azul."

"Shut. Up."

I had never seen the front of Paradiso in this light, still dark but with the night sky shading toward indigo. In the lobby, the new night guy sat at the desk with his head back and his arms crossed over his chest. This early, we didn't have to worry about running into Severino.

The engine of Ivan's truck was still running, and his eyes darted from me to the street in front of us and back.

"Next week?" I said.

"I can't make plans right now. I'm running late."

I nodded. "Text me later."

"Of course."

I thought I'd better get out before I said something I might regret like the time he threw me out of the truck. I leaned over and pecked him on the cheek. As soon as I did it, I wished that I hadn't. Fuck. A kiss on the cheek? That's what you did to your aunt. I opened the door and the harsh light spotlighted Ivan's face, revealing his forehead crinkled with concern, his eyes uncertain. I hopped out, leaving behind a false smile. "Have a good day."

"You too," he mumbled.

Ray's words echoed in my head. "Ride the highs, but be prepared for the lows."

In the next week, I continued with the manuscript. Julian was moved by Edgar's emotional letter, and they began writing again. Julian reiterated his feelings and the romance continued to flourish despite not having seen each other in over a year and a half, or perhaps because of it. In letters they could be their ideal selves. Some COVID restrictions began to lift, and they fantasized a rendezvous in Florida, though Edgar lived with his aging mother and was still reluctant about traveling. I went to the internet and researched the timeline of COVID restrictions, particularly for Canada, to make sure the writing was accurate.

Edgar wrote about the failed relationship with his girlfriend. Julian stayed quiet about his wife. As long as I immersed myself in the book, I could forget what was happening in my personal life. Two days went by without hearing from Ivan, and on the third day a text ambushed me, taking me away from my work.

Pensando en ti.

After the initial surge of joy that Ivan was thinking of me, my thoughts verged into the cynical. Thinking of me how? Pondering the difficulties? Plotting how he could let me down easily? But what would be accomplished by responding suspiciously?

I look forward to seeing your smile.
Will Saturday work for you?
Sí, señor.
I must take Isa to a birthday party. I take her home about 6.

I assumed Ivan would spend the night and upgraded our single night accommodations to a small hotel near the beach in 5 de diciembre that had air conditioning. It was late September, and though we were nearing the end of the rainy season, it was still hot and muggy. High season rates hadn't kicked in yet, and it was a small price to pay for the comfort, though a tryst in a hotel in the town where I lived still had a tawdry feel to it. In the afternoon, I checked in with my toothbrush and stocked the mini fridge with beer. I stared at the bathtub and imagined the two of us in it.

Ivan arrived in a cheerful mood after having spent time with Isa. There was no hesitation in hugging and kissing me upon entering the room.

"There's a bathtub," I said.

"A little hot for a bath, no?"

"We can crank up the air and pretend it's winter."

I convinced him to try it, and we sat in the warm water, facing each other in the tub, beers in hand. I compulsively stared at him, a smile frozen on my face.

"Why you look at me so much?"

"It makes me happy. I never would have imagined this in a million years when I first met you."

He closed his eyes. "I think ten minutes ago I don't imagine this bathtub thing. I never do this with anyone. So many first things with you."

"I can think up a lot more." I glided my foot along his inner thigh, squeezing my big and second toe together, grabbing a tuft of hair and pulling.

"Ay!" He opened one eye and raised an eyebrow as he took hold of my foot, stopping its progress. "I think you only want me for sex."

Since that first kiss, I had been able to tick off several things on my wish list of things to do with Ivan: sex on the beach under moonlight, a night in a bed with limbs entwined, and now lounging in a bath, gazing into those dark eyes, resting a hand on his hairy knee. There had been significant non-sexy things as well: playing in the waves, meeting his daughter, going to a restaurant as if we were a little gay family. But it still felt like what we had, this unnamed thing, was hidden from the world. We had no declared status.

We were friends.

Each time we were together now, the joining of bodies brought us not only to new levels of pleasure but also trust. Yet in the morning, the awkward separation made me anxious as well as sad, wondering if another week of uncertainty about the next secret rendezvous was worth the reward. But, of course, in the throes of it, it was. *Ride the highs.*

My work gave me an escape from thinking about Ivan, and a massage with Matthew was another way to disconnect during the weekdays away from him. The period of using me as guinea pig for his nascent massage skills was over, but he still gave me a discount.

Lying on Matthew's table with his hands running up and down my body, I truly relaxed, and in the new-age ambiance of the room, listening to the twanging strings of a sitar, I felt connected to my parents. When Matthew lit a stick of incense, it was like a sense-memory superhighway to the past, conjuring up my mom, sitting on the floor in lotus position with her eyes closed. As a child it used to irritate me as if she was shutting me out. But later I was glad she was too engaged to criticize me for being overly focused on material things or my obsession for "getting ahead" she would always frame in finger quotes.

Now that I was used to Matthew's peculiar brand of flirtiness and was no longer confused by it, the young man's hands on my skin were just that, a manipulation of soft tissue to boost mental and physical health.

The weekly escapades with Ivan continued, my body craving the highs of Saturday, my mind preparing for the lows of Sunday. October flowed in on the muddy, turbulent Cuale River, swollen with daily downpours, and more rain was on the way with tropical storms looming out in the Pacific. The green of the jungle was dense as if the artist's painting that had begun early in the summer with the sparse under layers of a forest was now nearly finished, the final deepest layer of green laid on the canvas. The sunsets were like forest fires on the horizon, heralding a blood red rage of a storm.

One Friday Ivan notified me that we couldn't get together on Saturday because he had to go to a wedding. It annoyed me that he waited until the day before to tell me. "Fine," I shouted after reading the text. I booked a massage with Matthew, made a dinner date with Ray and Stef, and walked along the Malecón toward the Zona Romántica, trying to remember the exact location of the store that sold a certain whole grain bread that I liked. I would pick up a loaf, and on my way back, go to Matthew's for my massage.

When I got to the point of the Malecón with a view down the narrow street that led to the main church, I saw a large crowd of people dressed for an occasion, gathered on the steps. Despite the muggy, gray day—the rains had so far held off—there was joy in the air, the particular variety of joy that was the result of a wedding. The pieces slowly came together in my brain made sluggish by the heat: Saturday, wedding, Ivan. Could this be the wedding?

I crossed over to the plaza and into the narrow street, stopping in the shadow of one of the small trees planted in a row. In the gauntlet on the church steps, waiting for the bride and groom to emerge, stood Ivan in a solemn pose with his hands on Isa's shoulders. His hair was swept back with product, and he wore sunglasses, a light blue polo shirt, and navy slacks. Isa had on a yellow dress with her hair pulled back, and she carried a small bouquet of flowers. Ivan bent down and said something to a woman who leaned forward, coming into view. It was Sara in an identical dress to Isa's. I stood frozen, watching as best I could from behind the thin trunk of the tree, my heart thumping an irregular beat like I was having a heart attack. After torturing myself for several minutes, I forced myself to turn and flee back through the square, past the gazebo, and along the main street.

I abandoned the idea of getting the bread and wandered the streets, beating myself up for being ridiculously emotional. I struggled with the notion that I was a terrible person, a homewrecker, destroying this perfect family. Then I remembered that they had divorced long before I met Ivan. Still, thoughts and emotions swirled around in my head, none of them making me feel like I deserved Ivan's affections, those stolen moments of pleasure in hidden locales. I concluded it would be best if I ended this affair. God, affair sounded so cheap. We were friends and had sex we both enjoyed. No strings attached. Why was I trying to make it out to be something it wasn't? And so what? Ivan went to a wedding with his ex. She probably needed someone to go with and it wasn't appropriate to invite the boyfriend. It didn't mean she and Ivan were getting back together.

My wandering led me to Matthew's door, where we hugged, and he asked why my body was so tense. I said it must be the extra hours working intensely on manuscripts at my desk. I needed to stretch more. He worked his magic and after a few minutes, I settled into being stretched and kneaded and stroked.

That night I arrived at the dinner with Ray and Stef, feeling relaxed and rejuvenated until Ray asked about Ivan. I said everything was fine. Stef looked at me skeptically, opened her mouth to say something, and then seemed to have second thoughts. I ordered the fried chicken in an attempt at comfort food but now found the grease on my fingers annoying. As hard as I wiped them on the napkin, I couldn't get the oil to go away. I changed the subject.

"My sister might come to visit for Day of the Dead."

"Your sister? I didn't even know you had a sister," said Ray.

"We're not close. Well, we haven't been since we were little. In my rebellious period, I said some horrible things to my parents that she never forgave even though they did. She idolized them and thought our bohemian upbringing was just peachy, the moving around, seeing new things, spending time in nature and around animals. I hated it. It would take me a long time to get settled in a new place, in a new school. As soon as I would make a friend, we would move again. We usually lived in rural intentional communities, often with goats and chickens and pigs. A billy goat knocked me down one time. Another one ate my favorite shirt I left outside. I hated goats. I hated collecting eggs that sometimes had poop on them and wouldn't eat them. The pig pens made me sick. Of course, it wasn't the animals I hated. I hated our life. My sister, Nell, took the experience of our childhood, embraced her love of nature and animals, and made a career of it. She now works for the National Park Service and lives with a number of rescue animals in Colorado."

"Sounds like you two are very different," said Stef.

"We are, but she's all the family I have and I admire her for taking our upbringing and making it into a good life. I've been thinking about my parents a lot lately and decided to contact her. I told her I was living in a place surrounded by barking dogs, crowing roosters, and scary iguanas. It was my punishment for being shitty to my parents. She laughed and said she'd love to see it."

Nineteen

I woke to noise coming from the apartment next door after months of silence. The migration was starting, like birds coming south for the winter. Snowbirds they were called, northerners flying to Mexico to be warm. By the winter holidays, the building would be full. It would be rare for me to have the pool all to myself, and the sounds of humans going about their daily business would come from above, below, and in the hallway. At least the snowbirds returning heralded the season of lower temperatures, though not by much, and we would get some respite from the debilitating humidity.

In the midst of this new activity in the building, I had been approved by the other board members to take Patrick's seat, and Trixie had scheduled an online meeting to introduce me, discuss changes in the building, and prepare for the general meeting that would happen in the winter when all the residents had returned. I deliberated over how hard I should push for us to fire Severino and how much I should reveal about Severino's vindictive behavior.

The meeting began with everyone welcoming me. Most of them knew me, at least by sight, but hadn't interacted much with me or known my opinions. Some of them had questions about points I had made in my letter requesting the board seat.

"I'm confused," said Ed, "why you have so little confidence in Severino. I think he's done a stand-up job."

Mary chimed in with a hoarse voice from a cold she had been nursing. "It's not COVID!" she rushed to assure us. "I've tested several times. Anyway, Severino has been so helpful to John and me, carrying groceries for us, those little things like holding the door open for us."

Trixie pursed her lips as if assessing the lay of the land. "Well, he did step in when we needed him."

"It was so irresponsible of Ivan to leave us in dire straits after the... um...mess," said Ed.

Everybody nodded in their boxes like bobbleheads. "I'd like to remind everyone," I said, "that we aren't here to bash Ivan but to discuss Severino."

All the board members except for Trixie, recounted ways that Severino had helped them, ignorant of his ingratiating agenda. They whined about how problematic it would be to replace him even if they wanted to. I sent a private message to Trixie. "WTF?" It was clear that we didn't have the votes to get rid of him, and I began to doubt if Trixie was on my side. She sent back a shruggie emoji.

I was so close to laying out in detail the attacks on Ivan and the audacity of threats Severino made to me, a resident and now board member he was supposed to work for. How would they like it if Severino turned on them? If I laid it all out for them, it would involve a lengthy discussion about Ivan, force everyone to relive the night they all wanted to forget, and reveal certain elements of my own behavior that were less than exemplary. They might wonder how I had recent knowledge of Severino's behavior toward Ivan and be curious why I defended Ivan so vehemently. Ed might bring up the tired rumors again. I would also have to acknowledge I had no proof to back up my claims. It would be my and Ivan's word against Severino's, and none of the others wanted to shake things up just as "the season" was beginning.

"Shall we move on?" said Trixie.

I seethed and remained quiet the rest of the meeting. Severino had won. I anticipated the sneer on his face when I next entered the lobby. After the session ended, I sat at my desk, and for the first time, entertained the thought of selling my place, maybe getting a little house like I had rented in San Pancho where Ivan could visit. But wait, I was ending things with Ivan, right? Was my desire to buy a little house outside Puerto Vallarta only part of a fantasized future with him or would there be other advantages?

In my head I prepared a PowerPoint presentation, going over item by item why it was ludicrous for our relationship to continue. If my new life in Vallarta was to include a relationship, there were plenty of men to choose from. Rafael wasn't the right one, but I shouldn't be discouraged. And if I only wanted sex, the possibilities were endless, men passing through, hot for a good time, or residents who moved to the town because of the freedom to cruise and be cruised. Though I dreaded the thought of wasting time in bars, there had to be other ways to meet people that didn't involve friends setting me up with a gay friend who they insisted would be a match. Sure, Ivan made me feel things I had never felt before, but the price was too high and the payoff too uncertain. In the middle of this heated debate between Dawson-the-practical and Dawson-the-emotional, I got a text as if my high frequency ruminations traveled the miles and provoked a response.

I miss our weekend together.

"Motherfucker!" I screamed.

Why was my reaction so immediate and rabid? How could I love and hate someone in equal measure? Yes, I'd used the word love again, at least in the uncensored part of my brain. It felt both liberating and terrifying. My first impulse was to call Ray as if he was my sponsor. and I was about to take that sip that would send me over the edge, tumbling into the valley of forbidden pleasure and extremely difficult to climb out of. And yet Ray might have been incapable of providing unbiased advice. He was too close to the dilemma. I was Ray's dear friend, but Ivan was in the position Ray had undoubtedly found himself many times.

I concluded that my best option for the moment was to do nothing about Ivan and return to my work. Susan had sent me a nonfiction manuscript that another editor hadn't been able to finish. She needed it sooner than the "moonstruck boys" book, and if I didn't mind, I could put that aside for the time being. Or work on them both at the same time as I wished. I was more than happy to get a respite from the romantic letters. I dove into the work written by a journalist who went to Vietnam searching for Americans who stayed in the country after the war. It was called *Vietnam Dialogues* and wasn't about the POWs who were unaccounted for, but rather people who served the American war effort in some capacity in Vietnam and stayed in the country voluntarily, disappearing into the postwar society. Most of their relatives had never heard from them again.

I worked full days on the new book, keeping my brain occupied and, as much as humanly possible, free of thoughts of Ivan. I felt great pride that I'd managed to resist answering the text. However, by mid-week I was lonely and sent a message.

How does your weekend look?
It look like a room by the sea. Sí o no?

"No" was such a small word. Two little letters. It could be the gateway to moving on. But of equal length was the word "sí." It was yes to kisses and holding him in my arms, and yeah, the sex part, too. It did not need to be nearly as complicated as my pinballing head made it out to be. Pleasure, sharing, fun. I deserved that, didn't I? That was all it seemed to be for Ivan, so I could strive for the same frame of mind. Friends. Simple. Dilemma resolved.

The surf pounded the beach as we lay in bed side by side, bodies spent, hands touching. After my conclusion that I accepted a purely physical connection and Ivan's willingness to try new things—he still had his limits, things he didn't think he'd ever be able to do—I had no problem saying it was the best sex I'd ever had, and I had no doubts that he enjoyed it nearly as much as I did. We drifted in silence, and I looked forward to a restful sleep, curled up next to him, taking in his scent. I was in the initial phase of falling when his movement turning toward me forced my eyes open.

"You asleep?" he asked.

"Almost."

"I want to tell you something."

With the seriousness of his voice, I was fully awake. "Okay."

"It is not a problem with this, you and me, but I think is important you know. I don't want you be angry."

"Just tell me. What is it?"

"When I go to the wedding, I go with my ex-wife."

As I already knew that, I had to find the right tone of my response. "That's what you wanted to tell me? I have no problem with it." At least, not in my new resolve to treat our time together as nothing more than friends who had sex.

"Is her cousin who got married." His voice was anxious, and the air in the room had gone from dreamy post-sex bliss to tension.

"Ivan! Just say what you have to say."

"We get drunk and...uh..."

"You fucked?"

"I don't like this word."

"You had sex. Fine. You are a free man." I tried to keep my voice moderated, but the churning inside belied my relatively calm exterior.

"See? You get angry. It change nothing with us."

"Are you getting back together?" As soon as the question was out of my mouth, I was hit by the dissonance between what my heart expected when involved with someone and what was possible with Ivan. I was willing to let great sex cloud my vision at least for now, but an expiration date seemed looming. "Actually, I don't care. It doesn't matter."

"Not together like before. For Isa is better I move back to my house. I can see her every day. Bad part I must drive a long way to work."

I wanted to ask if Sara knew about me, but I was nearly certain of the answer. "We will live in the same city again," I said, trying to sound upbeat, but my voice faltered with the realization there would be no more overnights.

"I know what you thinking. I can say sometime I have to do double shift, work all night."

I faked a laugh. "And a lot of work it is."

Ivan chuckled. "I enjoy this work."

"We should sleep. Early morning for you."

"Thank you for understanding."

Rational me did understand. Another part of me hated it, hated the thought of him having sex with his ex, living with her, lying and sneaking around so we could be together. "It won't change anything," says every man to his lover when he decides to get back together with his ex.

A short time later, Ivan was dozing in the serenity of being able to have his cake and eating it too. I stared at the ceiling fan, wondering why it didn't come crashing down on us. My mind jumped back and forth from giddiness at lying next to someone whose body I craved to touch whenever he was near and downright self-loathing for allowing myself to be the side squeeze.

In the morning, I pretended everything was normal. Any grumpiness I could blame on not having my cup of morning java. We kissed when he dropped me off at my building. As I got out of the truck, my lips curled up into a grin and produced a cute wave in an Oscar-worthy performance of my acquiescence to the new order of things.

I got through the week by working every day, going for swims in the pool, and walks on the Malecón. Late in the week I got a text from Ivan. **Moving this weekend. Sorry. No time.**

The text made me furious as if Ivan thought I sat around waiting to be summoned. Would no response be an answer to how I felt? I didn't have the energy to compose a pithy reply. Mostly I felt an urge to go out and get drunk, not something I regularly indulged in as a problem solver who confronted things head-on. I wouldn't go to the Zona Romántica bars because a one-nighter was not my goal. Any sleazy bar in Centro or 5 de diciembre would do, a place where I could be anonymous and not bothered by flirty smiles and cruisers striking a pose.

I had a couple of shots of tequila before I left the house, letting the little buzz lead me. The violins of ranchera music like sirens pulled me into a Mexican equivalent of a sports bar. I wasn't fond of the music, but it set the right mood of love, betrayal and death. It was a local bar where Mexicans could feel the neighborhood was still theirs, but a foreigner's money wouldn't be rejected. On one side of the room were small tables and on the other, a pool table where a young woman in skin-tight jeans leaned on a pool cue taller than her, waiting for a rake-thin older man to finish his shot. There were two medium-sized screens showing soccer. The place smelled of tortillas and crispy meat. I walked around the pool table and sat on a stool at the end of the bar. A few heads turned toward me and then back to their conversations. People gathered in groups of two or three, drinking beer.

The other patrons left me alone as I sunk deeper into my funk with each tequila, and the lyrics of the music assisted me in wallowing in heartbreak. I nearly burst out laughing when Vicente Fernández sang, "Y yo caí en tu trampa ilusionado."

"I fell into your trap of illusion," I said to an imaginary Ivan sitting next to me.

Later in the song, Vicente sang, "Y pa' qué quiero la tumba si ya enterraste en vida." *Why would I want the grave when you've already buried me in life?*

If I knew how, I would have produced the loudest grito mexicano anyone had ever heard, the drawn-out, high-pitched yell that is part pain and part laughter, often heard from mariachis.

Down the bar, I caught two men staring at me, one of them classically handsome with a mustache, a five o'clock shadow, and a square jaw. He wore a tight T-shirt, faded jeans, and boots. He turned and said something to his friend. The menacing-looking friend with tattoos on his neck laughed, and the hot one turned to me with a smile blooming on his face and a slight jump of his eyebrows. I was just drunk enough to think for a moment it was a real smile of seduction that could lead to a hookup. Though I wasn't seeing things clearly, there was a tiny part of my unwaveringly steadfast rational brain that pinned the smile as a hustler smile, one I had seen in other cultures across other borders, someone looking for something. It could be as simple as a free drink or as involved as sex for pay, most often bad sex. The proverbial struggle between my dick on the march and frank reality.

I stared a moment without returning the smile before turning back to the drink in front of me and the mottled surface of the bar, picking out shapes that looked like countries or states. I had achieved the absurd goal I set for myself—getting drunk—but I didn't know how well I'd reached that goal until I stood up and saw the path I would have to negotiate to get to the door. I shook out my shoulders in an attempt to look sober, but I felt the two men staring at me as well as several other patrons of the bar. Weaving an escape route, and only once slowing to steady myself by grabbing the back of a chair, I reached the outside. The air was not fresh as I had hoped, but rather warm and moist, still better than inside the stuffy bar.

A taxi sat on the other side of the street, and considering the hour and the walk up the hill, it looked inviting. But the thought of being in a moving vehicle nauseated me. I would walk, or at least stagger to my street and then up the hill.

Twenty

I stumbled on my journey home but made steady progress over uneven sidewalks, not bothered by the never-ending traffic and crowded streets, or the heat and humidity of the night. Near the Malecón, people were in a festive mood, and I greeted several passersby with animated holas. As soon as I started up the hill, the crowds thinned until I approached the corner where the boys hung out. I had a moment of fear that the group of five or six might mess with me in my vulnerable state, but they were glued to their phones between gulps of beer and barely seemed to notice my passing. One boy glanced at me and nodded with a look that said, "You're fucked up just like me."

The sidewalk here was even more irregular, and at times reduced to chunks of concrete while unconnected electrical wires dangled above it like strips of black licorice. I moved to the middle of the street as I often did when there was no traffic. A car came up behind me, and I moved over to the sidewalk. The car stopped, and two men got out and approached me. The two men from the bar.

"Are you offering me a ride home?" I said in slurred speech, grinning, not yet grasping the danger.

"Yeah, sure," the handsome one said with a sneer. "But first, phone and money."

"Come on, man. Seriously?"

"Give me your fucking phone and wallet!"

I laughed. I couldn't believe this was happening.

"Vamos, pendejo! I don't wanna hurt you." He grabbed the front of my polo and balled it in his fist.

With the handsome face close to mine, now ugly in its intent, the fact that these idiots had singled me out and stalked me had a sobering effect, but more than that left me with a burning anger, flames stoked by drunken recklessness. I took my phone out of my pocket and held it up.

"You mean this phone?" I threw it over my shoulder into the weeds beyond the sidewalk in an overgrown section between two buildings.

"Puto!" yelled the one with tattoos on his neck. The other, with my shirt still bunched in his fist, shoved me hard. I fell back and hit my head on a parked car and landed in a slump on the ground. With the crashing thump, I thought my head had split wide open.

The two argued about who would retrieve the phone from the weeds but decided to get my wallet first. It was in my back pocket that was closed with a zipper. I struggled to stay on my back, trying to push and kick them away. Despite the intense pain in my head, I needed to fight, as stupid as it seemed later in sober reflections. I wasn't thinking rationally. The good-looking one straddled me, grabbed my wrists in one hand, and punched me with the other. The tattooed one kicked me several times in the ribs, each punch and kick like a red flash of pain in my brain.

"Stop fighting, puto!"

I was at the point of giving up when shouts came from down the street, multiple pairs of feet running toward us. A rock hit the back of their car stopped in the street, the doors still open. Another hit the glass of the back window and bounced off. The two men abandoned me, ran to their car, jumped in, and sped up the street.

One of the boys hunched down over me and lay a hand on my arm. We had seen each other many times in quiet acknowledgement of our crossed paths. The other boys hovered over us with saucer eyes. One of them asked if I was going to die.

"You okay, man?"

I put my hand to the back of my head and felt blood. "No."

"Sorry for this. We take you to the hospital." He took off his T-shirt and wrapped it around my head. "What your name?"

"Dawson."

"Dog Son. Cool name!"

I began to laugh, but it hurt so much I grabbed my ribs.

"Tranquilo," the boy said.

"Please," I gasped. "My phone." I pointed at the weeds.

A few of the boys turned on their phone flashlights, searched the weeds, and found it. They slipped it into my pocket. Others shouted for someone to call Pepe who had a taxi and lived nearby. They discussed the taxi versus calling an ambulance but decided an ambulance would take too long. Neighbors came out on their porches and balconies, expressing concern and deriding the hoodlums who had gotten away. One boy shouted he had gotten their license plate.

As the shock wore off, the pain became unbearable. My head throbbed, my face burned where they had punched me, my ribs smarted where they had kicked me. The taxi arrived, and the boys lifted me as gently as possible into the back seat. The shirtless boy rode in the front seat while the people of the neighborhood stood at the windows, waving and sending wishes for a speedy recovery. As we passed over the cobbles, my bones and insides rattled so much I thought I was going to die.

I woke up in a hospital bed, not knowing if it was day or night since the curtains were closed, and I was unable to recall much after being lifted into the taxi except that the driver was Pepe. I never got the boy's name who helped me. I laughed inside, imagining the boy telling all his friends he had helped a foreigner named Dog Son, like I was an anti-hero in an apocalyptic video game.

A nurse walked by my door, and when she noticed I was awake, asked if I spoke Spanish. When I said yes, she enquired if there was a family member I wanted to call. I had been too out of it the night before to give them a name for the form. The first person who came to mind was Ray, who, along with Stef, had in a short time become family. The nurse brought my phone, which they kept in a safe place while I slept. I opened the phone and saw that it was five in the morning alongside three missed call notifications dancing on my home screen. From Ivan. It was rare that he would call once. I was still groggy from the pain medicine they gave me and hungover from the alcohol, and I wondered if I was hallucinating. I switched off my phone and turned it on again. Still there. I could erase them without listening to the messages. I could pretend my heart didn't skip a beat when I saw them.

I thought it was too early to call Ray, so I sent him a brief text explaining that I had been mugged and was in the hospital. I had to ask the nurse the name of the place. Ray was an insomniac. He called immediately.

"I'm coming right over."

"You don't have to."

"Stef's not up yet, but I'll be there in a few minutes."

"I might be asleep." I could barely keep my eyes open.

"Sleep, my friend, if that's what you need. I'll be there regardless."

I opened the camera app and switched to selfie mode. I had a bandage on my head and my face was bruised and swollen, looking like I'd just come back from a war. I snapped a picture with the intention of sending it to Ivan with the message that it was all his fault. Before I could press the send button, I drifted into sleep with the phone in my hand.

The next time I woke up, Ray and Stef were by my bedside.

"Hello, handsome," said Ray.

I clutched my side. "Don't make me laugh. It'll kill me. My ribs."

"Looks like you've got three fractured ones. They really did a number on you."

"I fought back."

"Not a good choice," said Stef.

"But they didn't get my phone or wallet. Of course, I got a little help from the corner boys."

"The who?"

"Didn't I tell you about the boys that hang out on one corner of my street? I used to worry they might be dangerous, but now I see they've got my back."

"How many times have we told you not to walk home alone late at night, especially after drinking?" said Stef. "It's just asking for trouble."

"They followed me from the bar."

Ray was smirking and shaking his head.

"What, Ray?" I asked.

"You were in some dive bar, getting stinking drunk, which we've never seen you do, or anything close..." Stef gave him a look. "Okay, the night we went out with Rafael. The point is I've got a big question mark in my head about why you would do such a thing. Is there something new you need to tell us?"

"Nope. Same old, same old."

"You can lie to yourself, but you can't lie to me. I know damn well it's related to something that begins with I and ends with van. What did he do this time?"

"He's moving back in with his wife. For his daughter's sake, he says."

Stef groaned as if in pain. "I can't listen to this." She went out into the hall.

"I'm sorry," I said.

"Don't worry about her," said Ray. "She cares about you a lot."

"I know. But it's a fine line between caring about someone and judging them."

Ray pointed his finger at me like a professor letting a student know he had made a good point. "You're a big boy. You'll figure this out, but please don't do anything stupid like this again. You can call us at any time of day or night. I would have come and picked you up. I'm usually awake anyway."

Stef came back in the room with tears shimmering in her eyes. She put a hand lightly on the less damaged side of my face. "My beautiful boy." She had a lot more to say but kept it to herself. "We can go by your place and get you some things. I think they want to keep you for a few days."

I spent the rest of the day falling in and out of sleep. They woke me up for lunch, and I saw Ray and Stef left some toiletries, clean underwear, and my laptop. I ate a few bites, but that was all I could keep down. I drank lots of water, though, and someone had to help me get up to go to the bathroom a few times. They offered me a bedpan, but I insisted on getting up despite the pain it caused me.

At one point two police officers woke me up to interview me about the attack. I gave detailed descriptions. I was glad they were not the same officers who had come to the building on the night of the boy's death.

In the evening, I woke up to someone holding my hand. I assumed it was Ray. I opened one eye, concluded it was a dream, and closed them tightly with a grimace.

Ivan squeezed my hand. "I see you."

I attempted to pull my hand away, but he held on tight. "Go away."

"No. I am here for you."

"Who told you? Ray?"

"You don't listen to my messages?"

"I deleted them."

"Sure." He grinned like he didn't believe me.

"So, who?"

"You are not going to believe."

"Who?"

"Severino."

"No fucking way!"

"The night guy call him cause everybody in the neighborhood know what happen. Somebody come to the building to tell him."

"And Severino called you?"

"Sent me text. He say my friend is in the hospital."

"Unbelievable," I mumbled.

"I try calling you many times. Leave messages. Sara is very angry. Confused. She think I have a secret amante."

"Had!"

"When I come in here and see you in the bed, it is like a knife in my heart. I think is because of me."

"Don't flatter yourself."

"I know you only short time but never see you get so drunk and do something silly like this."

"It could happen to anyone."

"I am very sorry it happen to you. If I am with you, I don't let these bad people hurt you."

"Yada, yada, yada. I can take care of myself."

"It seems no. Of course, I don't see the other guy."

"Please. Don't make me laugh. It hurts."

He squeezed my hand again and ran his other hand along my arm. "You don't believe you are important to me?"

"I don't know. Maybe?"

"Already I think this don't work living with Sara. One day! Already problems. I come here directly from work. She call me like ten times."

"Sorry. I screwed up your life. Again."

"I only do it for Isa. I swear. She ask me other day at the wedding where is Dawson, if you are coming to the wedding. My wife hear it."

"And you said?"

"I tell Isa that you don't know these people. I am waiting for Sara to ask something, but she say nothing, only look at me with eyes of confusion."

"When you go home tonight, what will you tell her?"

"How do you know I am going home?"

"They will kick you out when visiting hours are over."

"I just say I am your husband." He produced a gurgly laugh that turned into a cough.

"Is that so funny?"

He rested his head on the hand that was still holding mine and looked up at me with sorry eyes. "Not a good joke?"

"No."

"You have a husband before, right?"

"We weren't married."

"You don't love him enough?"

"None of your frickin' business."

"I am curious about things...since I meet you."

"Everything you want to know is on the internet."

"But I want you to tell me. I don't care about this people on the internet."

"I'm too exhausted to be your teacher right now."

"Go to sleep. I won't bother you." He let go of my hand and settled back in the chair with his arms crossed.

I closed my eyes but opened one after a minute. "You should go home."

"I stay until you go to sleep."

I sighed and opened both eyes. "Okay, but do you have to stare at me?"

"I am thinking. Before your face is like an angel. So innocent. Now, when you are better, it will have more character."

My eyelids felt like heavy shutters. "Okay. If you say so. Now be quiet and let me sleep. I really can't keep my eyes open."

When I woke up around midnight, Ivan was gone. It had been a dream, right? The hand holding? The joke about being my husband? The promise to protect me? The little fire inside me fanned by him watching over me while I slept? But the strangest thing of all was that Severino had been the agent that brought Ivan to the hospital. Was he plotting something new or did a shred of human decency slip through?

Twenty-one

I lay in the hospital bed, the back adjusted to an upright position, staring at the words on my laptop that blurred with the pain medication. I felt dopey and listless, but the pressure was mounting to complete my editing work. Out of fear that Susan would worry I couldn't get things done, I hadn't told her about being laid up in the hospital. She had already made several statements insinuating that I worked slower "down there" and once made a joke about me working "on Mexican time." I rubbed the sleepies out of the corner of my eyes and tried to focus.

I opened up *Vietnam Dialogues* and picked up where I had left off. In this chapter, the author had been led down a narrow alley in the old part of Hanoi to interview a Black woman in her late seventies. She served as an Army Corps nurse, but as the war went on, she soured on the U.S. involvement. Then she got word that her brother, who had also served in Vietnam, was shot by the police in Philadelphia. Her disillusionment with the war and the devastating news of losing her brother at the hands of the police made her furious with her country. When the war ended, she decided to stay in Vietnam and use her nursing skills to help the Vietnamese people. She lived with a Vietnamese woman for thirty years.

When Ray stopped by the hospital for a visit, we talked about the books I was working on. He was fascinated by the Vietnam book and filled me in with some of the views at the time and his perspective of being a Black man. Then I switched the conversation to ask Ray's advice on the tone, rather than content, of *Between the Lines*. I was particularly interested in Ray's reaction to Julian, who was married and kept his wife completely in the dark about his communication with Edgar. Julian wrote the letters late at night after his wife went to bed. He would post them on his way to pick up a few things at the store. He rented a private mailbox and snuck the letters he received into the house, locking them in his desk drawer.

"As the book goes on, Edgar can't juggle pouring his heart out to a man while maintaining a relationship with a woman and breaks up with his girlfriend. Julian, on the other hand, is comfortable not only juggling his emotions, but keeps his wife—and Edgar—in the dark."

"I can't imagine being in a situation where you have to lie all the time. Though, and we've talked about this before, I believe that's the norm rather than the exception," said Ray.

"The author does a good job of communicating Edgar's frustration, but he's less convincing when it comes to Julian. In our communication, he admitted that the Julian character was more difficult to write."

"There are certainly plenty of examples of closeted men in literature often written by closeted authors. E.M. Forster's *Maurice* wasn't published until 1971 after his death. Of course, there's the classic one in the character of Aschenbach in *Death in Venice.*"

"Is the message there that being closeted leads to death?"

"A lot of tragic stories, for sure."

"I sometimes think about how great this book would be in your hands."

"I've been out of the game too long," he said definitively as if to end the conversation.

"A talent like yours doesn't just wither away. You're living in a new country, new culture, new smells, a host of new characters ready to take their places on the page. You must think about it."

"Why don't you do it if you're so keen on it? Or do want to be the behind-the-scenes guy the rest of your life?"

"I feel like I could craft a well-written sentence or two, certainly better than a lot of the people who get published, but a whole book?"

"If you think of it as a finished book of so many pages and thousands of words, it's daunting. The trick is putting one word after another and realizing you have a sentence, and then sentences into paragraphs, one after another. You put in the work just like you put in the work at editing."

"Maybe if I'd had you as my teacher..."

"Yeah, that would have been fun." Ray widened his eyes, and I imagined how it would have been in Ray's class, how I might have discreetly flirted with him, visited him during office hours.

Ray's smiling eyes indicated he might have been having the same mini fantasy before he changed the subject. "So, he came to visit you, huh?"

"I woke up to him holding my hand. That shouldn't be allowed. Doesn't he know about consent?"

"It felt good though, didn't it?"

"I tried to shoo him away like a pesky fly, but he was so fucking charming. He even made a joke about telling the nurse he was my husband so they wouldn't bother him about visiting hours. All this right after he's moved back in with his ex-wife. It's maddening, I tell you."

"Yes. That is cruel and unusual punishment," Ray said, holding back a grin. "He should be reported to the authorities."

"Now he wants me to educate him about relationships between two men. I told him to go look it up on the internet."

"Next thing he'll be going to gay porno sites to get pointers."

"He's already done that!"

Ray howled. "Is he a good learner?"

"I will *not* discuss what happens in the bedroom...or on the beach... or in his car."

"You are a tease. But seriously, I get what you're saying about not wanting to educate him. It's not quite the same, but I'm exhausted trying to educate my white friends and acquaintances about being a Black man in our society, how it's not enough to be non-racist. They have to be an anti-racist. If they're serious, they need to do the work. Like I used to tell my students all the time, 'I'm not here to hold your hand.' I can give them some tools, maybe a little inspiration, but they have to walk the walk."

"Kendi's book was an eye-opener even after growing up with progressive parents who taught me to treat everybody the same. I always feel like I'm not doing enough."

"If you can say that, you're on the right path. One reason Stef and I are in Mexico is to get away from that constant undercurrent of racism in the States, day in and day out, even when it's not obvious, and no matter where you are, it's there. Have you noticed how many Black expats are coming to Mexico? A lot more are coming down on vacation. It's not that things are perfect here, but I can feel the relief of pressure as soon as I get on the plane to Mexico."

"I did notice that. A lot of Black gay men and lesbians, but I also see a bunch of Black families walking around. When I was making the decision to move to Mexico, it entered my thoughts why so many Black people felt comfortable here. It had to be a good sign, right?"

"I'm afraid I got us off topic, talking about my shit. We were supposed to be talking..."

"Speak of the devil," I said in a low voice with my eyes zeroing in on the doorway.

Ray turned around and saw Ivan.

"I can come back later," said Ivan.

"Absolutely not. I have to leave soon anyway," said Ray.

"Come in. Ray, could you find another chair?" I think I sounded smooth and unbothered, but inside I was tripping. I wanted these two men to meet for a long time. I wanted to sit back and watch the show. Too bad there was no popcorn.

Ray and Ivan shook hands.

"Nice grip," said Ray.

"Hehe," said Ivan. "Nice to meet you. Dawson say many good things about you."

"Likewise. I'm glad we finally get to meet."

"I hope to meet your wife someday," said Ivan.

"Oh, you will."

"I just come from work. That's why this clothes."

"I appreciate a man in a uniform," said Ray with a laugh.

I cleared my throat. "Excuse me. I'm the one barely alive in a hospital bed."

"Sorry, D." Ivan walked over to the bed and awkwardly took my hand.

"Did you just call me D?"

"It come to me like that."

"How quickly we went from señor Dawson to D!"

"If you prefer the señor, I can..."

"D is good. The boy who helped me when I was attacked thought I said Dog Son when I introduced myself."

"You want I call you Dog?" said Ivan.

"Definitely not," Ray chimed in. "Not Dog or Dawg or anything like that. Sorry, I shouldn't answer for you." He left the room to find another chair.

"You look better today," said Ivan.

"Bullshit! I saw myself in the mirror. I don't know how you can even look at me."

"Yes, is difficult but I manage." He smiled and squeezed my hand.

"My face is going to have so much character I won't need a Halloween mask."

Ray came back in with a chair and placed it close to me, moving his out of the way.

"Not necessary to move," Ivan said to Ray.

"Please," said Ray, motioning to the chair closest to the bed.

"Boys. Boys. No need to fight over proximity to the royal bed," I said.

Ivan turned to Ray. "He is always with the jokes."

"I know," said Ray. "So annoying."

My smile was so wide it hurt my face, watching the two of them interact, to see them already showing signs of liking each other. I imagined for a moment if they could be fused into one, Ray with his intellect, life experience, and kindness mixed with Ivan's playful sexiness, his ability to surprise, his affectionate nature, making a perfect man anyone could love. There was that word again. I put a hand on my chest, feeling the warmth expanding within.

"Are you okay?" said Ray. "You look like you're having a heart attack."

"A heart something," I said.

Ray and Ivan turned to each other. "Your friend is very strange," said Ivan.

"My friend? I thought he was your friend. I'm not sure I'm in the right room."

"What a pair of jokers!" I said. "Sit, Ivan, and tell me about your day."

"Very exciting. One water heater break, and a lady is crying because she can't take a hot shower."

"In this heat?" said Ray. "I rarely use the hot water."

"Not everybody is so macho like you, Ray," I said.

"Ray macho?" said Stef from the doorway.

Ivan looked toward her with innocent surprise. Ray and I both clenched our jaws.

"Stef said she'd come by and pick me up," said Ray.

"I guess I'm late for the party," said Stef, still reading the room as if keeping her options open, assessing how much she wanted to squash the vibe.

Ivan stood up. "Here, take my chair. I am Ivan." He stuck out his hand.

She took it loosely. "I'm Stef, but I imagine you guessed that."

"It is my pleasure. Please. Sit."

Stef sat down and lay a hand on my arm. "How are you, my dear? Hope these guys aren't tiring you out."

"They've been very entertaining. You know, like those clowns who go around hospitals to cheer up dying patients."

"Hah!" said Ray. "I was wondering what I was going to do in my retirement."

Ivan moved to the other side of the bed and stood over me like a guard. "Sometimes my friends call me payaso. Now I know I have this talent I don't must pay for one at my daughter's birthday party." His chuckle died quickly into the silence of the room. Without meaning to, he had reminded us he was a father, had a wife—an ex-wife—was from another culture, and distinct from the other three people in the room. He looked at me pleadingly to know what he had said so wrong.

Stef jumped in. "How old is your daughter?"

"She is eight," he said quietly.

"She likes to swim in the ocean," I tossed in to keep things moving.

"You've met her?" asked Stef.

"I joined them at the beach one day."

"And then we go to lunch," said Ivan.

"I haven't been to the beach in a while," said Ray. "Where do you like to go, Ivan?"

"We like the beach in Conchas Chinas near La Playita restaurant."

"That's a nice one," said Ray. "I love La Playita's pescado al ajillo." He turned to his wife. "Are we eating at home tonight or going out?"

"It's a little late to cook. We should go out. Maybe Ivan would like to go with us?"

My jaw fell. Was she being friendly or deliberately putting Ivan in an awkward position, knowing he was probably expected at home?

"I...um...need to go home. Thank you."

Ray gave his wife a suspicious look. "That's fine. Another time."

Stef came to the bedside and gave me a kiss on my head.

"I should go too," said Ivan.

I took his hand. "Wait a few minutes. We hardly got to visit."

"My fault," said Ray. "Let's go, Stef."

She hesitated like she was reluctant to leave me alone with Ivan. Ray put his hand on the small of her back and ushered her out.

Ivan let out a puff of air through puckered lips. "She hate me I think."

"No. She's being protective."

"You need protection from me?"

"Not from you. From hurt."

"And who is hurt more in this? I'm sleeping on the sofa now."

He had a point. Since that night on the balcony, he had lost one job, nearly another. He had finally gotten back in the house he'd built, and now he was sleeping on the couch. "Sorry about that. I wish this bed was bigger. Be happy to share since you're practically my husband and all."

"Why you must make everything a joke?"

"Better to laugh than cry."

He sat in the chair next to the bed and took my hand. "No more crying. We must enjoy the life."

"I need to get out of here. I'm going crazy."

"I think Ray is a cool guy."

"He liked you. Stef is...she's harder."

His phone rang. He looked at the screen, twisted his mouth, and sent it to voicemail.

"Sara?" I asked.

He nodded. "She is very angry with me. She can't understand why I must go to the hospital."

"And why do you?"

"So I can see your ugly face, bobo!"

"Thanks for that. You always make me feel sooo much better."

"How much longer are you here?"

"I think I go home tomorrow."

"Do you have a ride?"

"Ray and Stef can take me. Anyway, you have to work."

"But if it is later after work, I can do it. We could walk in front of Severino and say hola. Watch his face."

"That would be fun. I will text you tomorrow. You should go, so you have time with Isa."

He leaned over and kissed me on my lips, the lower one cracked and swollen. "Sweet dreams."

"Not if I dream of you."

"Haha. Then it will be a sexy dream."

"Goodbye, Ivan."

"Bye, D."

I lay back, exhausted and still in pain but content. Having Ivan, Ray, and Stef in the same room wore me out but in a mostly good way. It wasn't how I had hoped for Ray and Stef to meet Ivan, though having me busted up in a hospital bed kept them at their best behavior, even Stef who struggled to be civil.

The nurse came in with my evening meds. She tried out the little English she knew. "I see you happy. Your friends very nice."

"They are."

She raised the bed to check the bandage on the back of my head. "Is okay. We change tomorrow."

"Good. I want to go home."

When the nurse left, I reached for my laptop. Despite my low energy, I hoped to get in a couple of hours of work before I went to sleep. I opened the *Between the Lines* manuscript after not having worked on it in a week since I had been focusing on the non-fiction book. Edgar is again worried as he hasn't received a letter from Julian in a couple of weeks. At the beginning of the pandemic, mail service could be blamed for the delay, but now delivery was back to normal. He reread the last letter from Julian multiple times, searching for clues. He waited another week. Still nothing. They hadn't exchanged any social media info and promised they wouldn't seek information about each other on these superficial platforms. What they had in the letters was true. But something was wrong, and Edgar felt he had no choice but to search Instagram where he found Julian's profile. There was a recent addition to Julian's story, a short video of him standing behind a woman Edgar assumed was his wife. Julian's hands wrapped around her big belly, beaming like he couldn't wait to be a dad. Edgar tumbled to the floor, all the lies falling on top of him like a ton of bricks. Edgar was devastated, and I felt a sympathetic pain as if it was happening to my best friend. Tears shimmered in my eyes.

I reminded myself that it was a novel I was supposed to be objectively editing, not getting emotionally involved in the story. I made some line adjustments, added a couple of commas, and caught a typo, but I couldn't stop thinking about it, the pathos that was a bit too close to my reality. What if Ivan's wife got pregnant again, giving Isa a little sister or brother? It could easily happen, and I could see Ivan being badgered into "doing the right thing" and marrying her all over again.

Twenty-two

Stef and Ray brought me home from the hospital, loaded my refrigerator with food, and installed me in my favorite armchair with my pain meds on the end table next to my water bottle.

"Are you sure you don't want to come stay with us?" said Stef. "We have room."

"And you have stairs. At least here, I can take the elevator up to the roof and sit by the pool for a change of scenery."

"Do not hesitate to call at any hour," said Ray. "In any case, we'll come by every day to check on you."

"Don't worry about me. I'll be fine."

When they closed the door, I let out a sigh of relief. I was alone for the first time in days, no nurses bopping into my room without warning, no staff running up and down the halls responding to alerts on the intercom, no moaning coming from the next room.

I sent Ivan a text, telling him I was home. Despite his bravado about walking into the building right in front of Severino, I didn't expect a visit.

I can bring you anything you need, Ivan texted.

Maybe in a couple of days. Right now I need to rest and work when I have the energy. Stef and Ray left me with a lot of food.

My sister, Nell, was scheduled to arrive in less than a week. When she phoned, I told her about the mugging, and she offered to cancel. But I knew that the longer my sister and I waited to reconnect, the harder it would be, and I didn't want to lose contact with my last remaining family member. She was two years younger and the only person on the planet that shared the experience of our exceptional upbringing, although her take on it was quite dissimilar.

As a child, I loved school, an escape from whatever rural community we were living in at the time. Schools had libraries where I could further escape into books. Nell hated school because it took her away from whichever animal she had adopted and needed to care for or whatever discovery she made in the woods: a bird's nest where babies were hatching or a hollow in a tree where she could hide things like bird feathers or funny shaped rocks. Sometimes she would bring home garter snakes and taunt me with them while I tried to read, sitting under a tree. The one thing I enjoyed about the rural communities was planting things and watching them grow. Working in community gardens was normally part of the living arrangement. But as soon as I finished working in the soil, I would rush to scrub my hands so as not to sully the book I was reading. Nell always had dirt under her fingernails. As adults, I ended up working with books, and Nell with nature and animals.

I paced the airport waiting area, awaiting the arrival of a sister who I hadn't seen since our father's funeral. She came out of the sliding glass doors wearing her blond hair long and unstyled, a hooded sweatshirt, khaki trek pants, and Birkenstocks. Her luggage consisted of one medium-sized backpack. I raised a tentative hand and waved at her. After a brief hesitation, we hugged loosely.

Nell peeled off her sweatshirt. "Guess I don't need this here, like ever."

"Maybe in mid-winter if you're out late. Maybe."

In the taxi back to my apartment we eased into getting reacquainted, small talk about the flight, where my place was in relation to the airport, the population of Vallarta. Traffic crawled on Francisco Medina Ascencio, the main thoroughfare from the airport into town. There were uncomfortable minutes of silence. Before we were halfway to my building, Nell checked her phone three times.

"Are you seeing anyone?" I asked.

She turned her phone screen toward me and showed the doggie watcher app where she could follow her dog's activity at the pet hotel. "That's Charlie. Isn't he adorable?"

I wondered if adorable was the right word—I had a tendency to carry my editing of words on the page to other people's speech, especially when I was nervous—to describe a large golden retriever with his muzzle flocked with white, making him look to be in his later years. "Are you worried about him?"

"He's the love of my life. The separation anxiety is killing me, but I wanted to do this." She patted my leg.

"Me too." I already had a feeling this was going to be easier than I thought.

"Anyway, relationships and sex aren't really things I'm interested in right now. Haven't been for a long time."

"I didn't know that."

She turned to me and grinned. "I'm sure you have enough sex for the both of us."

I jerked my head back like she'd slapped me. "Meaning?"

"Isn't that why you moved to Puerto Vallarta? All the partying and gay boys?"

"How do you know about that?"

"I may live in the boonies, but I do know what's going on in the world. When you said you were moving here, I did my research."

"Though being a town where two guys can walk down the street holding hands and not get bashed or even looked at funny is certainly something I appreciate, it wasn't in my top three reasons to settle here."

"And those are?"

"Several things come to mind. Beach and climate. Not a big city, but with a lot of city things in terms of entertainment and shopping. And a community with a nice combo of Mexicans and foreigners here to enjoy life. A lot of people think of Vallarta as a foreign tourist town, but what they don't know is that Vallarta is a very popular destination for Mexican tourism as well."

As the car headed up my street, Nell looked out at the humble buildings and houses along the way, the garbage pickup sites with trash strewn over the street, the tall weeds between buildings, and the dimly lit little stores.

"I imagined you living in some fancy place in a gayborhood," said Nell.

I laughed. "I try not to be a cliché. Did you remember the T-shirt I asked for?"

She pulled the shirt out of her backpack and unrolled it.

It had the face of a German shepherd on the front with its tongue hanging out. "Thanks. That's perfect," I said.

I asked the driver to pull over at the next corner for a moment. The usual crowd of corner boys was sitting on low walls across from a store. I motioned for one of the young men to come over to the car, the one who had been the first to help me that night. I hadn't seen any of them since the mugging.

"What's up?" I said when the boy came to the window.

His eyes were suspicious until he recognized me. "Hola, Dog Son."

"I never got your name the other night. Cómo te llamas?"

"Son of Satan." He laughed. "Just kidding. Liam."

The other boys stood at a distance but watching. I waved them over, and there were fist bumps all around.

"Liam, I got you a new T-shirt for giving me yours. I don't know what happened to it at the hospital." I passed the T-shirt through the window.

Liam unfolded it and showed it to his friends. "Qué chido! Gracias."

Feeling bad that I didn't have a gift for the other guys, I pulled a couple of bills out of my wallet and put them in Liam's hand. "Cervezas para todos!"

The driver looked over his shoulder with an expression that he didn't have all day. "Hasta luego," I said to the boys. "See you soon."

As we pulled away, I looked back and saw Liam changing into his new shirt.

"Were they calling you Dog Son?" asked Nell.

"When they asked my name that night, that's what they understood. I wasn't exactly in a condition to correct them and spell it out, so I just let it stand. I thought it was funny. I never really had a nickname."

"And you gave these guys who hang out on the corner money for *beer*?" said Nell, shaking her head.

"I should have given them more. They saved me. Things could have been a lot worse. Thanks to them, the muggers didn't get my phone or wallet."

Nell gave me a look just like our mom would have. I heard our mother's voice in my head, saying with disgust and raising her eyes to the sky, "Material things!"

"You can replace things," said Nell. "You've only got one life."

"I know it was stupid, but maybe because of the way we grew up, I like to hold on to the few things I have."

"Few things? Two houses?"

"What can I say? I'm a material girl," I said. "You have a nice home in Colorado. It's not like you're living in a yurt."

Nell laughed. "Been there. Done that. Okay. I have to admit I love my home and being able to stay in the same place year after year."

"You're getting old," I teased.

"Hah! You'll always be older."

The taxi pulled over in front of my building. "Here we are."

"I noticed places getting classier as we climbed the hill. This looks nice."

I paid the taxi and got out. As I put in the code to open the door, I said in lowered voice, "Not sure how much longer I'm going to be here."

"Oh, really? Why's that?"

"Long story."

"I've got time. A week here and no agenda."

"That's..."

"Señor Dawson!" Severino shouted in an overly enthusiastic voice. He stood up upon seeing Nell. "Hello," he said in a tone that managed to be mawkish and suggestive at the same time.

"Severino," I said curtly.

"Who's this? Is she your girlfriend?"

I wanted to say, "fuck you" but smiled grimly instead. "This is my sister. She'll be staying with me for a few days."

Once we got on the elevator, I snorted. "That's one of the reasons right there."

"For what?"

"Moving. That girlfriend comment. He said that deliberately to goad me. He knows perfectly well I'm gay. He's an asshole."

"Are you souring on Mexico?"

"Not at all. Most Mexicans I meet are wonderful. You can find assholes in every country. He's done some fucked up things."

"Your whole demeanor changed when we got in the lobby. It surprised me. You're so easy to get along with."

"I'll tell you the story if you want to hear it, but let's get you settled in first and have a bite to eat."

Nell was staying in the flex room I used as an office, forcing me to set up a makeshift desk on the dining table. She came out in shorts and a sleeveless V-neck shirt. "Is this too cazh?"

"Not at all." But I was focused on how fit she was with a body that was stockier than mine. I imagined that if I had her body type and went to the gym a lot, I could be a muscle guy. I laughed inwardly. Did anyone but gay men have such thoughts?

"What?" she said.

"You keep really fit."

"I walk and hike, ski in the winter, ride my bike in the summer."

"Stop! You're making me feel like a slug."

"Speaking of slugs, I'm starving. I couldn't eat that crap they served on the plane."

I shivered at the bizarre segue only my sister could make. "Yeah, well, I can take you to my favorite place. They don't serve slugs, but seafood is their specialty. Do you eat seafood?" One of the many things I didn't know or had forgotten about my sister.

"Yes, I do."

"They have unusual takes on tacos, tostadas, and burritos, plus other fish dishes. It's very relaxed."

Just before we left the house, I checked the weather app as the restaurant was open-air. It said a thirty percent chance of rain around seven o'clock. Shouldn't be a problem as the patio was covered.

"I like eating outside," said Nell as we sat down. "All the plants are nice. Things must grow very easily here."

"Lots of rain and sun."

The server came to the table and smiled at me, recognizing me from my many visits there. I ordered a bottle of pinot grigio and a few small plates to share.

"Well, you've got me intrigued," said Nell.

"About what?"

"The guy at your building you're so upset with."

I blew air out of pouty lips. "It all began on what I call the night of the iguana. You may think I'm a slut...well, that was the night I shouldn't have been one."

"I was teasing." We both grinned.

Between sips of white wine, I told the story of the storm, the dead iguana, the seduction of a straight man who worked in my building, and the kiss while a body fell through the air beside us.

"What an incredible and devastating story!"

A light rain began to fall and the palm trees around the patio swayed with the wind.

"When did you realize you were attracted to Ivan?" asked Nell.

"It was months of built-up tension. I thought he hated me. I know it sounds naïve, but that night we both realized that the nervousness we felt with each other was something else. We had the opportunity to do something about it."

"It sounds a bit like a Victorian novel."

I giggled. "Now that you mention it. A brutal storm. Hidden passions. Howling dogs. And a tragic death."

"What's the current status?"

"He has moved back in with his ex-wife, but he insists it's only to be close to his daughter, and he sleeps on the couch. Every time I think it's over, he pops up again. He came to the hospital, and I tried my best to make him go away."

"Sure you did."

"He has difficulty talking about his feelings and what our little affair means in terms of his sexuality. At best, he can joke about it."

"I'm shocked. A man who jokes instead of talking about his feelings."

"But in other ways, he's not macho at all. He's sweet, affectionate, and caring. It's not how you would think of him when you first meet him. He's a little rough around the edges."

"Not that I knew Jacob very well, but this seems quite a departure."

"Nail on the head! I guess I was ready for something different. Way different."

"I'm fine on my own."

"You've got Charlie."

"I do."

The rain now drummed the corrugated patio covering, and the awnings around the edges danced wildly. Workers brought out a contraption and unrolled the awnings to the ground to keep the outside tables dry.

With a break in our conversation while we watched the servers prepare the restaurant for what appeared to be a much bigger storm than predicted, I tried to recall people Nell might have been attracted to in our growing up. "Hey! I just remembered that guy you had a crush on when you were a teenager. He was a couple years older. What was his name?"

Nell's face went pale, and she gripped her fork like she was about to stab someone. "Brock? That was like twenty years ago," she said quietly.

"What? Sore subject?"

She choked back an angry laugh. "You had no idea how miserable I was back then. Of course not. Your head was always in a book."

"I'm sorry. What happened?"

She began in a quiet voice, gaining strength as she went along. "He invited me over to his house to watch a movie when his parents were gone. He started touching me. It was okay at first, but he went too far. I told him to stop and tried to leave. He held me down, got on top of me, and you can guess the rest." She stopped and took a moment to breathe. "That's when *it* all began, the feeling that there was something wrong with me if I wasn't interested in sex. You know the usual bullshit that it was my fault, that I led him on. At least now I can talk about it. For the longest time, I couldn't."

"I'm so sorry, Nell, and I'm sorry I wasn't there for you. Did you tell Mom and Dad?"

"You know how they used to say we could tell them anything, that nothing was so shameful it couldn't be talked about? I seriously considered telling Mom, but no way in hell was I going to tell Dad that his precious daughter had been raped, putting him in the quandary of wanting to kill the guy or at least smash his face in when he had spent most of his life being a pacifist. Fortunately, we moved a few months after that, and I thought a new start would make it all go away. It didn't."

"Have you tried therapy?"

"Oh, yeah. They all wanted to fix me so I could have a relationship with a man, or a woman, or whatever. Finally, I found one who told me it was okay not to want a relationship, and it was fine not to want sex. Hallelujah! Someone gets me."

Lightning flashed followed by a loud crack of thunder. I pointed to the sky. "Not sure he...or she agrees with you." Nell looked relieved we returned to the teasing banter we'd fallen into before she shared that traumatic experience with me.

"Guess the weather app was a little off," she said. The lowered side panels of the awning billowed in and out with the wind, and rain blew in, making everyone stand up and move to the center of the patio. Half-eaten plates of food became drizzled with rain. The small palm trees in planters leaned precariously toward the ground, their fronds like cartoon characterizations of a powerful wind. Lightning lit the sky all around us, and thunder crashed as if it was a block away. One deafening peal of thunder sent the restaurant into darkness.

Twenty-three

The streetlights had also gone dark. Everyone took out their cell phones and turned on flashlights. They gathered their purses, hats, and umbrellas from the bag stands, preparing to exit when there was a break in the rain.

"Sorry about this," I said.

"Are you kidding? I'm a nature girl, remember? This is Mama Nature exercising her muscle. She's pissed. Can you blame her?"

A loud crack of thunder answered her question, causing me to jump.

"I'm going to settle the bill and try to get an Uber," I said.

The wind sent napkins flying around the patio as the staff brought out battery-charged lamps and lit candles. They collected plates of soggy food and carried them to the kitchen where workers put food away and began washing dishes by candlelight.

A small crowd had gathered at the entrance, and we walked over to see what the commotion was about. A utility pole on the corner had snapped near the base and it was kept from tumbling into the street by the wires it was attached to, causing it to lean and rock with the wind. The streets were now rivers, and the only vehicles attempting to pass were SUVs and trucks that rode high above the pavement. A taxi van crept down the street, causing waves that rolled over the sidewalks, and several patrons ran into the rain to flag it down. Multiple silhouettes inside the van turned to stare at the desperate people. I imagined them urging the driver to go faster for fear these crazies might storm the vehicle.

Rideshare apps were useless as no drivers picked up the fare. "I think we're stuck here for a while unless you want to swim home," I said.

"But seriously, could we walk?" asked Nell.

"It's not that far, it's just that in this weather we could get hit by a falling tree, especially in this neighborhood, known for its number of trees."

"Or falling utility poles," added Nell, pointing toward the entrance.

"With electrical wires," I said with humorously wide eyes.

We walked back to the center of the patio and sat down. The server came over with our bill. "What's this?" I said, pointing at the surprisingly small total.

"We only charged you for the bottle of wine. The owner's orders."

"Thank you. I love this place. Don't worry—I'll be back."

"What do we do?" said Nell.

"I guess I could call Ray and Stef. They have a car, but their compact wouldn't be good with so much water in the street." I thought of Ivan and his truck. *No, I couldn't.* A couple minutes later, a text came in.

I hope you are not out in this storm.

"Who's that? Are the corner boys coming to save you again?" asked Nell.

"Someone who has a truck."

"Are we playing twenty questions? Is he tall, dark, and handsome?"

"Not that tall. Dark and handsome, yes. Fuck. You probably guessed. It's Ivan."

"And you don't want to ask for his help?"

"Uh-uh."

"Would he offer?"

"Most likely. He would feel it was his duty."

Nell shrugged. "Your call. I can wait it out."

I wiggled in my seat, pursed my lips, and started typing. **As a matter of fact...**

No way.

At a restaurant in Versalles.

How is it?

The food is great here.

I mean the conditions, bobo.

The fish have returned to the water.

I come and get you.

Not necessary.

Text me the address.

I looked up from my phone.

"I can tell by your quirky smile we have a savior," said Nell with a twinkle in her eye.

"He doesn't know you're here."

"Here at the restaurant or here in PV?"

"I didn't tell him about your visit. We haven't communicated much lately, and I'm never sure how much personal info I want to share with him if this isn't going anywhere."

The wind continued to howl, and the rain pounded the roof. Despite the storm not letting up, the crowd thinned, and the momentary connections made in potential disaster—Nell had struck up a friendship with a woman whose daughter went to college near where she lived in Colorado—dissipated as people left without exchanging names. Some of the diners had cars nearby and took the risk they wouldn't stall while others called friends or family to pick them up.

Only a few people were left in the restaurant when Ivan pulled up to the corner. The rain had slowed, and the water in the streets had receded but was still deep enough to soak our feet as we stepped onto the cobblestones to get in the car. I opened the door, and Nell slid into the middle while Ivan scratched the back of his head.

"Surprise!" I said. "This is my sister, Nell."

"Nice to meet you, I'm Ivan."

"I know. Heard a lot about you."

His chin fell to his chest. "Probably much is true."

"Nothing bad," Nell assured him. "Mucho gusto en conocerte."

"You speak Spanish?"

"A little. It helps since I work for the National Park Service. A lot of our employees and, of course, visitors speak Spanish."

I remained quiet while Ivan asked Nell about her work. She turned the questions to his work. Once again, I found myself in a scenario I couldn't have fathomed a few months before, my sister visiting, which was major in itself, and then the two of us being rescued by the on-again-off-again object of my affection. Nell and I barely had a chance to catch up and find our footing with each other before this man of mystery was thrown into the mix. What would she think of this person who was now in my life in ways I was still trying to figure out?

We came to a street where water was geysering from a sewer cover and beyond that a large tree had fallen across the road. Ivan was forced to turn the truck around and find an alternative route. Lots of trees had toppled over and wires hung dangerously close to the ground and the water-filled streets.

After making several detours and moving slowly up streets in poor condition, we made it to my street, where water poured down as we climbed like a fish swimming upstream against a strong current. Conversation stopped as Ivan negotiated this last part of the trip, but in a few minutes, we were stopped in front of the building. The three of us stared at the wipers squeaking back and forth across the windshield as if a metronome keeping time in the awkward silence.

"This was really sweet of you," I said. I opened the door and rain splattered my arm.

"What?" said Nell. "You're not going to invite him in?"

"He...well..." I looked across Nell to Ivan, closing the door to stop the rain from entering. "Do you want to come in?"

"I cannot invite myself," said Ivan.

"I thought maybe..." I was still unsure.

"I should probably..." he said.

"For Christ's sake," said Nell. "Park the truck and come in. We hardly got a chance to talk."

"Dawson?" said Ivan.

"Yes...uh...definitely. Park the car."

There was no one at the desk in the lobby as the night man was probably making his rounds, checking how Paradiso fared in the storm. We entered the elevator, and Ivan squeezed into the far corner as if afraid to be too close to Nell and me. He had his hand at the back of his neck in what I had come to recognize as his nervous tic.

"This must be your first time back in the building since you left," I said.

He nodded.

Nell raised her eyebrows in surprise but didn't say anything.

As soon as we got in the apartment, I turned on lights and the air conditioning to get rid of the mugginess. I got beers for Ivan and me and a white wine for Nell. Nell and I sat on the sofa while Ivan took an armchair across the coffee table. I noticed a small stream of water that had run from the corner by the sliding doors to the center of the room. The leaks had still not been fixed. Ivan's eyes followed mine.

"I'll get the mop," he said, jumping up as if he relished having something to do.

"No!" I said, more forcefully than I meant to. "Don't be ridiculous. I'll do it."

I got up, and he followed me into the utility room off the kitchen.

"What are you doing?" I said.

"Just trying to help."

"You're always trying to help, but you end up making things more difficult."

"You want me to leave?"

The shimmer in his eyes made me bow my head, unable to look at him. "No."

He lifted my chin with the pads of his fingers, leaned in until our lips were nearly touching. In the stuffy room with the treacly smell of laundry detergent in the air, it was hard to breathe. He pushed me against the washing machine and kissed me.

I pushed him back gently, scrunching my face. "My sister."

"I think she has no problem with me. You have the problem." He kept his hands on my waist.

"Because you keep acting like all this is normal. You and me is not normal."

He chortled and squeezed my waist, pulling me a little closer. "I think you don't come to Mexico for normal."

"But I certainly didn't come down here to be with someone who lives with his ex-wife and who I can't invite to my home because of... circumstances."

Ivan looked around in an exaggerated gesture. "I am here in your home right now."

We heard Nell say in a loud voice, "I'm going to my room."

"No, wait," I said as I pulled Ivan out of the utility room.

Nell shook her head and grinned. "You two should have your little talk."

"He was just leaving," I said.

Nell turned to Ivan with a sympathetic look. "I'm guessing that's news to him. You guys need to sit and talk. I'm tired and want to lie down. It's okay. Really." She took her glass of wine and headed for the guest room. "Nice meeting you, Ivan. Hope to see you again while I'm here." She went into the room and closed the door.

I twisted my lips and shot him a hard look.

"This is my fault?" he said. "Why you don't tell me your sister is coming?"

I fell onto the sofa, and he joined me. "My sister and I've had a difficult relationship. It's not so easy for me to talk about it."

"This is something important, and you don't tell me."

I wasn't sure when this casual thing with him became one where we exchanged confidences and why he seemed to be pushing for that. "Are we talking about family problems now with each other?"

"I tell you what is happening in my family."

"Because it affects us directly. Not that I know what is really going on."

"You don't believe what I tell you?"

"I believe your daughter is very important to you. I have no idea what your relationship with your ex is like."

"I am here with you. It is ten o'clock at night. I am not running home to her. What else you need to know?" He reached over and took my hand. We interlaced fingers. I leaned my head on his shoulder.

"But you will go."

"I must work in the morning. I like to see Isa before I go." He put a cushion on his lap and coaxed my head onto it, running his fingers through my hair.

"You're making it difficult to let you go."

"I feel good like this. Believe me I don't want to leave."

On my first trip to Mexico, long before I ever imagined moving there, I wandered the streets of Mexico City where public displays of affection were everywhere, young people embracing on park benches often to the point of being soppy, more than anyone wanted to see, the sloppy kisses, the little whispers, the groping in the shadows. It had to do with the fact young couples had nowhere to be alone, but it also showed the deeply affectionate nature of the people. Now I was the recipient of that affection, causing my mouth to turn upward into a satisfied smile, sinking into this moment—here, now—when things were not complicated, a fragile bubble from the rest of the world. Something inside me broke, the good kind of breaking, allowing my emotions to flow.

I looked up at Ivan's serene face, his eyes focused on the rain running down the windowpane, the storm outside with its clouds and thunder, and the sea beyond. None of it seeming to frighten him. I wondered if he, too, was having some kind of breakthrough, a softening of resistance as we wallowed in the tranquility of the moment, the fitting together of two people who wanted each other. I didn't just believe it when Ivan said he didn't want to leave, I felt it as strongly as I already felt the sense of loss when he would be gone.

With Ivan massaging my head, my heavy lids fell shut, and my body settled as if in a nest. I woke up to Ivan kissing my forehead, unsure how long I'd been asleep. Minutes or hours? The rain no longer pattered, and Ivan looked down at me with apologetic eyes, telling me the moment of separation had arrived.

I rose up. "I know. You've got to go."

"Sí."

I walked him to the door. "Maybe Saturday?"

"No maybe. Sure. We can do something with your sister."

"What about Isa?"

"She's going to visit los abuelos this weekend. She come back for the celebrations of Día de los Muertos next week."

Twenty-four

I felt the sun reddening my neck as we stood in line on the Vallarta pier, waiting for the eleven o'clock water taxi to Yelapa. On the walk from Ivan's truck and now in line, I noticed that he kept Nell between us as if he was still reluctant to be out in public side by side with me.

Nell giggled as she practiced her Spanish with him, and I was pleased they got along. Nell and I wore wide-brimmed hats, sunscreen, and sunglasses to protect our pasty skin from the sun, while Ivan seemed unfazed by the sun beating down and the heat circling us.

The boat arrived and people crowded to get on it while a young man in charge urged everyone in well-spoken English and Spanish, and with a sense of humor, to be calm as there was room for everybody. He said his name was Fredi. "You will be happy to know my last name is *not* Kruger," he joked. When it came time for us to step onto the boat, which had room for about forty people, Ivan went first so he could help Nell from the pier down to the boat while I had to rely on the two young boat employees to give me a hand. I saw Ivan watching me over Nell's shoulder as I laughed and made jokes with the young men.

When the boat was full, five to a bench, and Fredi had given his speech about keeping hands inside the boat and securing hats so they don't end up flying to the moon, the motors roared and the front lifted up as the taxi sped away from the pier, increasing speed as it headed out to open water. People grabbed their hats or turned their baseball caps around with the bill backwards. A couple of times the boat bounced and landed hard on the waves, causing people to yell in unison like on a roller coaster ride.

Forty-five minutes after leaving the pier, we rounded a point and the boat slowed with a jerk as multiple buildings, colorful dwellings, and small hotels on the hillside came into view around a small bay, a community much larger than I expected for a place only accessible by boat.

We were dropped off, not at a pier, but on the beach where Fredi told everyone to remove their shoes as we exited the boat because we would have to wade the final six feet to the sand. Ivan again hopped out of the boat and helped Nell. I caught the toe of one of my water shoes on the edge of the boat and fell into the arms of a young helper, knocking him to the ground. I ended up sprawled on top of him as he stared up at me with shock on his face.

"Whoa, there!" said Fredi. "Be careful." Fredi offered a hand and helped me and the boy up while everyone laughed. Everyone except Ivan.

I apologized to the boy and covered my face with my hand as I walked over to Nell and Ivan.

"That was so embarrassing," I said.

"Hah!" said Nell. "I think you did that on purpose."

"Really, I didn't," I said to Ivan who stood by with a scowl on his face. It was the first time I had a feeling that he could be jealous. It seemed we had reached some kind of milestone that I wasn't sure I wanted.

We quickly learned why we had been dropped off on the beach rather than the pier where we were later picked up. Fredi explained that the beachfront restaurant right in front of us was associated with the same tour company, and we were free to use of any of the lounge chairs, umbrellas or palapa-covered tables in that area of the beach though it was clear that we were expected to consume. He also announced he could arrange for horses to take us to the must-visit waterfall above the town.

"Can we just hike to it?" I asked.

"Of course," said Fredi, and he gave directions how to get up to the town and then follow signs for la cascada.

"Are you afraid of horses?" Ivan asked me, still a little peeved.

Nell laughed. "Ivan told me how he grew up on a ranch in the interior and rode horses all the time."

Now I was annoyed that Nell knew facts about him that I didn't. "You mean you're a real live cowboy?"

"You think that is funny?" he said before storming off toward the town.

With Ivan walking away at a brisk pace, Nell and I hurried to catch up.

"You hurt his feelings," said Nell. "He's probably sensitive about growing up in the country. You're not helping by making fun of him."

"I wasn't. I bet he looks really sexy on a horse in hat and boots."

"Sounds a little like sexploitation of the less privileged."

"What? You're not serious? We grew up in the country. Remember?"

"And you hated it. You were always making comments about our redneck neighbors."

We walked along the water, following Ivan who continued at a determined gait. "I'm just saying you need to be careful. You're a foreigner with money. He's from a humble background and sensitive about it while at the same time trying to figure out what these new feelings are all about."

"Did he tell you that?"

"In so many words. Just because I'm not into relationships doesn't mean I can't have insights into the interactions of others."

"Of course." The thought that I was somehow using my white and foreign privilege on Ivan honestly upset me. I had always treated him as an equal, hadn't I? That night of the first kiss, I hadn't taken advantage of his position and vulnerability, had I?

We watched Ivan starting to wade across the river that ran into the bay. It was shallow enough to cross, but the current was strong, swirling around Ivan's ankles. He hesitated and dropped his shoulders. He turned around and waited for us.

I moved in front of Nell and approached him. "Sorry. Maybe we could go horseback riding sometime."

His face brightened. "Isa is going to ride a horse in the Día de los Muertos parade. She'll wear a traditional dress and have her face painted. She's very excited about it."

"Are you riding, too?"

"I will walk alongside her to make sure she's okay and the horse doesn't get spooked with all the crazy people."

"I can't wait to see it," said Nell.

"Follow me across the river," said Ivan. "It's not deep. You want to take my hand?"

"Yes," I said.

He shook his head. "I mean Nell, bobo."

"You have two hands."

"We'll all be fine," said Nell. "I wade across rivers all the time." There was a slight irritation in her voice that Ivan might be acting a little too solicitous of her as a woman.

The rushing water of the river was cooler than the sea but felt good in the heat. Once we reached the other side, we continued along the beach toward the steps that led up to the town. At the top of the steps, we walked along a narrow, cobbled street, only wide enough for ATVs, motorbikes, and horses, past walls painted with murals, small stores, and a church. The most modern storefront in town was a pharmacy with a sign out front advertising all the medications foreigners like to buy in Mexico, similar to the ones all over Puerto Vallarta.

Ivan pointed out a small hand-painted sign that said La Cascada, and we veered off the main street onto a path alongside the river. As we got closer to the waterfall, more and more stands sold souvenirs, but the catering to tourists didn't take away the simple beauty and relaxed atmosphere of the town.

The waterfall itself was the classic one from travel brochure photos with a pool below where you might have a romantic embrace with a loved one, the water streaming down behind you and mist in the air. Except the reality of this one was that the experience would have to be shared with about fifty other people. I was a hundred percent sure I wasn't going to have that fantasy kiss under the waterfall with Ivan while a crowd looked on.

"It is not usually so crowded," said Ivan. "But at least we have water falling. The last time I was here was no water. It was in the winter."

"One thing I've learned in my job," said Nell, "is that sometimes you have to share paradise. Beautiful places are for everyone. That's what national parks are all about."

"At least we can cool off," I said. "I bet the water is chilly." I took off my tank top and stuffed it into my backpack.

"You two go in," said Nell. "I'll watch our stuff."

Ivan shook his head. "I insist that no. You and your brother go. I go in later."

I knew there was no point in arguing with him. He was still uncomfortable about public situations where we might be perceived as a couple. "Come on, Nell."

She took off her white gauze blouse with a swimsuit top underneath, and we descended the stone steps into the water.

"Yikes!" I said. "It's cold."

"Don't be a baby. This is nothing compared to streams in Colorado." She dove under the water and came up with a satisfied whoop. "I haven't wanted to complain, but this heat is a bit much for me. The water is wonderful."

I was taken back to one of the communities we had lived in by a river. The water there was icy in the spring, but Nell would always jump right in while I would sit on the banks trying to summon the courage. The other kids would splash and taunt me until I finally waded in, realizing that the cold water couldn't hurt any more than the teasing.

"I tried to get you two to have your romantic moment under the waterfall," said Nell.

"Not going to happen unless you can find a way to make all these people go away. He can only be affectionate in private."

"He was jealous when you fell into the arms of that boat guy. That says something."

"I seriously doubt it. He was probably just embarrassed that I was making a spectacle of myself."

"My dear brother, don't sell yourself short. All the attention he's giving to me, he'd rather give to you but doesn't feel comfortable doing it in public. Yet. I have a feeling he'll get there."

I looked over toward the rocks where Ivan sat, staring at us, perhaps wondering if we were talking about him. I dove under the water and came up. "Shit! It's cold. I'm getting out."

"Go sit in the sun with your honey. That'll warm you up."

"Shut up! My honey?"

She laughed, and we swam toward the rocks to exit the water.

Ivan went into the water by himself, and when he got out, Nell insisted on taking photos of Ivan and me with the waterfall in the background. I threw my arm around his shoulders, and he didn't object. This was our first photo together, and deep down I hoped it would become iconic rather than fade into the hundreds of pictures that I never looked at, a day I went to the Yelapa waterfall with my sister and that guy, what was his name? Hah! Like I could ever forget his name.

We left the waterfall, and while Nell and Ivan walked ahead, laughing and chatting in Spanish through the town on the way back to the beach, I flipped through the various versions of the photo, as well as a selfie of the three of us together. In one photo, both Ivan and I were smiling, relaxed, leaning into each other, the sun and waterfall mist behind providing a magical aura around us. As I stared at it, my fears drained away, leaving me empty and vulnerable for a moment before a flood of warmth washed over me, making me, for a brief time, filled with happiness.

I stumbled on a loose rock in the cobblestone, bringing me back to reality, reminding me that the road to wherever we were going was not smooth. There were narrow winding paths and steep steps and rivers to ford and hot sand on the beach that burned our feet and dampness in the air that sapped our strength. It wouldn't be easy if it was to be at all. But I could look at the photo and recapture the contentment we had at that moment. We had made each other smile, and the smile was real, not a photo smile.

We escaped the sun and burning sand, plopping onto plastic chairs at a wooden table under a palapa where we had margaritas and fish tacos. We buried our feet in the sand and watched a small boat come to shore, filled with shiny green palms branches. The men dragged the branches across the beach, creating wavy patterns in the sand, toward the wood frame where two other men constructed a new palapa with rough-hewn poles.

After the meal, the hypnotic waves and the margarita and the heat made me groggy, and I went to a lounge chair nearby under an umbrella and stretched out. As I drifted in and out of a siesta, I could hear Nell and Ivan chattering in Spanish in low voices and occasionally laughing, probably at my expense.

A shout by one of the men building the palapa pulled me out of a dream. I looked over to see Nell had been replaced by her sunhat and colorful towel while nothing remained of Ivan but his T-shirt, hanging over the back of his chair. The high-pitched voices of children, romping in the waves drew my attention to the water where the upper parts of Nell and Ivan bobbed. My earlier happiness soured. *Great.* Maybe they would fall in love, and Nell could have her first boyfriend, and Ivan wouldn't have to be a homosexual. I wished them all the best.

Later I awoke to Ivan standing over me, dripping water and staring at me with a big sexy smile that challenged my previous surly supposition. "What are you doing, dormilón?"

"Dreaming of you."

"And what am I doing in your dream?"

"Terrible things."

"Terrible things you like?"

"Maybe."

Nell had returned to the table and was toweling her hair.

Ivan turned to look at her. "Your sister is very nice."

"Runs in the family."

He laughed. "I think you are still dreaming."

Nell came over to us with the towel wrapped around her. "We ran into Fredi. The boat is coming soon. He thought I was Ivan's girlfriend, but I set him straight. I told him that he wasn't with me. He was with my brother."

"I can't believe she do this," said Ivan.

"I'm sure Fredi wasn't shocked," said Nell. "They fly a rainbow flag on the boat."

"It's a private thing for me, okay?"

I could see that he was trying to control his upset out of respect for Nell. If I had said something similar, he probably would have stormed off again in a huff.

"Sorry, Ivan," said Nell. "I just hate it when people assume things in this heteronormative world."

He looked at her like she was speaking in tongues. "We should go over there," he said, pointing toward the pier, a ten-minute walk at the far end of the bay. "The boat will come soon."

This time, when we boarded the water taxi, Ivan helped Nell and then me get in the boat. I smiled as he gave me a hand. "Gracias, joven."

On the bench, Nell moved to the end and patted the seat next to her for me, allowing Ivan and I to sit next to each other. "This is new to him," I whispered in her ear.

"I know, but we all need a little push sometimes," she said. "He'll get there."

On the water, my legs and Ivan's were pasted together by the sweat that ran down them. At one point, Ivan moved his leg to the right a couple of inches. I moved mine in the same direction until they touched again. Ivan stared straight ahead while a grin tugged at his mouth. He leaned his leg into mine and put his hand on the seat, sliding it partially under my thigh. With the speed of the boat, the noise of the motor, and the wind whipping by, it was hard to have a conversation. But our legs and hands expressed everything that needed to be said at that moment.

Twenty-five

Nell, Ray, Stef, and I sat on a bench on Juárez Street, waiting for the Día de Los Muertos parade in which Ivan and Isa would make an appearance in the horse brigade. We sipped beers from the Oxxo across the street and looked around at the sparse crowd, laughing at our gringo behavior of arriving at the posted parade time. Mexicans knew to show up about an hour later. We had gone through a few beers by the time the first float came into view several blocks in the distance.

"I told you we didn't need to get here so early," said Ray.

"Oh, I suppose you're all Mexican now," I said.

"You were so afraid you were going to miss your boyfriend," Ray teased, taking a big gulp of beer.

"He's not my boyfriend."

"He's not?" said Nell. "I'm confused."

"We all are," said Stef in a dry voice, her eyes clearly showing she was not enjoying the conversation.

"Are you expecting a formal declaration?" asked Ray. "Good luck with that."

"Cut it out, Ray." Ray got a little frisky when he drank and sometimes crossed a line. I looked at Stef and noted her pained expression. I imagined it wasn't only that she was worried about my feelings but also uncomfortable with the boyfriend conversation concerning someone who had been married and had a kid. Maybe a little too close to home? I thought about Ray's boyfriend in Mexico City and wondered what he was like, how they handled the arrangement, how Stef felt when Ray went off to Mexico City. Did Ray use the word boyfriend with Stef when he referred to his friend?

"Don't get upset, brother. We all just want you to be happy," said Nell. It felt strange she was speaking for Ray and Stef. I hadn't filled her in on the complexities of Ray and Stef's relationship.

"I'm not upset," I said in a voice that sounded upset. "It's nobody's business but mine. End of discussion." I looked down the empty street. "I see something coming."

It was much more of a local affair than I expected with homemade floats covered in paper flowers. A couple of the floats were simply pickup trucks festooned with black and orange balloons, carrying children with painted faces in the back.

A drumming corps of local high schoolers marched by and stopped right in front of the Oxxo, increasing the pace and loudness of their drumming while a little girl in a flower headband and red party dress broke away from her parents and stepped into the street, bobbing up and down to the beat. The mother didn't panic and snatch her daughter away from the street, though she did stand up with a watchful eye. I had seen many examples of small children being able to wander away from their parents without the parents flying into panic mode as mothers and fathers tended to do in the States. One night around ten o'clock, I watched two little kids who couldn't have been more than three or four years old playing on a dimly lit street with no parents in sight. As I walked by the house, I saw the parents calmly watching TV in the living room.

A few nights before the parade, on Halloween night—the American tradition had a Mexican version where instead of knocking on doors, kids dressed up and adults carried bags of candy to give them on the street—huge numbers of children of all ages wandered the crowded Malecón, and at times it looked like they were separated from their family groups. Nell became upset when she saw a little girl of about five in a cat costume walking on her own. "Poor thing! She's lost. We have to do something." A minute later, her father arrived, casually took her hand, and walked her back to the group.

In the parade, another group of young musicians, their faces painted white with black accents, marched by, playing Mariachi music on violins, horns, and guitars. The men wore charro suits: white shirts with red bow ties, black pants with metal decorations along the outside of the legs, and shiny black boots. The women wore the same outfits except with long black skirts instead of pants. They were followed by a group of women, also with faces painted like skulls, looking like a troop of Frida Kahlos in flower headbands and Tehuanastyle dresses, wide ruffly skirts adorned with ribbons in multiple colors.

The horses were at the end of the parade, and Ray pointed out the logic to it. The marchers behind them wouldn't have to be stepping on their poop. I stood up to get a better view, craning my neck to spot Ivan and Isa. First came one group of horses, including a daddy in a Mariachi outfit and sombrero, his face painted, cradling a baby dressed like a mini version of him in his lap with one hand, and the reins in the other. Next to the father and son was another horse, ridden by a boy who turned and looked directly at me, his face painted skull-like with haunting, deep black circles around his eyes. He wore jeans, a sombrero, and a cowboy shirt with snap buttons, and his cell phone stuck half out of his breast pocket, making him look like a modern boy back from the dead.

At first, I didn't recognize Isa in the next group of riders. Her hair was braided and coiled on her head, crowned with a headband sporting colorful flowers. Her face was painted, and she wore a blue blouse with a gold ruffly skirt, draped over the saddle. I knew it was Isa when Ivan came into view, walking proudly beside her. His handsome face was painted like a ghoul under a cowboy hat. He wore an embroidered cowboy shirt with pearl snaps, tight jeans, and pointy cowboy boots.

"There's Ivan," said Nell excitedly.

"I see him," I said.

"Your very own cowboy," said Ray with a chuckle. He wouldn't let up.

"I didn't know I had that fantasy until right now," I said. "Ivan!" I shouted.

Ivan turned his head, staring at me with painted eyes of death, sending a chilling reverberation through my bones. And then he broke into a smile, making him appear a happy dead man, and I let the tension go. Whatever our relationship status was, just seeing him—here, now— gave me a thrill.

I pointed and gestured that we would meet at the end of the parade route a few blocks away. Ivan was distracted by something Isa said and didn't acknowledge if he understood my communication or not.

The last row of horses clopped past, followed by workers in brightly colored vests who scooped up the horse manure. The parade was over.

"Let's go meet Ivan at the end of the route," I said. "I want pictures. They went by too fast to get any good ones."

"Will he be joining us for dinner?" asked Stef, who had made a reservation for the four of us to go out.

"I doubt it," I said. "I'm sure he has horse stuff to take care of, and then he has to take Isa home."

"That's too bad," said Nell. "We had such a good time in Yelapa. I hope to see him again before I leave."

"When are you leaving?" asked Ray.

"Day after tomorrow. The time has flown by."

"We should hurry," I said. "You can say goodbye in case he doesn't have any free time in the next couple of days."

"We're going to swing by our place," said Stef. "We'll meet you at the restaurant."

Ray looked at me with raised eyebrows like he'd rather see my cowboy all decked out but followed his wife.

After Ray and Stef had left, Nell turned to me. "What was that all about? Stef seemed relieved that Ivan wouldn't be joining us."

"She's not happy that I continue to be involved with him. She's being protective, convinced that he's going to hurt me."

"What do you think?"

"If he's going to hurt me?"

"Uh-huh."

"Life is a cabaret, old chum. Come to the cabaret," I sang as we walked along, the drumming in the distance giving a beat to my song. "It has already been way more than I could have imagined at the beginning, mostly in a good way. Sure, there've been ups and downs, and there are issues, but I'm trying to focus on the part where someone enjoys my company and seems to care about me."

"I don't want you to be hurt either, but I do like him. Sometimes, it's good to go outside of your comfort zone."

I craned my neck toward her and furrowed my brow. "Really?"

"I know. Sounds strange coming from me. Maybe this trip will inspire me to go out of *my* comfort zone. Not making any promises, though."

"It's funny how Mom and Dad found this great love that lasted, what? Thirty years? And neither of us has come anywhere close to that."

"I've had a bunch of years to think about some of the things you said to our parents, the things that ticked me off so much back then. You were right about a lot of it. Maybe our upbringing did kind of mess us up."

"Looks like we've reversed roles with me leaning toward being more accepting and you more questioning. All in all, I guess we didn't turn out that bad. At least, that's the way I feel today. I'm enjoying being in Mexico despite all the shit that's happened to me here."

"I see the horses up ahead. Isa looks like a princess on that Arabian," said Nell.

"She's daddy's princess alright."

"Is the fact that he's a father make him more attractive to you?"

"Seeing the way he is with her gives me that warm gooey feeling inside. He's capable of pure love and would do anything to protect the people he loves. That raises the attraction factor up several notches. But at the same time, it makes things a lot more complex. Anyone who interferes with his bond with his daughter is a threat. Like me."

"But you would never do anything to come between Ivan and Isa."

"Not deliberately. Take the example of him moving back in with his ex. He swears there's nothing romantic or sexual going on between them now, and he did it only to be near his daughter. If I show any displeasure with that move because of the proximity he's in with his ex, it pits me against his being with his daughter. Who's going to win that battle?"

We were close to Ivan and Isa now, and several people were taking pictures of Isa, still on the horse, and Ivan standing by her. Nell and I took out our phones and started snapping pics as well. Ivan nodded at me, but his expression was hard to read with his face painted.

"Hola, Nell," Ivan said. At least she got a smile.

Isa expressed a desire to get down from the horse as she was tired, and Ivan lifted her to the ground. "Look who's here, Isa. You remember Dawson, no?"

She held onto her daddy's hand. "Sí. "

"And this is his sister, Nell."

"Hola," Isa said.

"English, mi vida," said Ivan. "Practice your English."

"What's your horse's name?" Nell asked Isa.

"Se llama Beauty," she said.

Isa's face quickly shifted from embarrassed to happy as she focused on something behind us. "Hola, Mami."

Ivan's face went in the opposite direction from a dead man's smiley face to a scowl, his white makeup cracking. "Sara."

Nell and I stepped aside and let Sara join the group. Isa ran to her mom and hugged her, seemingly relieved that she wouldn't be pressured to speak any more English.

"Hello, everybody," said Sara. After her five years in Los Angeles, she wasn't shy about speaking English or being around Americans. The grin on her face made it clear she also didn't mind breaking up our little party in the slightest.

Ivan introduced us to Sara.

"Did you get some good pictures?" Sara asked us. "So glad tourists get to experience our little town parade."

Ivan stood next to the horse and held the reins, which he twisted around his hand and gripped more tightly, causing the horse to move a couple of steps. "Dawson lives here, but Nell is just visiting."

"Oh, yeah. I think you mentioned something about that." It was obvious what she was doing, dismissing me as if I was of little consequence. Temporary.

I had only seen her from a distance a couple of times and made certain assumptions based on her petite size and my misguided notions about Mexican women being subservient to their macho husbands. I realized how wrong I had been as I watched Ivan cower in her presence.

"Ivan," she said in a stern voice, "don't you need to get Beauty off the street?"

"I was just going to do that," he said in an irritated voice. "Into the trailer and back to the ranch."

Sara put her hand on Isa's head. "Are you hungry, darling?"

Isa nodded.

"You didn't feed her?" Sara shook her head in disbelief and let out a frustrated groan like Ivan was the most hopeless person in the world.

"We had some tacos before the parade started," said Ivan. "She hardly ate anything because she was nervous."

"What were you going to do? Let her starve while you socialize?"

"Why you doing this?" said Ivan.

"I'll take her home and get her something to eat," said Sara.

"I could give you a ride," Ivan offered.

"What? On Beauty? Go take care of the horse. I'll see you at home later." She started to walk away. "Nice to meet you, Nell, and…"

"Dawson," said Ivan.

"Right," said Sara.

She steered Isa through the crowd, and Isa looked back with a sorry face that she had gotten her daddy into trouble.

Watching this domestic spat gave me a sinking feeling. I thought back to the conversation I'd had with Nell just a few minutes earlier. Now it seemed more absurd than ever to be involved with a man who was living with his ex, raising a daughter together with her, and they were snapping at each other over her care. At the same time, I understood how Ivan must relish those quiet moments with me when we could escape our day-to-day problems, enjoy each other's bodies, and drift into silence if we felt like it.

"I have to take Beauty back," said Ivan.

"Do you need any help?" asked Nell.

"Nell's really good with horses," I added.

"No. I can handle it. What time is your flight on Saturday?" Ivan asked Nell.

"One thirty."

"I can give you a ride to the airport and say goodbye," he said.

"You don't have to do that," she said.

"I want to." He turned to me. "We could go have lunch after."

"Sure. I'd like that," I said.

Twenty-six

I van and I stood at the bottom of the escalator that took Nell up to the boarding area. When she reached the top, she turned for one last wave, giving me a moment of sadness. Things had gone much better than expected. I had a family again, even if it was only the two of us.

Ivan insisted we park the truck and go inside to see her off even though she'd said she was perfectly fine with being dropped off, and again she seemed a little annoyed that a man thought she needed to be taken care of.

"No," said Ivan with a note of finality as he pulled into the parking area. "We take you inside."

It was one more act of kindness on his part, and I was pleased Nell and Ivan got along so well. Aside from the fact that they genuinely seemed to like each other, Ivan was much more relaxed in public with Nell as a buffer. Though he was making progress in accepting what we had, there were awkward moments when it was just the two of us. And even in private there were times when he didn't seem to know quite what was expected of him or what he should say. I tried my best to be patient, and I wondered how things would play out now, especially after recently witnessing Sara's behavior and Ivan's clueless reaction. I could feel how embarrassed he had been that I not only witnessed Sara's anger but also recognized how much Sara wanted me to feel her anger.

"Where should we go for lunch?" I asked as we walked to the parking lot from the airport terminal.

He took a long time to respond as if weighing the options. We arrived at the truck. "I know a good taco place."

"Can we have something besides tacos? I love tacos but not all the time."

He started the truck and turned to me with a face trying to stop itself from descending into a frown. "I don't want one of your fancy places at gringo prices."

He pulled out of the space, and we got to the booth where we had to pay the parking fee. I pulled out my wallet. "How much is it?"

He was now in full frown mode, the corners of his mouth definitely going south. "I got it." He grabbed some coins from a tray between the seats and paid.

"Don't worry about lunch. It's my treat for taking Nell to the airport."

He huffed. "Is not good you pay all the time."

"Why not? I'm happy to do it. Anyway, it's not all the time. Only when it's gringo prices," I said with a chuckle.

"I don't like it."

"When you said we're from different worlds, the only part I agree with is that we live in different economies. It's not your fault or my fault. It just is."

"Maybe I should just eat at home."

"Don't be ridiculous."

We got to a stop sign. Ivan's truck was a couple of feet into the crosswalk when an older woman stepped off the curb. She looked at us and made angry gestures, indicating we were blocking her crossing. Ivan threw up his hands at her. "What do you want?"

She started yelling, but we couldn't hear everything she was saying with the air conditioning on and the windows up. She stood in front of the truck and wagged her finger.

"Fucking bitch!" said Ivan. I looked at him in shock, never having witnessed him react so strongly in anger at a stranger, especially when he was in the wrong.

When she was finally out of the way, he stepped on the gas and nearly hit another car while trying to merge into traffic. The other driver laid on his horn. He screamed at the driver, this time in Spanish. "Pinche cabrón."

"Ivan!" I shouted. "Pull over. You shouldn't drive when you're angry like this."

"Fuck!" He thumped the wheel with the palms of his hands but did what I told him and pulled over on the shoulder. He hung his head. "Sorry."

"Take a breath. What's going on?"

He leaned over the steering wheel and put his head on his arms. "This morning Sara say me something."

"What did she say?"

"I can't tell you."

"Come on. You brought it up."

"She is angry I'm going to the airport. She ask why I spend time with you."

"Hah! She knows who I am. Why did she act like she doesn't?"

"She say we are friends because you buy me things."

"Really? The shoes?"

Ivan, Nell, and I had gone to a department store soon after she arrived because she needed flip-flops, something she never owned in Colorado. Ivan said he wanted some new black sneakers for work. After trying on an off-brand, I encouraged him to try a pair of New Balance, which looked really good on him, and he smiled when he saw them in the mirror.

"How do they feel?" I asked.

"Great, but I can't," he said. "They are too expensive."

I knew it would embarrass him if I offered to pay for them. Ivan bought the shoes that were less than half the price of the New Balance. A few days later, I went back and bought the better shoes and gave them to him the next time I saw him. It was the first gift I gave him.

"I haven't worn them," said Ivan. "I want you to take them back."

"You're still letting her control your life."

"That is not true," he mumbled, his voice sounding defeated, his head still on the wheel.

I chuckled in frustration. Nell wasn't even in the air yet, and we were having an argument. About money. I thought of all the millions of couples who were destroyed by financial issues.

"Let's not do this," I said. "It's cliché. A typical couple arguing about money."

"We're not."

"Not arguing about money?"

"Not a couple."

"I just meant..." I thought a moment. "Is the idea so frightening to you?"

"I can't talk about this."

"You like me."

"I like you when you are quiet. When *we* are quiet."

I knew what he meant. Those tender moments in the silence, lying in bed after sex, our breathing slowing, our bodies stuck together.

"We could skip lunch all together and…"

He raised his head off the steering wheel. For a moment, I thought he was going to throw me out of the truck again. But he broke into a gnarly laugh.

"This is one thing we have, no?" said Ivan. "You want my body."

"And you keep coming back for mine."

"Maybe I only want a new pair of shoes."

"Shut up. And I'm not taking them back. You are going to wear them the next time I see you, and I'm going to take them off your feet. And then your socks. And then your pants…"

"I think you need to see a doctor."

"There is only one cure for this."

"Sadly, I have to be with Isa at three o'clock. Sara has something to do."

"Let's go to your taco place then. And you're buying me lunch."

We sat on stools at the taco stand with carne asada tacos on scratched and faded plastic plates and a tray of red and green salsas of various heat levels in front of us. We both drank beers. Between bites, we watched the cook frying the meat on the grill and then chopping it up into little bites with a cleaver. We were the only ones at the counter.

"Your sister is nice. I like her very much."

"Maybe you want to go live with her in Colorado and freeze your ass off."

"This is good idea. Then you don't be bothering me all the time."

"I used to wonder if she liked women but couldn't admit it to herself. But she says she's asexual, so I have to respect that."

"Hard to believe she is your sister," Ivan said with a guttural laugh.

It wasn't the first time he had teased me about being a sexual being.

My journey to acting on my sexuality hadn't come easily. I thought back to my time in college where circumstances resulted in a nearly non-existent sex life. I studied hard to keep up my scholarships and worked at the same time because my parents hadn't put aside any money for school. That, combined with my confusion about my sexuality, made it nearly impossible to explore sex. At graduation, I arrived at two conclusions. I was gay, and I was going to take the summer to have, if not a gap year, at least a gap summer with the proverbial backpack trip through Europe before I began graduate school in the fall. I came out to a friend and told him I was going to fuck my way through the capitals of Europe. The friend encouraged me, saying with my looks and blond hair, the guys would be all over me.

I struck out in London and Paris. I went out to bars but didn't know how to talk to people, never having learned the mechanics of hooking up. In Madrid, I went to a hot, sweaty dance club in Chueca where I stood at the edge of the dancefloor mesmerized by a guy dancing with his shirt off, his muscular body glistening. The young man must have noticed me staring and dragged me out on the dancefloor, rubbing his body against mine. Because of his olive skin and dark hair, I assumed he was Spanish, but in a brief conversation shouting over the music, I learned he was Dutch. We went to his hotel, a much better option than my cheap hostel. I still remembered his name, Aat, the shape of his body, and all the places in the room where we ravaged each other: the bed, the chair, leaning over the desk looking out the window. Something awakened in me that night.

I took a train to Rome where the boys were as pretty as statues and just as cold. In Athens, at an outdoor cruising area near ancient ruins, I met a man and invited him back to my hotel. It was a good night, but I didn't remember his name or anything about him except what he revealed in the morning. He was married and had two children. In Munich, I met two Lebanese men in a bar and went back to their hotel. They were rough and wouldn't kiss me. I ended up going soft while they leaned over me and came on my chest at the same time. I got up, wiped myself off in the bathroom, and fled the room.

I came back to the States a different person, the beast in me awakened, but I was also confused. Sex could be perfect as it had been in

Madrid, confusing like in Athens, and frightening like in Munich. Although it took more time to figure out what I enjoyed most, once I roused my dormant sexuality, there was no way I could make it go back into hibernation, even with all the demands of grad school.

"Well, anyway," said Ivan, bringing me back to the present. "You are cuter than she is."

"Thank you...I guess."

"She warn me to be good to you."

"I think you should follow her advice."

"I am not good to you?"

"Sometimes you are very good to me."

Ivan shook his head. "You want me to jump into this life, but you are the one who is never serious, always making the jokes."

"Oh, are you ready to get serious?"

"I don't want to fight. I am a lover not a fighter. And, yes, I like you. I enjoy with you."

"But?"

"You know. These feelings are new for me. I worry about Isa. I have problems with my ex. Maybe moving back to the house is not such a good idea."

"I didn't want to say anything, but..."

"And the sofa is not good for sleeping. Yes, I am on the sofa in case you wonder."

"You made it clear we're just friends, so you're free to do what you want. And I am too."

"I see how you are with these boys on the boat to Yelapa."

"You were jealous."

"No way. I am only embarrassed for your sister to see you like that."

"Uh-huh." I dropped my hand onto his thigh under the counter and squeezed.

"I told you," said Ivan in a low voice. "I must take care of Isa later."

"And tonight?"

Ivan parked his car on the street outside Paradiso, and I gave him my bucket hat to wear. He looked askance at it like he was being offered an Easter bonnet but eventually put it on with sunglasses in an absurd ruse to avoid prying eyes. Jose, the night man, was snoring when we entered the lobby, startled awake for a moment, offered a small wave, and was back asleep by the time we got to the elevator. Ivan knew where the video cameras were and tried to avoid them. Then he slipped out of the building while it was still dark and before Severino arrived. Though things with Severino seemed to have been resolved, there was no reason to give him fodder for further scandal or to get other residents gossiping.

After Ivan left, the hour of rosy light between dawn and daylight found me at my desk making a mental checklist. Re-establishing a bond with my sister? Check. Spending the night in my bed with Ivan and wallowing in the post-sex quiet in his arms, even though I had a thousand things I wanted to say and biting my tongue because, well, this was our quiet time? Check. Catching up with my editing projects? No check.

With Nell's visit and all the festivities around Day of the Dead, I had fallen behind. My boss told me that the release of *Between the Lines* was pushed back again as the author was revising the ending, the ending I had been avoiding.

"What happened in that book with the two guys writing letters?" Ivan had asked me the week before.

"I don't know. Never got to the end because I was told to prioritize other projects."

I finished *Vietnam Dialogues,* a book not only well written but full of the sights, smells, and mysteries of Vietnam. It took the reader into a niche of post-Vietnam-war society, that of Americans who had abandoned their country. The interviewees expressed their feelings about the United States and, in many cases, the desire never to go back. Even as a white, privileged man—a lot of the characters in the book were Black or mixed race—I could sympathize with some of their anxieties about my native land. And though I returned to Los Angeles frequently, with each visit I envisioned staying away for longer periods of time. My life was in Mexico now.

My newest editing project was a historical novel based on the true story of Edward James, a British eccentric and collector of surrealist art, who built a sculpture garden in the jungle near Xilitla, Mexico with the help of a handsome young Mexican, Plutarco Gastélum. James was known as bisexual, or homosexual as his ex-wife claimed in the divorce proceedings, but his relationship with the young Mexican was left to speculation as Plutarco later married and had four children. The novel focused on the part of James' life in Mexico when he lived with and adopted Plutarco's family. The novel offers a fictional version of what might have been the relationship between the two men.

"This is perfect for you," said Susan. "You live in Mexico, speak some Spanish, and are gay. Have you met anyone down there, by the way?" For a time in Los Angeles, Susan and I were friendly, even social, going out for drinks. When Jacob and I were together, occasionally the three of us went out together. During the COVID years and now with the geographical distance, I no longer felt close enough to Susan to share my personal life and told her nothing about my flirtation with Ivan.

"Haven't really been looking," I said.

While she explained the gist of the Edward James novel, which had the working title of *Garden of Delights,* I had the same queasy feeling as when I read about how Edgar and Julian met in *Between the Lines.* Art imitating life. My life. I immediately went to the internet to research Edward James, but it was nearly impossible to find any information on his relationship with Plutarco, referred to as his secretary or friend or factotum or collaborator. In one article, the writer went so far as to say that the personal relationship of the two men could be left to imagination. The author of the book I was tasked to edit had apparently gone with his imagination, and I looked forward to working on it.

I sat at my desk with every intention of starting on *Garden of Delights,* but my brain was caught up in the notion that changes were necessary in my life. Having Ivan in my home was beautiful once we closed the door, but the idea of sneaking around was not something I could tolerate for much longer. The thrill of buying my first getaway home in Mexico had faded some in recent months: the boy falling off the roof, Severino's meddling and Ivan's forced exit, my mugging on the street I walked every day, and the fact that I hadn't made friends with anyone in the building, most of them being retirees with different interests and older than my parents would have been. With Patrick gone, I was now the only gay man. I hoped at first that whoever bought Patrick's apartment would be someone I could better relate to. Instead, it was a demanding couple from Memphis who pestered the board with complaints and special requests, all the while their yippy little dog drove everyone crazy. The thought of selling seemed too extreme less than a year after I bought the place, but I considered the option of listing it as a short-term rental, giving me enough cash to rent another place while I decided what to do.

I went to rental listings and saw an apartment in a building I looked at in my initial search to buy. It was in the Versalles neighborhood with a view of the mountains rather than the sea, but it had a rooftop pool. It wasn't close to my beloved Malecón, but not so far I couldn't get there often. The area was full of good restaurants and cafes, and close to shopping. It was also flat, making having a bicycle more practical. I made an appointment to go look at it.

Twenty–seven

Severino walked through the garage and stopped to watch me putting the last box in Ray's car. Since the new place was furnished, I could fit all I was taking into the car—my clothes, books, sheets and towels, and other personal things. Severino started toward me like he was going to say something, so I quickly slammed the trunk and jumped in the car. The only thing I might want to hear from Severino was an apology for the part he played in leading to my moving out, but I knew it wasn't going to happen.

The day before, Severino and I discussed how the short-term rental would work and how I would keep him informed of who was renting my apartment. I would take care of the checking in and checking out. I hired one of the building's cleaning ladies to get the apartment ready for guests. And though I didn't like the idea that Severino would have any involvement whatsoever in my rentals, as the day manager, he needed to be informed.

As we pulled out of the garage, I felt relief and a fair amount of excitement about the new place, a new beginning, and, I had to admit, a large part of my excitement was the fact that Ivan and I could come and go as we wished.

"I thought I would feel sadder," I said as I watched Paradiso recede in the side mirror. "I will miss the view and the proximity to the Malecón."

"It's just temporary. And you're not that far away."

"Paradise was hell," I said with a laugh.

"That would be a great title for a song or a movie."

"Or a book?"

"Yeah."

"I hope you guys will come and visit."

"Of course, we'll venture to the flatlands. You've got great eats over there. Stef and I also volunteer at the Biblioteca over on Francisco Villa, so we're in the area fairly often. And what does Mr. Ivan think of your move?"

"He'd better be happy about it."

A few nights before, I told him by phone that I rented a place in Versalles. He sat in his truck to talk, so Sara wouldn't hear him.

"I'm happy for you," he said, but neither of us expressed the obvious. We wouldn't have to go to hotels or vacation rentals anymore if we wanted to sleep together. The days of clandestine rendezvous were over, but I had to admit there had been something titillating about our trysts in hotels, even the sleazy no-tell motel we went to. From one week to the next, I had a hard time summoning confidence that we would continue seeing each other, but we carried on against the odds. At least one of the obstacles to our being together had been removed.

"I'll be happy to be out of this building, not to have to see Severino every day, not to be reminded of the tragedy every time I go out on the balcony," I said to Ivan.

"I am maybe moving soon too. This isn't working out."

I was so close to telling Ivan to move in with me. That's what my heart was saying anyway. Practical me knew it was too soon. "Is she making it difficult for you?"

"I told her about us."

"What did you tell her? Because I'd like to know too."

"Don't, Dawson. Not now."

"I know. Sorry."

"I tell her we are more than friends. She say she want me to move out. But I remind her she can't make me move out of my own house."

"But you want to, right? I mean, I know you don't want to leave Isa, but if you are close by, you can see her often." What I didn't say was that my new place in Versalles was a walkable distance from Ivan's house in 5 de diciembre.

"Yo, Big D," said Ray, breaking into my thoughts.

"What?"

"I know what you're thinking about."

"Yeah, I'm making a mental shopping list of what I need at La Comer."

"Bullshit. You're thinking about inaugurating your new place with a little Ivan action."

"That's what you think of me?"

"Nothing wrong with that. You deserve it." I was trying to keep my excitement in check, though Ray seemed to have enough for both of us. I detected on Ray's face a certain amount of jealousy mixed with a bit of vicarious pleasure at what Ivan and I had.

"How are things with you?"

"Don't ask. I was supposed to get together with my friend in Puerto Escondido over the holidays, but he canceled."

"Sorry about that."

"No biggie. This is the life I chose. Comes with the territory."

"Aren't we a pair? Seems like we could make things easier on ourselves."

"It's a challenge for sure."

After a brief stop at La Comer for a few staples and a six-pack of beer, we arrived at my new building. I opened the gate to the garage with the remote and directed Ray to my assigned space. "I guess I could rent out the parking space since I don't plan on getting a car."

"Or keep it available for visitors."

I palmed my forehead. "I'm still not thinking like a person with a boyfriend. Am I a person with a boyfriend?"

"This thing's been going on a minute."

"It's not working out living with his ex."

"Of course, it's not."

"He told her about us. Wish I could have been a fly on the wall. Would love to know what word he used to describe it. Amigos con derechos? Amantes? Novios? He probably just said amigos, and she could fill in the rest."

"Did he ask to stay with you in the new place?"

"He would never do that, and I don't think we're there."

"I know you've imagined what it would be like to live with him."

"Sure I have. If I took all those thoughts and wrote them down, I'd have a book. Doubt it would be a best seller, though."

"I could help you spice it up."

"If I thought it would get you writing again, I'd let you tell my story. Changing the names and putting your spin on it, of course. You could make me dashing and irresistible."

"But you are, my dear." Ray laughed. There was a little light in his eyes like the book wasn't an absurd notion. "Let's get these boxes out of the car and set up your love nest."

Once we had all the boxes and suitcases in the apartment, we cracked open beers and toasted. "To your new digs," said Ray.

"It's not bad, right? Not as nice as my other place, but it'll do for now."

"Do you need help unpacking?"

I looked at the sweat on Ray's forehead. "No, you've done enough. Just relax. Have a look around. I'm going to take some of this stuff into the bedroom." I grabbed the remote from the island counter, turned on the air conditioning, and then rolled a couple of my bags into the bedroom.

I stood at the sliding doors that led out to the balcony shared by the bedroom and living room. The view of the mountains rather than the sea had its own appeal, the dense jungle green holding a sense of mystery. From here, I would see the sunrise rather than the sunset. I imagined Ivan in bed and the morning rays lighting up his face.

In the reflection of the glass, I saw Ray enter the room and come up behind me. He stood close, his eyes not focused on the jungle but my face in the glass, our two faces, Ray's half a head taller. I sensed the power of his body but also his mind, his passion for life, his hunger. At times, Ray's intensity was like the sun, and I was just a planet in his orbit.

"The vast green of the jungle overwhelms me sometimes," said Ray. "I feel small and...and lonely."

"I know what you mean."

"Do you?"

"I think so."

"I sometimes wonder if back in those days when I met Stef…I mean, there was no one like you around. My life could have been different."

"Ray, I…"

"It seemed like the right thing at the time. I felt…I feel…a strong connection with her."

Ray's sigh was so strong, I felt it like a blanket thrown over me that I didn't want. I was afraid what Ray might do.

He moved a step closer and put a hand on my shoulder. The heat of Ray's palm burned through my T-shirt into my skin. I closed my eyes, wishing to be someplace else and yet my feet wouldn't move. Ray's breath tickled my ear.

My phone sounded. "I should get that." Ray dropped his hand and stepped back.

"Yes, you can send him up," I said. I had a visitor.

"Ivan?" said Ray.

"I told him to stop by on his way home from work."

"Saved by the bell," said Ray with a chuckle.

"There was no saving. Nothing was going to happen. It's much better the way things are. You know that."

"Ivan is a very lucky man."

"You need to get laid." My face reddened. I had just told this older, powerhouse of a man, who I respected beyond measure, that he needed to get his rocks off.

Ray winced at my bluntness. "You think that's all this is?"

There was a knock at the door, and I headed for the other room.

I took a deep breath and opened the door. "Hola, Ivan." We hugged. "Would you like a beer?"

Ray came out of the bedroom, cradling a beer in his large hands.

"Hello, Ray." Ivan's eyes narrowed and darted from Ray to me.

"Ray helped me bring over my stuff." I stood at the open refrigerator, avoiding Ivan's stare, enjoying the coolness as I wrestled a beer from the pack.

"I also offer to help you," said Ivan.

"I appreciate that. Ray wasn't busy this afternoon, so…"

"Anyway, congratulations!" said Ivan. The three of us clinked bottles and put on awkward smiles. I had a bizarre fantasy that the three of us should go to the bedroom and fuck each other's brains out to cut the tension in the room. I mentally slapped myself.

Ray took a big swallow of beer. "I have to go. I'm cooking dinner tonight."

"It is not necessary for you to leave. I only stop by for a minute to see the place."

"No, you guys drink your beers. Check out the view. I really gotta go." He put his half-finished beer on the counter.

I hugged Ray at the door and then closed it. I turned around to face Ivan.

"What is going on?" he said.

"Nothing."

"I feel if I come a few minutes later I find…"

"Don't be ridiculous."

"There is something between you two. I see the way he look at you."

"I respect and admire him for what he has accomplished in life. We are good friends, but I promise there is nothing more and never will be." I couldn't explain to Ivan what it meant that Ray had reached the top of the mountain and written a book that made the world take notice. And even if he slid down the other side with his later attempts, and even if he never wrote another word in his life, he achieved something that few writers did. No one could take that away from him. Yes, I was dazzled by Ray's light and found him attractive in so many ways, but I knew in the depth of my soul that Ray was not the man for me. Ray had been clear that he never believed in fidelity, that monogamy was not for him. Even if we had met years before when he was in his prime, and I was an impressionable young man trying to figure things out, he would never have been satisfied with just me. He was a man that had a lust for other bodies, and I wouldn't have been able to accept that, or I might have accepted it and hated myself for it.

I asked myself why, then, I would accept something casual (for now) with Ivan. Despite his having sex with Sara, which he assured me was only once, he hadn't been with anyone else since we started sleeping together. And I believed him. He didn't have the same unquenchable lust for life that Ray did.

Ivan's face was still hard, his eyes asking questions. "He is better for you. I have done nothing. My life is nothing important."

"You don't choose someone like ordering on the internet, the right size, the right color, the right design. Sometimes people come into your life, and it feels right. What you mentioned the other day about the quiet times, it hit me. That's it. We have that beautiful thing, and I want more of it. That's part of the reason I changed apartments. I choose you."

He nodded, but his shoulders were still tense as if he didn't believe me. "When I come here and see you two together, I have this feeling like jealous. You understand how strange that make me feel? I am jealous of another man with you. My head want to explode."

"It's not so bad, is it? To have feelings? Even if it's another man?"

"You grow up in a different environment. It is against everything my parents and teachers tell me. I am staying with my brother now. Sara tell him something. Now every day, I must listen to him say terrible things about me, how I am an abomination in the eyes of God."

"I know you don't believe that. You are here standing in front of me now because you believe something else. You believe we have something. You believe in the quiet time, in *our* quiet time. During those times, I see it in your eyes, your face, your funny little smile, that it's a good thing."

"What about Isa?"

"You said yourself that she can tell when you're happy. I'm sure she wants you to be happy."

I put my beer on the counter and threw my arms around Ivan. His body was stiff but slowly began to relax.

"I don't think you are bad like my brother say," he said.

"Thanks...I guess."

"You know what I mean. I think you are good."

"If it gets to be too much with your brother, you can always come over here."

He pulled back a little. "I'm not moving in with you."

"I didn't ask you to, but I want you to know you have a place to go."

He rested his head on my shoulder. "You are more than good."

We separated, and I retrieved my beer from the counter. "Let me show you the apartment. The view from the bedroom is great."

"This is a trick."

"I want you to see what you would be missing if you decide we can't continue."

"I never say that."

I stopped and turned around. "You said that lots of times."

"That was before."

"Before what? You got a taste of the good stuff?"

"I really hate you sometimes," he said with a smile and in the most charming way possible.

In the bedroom, we stood where Ray and I had been only a few minutes before. I gestured with my hand, offering the view. "It's the mountains, not the ocean."

"Yes, I can see that," he said, turning to me with a grin.

"You can wake up looking at that."

"And at you."

I snorted. "A minute ago, you were making me out to be the devil, leading you down a path of sin. Now you're flirting with me."

"Yes, D. D for diablo."

"And what are you? An angel?"

"A fallen angel, I'm afraid."

"Then you might as well kiss this devil and keep on falling."

"Falling into you."

"I think that's a song. Celine Dion."

"She steal my idea."

I kissed him quickly before he could protest and then opened the door to the balcony. We stepped out and sat in the chairs on the living room side of the balcony, drinking our beers.

"You told Nell you play guitar and used to be in a band. You never told me that."

"I don't play anymore. The band was a long time ago."

"That's too bad."

"When do I have time with work, the long commute, and time with Isa? Oh, and I have this American guy who is constantly bothering me."

"If you can't play a song for that terrible American guy, I'm sure Isa would like to hear you sing."

"When she is a baby sometimes I sing to her, and she fall asleep."

"And look, she turned out okay, so I guess your singing isn't that bad."

"Funny. And you remind me I promise to take Isa some dinner. She ask for pizza."

"Maybe you can bring her over here on Saturday, and we'll go to the pool on the roof."

He turned to me, biting his lower lip like I had suggested the impossible. "I don't know. Maybe."

"Why maybe?"

"If Sara find out, she would go crazy. Isa is not so good about keeping secrets."

He chugged the last of his beer and got up to leave.

"The devil can't make you stay?"

"Hmm. You haven't really tried."

I stood, took Ivan by the hand, and pulled him toward the bedroom. Ivan resisted. "I can't. When I have more time, I come back. I promise. We must... how you say? Inaugurar your apartment."

"Inaugurate."

"Oh, same."

"I'll get some champagne."

"Champagne goes right to my head. If I drink too much, I maybe fall into you...like for real."

"I hope so."

Twenty-eight

I sat at the desk in the corner of the living room where I set up my computer, books, and other materials I needed for work. Though I would miss the small room I used as an office in the old place, in general I felt a sense of relief. Ivan visited, and there was no sneaking him into the building. The people downstairs would get to know him. He would be my regular visitor. No one would care. No one would be watching.

Although the flirtation with Ray in my apartment still left me with a disquieting feeling, Ray sent me an apology text later that evening. **Sorry if I made you feel awkward. Your friendship means the world to me.**

Hope to see you soon, I answered.

I told Ray that nothing would have happened regardless of being "saved by the bell," but I wasn't sure of that. In those few seconds, the urge to give in to Ray's magnetism fought a fierce battle with what I knew was right, and what I knew I really wanted. I wondered if sometime down the line I would look back with the regret of a missed opportunity.

With my brain steeped in coffee and thoughts of my wobbly personal life, I jumped into the *Garden of Delights*, a book of eccentric personal lives in a time where stakes were even higher for queer men to keep things hidden. The story was narrated in the voice of Plutarco Gastélum's neighbor, a character invented by the author. After making a trip to the remote town of Xilitla, the author managed to speak to some of Plutarco's decedents but found that the personal relationship between the two men was a taboo subject. The fictional neighbor, more worldly than other residents of the small town—Gastélum was also an outsider who arrived in Xilitla with James in 1945—became Gastélum's confidant, and he shared things with her that he never told his wife and children. The book began the day the neighbor receives Gastélum at her door, distraught with the news of James' death while on a trip to Italy.

He appears to accept the news stoically, but immediately the two of them set off for Las Pozas, the sculpture garden in the jungle that he and James created outside the town. Gastélum recounts his memories of James, telling the story of each sculpture and the landscaping, each component revealing an emotional journey through their life of collaboration. According to the author, it was only in the isolation of Las Pozas that the two men could be intimate, and the sculpture garden was, in fact, a physical manifestation of their love for each other.

Despite the initial feeling that Susan was being patronizing in assigning the story of male-male love in Mexico to me, a few pages into the manuscript I was very glad she did. The writing needed work, but the well-researched and intriguing content left me excited about the project, and I hoped the eventual readers would react with the same enthusiasm. I imagined taking a trip to the town in the state of San Luis Potosí with Ivan and bathing in the pools of Las Pozas surrounded by butterflies, a re-creation of a scene recounted early in the book of what James and Gastélum experienced on their first visit to the land.

I planned to spend the rest of the week settling into my new apartment and working on the book, hopefully without distractions, unless it was a chat with Ivan or a dinner and Malecón walk with Ray and Stef. Midweek my plan was ruined by a call from Jacob. We rarely communicated. He sometimes stopped by the Sherman Oaks house to check on it, so when I saw the caller ID, I assumed it had something to do with the house and hoped it wasn't bad news. I was right in my assumption about it having something to do with the house. Whether it was good news or bad news depended on how I looked at it.

Jacob broke up with his boyfriend, and not only did he want to move back into the house, he also wanted to buy out my share. When we bought the house over six years before, Jacob put down the larger share using his trust fund, but I had also put in a significant chunk of my savings. Jacob's offer would take into account the appreciation of the value and give me the percentage I put in. He gave me an approximate figure of over $200,000. Though I knew Jacob wasn't giving me a gift, I also had the feeling he wouldn't screw me over. I said I would think it over and get back to him.

I immediately started fantasizing what kind of home I could buy if I put that money together with what I would gain by selling my apartment at Paradiso. The downside was that I would have to go to Los Angeles to take care of the paperwork and clear out my possessions, either getting rid of them or putting them in storage. I also would no longer have a place to stay when I went back for work or to visit friends. Jacob would probably let me stay at the house, but I didn't want to assume anything.

Ivan said he couldn't bring Isa over for a swim on Saturday in hopes of keeping the peace. It seemed that deep down he still felt what we were doing was wrong, and Sara was going to find a way to use it to deny his rights with Isa. So, I ventured up to the roof alone. The pool and the area around it were as nice or nicer than the rooftop at Paradiso, and the bonus was that it didn't have the bad memories. Stretched out on lounge chairs was an interracial gay couple, and when I walked by, the white guy moved his Gucci sunglasses to the top of his head.

"Excuse me. Where are you going?"

"I...uh...over there." I pointed at some empty chairs. There was only one other couple at the far end of the row.

"I'm afraid those are all reserved. The only free one is right here."

"Next to me," said the dark-skinned man with a giggle.

I knew they were playing with me, but it was an opportunity to meet some of the new neighbors. I put my things down on the empty chair and played along. "Thanks for telling me. I'm new in the building."

"Oh, we thought you might be one those renters."

"I am but not short-term."

The two men introduced themselves. Alonso was from Panama, but he and Trevor had been living together in Vancouver the last ten years.

"Though we don't get much snow in Vancouver, I guess you could call us snowbirds," said Trevor. "We love the winters down here and the summers up there." It was obvious from his slurred speech they had been drinking a while.

I stared as Trevor filled their glasses from a thermos.

Alonso clicked his longish nails against the glass. "They're plastic in case you wondered."

"I live in PV full time," I said. "I've got a six-month rental contract here. See how it goes." They didn't need to know my whole story.

"Don't tell me a young thing like you is retired," said Alonso. They appeared to be in their early fifties.

"Thanks, but I'm over forty now, so I don't think young thing applies."

"Babe in the woods," said Trevor. "Stop gawking, husband."

"I work remotely," I offered.

"You're going to think we're terribly nosy, but do you have a partner? A husband?" said Alonso.

"Not really. I'm sorta seeing someone, though."

"We're right across the hall and happened to notice, I swear just by chance, this guy coming out of your apartment. We got all excited."

"Why's that?"

"We thought, hoopdy-do! We got another intergaycial couple in the building."

"What? Oh, no. That was my friend, Ray. He's married...to a woman."

Trevor gasped. "No! He is such a fine-looking man. What a waste!"

"Now, now," I said. I thought of mentioning that Ray occasionally batted for our team, but I didn't want to get them too excited.

"So, come on. Who's your sorta kinda whatever?" said Alonso.

"Soso, leave him alone," said Trevor. "We just met. He probably thinks we're a couple of busybody gossipy queens."

"But'cha are, Blanche!" Alonso laughed so hard he started making choking noises.

"Don't choke on me, girl," said Trevor. "There's no hunky lifeguard to give you artificial restitution, and I'm not about to be calling 911 or whatever it is here."

"Respiration, dear."

"What?"

"Artificial respiration."

"Whatever." Trevor turned to me. "His native language is Spanish, but he speaks better English than me. He also speaks French and Eye-talian."

"Ignore him," said Alonso. "Now back to you, sweetlips. What did you say your name was?"

"Dawson."

"Okaaay, Dawson Creek. Tell us about your beau."

"He's a local guy."

"Qué bueno!" said Alonso. "Best way to learn the language."

Trevor rolled his eyes. "All I learned from you is 'Ay, papi, ay. Sí, eso!'"

"Shut up. I'm cutting you off. Dawson, I'm so sorry. We're not like this all the time."

"Just most of the time," said Trevor with a giggle.

Alonso took Trevor's glass and downed what was left before grabbing the thermos and putting it in his Louis Vuitton bag. Then he took it out again. "I'm sorry, Dawson Creek. Can I offer you a drink?"

"What is it?"

"It's supposed to be a margaritas," said Trevor. "That crappy mix from Costco and some cheapo tequila. I told Soso not to buy that junk. Look what it done to me." He tried to fluff up his wispy hair. "That cheap shit is making my hair fall out."

"Thanks, but I'll pass," I said. "Mostly stick to beer and wine."

"Anyway," said Alonso. "I'm taking this one home before she makes a fool of herself. Oops! Too late."

Trevor stood up, adjusted his speedo, and slapped a straw hat backward on his head.

He draped a striped gauzy wrap over his skinny, sunburned body. "Ouch! That PF-50 didn't do shit!"

"Great. We now have a ten-year supply of it from Costco," said Alonso. He wrapped a large towel around him, tucking it in high over his chest like a sarong. "Ciao, bello," he said to me with a wink. "Sorry, again. We're starting AA on Monday," he cackled. "Not!"

I watched Alonso and Trevor snip at each other as they weaved their way to the exit, each one probably blaming the other for giving the new neighbor a bad impression. When they were out of sight, I let out a big breath and lowered my shoulders. It could have been a disaster if Ivan had shown up with Isa. Ivan might have run away to find the nearest closet, lock himself in, and throw away the key. Or was I projecting my own discomfort with out, campy behavior onto Ivan? Just because he was reluctant to slap the homosexual or bisexual label onto his own forehead didn't mean he would be disgusted by those who did. Even more frightening was the possibility that if Isa had shown up and somehow leaked to her mom about the funny people at Dawson's pool, Sara might have accused Ivan of taking her to a drunken queer pool bash.

And then I started getting on my own case for being uptight and stopped the runaway internalized homophobia in its tracks. Would I rather be sitting around the pool back at Paradiso, listening to women sharing bean dip recipes and talking about which dental office was offering the best price on implants while their husbands talked about sports teams that were playing thousands of miles away in another country? *Give me the queens. They are my people.*

A few hours later, my head lay on Ivan's chest as we sprawled across my bed, and my ear picked up the slowing beat of his heart. It made me smile to think I had made Ivan's heart race and now was responsible for slowing it down. It gave me a sense of power, the same power Ivan had over me and my heart. None of my earlier preoccupations mattered: my new neighbors and whether Ivan would be comfortable with them, the house negotiations with Jacob, the near jeopardy of my friendship with Ray. "Be here now," my mother's voice said again. I wondered what she would think of me, sharing the quiet time with a man who held me in his arms and gave no signs of leaving. I had a feeling she would be pleased.

"I was just thinking..." I began.

"Tut!" Ivan opened one eye and put a finger to his lips. "Shh."

"Sorry."

"Shh."

With heavy eyelids, I gazed down the length of Ivan's body toward the glass doors of the balcony and the mountains beyond, thinking I should close the shades. If I only had the energy to get up and do that. And what seemed like a minute later, I awoke to the sun peeking over the crest of the mountain and the knowledge I was alone in the bed.

Ivan came in with a towel wrapped around his waist while drying his hair with another. "Hey, mi diablito."

"Did you just call me your little dolly?"

"What? Oh, you mean the little hand truck thing dolly, not like Parton."

"Obviously. You taught me the other meaning of diablito."

"Me?"

"The day they moved in my washer and dryer at Paradiso, you came to my door looking for your diablito. I had no idea what you were talking about. You pointed at the dolly. Now I see you meant me all along."

Ivan sat down beside me and used his towel to rustle my hair. "Maybe with the right wig..."

"Please tell me you don't want to see me in Dolly drag."

"No, D." He put his hand to his chin as if imagining. "Hmm. D for Dolly?"

"I will never apologize for saying silly things again. You take the cake, as my mom used to say. Now, I'm telling you, shush and get back in bed."

"Can't. Work." He stood up, dropped the towel, and put on his underwear.

I feasted my eyes on Ivan getting dressed and sighed heavily. "Do you ever call in sick?"

"Never. Not even for you."

"I guess I don't mean that much to you."

"I guess not."

I threw a pillow at him, and he dodged it. "You're a tease."

He sat on the bed again to put on his shoes. "Don't know what you mean. You see my English not so good," he said in an exaggerated Mexican accent.

"Hah!"

He leaned over and kissed me. "Have a good day, my Dolly."

I groaned. "Don't you ever call me that again!"

Ivan stood up and hurried out the door with a lofty wave, trailing, "Besos."

What the hell was that? I had been amused and slightly disconcerted by the campy queens by the pool, and my own macho boyfriend had just gone campy on me. I took the pillow and put it over my head, blacking out what felt like center stage with the sun spotlighting me.

"Dawson," Ivan shouted.

I pushed the pillow off my head and turned over quickly. "God, you scared me. I thought you'd left."

"What you want to talk to me about last night?"

"I can't talk about it in two minutes."

His face went into serious mode. "Is it something bad?"

"No, not at all. It could be really good. You have to go. We'll talk about it later."

"You are sure everything is okay?"

"Sure."

"I call you later."

I heard the door close and felt the impact like a double punch, one soft to my gut like I always felt when Ivan left, the ache of already missing him and not knowing if he would come back. The other was a little knock on the door to my head, reverberating like a wake-up call. Ivan cared. He worried that a talk might mean something about us, some change to what we had.

Ivan called me that night on his way home from work. "Hola, D. Can you talk now?"

"Here's the deal. Jacob, my ex, called. He broke up with his boyfriend and wants to move back into the house. He has offered to buy out my interest. I'm excited about it. More and more I see my life here. The only problem is that I have to go back and deal with all the papers and move out the rest of my stuff."

"Where are you going to stay?"

I had just given him significant news about a major change about to happen in my life, expressing my commitment to Mexico—and by extension, to him—and all Ivan wanted to know was where I would be staying in California. "At the house."

"So, you stay at the house and your ex stay at the house."

"Yes. There are two bedrooms. Actually, there are three bedrooms."

"Maybe he want you back."

"He's the one that left."

"Maybe you want him back. You seem excited about going to Los Angeles."

"Are you serious right now?" I heard honking in the background. "What's going on?"

"Some asshole think I drive too slow."

"Ivan. I'm excited about cutting the last tie with my ex. I absolutely do not want to get back together with him. My life is here. You should know that staying with an ex doesn't have to mean getting back with an ex."

"How long are you gone?"

"As short a time as possible. Ten days. Maybe two weeks."

"Two weeks!"

"Are you going to miss me or something?"

"You better come back."

"What would you do if I didn't?"

"I would hunt you down and drag you back."

I assumed by the tone of his voice he was joking, indicating that his suspicions had waned. Admittedly, the possibility that he was serious was both thrilling and scary. "You sound like a caveman."

"Me Tarzan. You..."

"Don't say Dolly. I'll kill you."

"I'm coming by your house for a minute. I want you to tell me to my face you're coming back."

"A sus órdenes, jefe."

Twenty-nine

His visit on the way home turned out to last more than a minute. We ended up a heap of sweaty nakedness on the bed after I swore to his face I was coming back from my trip to California and swore again there was no way in hell Jacob and I would get back together.

With his skeptical mind appeased and bodily desires satisfied, he sat up. "Sorry. Got to go."

"You'd better take a shower before going back to your brother's. He's going to smell the scent of the devil on you."

"Ay, mi diablito."

After Ivan left, I went up on the roof to watch the sunset, and when I came back down, I went to my computer to read a few articles about Edward James. Though, as an editor, I liked to fact check, I didn't normally do such extensive research about the subject of a book. That was the author's job. But if the topic of a book interested me, it didn't hurt to know some background to what I was editing. In the articles, James was described as a dandy—flamboyant, eccentric—and didn't seem to care what people thought of him. I was amused when I realized that the same adjectives could be used to describe Alonso and Trevor. My research left me with an appreciation of Edward James, admiring what he accomplished, his patronage of the arts, the surrealist artists he supported, the crowd he associated with, including Salvador Dalí, Christopher Isherwood, and Aldous Huxley, as well as the fantastic sculpture garden at Las Pozas.

But if I had met him in person, would I have felt the same awkwardness I experienced in the company of Trevor and Alonso?

In the articles, Plutarco Gastélum, James' supposed companion, secretary, or collaborator (depending on who was asked), was described as handsome. He was a photographer with ambitions of being an actor, the brawn to James' brain in making the phantasmagorical landscape and cultural drawings a reality in the jungle. Whatever the exact relationship between them, Gastélum was able to juggle his commitment to James and the building of Las Pozas with a wife and four children. I became obsessed with learning more about James and suddenly realized I spent hours on the computer without doing a lick of editing. And I hadn't eaten dinner. I sent a message to Ray and Stef.

You've probably already eaten. Any chance you would want to meet me for a drink while I eat something? I'm going to the Greek place, Opa.

One thing I loved about Ray and Stef was that they were always up for a drink, a dinner, a walk. We met at the restaurant just a few blocks from my new building. It was the first time I was seeing Ray since the awkward incident. Though Ray supposedly told Stef everything, I suspected he kept it a secret. Stef acted like she was thrilled to see me, mentioning she hadn't seen me since my sister's visit as if it had been ages when it hadn't even been two weeks.

I launched into the latest development with Jacob and the house in California.

"You don't get a break, do you?" said Ray.

"I think it's good thing. I'm just not overjoyed at going back to LA right now. Ivan made me swear up and down that I would come back. He's afraid Jacob and I are getting back together since he broke up with his boyfriend."

"The ground is shifting!" said Ray.

"Meaning?"

"He wants you to come back, and he's worried about losing you," said Ray. "That's like a movement of tectonic plates compared to a few months ago."

Stef sat quietly, a blank expression on her face.

"And you wouldn't be coming back just for Ivan. You'd be coming back to your friends. Right, Stef?"

"I do enjoy our discussions, dinners, and walks," said Stef.

"It's clearer to me than ever," I said. "My life is here."

A smile crept onto Stef's face, and she sat up. "Sounds like you and Ivan are really making it. I had my doubts, but you sound so happy, which makes me happy. You guys do make a cute couple."

Talk about tectonic shifts. Was she now being supportive because she worried about Ray's feelings for me? Or did she finally believe in a more permanent future for Ivan and me? I mused at how my relationships had gotten complicated in Mexico. In California, before Jacob's affair, my life was straightforward. Jacob and I had our routine. We were involved with our jobs and had a few friends, some work acquaintances, and two couples in long-term relationships we socialized with. The dinner parties or evenings in restaurants were formulaic. I often sat quietly, trying to appear engaged but with my mind frequently drifting. I wasn't unhappy, necessarily, but my life was predictable. As shocking as Jacob's affair was at first, it quickly turned into a blessing. It was my ticket to a new life, and that new life was messy and challenging. In a mostly good way.

I told Ray and Stef about the latest book I was working on. They had never heard of Edward James or his surreal Garden of Eden near Xilitla, so I proceeded to fill their heads with descriptions of the out-of-this-world sculptures of Las Pozas. I pulled up images on my phone, showing them the bathtub in the shape of an eye, where James used to bathe with white carp swimming about and the "Sarcophagus" where he would meditate, the shape of his body marked in the concrete. Some of the structures were huge, like "The Bamboo Palace" and the "Tower of Hope." All the organic-looking cement creations were nestled in jungle vegetation surrounded by waterfalls and pools.

"We have to go there," said Stef. "Where is it?"

"It's in a remote area in the state of San Luis Potosí. It's a long bus ride from Mexico City."

"I'm in," said Ray.

"Great," I said, though my fantasy was still to go there with Ivan and bathe in the pools surrounded by butterflies. "I haven't told you the best part. This surrealistic Garden of Eden was created by James along with his 'secretary,'" emphasizing the point with air quotes, "a handsome young Mexican named Plutarco Gastélum. Few of the things I've read care to speculate on their relationship, but one suggested their thirty plus years of collaboration on the garden was a testament of their love for each other. There are also letters and a few of James' poems that a good read between the lines tells the score."

"Oh," said Stef.

"Fascinating," said Ray.

"But all the articles also mention that Plutarco married a local woman and had four kids."

"More fascinating," said Ray. "Living up to the Greek tradition of his namesake."

"Are you saying Plutarch had male lovers?" I asked.

"They all did," said Ray.

"I doubt they all did," said Stef with a sniff, "though it was common."

We spent the rest of the time at the restaurant scrolling through our phones, looking for information on how to get to Xilitla, the best time of year to go, and places to stay. We decided that around my birthday in March would be a good time.

A week later I was on my way to the airport. Jacob had already started the process of a quitclaim deed and insisted that the paperwork would be ready to sign in a few days, and then we would have to go to the county recorder's office. In the meantime, I could take care of my belongings in the house. I also planned to stop by the offices of Caliber to meet with Susan, hopefully getting a face-to-face agreement that the current arrangement of remote editing could continue indefinitely.

Since Ivan wasn't able to drive me to the airport as my flight was in the middle of the day, we had said our goodbyes the evening before when Ivan stopped by, supposedly for a beer but ended up spending the night.

Before we crawled into bed, I suggested he stay in my apartment while I was gone. "You might as well stay here. It would give you a break from your brother's fire and brimstone lectures."

"You trust me?"

"What? Like you're going to have wild parties and destroy the furniture? Of course, I trust you. I can give you a key and tell the people at the front desk you will be staying here and parking in my spot."

His face showed uncertainty as if he was making a huge life decision. "Are you sure? A key to your place?"

"It's temporary. Don't think of it as a big deal. It makes sense."

"Don't worry. I will return your key as soon as you get back," he said with an element of hurt in his voice.

"Ivan, look at me. I trust you, and I...I enjoy the time we spend together. I know your life is complicated right now, and I don't want to put any pressure on you...on us to...I don't know. Where do you think this is going?"

"People don't want to accept us as, you know, like, together."

"People who?"

"Everybody. Your friends. My family. The people in the street."

"I don't give a fuck about the people in the street. Anyway, nobody cares in this town. As far as my friends, Ray has always been supportive, and Stef said something interesting recently. She said I seem happy, and she knows why."

"Why?"

"Ah, you want me to say it. You! When you're not worried about what other people think, you make me happy."

He nodded his head. "The quiet times."

"Now, your family. I hate to say it, but Sara and your brother might never accept that we have something. Isa adores you and knows when you're happy."

"It would kill me if she rejected me for...this."

"Let's forget about *this* for now. Enjoy the apartment. When I get back, we'll talk about wedding dates."

He grimaced in frustration. "Always the jokes!"

I put a hand on Ivan's leg as we sat side by side on the edge of the bed. "Sorry. Believe me, I take everything that has happened between us very seriously. And yes, sometimes my jokes are to push away my true feelings."

"What are your true feelings?"

I thought carefully about what to say. Was he ready to hear how enamored I was, how much more enamored I had become in just these last few weeks? The desperation I felt when it looked like he was going to call it quits? The amount of time I spent thinking about him and what was going on in his head?

"You are the person I didn't know I needed. I thought I wanted to be with someone like my ex. He was handsome, formally educated, had an expensive sense of style, worked in Hollywood, and had lots of money. I had nothing growing up. But the importance of those things faded with time, and it felt empty. Then, when I met Ray, I was so impressed with his mind, what he accomplished as a writer, his kindness, and his strength. But I quickly saw how his situation was even more complicated than yours. I don't think he could ever be faithful to just one man as much as he might desire it. Stef is a safe space for him. And I didn't tell you that they set me up on a date with a friend of theirs, a Mexican guy. Very nice, but he reminded me too much of Jacob. Nothing felt right about it."

"This is after or before you met me?"

"Does it matter?"

"Yes."

"It was after the moonstruck night on the beach," I said with a big grin.

Ivan stood up, and I thought for a moment he was going to leave. "You have sex with him?"

"No. Had no desire. At that time, I didn't believe things would work out with you, but I wanted to give it a chance."

He hung his head. "You should forget about me."

"That is *not* going to happen." I reached for his hand. "Come here." I pulled him down on top of me as I leaned back on the bed. "Hey. I said a while ago we should stop thinking about this. Let's enjoy tonight together in the quiet. Tomorrow, you become my house sitter. You can tell people you are watching a friend's house. And if you're not here when I get back. I'll hunt you down and drag you back like you said you'd do to me."

He was on top of me, straddling me and shaking his head. "Huh!"

"And by the way, I'm not the only one who makes jokes to hide his feelings."

"That wasn't a joke!" Ivan said with a serious look, eyes glaring at me. I decided it wouldn't be helpful to point out how our roles were seemingly reversing.

"Enough talk, tough guy." I pulled him down until our mouths met.

As many times as I assured him that I no longer had feelings for Jacob, as I waited for the plane to take off, I acknowledged that Jacob had been an important person in my life. We were together close to ten years, and, at least at the beginning, I thought I was in love with him. Now, after my time with Ivan, I realized I wasn't. Was I in love with Ivan? I still hadn't really allowed myself to use those terms, but the feeling of wanting someone—it's curious that Spanish uses the same verb for love and want—was much stronger with Ivan than I ever felt with anyone before.

The flight passed quickly, and I managed to get some work done, further amazed how the author seamlessly wove what was documented about James' life in Mexico with the fictional creation of an intimate relationship.

Jacob picked me up at the airport, an extremely magnanimous thing to do considering the traffic in Los Angeles. Jacob had always been, if nothing else, very generous with me, but as soon as I got in Jacob's Tesla, I realized there was absolutely no chance of rekindling any feelings for him. He wore a beige silk collarless shirt and white jeans. He was still quite handsome, but I knew he used a lot of products to keep looking that way. Not a curl on his head was out of place.

"You know you're not supposed to wear white after Labor Day," I said, resorting to humor in awkward moments.

"Listen to you. I taught you everything you know about fashion. In case you forgot, we're in LA. Rules don't apply." Jacob gave me the once over before pulling away from the curb. "You look good. You've even got a little tan."

"I try to stay out of the direct sun."

"Yes, you need to protect your creamy white skin. I hope you're using a night cream. I don't want you to end up like my gran, whose face reads like a roadmap."

I couldn't believe this was the conversation we were having after a couple of years of not seeing each other: fashion and skin care. Jacob always paid attention to his looks, but I didn't remember him being so obsessed about it. Of course! The boyfriend he just broke up with was a makeup artist for the studios. As the years of our relationship passed, Jacob seemed to change, or at least, the person inside Jacob that was dazzled by pretty things and pretty people was allowed to flourish in the false bubble of Hollywood. Later in the relationship, Jacob took me to a studio party. I was uncomfortable and said I wanted to leave but that he should stay. It caused an argument. Soon after that, Jacob announced his affair. All the memories made me want to jump out of the car and get on the next plane back to Mexico.

But I knew I would get through this. I had to get through this. I would be going back to Mexico with a fat check and the means to take my life in Mexico to the next level.

"What do you plan to do while you're here?" Jacob asked. "I mean, aside from the business we have to take care of."

"I'm going to be busy cleaning my stuff out of the house, and I have to work. I'm behind on my latest project."

"Me too."

I had to stifle a chuckle and the urge to make a sarcastic comment. I didn't have a trust fund to fall back on if I didn't work. When Jacob and I first got together, I was impressed when he told me he was a screenwriter at Universal. I later learned that he had gotten the job through his father's influence. While we were together, Jacob worked on a few films, and it was exciting to see his name in the credits. The last time we talked about it a few years before, Jacob admitted that he hadn't been involved in many recent writing projects.

"I've had a lot of distractions this past month. My sister, Nell, came to visit."

"So, you guys are back in communication? How is she?"

"We had a great visit. She's family."

"I hope you think of me as family."

The comment took me by surprise and made me wary why he would say that. "Of course." *Keep things light and cordial.*

"What's that scar under your eye?"

"Nothing. I fell. The street where I live gets slippery in the rain."

"Glad you didn't say you had an abusive boyfriend. Do you have a boyfriend?"

"Uh...is this something we do now? Talk about other people in our lives?"

"I told you about what happened with Clive."

"You told me you broke up because he wanted an open relationship. That's all I know."

"And you didn't answer my question."

"I'm sorta seeing someone." I had to stop saying that. I should either say I was madly in love, or nothing was going on. My go-to answer was starting to sound pathetic and that was the last way I wanted to appear in front of Jacob. I was desperate to show him I was a different person now.

"Is he Mexican?"

"Yes. He's a really cool guy. He plays guitar and rides horses. He's a manager at a condominium complex." In not wanting to focus on how good-looking and sexy Ivan was, I embellished some details.

"Oh. He sounds colorful."

"He's not a stereotype, if that's what you're thinking."

"I just meant that it seems you've really gotten into the whole Mexico thing."

"I'm happy there."

"Good. I was afraid my house proposal was going to screw you up in case you wanted to come back."

"I don't want to come back."

"You can always stay at the house. Mi casa es tu casa and all that."

"It's still nuestra casa for a few more days."

"Right. Is your boyfriend the jealous type?"

"Not at all." I continued to lie or evade questions about who Ivan really was. "So, are you seeing anyone?"

"I just got out of a relationship. I'm going to be on my own for a while."

"You've never been on your own."

"That's not...I guess you're right. We do know each other pretty well. I have some regrets. I mean, about us."

"Don't. It was for the best."

"That's a bit harsh. Sounds like you were happy to be rid of me."

Again, I smiled inside, not wanting to seem like an asshole. The breakup was the best thing that ever happened to me. My life was so much better now despite the chaos. "It forced me to grow up."

Jacob took his eyes off the road a minute to glance at me and see if I was bullshitting. "You do look more grown up. I don't mean old. You've aged well. And with that scar, you look more...manly."

"Thanks."

"Whoever you're seeing is a lucky guy."

I stared out the window at the bumper-to-bumper traffic going both directions on the 405. Was Jacob flirting with me? "Why are you being so nice?"

"Do you still think I'm an asshole for what I did?"

"I'm way past that. I used to think we had a lot in common, but I'm not so sure anymore. I just attached myself to your star, let you dress me up and take me out because you always said we looked good together and people told us we looked good together. I'm not saying you didn't teach me a lot. You did. About style and food and design. But I constantly questioned my self-worth, and I was working that crappy job copyediting. Things started to get better when I got the job at Caliber House, a real editing job."

"I can't believe you questioned your self-worth. Didn't I always tell you how handsome you were and sexy in your understated way?"

"That's physical stuff. The luck of the draw. I admit you showed me how to better present myself. Might have even helped me get the job at Caliber."

"I always said Susan had the hots for you. But you got that job because you're good at what you do." I felt like a bitch for not returning the compliment, and every second the cars weren't moving made me feel trapped in a conversation I wasn't comfortable with. From the looks of the traffic, we would have time to rehash our whole lives, and I wasn't interested in doing that. Where was all this validation from Jacob back when I wanted it?

As the car crawled and the silence within grew to be oppressive, I felt compelled to break it. "What are you working on these days?"

"The studio put me on a writing team for a new rom-com that I'm excited about. One of the problems with Clive was that I wasn't focusing enough on my career. Makeup people are the biggest partiers on the planet."

I realized that I might have been insensitive, and it seemed Jacob had his own come-to-Jesus moment. "Does that mean you're off coke?"

"Definitely. And I've cut back on the drinking a lot."

I continued having the feeling that Jacob was hinting he had hopes of getting back together: the outfit, casual but flattering; the supportive comments; the questions about a boyfriend; admitting he had regrets about us. I was absolutely certain I didn't want that and hoped Jacob wouldn't throw any curves into the path through the house process.

Thirty

Going through my belongings took me to places I didn't necessarily want to revisit, and yet, it was my life, at least my material life, up to that point: the clothes I'd worn, the books I'd read, the glossy family photos before everything was digital, and objects I'd accumulated over the years, like my sea glass collection. Next to my books, my sea glass collection was my most prized possession, representing something pivotal in my life. Jacob laughed at my sea glass. He collected unique and expensive watches, some of them quite old, which he considered an adult and sophisticated hobby. I often mused that what we collected summarized the differences between us.

When I was sixteen, my family moved to a community near Fort Bragg, California. I started at the local high school as a junior, and my fellow students pegged me as a weirdo for being a transfer, for being introverted and quiet, for wearing secondhand clothes, and for living on what my schoolmates called a hippie commune. It wasn't exactly a commune. My family rented a house on a plot of land with other renters and owners where we shared in the upkeep and duties of the land, and yes, the people who lived there were artists and creative types devoted to Mother Nature.

It was hard for me to make friends at school, and I became an easy target for a bully who tried to pick a fight with me to impress his friends. When he got no reaction after calling me a series of names that included faggot, the boy shoved me so hard I fell and broke my wrist. A few days later, with my arm in a cast, my mom drove me to the beach for a talk.

"Let's walk," said Mom after she pulled our VW bus into the parking area, and we sat there a moment in silence. I agreed, though it was the last thing I wanted to do. I was still smarting from my difficulties at school and confused by the nervous tension on her face. We got out and started toward the shore.

It was a foggy day, as it often was on the coast, and I wished I was at home with a book stretched out on my bed with the door closed. I had just started reading *One Hundred Years of Solitude* by Gabriel García Márquez and was mesmerized by the language unlike anything else I had read.

"Are you in any pain?" asked Tess.

"I'm fine. What are we doing here?" I said in my irritated-with-the-world teenage tone.

She pointed at my cast. "The people at your school and the boy's parents promised your dad and me this wouldn't happen again, but the truth is you're going to have to figure this out on your own," she said. "School authorities are rarely very successful against bullies, mainly because teachers and counselors can't be everywhere all the time."

"I know, Mom." Now, I felt irritated *and* embarrassed.

"You're smart. If I were you, I'd find the biggest, toughest looking guy, maybe a football player, and make friends with him. Offer to help him with his homework. We have taught you nonviolence, but bullies need to be put in their place, and if someone else does it, well..." She raised her hands in a what-can-I-do gesture.

"Seriously?" Not only did I cringe at her suggestion, but my general frustration with my life, the constant moving, and strange upbringing made me seethe inside. But true to my nature, my impulse was to run and hide rather than express what I was feeling. All I wanted was for this conversation to be over so we could go home.

"Doesn't the fresh air make you feel better?" she said.

"Yeah, right."

Seagulls screeched above us, and the wind cut through me, making me wish I had worn a heavier jacket. I was miserable.

In later years, I understood she was thinking of her best friend in high school that had been bullied, leading to his drug overdose—my namesake. She was devastated that she hadn't been able to do anything about it. It was probably the strangest, not to mention the most successful, piece of advice my mother ever gave me, and it seemed significant that my father wasn't around when she gave it. He probably wouldn't have approved of my mother telling me to throw myself at another boy in a scheme that could run contrary to their typical nonviolence. It wasn't the usual way parents proposed to counter bullying in high school, sounding more like advice you would give a son going off to prison.

But follow her advice I did. I "seduced" Melvin who sat next to me in Spanish, the language jocks usually signed up for to fulfill the course requirement. For me, it was the beginning of my fascination with every-thing Latin. I initiated my campaign by moving my quiz paper within eyeshot of Melvin's desk and pointing with my eyes. No words were exchanged until one day, as we were leaving class side-by-side, I offered to help him study. I was surprised how quickly Melvin jumped at the chance, a young man a lot like Ray it turned out, playing the tough foot-ball jock because societal pressures forced him into the role rather than a true desire to be that person. Though my friendship with Melvin never ventured into the physical, we became more than just study buddies, and I never had a problem with bullies again, making my last two years of high school tolerable.

At a graduation party where Melvin and I were both drunk, I watched him weaving toward me with a soft grin like he was going to pick me up and carry me off into the sunset. Since we both knew we probably wouldn't see each other over the summer because of our completely disparate lives outside of school, and we would be going to different colleges in the fall—Melvin to Oregon on a football scholar-ship and I to UC San Diego on an academic one—emotions leaned to the maudlin, facilitated by the alcohol. I braced myself as Melvin pulled me into a bear hug so thrilling and unexpected that if I had to pinpoint a moment in my life when I turned gay, that would be it.

"I'm going to miss you, man," said Melvin in an emotional voice that threw me off.

"Me too," I choked out.

That was the last time we saw each other.

Many years later, the first time I hugged Ray, it was exhilarating beyond the fact that I was in the arms of a large, sexy man who happened to be a damn good writer I felt privileged to know. The level of warmth and familiarity of it, I realized, was sparked by the sense memory of that hug with Melvin.

Something else happened the day my mom took me to the beach. I kept being distracted from her peculiar advice by the activity around us.

Many people were combing the beach, eyes focused on the ground. I imagined they were searching for lost jewelry or money buried in the sand though none of them had metal detectors. Then a young woman right near us squealed and held up what looked like a large ruby.

"What is it?" I asked.

"Sea glass. It's my first red one!" She explained what sea glass was and showed me the others she had found that day, green ones and blue ones and clear ones, and several of a mossy color, ranging in size from a dime to a quarter.

"How do you find them?" I asked.

"Just keep your eyes peeled for something shiny and scoop them up," the woman said.

When my mom announced we needed to get back for dinner, I surprised her by begging to stay a little longer so I could find some pieces of my own. That was how the collection began. A lot of my pieces were from those northern California beaches, but in later years when I moved south, I found beaches in Laguna and La Jolla ideal for collecting the jewels of the sea, though Fort Bragg remained the mecca for sea glass collectors.

In the bedroom Jacob and I had shared for years, I pulled the wooden box where I kept my sea glass collection off the shelf in the closet and sat with it on the floor. I lifted the lid, delighting in the hundreds of pieces I had collected and stuck my hand in like it was a treasure chest of precious gems, picking up handfuls and letting them slip through my fingers. I caressed the smoothness of the edges as if they could take me back to the day I first discovered sea glass, the day my mother basically told me to go find a big hunk of a man to protect me because she couldn't stand the thought of losing another person she dearly loved to bullies. In the stones, there also seemed to be a lesson about time and patience. They started out as shards of broken glass that could slice your hand or cut into your feet if you stepped on them. With time and the constant motion of sea and sand, they became harmless, beautiful objects.

These colorful beach stones were also the gateway to my love of the beach. Before my family moved to Fort Bragg, I never lived close to the ocean. I didn't take to the beach right away, especially in northern California where it was often foggy, windy, and cool. But collecting the glass took me back to the sand again and again, each time appreciating more the solitary and meditative search while surf pounded, and the seagulls screeched overhead. I carried this love of the beach to southern California, and then to Puerto Vallarta where living near the ocean was one of my top priorities in moving there. No way could I leave the collection behind, and I closed the box, setting it aside as one of the things I would take back with me.

While Jacob was at work, I wandered around the house trying to decide what else I might take. Most of the furniture Jacob picked out, and the few things I acquired pre-Jacob wouldn't be worth the shipping costs to Mexico. I had contributed to the kitchen utensils and appliances, but I didn't need any of them. Jacob promised to compensate me fairly in the final figure of the settlement and had also offered space in the garage if I couldn't part with a few things but didn't want to take them to Mexico. I preferred a clean break, and one thing I refused to engage in was the American habit of paying for a storage space year after year and never looking at the accumulated articles again. I would only keep what I could carry on the plane.

I packed some of my favorite books—I already had the books I used for work to Puerto Vallarta—and the rest would be donated to the library.

In the purge of my few cooler weather clothes, I came across a Hugo Boss leather jacket Jacob gave me one Christmas, the material a soft pliable brown that felt like a second skin. I slipped it on and rubbed my hand up and down the sleeve as I looked at myself in the mirror. The leather had softened to the perfect worn-in state but still held a rugged elegance. Despite the clean break from Jacob I'd promised myself, this was an article of clothing I felt extremely comfortable in, always pulling it out the first evening it turned cool in Los Angeles and wearing it into the spring year after year. "I know, Dad," I said out loud. "The clothes don't make the man, and we shouldn't be killing animals so we can wear their skins. But I love this jacket."

I thought of trips to Mexico City where the nights were often cool or to other parts of the country where I might need a jacket. I put it in the pile to take back with me, along with a couple of sweatshirts and a few pairs of jeans, which I almost never wore in Puerto Vallarta but might come in handy when traveling around Mexico. I fit everything I was taking back into a duffel I would check and a carry-on bag. The rest would be donated.

I arrived at the airport feeling relieved that the last connection with Jacob had been severed, and a check would soon be deposited in my account. The night before I left, Jacob and I planned to go out to dinner to celebrate that both of us had gotten something we wanted. Jacob canceled at the last minute with the excuse that he was trying to make a deadline on a writing project. In the morning, I sat at the kitchen counter having coffee, looking out at the foxtail palms and the Tesla across the street for probably the last time. Jacob trudged into the kitchen in a Versace bathrobe with hair awry and frightening breath, hugged me goodbye, and went back to bed. I was relieved he didn't offer a ride to the airport. I'd already booked a rideshare.

Back in Puerto Vallarta I gathered my checked bag and headed out to find Ivan, who agreed to pick me up, all the while trying to reel in my excitement, the ramped-up heartbeat, the fitful breathing...and the flashes of doubt after not having seen him for a period of the time. I could not remember the exact contours of his face.

While I was in LA, we spoke twice by phone. Once Ivan called to let me know I should contact the landlord because the washing machine was acting up, and a second time to offer me a ride from the airport. Those tasks could have easily been handled by text, and I wondered if it was just an excuse to talk to me, to check up on me. Both times we spoke, Ivan's innocent-sounding questions seemed to be thinly veiled probes for confirmation I was coming back and not running off to a wedding chapel in Las Vegas with Jacob. It made me smile with amazement that Ivan could be jealous. And then another part of my brain reminded me how jealousy functioned in a relationship, the coin with two faces, proof of interest on one side and a dire warning on the other.

As I sauntered down the hallway to the exit, I also wondered if I would be afforded the same courtesy as my sister when Ivan parked the truck and came inside the airport. I got my answer, easily spotting Ivan off to one side near the back of the waiting crowd, discreet but expectant. My smile was unstoppable, even though Ivan's was less obvious and took its time to arrive. We hugged loosely.

Ivan took hold of the duffle I had dropped to the ground. "This is it?" he asked.

"Yeah."

He looked perplexed. "You are cleaning out your house, no?"

"Done. Everything I need is here." I bounced my eyebrows at him.

"Everything?"

"I hope so."

We walked out the doors into the afternoon and instead of the usual shock of heat and humidity, it was pleasantly warm and relatively dry.

"Nice weather," I said as we weaved through groups of people with large bags, waiting for taxis.

"Yes, it's broken."

"What?"

"The humidity."

"Oh, it broke."

"Sí."

On the way to my apartment, I asked about Isa, his work, and how he liked staying at my place.

"I enjoy very much."

He gave short answers without elaborating, his face serious.

"Are you sure everything is okay?" I asked. "You're so quiet."

"I am driving. Sure you don't want to have an accident."

"I'd prefer not."

We came up to a traffic light with a long line of vehicles in front of us. He opened a music app on his phone and connected it to his car system. It was a Maná playlist, and the song "Falta Amor" came on. I let out a knowing chuckle.

"What?"

"Of course, you're a Maná guy."

"You know this group?"

"You mean the number one rock en español band in the world? Yeah."

Ivan's mood immediately picked up as he sang along to the music, tapping the steering wheel with his fingers and bobbing his head to the beat like a rooster strutting around the barnyard. When the song got to the chorus, he shouted out, "Falta amor, mucho amor."

"Are you missing love?"

"No. I have Isa. Isa me quiere."

"Only her?"

"Who knows?" He continued singing along with an enigmatic grin on his face.

I was on the edge of saying something emotional but feared making him ill at ease. I never knew which Ivan I was with. The one who sent me a text one night? **In your bed is almost like you are here.** Or the Ivan of now, pensive and unsure?

"It's nice to be back," I said.

"Nice?"

"It's like coming home." It was a feeling without a physical abode to encapsulate that feeling. The place in Versalles was still new and my apartment at Paradiso tainted with bad memories. But, when Ivan fished the door opener out of the tray, pulled into the garage, and navigated directly into my parking space, it felt as if I was home, our home.

It all felt normal and easy until we got inside the door, and I saw his packed bag sitting in the hall and a guitar next to it, leaning against the wall.

"Going somewhere?" I said.

"My vacation is over. I must go back to my brother's." He set my bag in the middle of the room.

"There's no rush. We can spend some time today, can't we?" Everything that came out of my mouth was a diluted form of what I really wanted to say, a safe path on the edge of a precipice where one wrong move could send us tumbling down the mountain we had managed to climb, but with great difficulty.

"I think maybe you are busy."

Play it cool. Play it safe.

"No plans. Only to unpack." I dropped my backpack on a chair.

"This morning, I go to the market and buy a few things for you."

"Thank you. That was sweet." I walked past the bowl of fresh fruit on the counter and around the sofa to the sliding doors and opened them to the balcony. I stepped out and took a big gulp of the air. The jungle was a slightly faded shade of green with the dry season having begun, not the dewy green of when I had left. Ivan followed me out and stood next to me at the railing. Here we were again. Like that first night standing at the railing. But so much had changed.

"I missed you," I said.

"Me? You don't call me."

"I wanted to give you time to think about this."

This time it was Ivan who reached out and touched my hand. It seemed that the wheels in his head were turning but couldn't produce any words, though his lips acted like they wanted to speak. The best he could do was a long sigh from somewhere deep inside him. I moved closer and let my head fall on his shoulder.

"Let's go for a walk on the beach," I said. "I missed the beach."

"First, I want to do something."

I turned to him with a smile. "Okay."

"Not what you're thinking. Go sit down in the living room."

We went inside, and I sat on the sofa while he retrieved his guitar from near the door. He took it out of the case and sat in an armchair across from me. He set up his phone on the coffee table and scrolled until he found what he wanted.

"Have you been practicing?"

"A little. Don't laugh at me. I want to play something."

He plucked the strings and appeared pleased that it held its tune since the last time he played it. He began strumming chords that hinted at a song I had heard. His voice came in, soft and a little patchy, the lyrics hard to capture until he got to the chorus where his singing got stronger. "Falling into you," he sang.

All the awkwardness hanging over us since I arrived faded with the realization that he was singing me a romantic song by Celine Dion that said things about seeing us inside each other and dreams coming true. It was both the cheesiest and most beautiful thing I ever heard, shaking me with a glut of emotions.

At the end of the chorus, he stopped and looked up. "I told you not to laugh," he said with pouty lips.

"I'm not laughing. I'm smiling all over. Please continue."

"No. I'm finished."

"No, you're not. I could listen to you all day."

"Hmm." He squinted his eyes at me as if he didn't believe me. He patted the body of his guitar nervously.

"I'm going to be very upset if you don't finish the song."

He went into the second verse with more confidence, and by the time he got to the chorus again, his voice was rich and resonant, tender and masculine. He got to the outro and his voice faded softly. He tapped his palm twice on the guitar and, without looking at me, slipped the instrument into its case.

"That's it?" I sniffled back my emotions.

"Concert over."

"Gracias con todo mi corazón," I said.

"It's just a song. I'm thinking of the conversation we have one day, so I learn it."

"It was beautiful. Really, really beautiful."

"Let's go for the walk now." Ivan stood up and started for the door.

I caught up with him in the hallway. "Come here a sec." I put my arms around him and brought us face to face. "I'm serious. Your song was like a punch in the stomach...in a good way. It left me emocionado. Falling into you." We stared at each other for a moment before leaning into a kiss.

"This is what I must do for you to give me a kiss?" he said with a chuckle.

"If you play me another song, who knows what you might get?"

We heard someone outside the door and then a knock.

Thirty-one

I recognized the woman police officer from the night of the boy's death but couldn't fathom why here and why now. It was as if I had almost reached a destination on a difficult trail and, in a moment of distraction, taken a wrong turn.

Ivan took a step back as if to flee, but it was too late. She had seen him, and a sardonic grin crossed her face. The three of us stood a moment, looking at one another.

"I assume you remember me. May I come in?"

"Of course," I said, waving her in.

"Officer Vázquez, I believe," said Ivan.

"Correcto," she said.

I couldn't remember if either of the officers introduced themselves to me that night.

We went into the living room.

"This is my lucky day," she began. "I wanted to talk to both of you, and here you are together."

"I just returned from the States, and Ivan picked me up at the airport."

She stared at the guitar in the open case. "Who plays? Have I missed a concert?"

Ivan carefully closed the case and snapped the latches shut. "I play a little."

"You don't mind if I speak in English, do you, señor Ivan? You seem quite proficient."

"Not like you."

"I had the good fortune to live in Canada for a while."

"That must have been a great experience," I said.

"For the most part," she said with a half-smile.

"Please sit," I said, indicating an armchair.

She sat on the edge of the seat as if afraid of getting too comfortable.

She ran her fingers on either side of her head, moving her short hair behind her ears. "Let me get to the point of my visit. As you know, Benito Perez's demise was ruled an accidental death. I wasn't completely comfortable with that. I thought it needed further investigation, but I was overruled. Still, I had trouble letting it go. Whenever there is...what should we call it...people movement after a tragic event, it just makes me ask questions. The other young man on the roof disappeared, and Mister Patrick sold his condo and returned to the United States. You, señor Ivan, left your job at Paradiso, and you, Mister Dawson, went back to the States, and now it seems you've moved into a rental away from the property you own."

"I had some business to attend to in the United States. And I find Versalles more suited to my lifestyle. I learned I could rent out my place in Paradiso for more than I'm paying here."

"So, it was a sort of economical move?" said Vázquez in a skeptical voice.

I shrugged. "I guess you could say that."

She turned to Ivan. "I went by your house and talked to your wife..."

"Ex," said Ivan.

"Ex-wife, and she didn't know where you were staying. I assume you wouldn't have appreciated me showing up at your place of work in Sayulita."

"What is it you want to talk about?" His tone was annoyed like he was tired of this little cat and mouse game.

"I managed to locate Ramón Salazar, the other young man on the roof. We had a very interesting chat. You see, the story that Benito Perez accidentally fell through a previously damaged panel in the corner of the rooftop that was not close to the pool area where they were socializing didn't make a lot of sense. I was finally able to get the video footage that shows the pool area, but the camera doesn't reach the covered area where something took place or the corner of the roof where he fell. Why would the young man leave the covered area in the pouring rain and go to a remote area of the rooftop where yellow tape clearly indicated it was dangerous? After a number of questions, señor Ramón came out with a slightly different version of the story and seemed very happy to get it off his chest. There had been an argument in their kind of...how do you say...love triangle, and Mister Patrick was breaking off with Benito Perez. I am not judging." She stopped to look at both me and Ivan as if to indicate she wasn't judging us either. "I am just trying to get the facts."

"Can I get you something to drink?" I said, anxious to get up and stretch my shaking legs.

"Just some water."

"Ivan?"

"I'm good."

I opened the refrigerator and was momentarily distracted by the food Ivan bought for me: milk, butter, orange juice, and eggs. I wished I could rewind the day to about fifteen minutes before where we seemed on the brink of a breakthrough. I grabbed the pitcher and poured a glass of water.

"Thank you," she said when I handed her the glass. "Muy amable."

"I don't understand. Where are we going in this conversation?" said Ivan.

"I will explain in a minute," she said. "Where was I? Yes. The young man admitted that they were drinking a lot. The toxicology report showed that señor Perez was doing drugs as well. Señor Salazar couldn't remember the sequence of events precisely. He said that Benito was quite distraught and screaming that he couldn't go back to his village. They would kill him. Apparently, Mister Patrick had been supporting him as he had no work. Señor Ramón painted a picture of what sounds more like a suicide than an accidental death, which leads me now to you two. I would like to return to that night and your statements of where you were exactly and if you heard anything you neglected to mention." She pulled out her phone and scrolled to her notes. She looked at Ivan. "You said you were in the building because the management asked you to go around to the apartments and check on leaks."

"That is correct."

"I can confirm that," I said hurriedly.

Officer Vázquez held up a hand. "I will get to you in a minute. Señor Ivan, where exactly in the building were you at the time of the incident?"

"I think I am between apartments, possibly in the stairwell. The elevator wasn't working."

"I spoke with señor Severino the other day. He said you might have been on the rooftop."

"That is a lie!" I shouted.

"Please, Mister Dawson. You will have your chance." She turned to Ivan again. "Well?"

Ivan's hesitation was making him look bad, and my legs were jittery again. "He was with me," I interjected. "He was in my apartment. He came to check on leaks and helped me mop up the water. I offered him a beer. We went out on the balcony. We heard loud music and shouting, an argument. Ivan wanted to go upstairs to check it out right away. It's my fault that he didn't."

She let out a big breath of air. "Your fault, how?"

"I asked him to stay. We were enjoying the moment, having a beer, watching the storm. It really wasn't our business. Ivan was in the building to check for leaks. Severino was the man on duty, and it was his responsibility to monitor any disturbances. And then we saw him fall. That's it. That's the truth."

"Ivan?" she said.

He nodded.

"Enjoying the moment," she repeated my words, nodding her head, scratching her temple. "I'm sorry you didn't tell me this before, although I suppose you wanted to keep your 'enjoyment of the moment' a secret."

"Ivan was an employee of the building, and it might look funny to some people that he was in my apartment socializing. And you should know that Severino is a liar who holds a grudge against Ivan because he was passed over for the day job."

She looked momentarily flabbergasted by this new information I blurted out and worked her face into a frown. "This is not good. You both withheld information that hindered the investigation. I could report you."

Ivan cowered in his chair, but I sat up straight. "Respectfully, this is the way I see it. You said yourself that the authorities are not interested in further investigation. There were two witnesses to what happened on the roof at the time. Maybe Ramón is telling the truth. Maybe he's not. And Patrick will probably never return to Puerto Vallarta to give his version. What is the point of pursuing this? Will we ever know what really happened?"

Officer Vázquez thrust her head back like she'd been thrown a punch. "Don't push me. I could make things difficult for you."

"Por favor..." said Ivan in a desperate voice.

"But I have no intention of interfering in your enjoying the moments," she said with a smile back on her face. "I want you to know, however, that it is serious business to withhold information from the police, but I do think I understand why you did it." She sat quietly with her hands on her knees, her phone resting on the arm of the chair. She had not entered any of the information we gave her into the notes on her phone.

I started to suspect she was a lesbian who understood discretion. "What are you going to do with this new information?"

"You are right that Mister Schell has no interest in further questions. I sent him a message asking him if he would agree to a video call to clarify a few things. I got a response from his lawyer, saying he answered all of our questions to the best of his knowledge and wouldn't have anything to add. There is a part of me that still believes there was some foul play. A push instead of a jump perhaps? Regardless, I thank you for your answers to my questions today. It wasn't my intention to trap you in a lie but rather to get information to disprove or corroborate my hunch. I'm afraid what you told me doesn't change anything. All we know is that there was definitely an argument, and a young man fell to his death. I won't bother you any longer." She stood up. Ivan and I did as well.

She looked back at Ivan. "Don't worry. I won't tell anyone."

I wanted to ask her what exactly she wasn't going to tell. About withholding information from the police? About us? About socializing, or whatever she surmised was happening with a resident of a place where he no longer worked?

When the door closed, Ivan and I looked at each other. "What the fuck?" I said.

Ivan went back into the living room and slumped on the sofa. "This nightmare is never over." There was the still simmering accusation in his voice that the nightmare went back to the night we had our first kiss.

I joined him on the sofa. "At least she knows the truth from our side, and I believe her when she says she won't do anything with that information."

"I hope you are right."

"I'm not feeling a walk right now."

"I am feeling a tequila," said Ivan.

"Coming right up." I opened the cabinet over the fridge. "Only have mezcal. Will that do?"

"Better."

I pulled down a bottle of 400 Conejos reposado. One shot led to another led to the bedroom where we rediscovered each other's bodies in the golden light of late afternoon, which we should have done after his song brought me to tears and not answered the door, letting in the nightmare of that night, which managed to find us even here, in this new place, and continued to play with us like a beast with its prey.

Though the new place offered no protection from the past, nor a view of the sunset, there was peace in looking out the window at pink clouds, looking like swirls of cotton candy spread across a pale blue sky. I lay my head on Ivan's sweaty chest, listening to his heartbeat and breathing the briny odors of his chest hair mixed with the remnants of soap from the shower he must have taken before going to the airport to pick me up. "Sorry for all the problems I've caused you," I said.

"In this moment, I don't think about the problems. Only how nice I feel right now."

"Nice? I must do better than that."

He kissed the top of my head and pulled me closer. "See those clouds? I feel like I am floating on one. With you. And I must hold you tight, so you don't fall off."

"Thanks for that. It's a long way down."

Christmas crept up on me like a dental appointment I had forgotten and was not thrilled about. I always hated going to the dentist. I went out for a walk one evening to find that a giant artificial Christmas tree with lights and baubles had been erected on the Malecón, as well as a life-size creche scene with plaster animals, real hay, and twinkly lights on the roof, not to mention a stunning view of the sea out the back of the shelter. Down the way, worn and faded statues of The Three Kings made their way alongside a camel, a horse, and an elephant, gifts in hand, toward the manger. And then I noticed, as if it had happened overnight, Christmas decorations everywhere, in stores, on balconies, and in restaurants.

Christmas was always a weird time for me growing up, my parents railing against commercialization and the mad rush to buy things we didn't need for people who wouldn't appreciate them. My father was often grumpy around the holidays, but he would usually slightly soften his stance and take part in a large dinner on Christmas eve and a modest exchange of gifts organized by whatever community where we lived at the time.

When Jacob and I were together, we didn't celebrate because he was Jewish. After Jacob left, I often spent Christmas alone. It was just another day, and I usually had manuscripts I needed to work on.

Ivan was now spending several nights a week at my place, but for Christmas he was taking Isa to his parents' house. It looked like another Christmas alone until I got a message from Ray and Stef, asking if I wanted to be miserable together on Christmas. Stef was also Jewish and suggested we do what her family always did, go out for Chinese food.

At Archie's, Ray, Stef, and I ordered all our favorites, and the table was soon covered with way more food than we could possibly eat—fried calamari, egg rolls, spicy shrimp and coconut soup, drunken noodles, fried rice, and cashew chicken.

"Do you have any plans for New Year's?" I asked.

"One of our neighbors is having a get together," said Stef.

"Doesn't sound that exciting," said Ray. "We'd rather hang out with you if you don't have plans."

"A couple of people in our building, Trevor and Alonso, are organizing a party on the rooftop. We should be able to see the fireworks from there. I don't know them well, but I have a feeling it will be fabulous."

"Will Ivan be able to make it?" asked Stef.

"He has to work that day and go to an early celebration with the people of his building. Then he plans to rush back to the party."

"Has he moved in yet?" asked Ray.

"No. He's at the two-drawer and toothbrush-in-the-bathroom status."

"And psychologically?" said Ray.

"He's been occupying the master suite in my head for a while now."

"I mean, in *his* head."

"He no longer wears a disguise to enter and leave my apartment."

"What?" said Stef.

"Kidding," I said with a laugh. "As I mentioned before, he told his ex about me, but I doubt he's said anything to his parents. We do things in public together, but no PDA. I'm okay with that. When we are at home alone, he's the perfect spouse, even cooks sometimes. He makes some mean shrimp tacos, cleans up after himself, and is wonderfully affectionate. And sex is still mind-blowing. Sorry, maybe that's not what you asked."

"Good to know," said Ray with a chuckle.

"And how is Isa with all this?" asked Stef.

"She's still very shy with me, but I'm occasionally able to make her smile. Contact has still been limited as he's trying not to piss off his ex. Well, she's already pissed, but he doesn't want to make it worse."

Stef shook her head. "She wouldn't do anything..."

"Don't even say it," I said. "It's his worst fear that she would go all vindictive like Severino did. He can't blame that on me since they were divorced before I came along. Well, I guess I have made things worse."

"Yeah," said Ray. "Divorce is one thing, but learning your ex is in a same-sex relationship can turn the knife a bit."

"Anyway, I hope you can make it to the party. There are some pleasant though not terribly interesting people in the building, but Trevor and Alonso are a hoot. And I have no doubt about their abilities to throw a fab party."

A couple days after meeting Trevor and Alonso at the pool, I came home to find a bottle of wine at my door with a note. "Sorry if we were a bit much the other day. Happy to have you in the building. Bien-venidos."

We were now friends, and I felt like I could count on them if I needed anything. Though they mentioned several times they wanted to have Ivan and me over for dinner, I kept finding excuses each time a potential date was discussed. Most evenings were difficult because Ivan usually stopped to see Isa after work or take her out for pizza or tacos. It was sometimes late by the time he got to my place.

Against all odds, we settled into a kind of tenuous domesticity. But there were evenings when Ivan would go to his brother's and suffer the love-the-sinner-hate-the-sin abuse. I couldn't fathom why he would subject himself to that atmosphere. Perhaps there was an element of self-flagellation to it, combined with the pull of family. I'd recently come to my own family moment with Nell after years of disconnect. Now we spoke or sent messages regularly, and I kept her up to date about recent developments. The fact that she met and got along with Ivan made me feel a little less like I was bumbling around in the dark in my relationship.

Thirty-two

To complete my New Year's party outfit, I dove into my sock drawer for one of my pairs of message socks. I chose a pair with famous books scrolled in bands up and down the right sock while the left one had the same books redacted with a black bar over them, a not too subtle statement about the current wave of book banning. In the same back corner of the drawer, I discovered a little baggie containing a piece of a chocolate bar laced with psychedelic mushrooms. Without thinking about it too much, I popped it in my mouth. Matthew gave it to me when I ran into him on the street, where I also invited him to the party when he said he didn't have any New Year's plans. For the first time, all my peeps—Ivan, Ray, Stef, and Matthew, plus my new friends, Trevor and Alonso—would be together in a social gathering. I worried how they would all get along. I had a brief bout of spontaneous drug ingestion remorse, but it was too late to do anything about it unless I was going stick my fingers down my throat and purge.

None of my friends had yet met the flamboyant Trevor and Alonso. Ray and Stef had a negative impression of Matthew—my fault—and Ivan only recently learned that Matthew existed. A few nights before, Ivan asked about my day. I said my shoulder had been acting up, so I had gone to get a massage.

"With who?"

I smiled innocently. "My regular guy. Just a therapeutic massage, I swear."

His mouth twisted and his head bobbed like he didn't want to care but couldn't stop himself. "You have a regular guy?"

"I'm hunched over a computer all day. Occupational hazard. The massage helps."

"You are naked?"

"Well, yes. But I have a towel over my...down here." I swiped a hand over my crotch.

"And with his hands on your body, you don't...?"

"Ponerme duro?"

"I know about these boys in Zona Romántica."

"He's not in the Zona Romántica, and he's not gay."

"I think the ones there are not too."

"You have nothing to worry about."

"I can't believe you don't..."

"Stop. Next time I'll take you with me. Maybe he'll give us a two-for-one deal."

"No way. I do not let a stranger put his hands on my body."

Ray and Stef got to my place at around 10:30 already in party mode, and Ivan arrived a few minutes later. We all drank a shot of tequila before going up to the rooftop, which Trevor and Alonso decorated with LED balloons, strings of lights, and battery-operated candles on all the tables. Residents contributed money for wine, beer, and champagne, and Trevor and Alonso purchased two giant cakes from Costco. They hired a DJ and told him they wanted dance music for an older crowd.

"What about me?" I said when they informed me about the music request.

Trevor looked down his nose at me and raised his plucked eyebrows. "Girl, if you don't like the music, we're going to give you something else to focus on. We've got a big surprise."

"I hope it's not a naked boy jumping out of a cake," I said.

Alonso gulped, and Trevor gasped as if shocked. "What you must think of us!"

"Oh, no," I said. "We're going to have a naked boy jumping out of a cake. Are Burt and Sylvia coming?" Burt and Sylvia were an older couple from Saskatchewan, friendly but hadn't quite left their prairie conservatism behind.

"Now don't worry your pretty little head, Dawson Creek," said Trevor with an enigmatic smile. "Everything will be fine."

About thirty people were already on the rooftop when we arrived, and the DJ was spinning "All Around the World" by Lisa Stansfield.

Ray turned and cocked his finger at me. "Eighties!"

"Barely," I said. "She was really more nineties."

"Stop, you guys," laughed Stef. "Just so you know, I plan to dance tonight, and I don't care what decade the music is."

"And she can cut a rug," said Ray proudly.

"Ivan, are you with me?" asked Stef.

"Me? I don't dance."

"Liar," I said. "The other day I came home, and he was wearing his earbuds and mopping the floor. He was doing more boogying than mopping."

Stef put a finger in the middle of Ivan's chest. "I'm coming looking for you if they play any Michael Jackson."

"Who?" said Ivan with a straight face.

Stef looked at me. "Is he for real?"

"He's joshing you," said Ray, putting his arm around Ivan's shoulders. "Everybody knows MJ."

Ivan broke away from Ray like he was angry, walked away, then moonwalked his way back to us. Stef screamed. "I'm in love!"

I felt giddy about Stef's new attitude toward Ivan and wondered if the mushrooms were starting to kick in. Ray squinted his slightly bloodshot eyes at me a couple of times as if trying to read my state of consciousness. But it was possible I was being paranoid.

When I looked away from Ray's stare, the globe lights began to pulse with multi-colored flashing lights in perfect sync with the music. The next song sent chills up and down my spine. The soft piano, the violins, and finally Donna Summer's nasally vocals slid into "On the Radio."

As the song climbed to the disco beat, I started to move my feet. "I love this song."

"You weren't even born when this came out," said Ray.

"My mom used to play it when I was a kid. It was one of her favorite songs. We used to dance around the house to it." I shivered with happiness tinged with sad memories.

The Donna Summer song was the perfect time for Trevor to bring out the big surprise. The elevator doors opened, and Trevor led two young men to the end of the long, polished-cement bar. He helped them hop up on the bar where they began dancing. They wore long white gauzy beach pants, but their muscular brown torsos were naked. They held maracas in each hand and shimmied up and down the bar. Ray let out a scream of laughter.

"What, Ray?" I asked.

"That's perfect," he said, barely able to get it out between laughs. "Those are the boys from the movie *Night of the Iguana*."

"Oh my God, yes," said Stef.

I shrugged. I had never seen that movie, although I was getting a vibe like I had fallen into a Fellini film.

"You've never seen it?" asked Ray.

"Nope."

"It's mandatory if you're going to live in Puerto Vallarta."

Our discussion was interrupted by a shout from Burt. He and Sylvia were sitting at a table near the bar. "What the fuck, Trevor?" he said. "Go-go boys?"

Sylvia hissed at her husband. "Pipe down. It's a party."

The music changed to "Vamos a la Playa," the 1983 Righeira version.

"Your wife seems to be enjoying it," said Trevor.

"Why you son of a..." Burt stood up too rapidly and looked like he might fall, but his friends at the table caught him before he went down. They led him away from the dancing boys to another part of the terrace.

"Don't worry," Trevor shouted after him. "We have something for you too."

A moment later Alonso exited the elevator with a woman who looked like a young Ava Gardner. Her thick dark hair was piled on her head, and she wore hoop earrings. She had on a loose blouse with a deep V-neck over black capri pants. She climbed onto the bar and started dancing, sandwiched between the two boys as the three of them did a sensual dance.

Mollified, Burt wandered back to the table and sat down. Sylvia, mesmerized by the show, ignored him.

Ray guffawed again. "I can't believe this is happening."

"What now?" I said, not picking up the reference.

"That's the scene in *Night of the Iguana* with Ava Gardner and the two cabana boys at the beach."

"I'll watch it. Okay?" I turned to Ivan to suggest we watch the movie one evening, but Stef had dragged him out onto the dance floor. Was I dreaming? Stef and Ivan were dancing together and both seemed to enjoy it.

Out of the corner of my eye, I saw the elevator doors opening again, delivering Matthew in a splash of light. I hurried over to intercept him. "Hey, Matthew. Great you could make it."

"Are you high? Your aura is totally purple."

"I've had a few drinks."

"Bullshit. You are so fucking high. Mushroom high." I couldn't lie to him.

"Please, when you meet Ivan, just be cool. I only told him about my massages with you a few days ago."

"So, I've been your little secret," he said with a snort.

"It's not like that. Everything is still day by day with him, and sharing everyday life things wasn't always part of the deal. And none of this aura and chakra stuff." I watched myself saying the words as if from above, sounding much more profound than they really were.

His eyes probed my brain. "It's a party. I can be cool."

"Thanks." I turned around, and Ivan and Stef had magically materialized at my back, a moment ago over there and now here. Ivan must have been watching. A chill ran through me. "Oh! I was just coming over to find you."

"Hi," said Matthew.

"And you are...?" said Stef.

"Sorry," I said. "This is Matthew."

"Delighted," said Stef. Her being in a good mood would certainly make their first interaction easier when she wasn't inclined to think well of Matthew.

Ivan frowned but stuck out his hand. "Mucho gusto."

Matthew focused his curiosity on Ivan as if doing a five-second aura and chakra check.

"What do you think of the party?" I asked to distract him.

Matthew looked around. "This is amazing! DJ, go-go dancers, and good music. Buena vibra."

The current vibe felt more awkward than good. "Let's get drinks," I said.

Near the large tub where beer and champagne were on ice, we ran into Alonso. "Great party," I said.

"And who is this lovely?" said Alonso, staring at Matthew.

"Hi, I'm Matthew."

Alonso turned to me. "Is this the one you told me about? Good with his hands? Suddenly, I'm feeling aches and pains all over."

Ivan frowned and grabbed a beer. "Anybody else?"

"I'll have a white wine," said Stef.

"Beer for me," said Matthew. Ivan pointed at the tub and turned to find white wine for Stef.

"Enjoy!" said Alonso as he flitted away.

"D?" said Ivan, giving me a hard stare that cut through me.

"I'll have a beer," I croaked, even though I didn't really want one and wasn't sure how it would mix with mushrooms.

"Matthew," said Stef. "Let's go over there where it's a little quieter. I want to hear about your work. Dawson told me a little about it."

Thank you, Stef.

I took Ivan's arm. "Are you okay?"

"Of course."

"I want you to enjoy yourself."

"I am. Stef is a good dancer."

I glanced at Stef and Matthew talking in the corner. The go-go dancers were taking a break, and Ray was nowhere to be seen. "Oh, fuck."

"What?"

"Ray is kind of drunk, and I don't see him."

"You can't control everything. Everybody is adult here."

"You're right. I just want everyone to be happy. But mostly you."

"I'm good. Stop worrying. Let's go look at the view."

We stood at the railing, looking out over Versalles and the rooftop parties on several nearby buildings. In the distance, fireworks burst in the air all over the bay where a multitude of boats with twinkling lights were scattered across the water. A thunderous firecracker sounded from the street below, making me jump and my nerves rattle.

Ivan put an arm around my shoulders. "Poor baby. You are so sensitive."

His touch calmed me, and I interlaced my arm in his. "I'm glad you're here. I know it's not that comfortable for you."

He shook his head and put a finger to my lips. "Shh. Everything's okay." He pulled me closer. I took a deep breath and felt every synapse firing. When I let it out, I was afraid of ending up as a puddle on the ground. Without knowing why I needed extra care, Ivan was doing it. I lost myself for a minute in the closeness of Ivan while my eyes enjoyed the spectacle of exploding fireworks. I closed my eyes and still saw them bursting on the backs of my eyelids and felt the loud booms in my bones.

"Should we join the others?" I said lazily.

"I could use another beer." He looked at my bottle on a nearby table. "You've barely touched yours."

We turned around and Stef was walking toward us. "Get ready to dance. I made a request."

The fast drum beat and loose guitar notes introduced "Wanna be Startin' Somethin'."

Stef dragged us all to the dance floor. The dancers were back on top of the bar. The boys had taken off their long pants and now wore boxer-cut swim trunks. The girl shed her blouse for a bikini top. Ray was still missing.

"Where's Matthew?" I leaned forward and shouted in Stef's ear.

"He's talking to Alonso's niece. Probably needed the company of a younger woman."

"Bet she can't dance like you."

Stef laughed and spun around.

"And your husband?" I asked.

"He's over in one of the hammocks on the other side. He said to come get him before midnight."

"Oh." I noted it was the same area from which the dancers had emerged after their break.

Ivan danced close to me. "Stop worrying about everybody."

I looked into his eyes, and they calmed me. His smile cleared my head. "It's getting close to midnight. A new year."

"With you," he said.

The buzz inside me ratcheted up a notch, and I wondered if he realized what he was doing with his innocent yet explosive comments that set off fireworks inside me as powerful as the ones that echoed through the neighborhood and the rest of Banderas Bay.

Trevor and Alonso weaved through the crowd with plastic flutes and bottles of champagne, filling glasses and prompting everyone to get ready. The DJ went with a classic, Kool & The Gang's "Celebration," to usher in the new year.

Ray was back from his down time, looking revived and ready to party. Matthew joined us with Alonso's niece in tow. We continued to shake our bodies but moved toward the railing where we could better see the fireworks, now ramping up just before the midnight hour. The music was successful in getting even Burt and Sylvia to their feet, and the dancers came down off the bar to snake through the crowd. The DJ lowered the music and grabbed a microphone, beginning the countdown. "10...9...8..." while everyone joined in. Rockets shot up to the sky, one after another, and exploded in colorful flashes that quickly dissipated (in my vision dripped) into the sea below.

The moment arrived for the midnight kiss. Ivan's lips brushed mine but hurried to my ear, uncomfortable with a passionate kiss in public. "Feliz año, mi vida," he whispered.

"Te quiero," I blurted out. I hadn't meant to. It just happened.

"Cool," he said.

Cool? What did that mean? *Had I gone too far?*

With my words hanging in the air, I sensed the circle of friends around us waiting for their New Year's greetings. Ivan and I separated to begin the various pairings. Ray kissed me on the mouth, Stef on the cheek, Matthew a hug and a pat on the back. The music volume was back up and Pink sang "Get the Party Started."

By one in the morning, I was exhausted from so many emotions, my jaw hurt from so much smiling, and my whole body was sore from nonstop dancing since midnight. But as long as Ivan wanted to keep going, I would, because what could be better than spending the first hours of a new year dancing with the people I loved.

A week after the New Year's party, Ivan and I pulled into a spot above Palmares Beach. We took all the beach paraphernalia out of the back of the truck and began the trek down to the shore. At the bottom of the stairs was a simple palapa selling drinks and a few food items. My gaze went straight to an iguana on a leash stretched out on the sand at the end of the bar.

The bartender came out from behind the bar. "Do you want a picture with Lizzy?"

"No," I said.

The man pulled out his phone and opened the photo app. "Look. Lots of tourists take pictures with Lizzy." He scrolled through the photos, showing me several.

"I'm not a tourist," I said dryly. "I live here."

"You can pet her if you want. She won't bite." The man picked her up and put her on his shoulder.

I dropped the objects in my hands and ran one hand over the cool, scaly skin, remembering the night of the storm. I felt sorry for her, and if I'd had a knife, I would have cut the rope. "Have you thought about letting her go?"

The man glanced at Ivan in comradery with an oh-these-gringos expression. "I have her about ten years. I let her go one time. She is gone for a couple days but come back. I think she was hungry."

"Oh."

"She looks content to me," said Ivan.

"If you need beers or anything, let me know," the man said.

As we continued down the beach, I imagined Ivan thinking I ought to stop meddling in Mexican life.

"Is possible the money he makes from taking iguana photos with tourists put food on the table for his kids."

"I just thought..." I started. "I mean, it's supposed to live in the wild."

"Dawson," Ivan said in a warning tone.

"I know."

"It's okay," said Ivan. "I promise we don't get an iguana for a pet."

"A dog maybe?"

"Maybe. Isa would like a dog."

We? Dog? Isa? I had so many questions but held my tongue.

Upon arriving at a spot on the nearly empty beach, I struggled with the folding chairs I recently bought at Costco, dropping them angrily on the sand. Ivan stepped in and expertly snapped them into position. We also lugged a large umbrella down the path but didn't need it. The sun hid behind clouds despite the forecast of a sunny day. The sky hung low on the horizon, casting both points of the bay into hazy gray, Cabo Corrientes to the south and Punta Mita sixty-two miles to the north if you followed the coastline. If it had been summer or fall, we might have expected rain, but winter clouds, as ominous as they looked, were stingy in producing precipitation.

It was the first time I remembered not hugging the shade of an umbrella while at the beach in Puerto Vallarta, not rushing across hot sand to the water to cool off. Instead, we leaned back in our chairs, hypnotized by the rhythm of the waves pounding the shore, agitated surf producing larger than normal waves, a pattern that had persisted since the beginning of the year. The waves would build, sometimes crashing further out, sometimes closer to the shore where a deafening thud shook the ground, spray filled the air, and the water crept up the sand almost to our toes. And then there would be a lull, a moment of silent calm as the water receded and the next buildup.

"Winter waves," said Ivan. "Is rough for swimming."

The unexpected conditions couldn't dampen the fact we were at the beach together, happy and relaxed. Ivan spent all morning with Isa, putting him in a good mood. And now we sat back and drifted in our thoughts.

After a time, Ivan's voice broke into my drifting. "I never ask you. You finish the work on the moonstruck book?"

"I did," I said with a little sadness in my voice.

"Not a good ending?"

"Not a happily ever after, that's for sure."

"What happen?"

"In a short letter, Julian announces he's about to become a father and needs to focus on his family." I opened one eye and turned my head to peek at his reaction.

"And how feel the other guy?"

"Like his world is falling apart. He takes it very hard."

"It's just a story," Ivan said as if communicating a deeper meaning.

"It's just a story," I repeated. "Fiction."

I no longer felt that the story's ending portended an outcome for us. But the short conversation had shaken us out of our dreamy states. Our attention turned to a flock of pelicans enjoying the good fortune of rough surf rustling up fish for their taking. They skimmed the surface of the water or soared high into the air before nose diving into the sea when spotting a fish. After pulling their heads out of the water, they bobbed on the surface and opened their large beaks to drain the water from their throat pouches before swallowing the fish. In the process, the large birds had to contend with two thieves, the much smaller seagulls, which would land alongside the pelicans and nonchalantly wait for a chance to reach in with their beaks and grab a morsel, and the svelte frigatebirds with forked tail feathers, which glided overhead and watched for an opportunity to swoop down and snatch a fish right out of the pelican's mouth.

For a moment, the boy flying through the air flashed in my head as I watched the dramatic dive of the pelicans straight down into the water. I glanced at Ivan, wondering if he had any of the same thoughts, but his face remained serene with an amused grin playing with his mouth.

The pelicans normally flew in groups and dived one after the other. But two of them broke off, rose in tandem, and plummeted like synchronized divers, hitting the water at the same time. They did it several times in a row.

"Did you see that?" I said excitedly.

He turned to me with raised eyebrows, the same grin on his face. "And?"

"They are like us."

His eyes widened. "I am not a bird."

"No, you are not. You are a man. And I am a man. But sometimes we soar to new heights and plunge into the sea together, sometimes catching a fish, and at others coming up empty-handed or empty-billed as the case may be."

Ivan added a wrinkled brow to his enigmatic grin. "What a strange mind you have. I think you should be writing books instead of just editing them."

"Are you saying I live in a world of fiction?"

"Sometimes. And you have dragged me into this world not so real."

"Are you complaining?"

"No, corazón, I'm not."

"You called me corazón."

"Are *you* complaining?"

I reached over and took his hand. He didn't look around to see who might be watching and, in fact, lifted my hand and brought it to his lips, taking a little nibble of my knuckle.

I tingled from head to toe. "It won't be my fault if I fall in love with you."

"You are not already?"

"No way. I'm just in it for the sex."

Ivan dropped my hand and scooped up a fistful of sand. "The sand is coming." He moved his arm like a crane toward me.

"Noooo," I pleaded. I bolted from my chair and ran down the beach. Ivan quickly caught up with me, grabbed me around the waist, and sent us tumbling to the ground. He opened the top of my trunks and poured a handful of sand down into my crotch.

"I hate you," I said.

"Sometimes love and hate are very same." He rolled on top of me. We stared into each other, looking for signs of falsity or a way out. There were none. "You want this?" he said.

"I do. The question is do you?"

Ivan chewed on his thoughts, allowing a dramatic pause as if he needed a few minutes or days or weeks to consider it. I refused to be the first to blink and held the stare.

"I want you, yes," he said.

"Cool." I wobbled my head back and forth.

"I deserve that."

"Yes, you do."

I turned my head, breaking the stare, and saw movement on the beach back by our chairs. A creature with a long tail crept over the sand, trailing a rope still around its neck. "Lizzy is free," I said.

Ivan shook his head. "You got your wish."

My eyes rotated back to him. "In more ways than one. Now fucking kiss me already."

He did. *We* did.

On the beach.

In daylight.

Acknowledgements

First, I would like to thank my editor, Mat Mansfield. They have done an incredible job of understanding my story and helping refine it to make it clearer and more accessible. I appreciate the countless hours they spent, making this a better book as well as helping with memes and graphics.

Many readers along the way pored over early drafts, chapters, later drafts and all of them left in some way their mark on the book: Mary Hardcastle, Onia Wellman, Maciek, Kenneth Creech, Bevan Vinton, Brock Archer, R.L. Merrill, and Richard May. Also, the members of Write on the Hill Writing Group have provided valuable feedback and suggestions: Eric Peterson, Deon Bennett, Rebecca Baldwin Fuller, Da'Shawn Mosley, Traci Tait, Bill Brown, Tyrone Umrani, Gayla Cook, and Jerry Wheeler.

I must also acknowledge Natasha, who has tirelessly worked to help with promotion of my two previous books and has come on board again to work on this one.

My fellow members of BAQWA (Bay Area Queer Writers Association) have offered support, encouragement and suggestions about writing and promotion. A community of writers makes this solitary profession a better place to be in this world.

ACKNOWLEDGEMENTS

Hats off to J. Scott Coatsworth and Mark Marco Guzman at Other Worlds Inc/QueerRomance Inc for all they do for the queer writing community. They have helped me in several ways to bring this book to the light and find readers.

It is important to acknowledge my ethnically and racially diverse group of friends and family, particularly my husband, who give me inspiration to write characters from all walks of life.

And lastly, I thank the people of Puerto Vallarta, Mexico who have welcomed me into the community and been supportive of my writing. Local bookstores, A Page in the Sun, The Living Room and Casa de Libros have all graciously stocked my books.

About the Author

Vincent Traughber Meis is a fiction writer, a world traveler, and a former ESL community college teacher. When he's not traveling, he divides his time between writing and working in the garden. Most of the characters in his novels and short stories come from across the LGBTQ+ spectrum and are racially and ethnically diverse. He has published nine previous novels: *Eddie's Desert Rose, Tio Jorge, Down in Cuba, Deluge, Four Calling Burds, The Mayor of Oak Street, First Born Sons, Colton's Terrible Wonderful Year*, and *The Long Journey to You. Tio Jorge, Down in Cuba,* and *Deluge* have all won Rainbow Awards. *The Mayor of Oak Street* and *First Born Sons* and *The Long Journey to You* have won Reader Views Reviewer's Choice Awards and BookFest Awards. His short stories have appeared in several collections both in print and online, and have reached finalist status in several short story contests. A collection of short stories, *Far from Home,* was published in October 2021. He lives with his husband in San Leandro, California and Puerto Vallarta, Mexico.